SECRET WELLS

Let those whose Hearts and Hands are strong
    Tell eager Tales of mighty Deeds;
Enough if my sequestered song
    To hush'd and twilight Gardens leads!

Clear Waters, drawn from secret Wells
    Perchance may fevered Lips assuage;
The Tales an elder Pilgrim tells
    To such as go on Pilgrimage.

I wander by the Waterside,
    In that cool Hour my Soul loves best,
When trembles o'er the rippling Tide
    A golden Stairway to the West.

Such the soft Path my Words would trace.
    Thus with the moving Waters move;
So leave, across the Ocean's Face,
    A glimmering Stair to Hope and Love.

SECRET WELLS

THE
SPECULATIVE FICTION
OF
A. C. BENSON

COACHWHIP PUBLICATIONS

Landisville, Pennsylvania

Contents

STORIES BY 'B'

BROTHER ROBERT

The castle of Tremontes stands in a wood of oaks, a little way
off the high-road; it takes its name from the three mounds that
rise in the castle yard, covered now with turf and daisies, but piled
together within of stones, which cover, so the legend says, the bodies of three Danish knights killed in a skirmish long ago; the river
that runs in the creek beside the castle is joined to the sea but a
little below, and the tide comes up to Tremontes; when the sea is
out, there are bare and evil-smelling mudbanks, with a trickle of
brackish water in the midst. But at the time of which I write, the
channel was deeper, and little ships with brown sails could be seen
running before the wind among the meadows, to discharge their
cargoes at the water-gate of the castle. It was a strong place with
its leaded roofs and its tower of squared stone, very white and
smooth. There was a moat all round the wall, full of water-lilies,
where the golden carp could be seen basking on hot days; there
was a barbican with a drawbridge, the chains of which rattled and
groaned when the bridge was drawn up at sunset, and let down at
sunrise; the byre came up to the castle walls on one side; on the
other was a paved walk or terrace, and below, a little garden of
herbs and sweet flowers; within, was a hall on the ground floor,
with a kitchen and buttery; above that, a little chapel and a solar;
above that again, a bower and some few bedrooms, and at the top,
under the leads, a granary, to which the sacks used to be drawn up
by a chain, swung from a projecting penthouse on the top. From
the castle leads you could see the wide green flat, with dark patches

7

of woodland, with lines of willows marking the streams; here and there a church tower rose from the trees; to the east a line of wolds, and to the south a glint of sea from the estuary.

Inside, the castle was a sad place enough, dreary and neglected. Marmaduke, the Lord of Tremontes, had been a great soldier in his time, but he had received a grievous wound in the head, and had been carried to Tremontes to die, and yet lingered on; his wife had long been dead, and he had but one son, a boy of ten years old, Robert by name, who was brought up roughly and evilly enough; he played with the village boys, he lived with the half-dozen greedy and idle men-at-arms who loitered in the castle, grumbling at their lack of employment, and killing the time with drinking and foolish games and gross talk. There was an old chaplain in the house, a lazy and gluttonous priest, who knew enough of his trade to mumble his mass, and no more; women there were none, except an old waiting-woman, a silent faithful soul, who loved the boy and petted him, and mourned in secret over his miserable upbringing, but who, having no store of words to tell her thoughts, could only be dumbly kind to him, and careful of his childish hurts and ailments; the boy ate and drank with the men, and aped their swaggering and blasphemous ways, which made them laugh and praise his cunning. The Lord Marmaduke had been nursed back into a sort of poor life, and sate all day in a fur gown in the solar, with a velvet cap on his head to hide his wound, which broke out afresh in the month of May, when he had been wounded; when he was in ill case, he sate silent and frowning, beating his hands on the table; when he was well he muttered to himself, and laughed at Heaven knows what cheerful thoughts, and would sing in a broken voice, fifty times on end, a verse of a foul song; and he would suddenly smite those that tended him, and laugh; sometimes he would wander into the chapel, and kneel peeping through his fingers; and sometimes he would go and stroke his armour, which lay where he had put it off, and cry. The only thing he cared for was to have his keys beside him, and he would tell them one by one, and curse if he could not tell them right. And so the days dragged slowly by. He cared nothing for his son, who never entered the solar except for his own ends. And one of these was to steal away his father's keys, and to unlock every door in the castle; for he was inquisitive and bold; he knew the use of all the keys but one; this was a small strong key, with a head like a quatrefoil; and though he tried to fit it to every cupboard and door in the house, he could never find its place.

But one day when his father was ill and lay abed, staring at the flies on the ceiling, the boy came to the solar, and slipped in behind the dusty arras that hung round the room, making believe that he was a rabbit in its burrow; he went round with his face to the wall, feeling with his hands; and when he came to the corner of the room, the wall was colder to his touch, like iron; and feeling at the place, he seemed to discover hinges and a door. So he dived beneath the arras, and then lifted it up; and he saw that in the wall was a small iron door like a cupboard. Something in his heart held him back, but before he had time to listen to it he had opened the little door, for the keys lay on the table to his hand; and he was peering into a small dark recess of stone, which seemed, for the wail that the little door made on its hinges, not to have been opened for many years.

In the cupboard, which had no shelves, lay some dark objects.

The boy took out the largest, looping the arras up over the little door; it was a rudely made spiked crown or coronet of iron, with odd devices chased upon it; the boy replaced it and drew out the next; this was a rusted iron dagger with torn leather on the hilt. The boy did not care for this—there were many better in the castle armoury. There seemed to be nothing else in the cupboard. But feeling with his hand in the dark corners, he drew out a stone about the size of a hen's egg. This he thought he would take, so he locked the cupboard, let the arras fall, and stood awhile to consider. On the arras opposite him, over the door, was the figure of a man embroidered in green tunic and leggings with a hat drawn over his face and with a finger laid on his lip, as though he had cause to be silent, or to wish others so. The man had a forked beard and a kind of secret smile, as if he mocked the onlooker; and he seemed unpleasantly natural to the boy, as though he divined his thought.

He was half minded to put the stone back; but the secrecy of the thing pleased him. Moreover as he held the stone to the light, it seemed half transparent, and sent out a dull red gleam.

So the boy put the stone in his pouch, and soon loved it exceedingly, and desired to keep it with him. He often thrust it in secret places inside and outside the castle, in holes in a hollow elder tree, or chinks of the wall, and it pleased him when he lay in bed on windy rainy nights, to think of the stone lying snug and warm in its small house. Soon he began to attribute a kind of virtue to the thing; he thought that events went better when he had it with him; and he named it in his mind *The Wound*, because it seemed to him like the red and jewelled wound in the side of the figure of Our Saviour that hung in coloured glass over the chapel altar.

One day he had a terrible shock; he was lying on the terrace, spinning the stone, and watching the little whirling gleams of red light it made on the flags, when a man-at-arms stole upon him, and in wantonness seized the stone, and flung it far into the moat, where it fell with a splash. The boy was angry and smote the man upon the face with all his might, and was sorely beaten for it—for they had no respect for the heir, and indeed there was no one to whom he could complain—but he held his peace; and a week after the stone was restored to him in a way that seemed miraculous; for they ran the water of the moat off, to mend the sluice, so that the water-lilies sank in tangles to the bottom and the carp flapped in the mud; but the boy found the stone lying on the pavement of the sluice.

But the fancy for the stone soon came to an end, as a boy's fancies will; and he carried it with him, or put it into one of his hiding-places and thought no more of *The Wound*.

Suddenly the peaceful, idle and evil life came to a close. One day he had heard the tinkle of the sacring bell in the chapel, and had slipped in and found the priest at mass—the boy had a curious love for the mass; he liked to see the quaint movements of the priest in his embroidered robe, and a sort of peace settled upon his spirit—and this day he knelt near the screen and sniffed the incense, when he heard a sound behind him, and turning, saw a man booted and cloaked as though from a journey, standing in the door with a paper in his hand, beckoning him. Even as he rose and went out, it came into his mind that this was in some way a summons for him; the letter was from his mother's brother, the Lord Ralph of Parbury, a noble knight; he had been long away fighting in many wars, but on his return heard tell of the illness of Marmaduke, and wrote to bid him send his son to him, and he would train him for a soldier. They had great ado to read the letter, and there was much putting of heads together over it; but the messenger knew the purport, and the boy made up his mind to go, for he felt, he had said to himself, like one of the silly and lazy carp sweltering in the castle moat; so he dressed himself in his best and went. The men-at-arms were sorry to see their playmate go, though they had done him little but evil; and the old priest, half in tears, brought a small book and gave it to the boy; the old nurse clung to him and cried bitterly; but the boy felt nothing but a kind of shame at the thought how glad he was to go; indeed he would hardly have gone to wish farewell to his father, who was in one of his fits, and lay muttering on his bed; but the boy went, and, the door being ajar, he looked in and saw him, pale and fat, gibbering at his fingers, and almost hated him. And so he mounted and rode away, on a hot still summer afternoon, and was glad to see the castle tower sink down among the oaks, as they rode by green tracks and open heaths, little by little into the unknown land to the south.

The years flew fast away with the Lord Ralph; and Robert learnt to be a noble knight. It was hard at first to change from the old sluggish life, when he had none but himself to please; but something caught fire within Robert's soul, and he submitted willingly and eagerly to the discipline of Parbury, which was severe. He grew up strong and straight and fearless, and worthy of fame, so that Ralph was proud of his nephew; two things alone made him anxious; Robert was, he thought, too desirous of praise, too much bent upon excelling others, though Ralph tried to make him learn that it is the doing of noble things in a noble way, for the love of the deed done, and for the honour of it, that makes a worthy knight—

and not the desire to be held worthy. Moreover, Robert had but little chivalry or tenderness of spirit; he was not cruel, for he disdained it; but he was hard, and despised weakness and grace; cared not for child, or even horse or hound, and held the love of women in contempt, saying that a soldier should have no time to marry until he was old and spent; and that then it was too late. It even made Ralph sorry that Robert had no love for Tremontes or for his father, or for any of those whom he had left behind; for a knight's face, said Ralph, should be set forward in gladness, but he should look backward in love and recollection. But Robert understood nothing of such talk; or cared not; and indeed there was little to blame in him; for he was courteous and easy in peace; and he was strong and valiant and joyful in war. He made no friend, but he was admired by many and feared by some.

Then, when Robert was within a few days of twenty-five, came a messenger, an old and gross man-at-arms with rusty armour, riding on a broken horse; he was one of the merry comrades of Robert's childhood; but Robert seemed hardly to know him, though he acknowledged his greeting courteously, and stayed not to talk, but opened the letter he had brought, and read gravely; and when he had read he said to the messenger, "So my lord is dead." And the messenger would have babbled about the end that the Lord Marmaduke had made, which indeed had been a bitter one, but Robert cut him short, and asked him a plain question or two about affairs, and frowned at his stumbling answers; and then Robert went to his uncle, and after due obeisance said, "Sir, my father, it seems, is dead, and with your leave I must ride to Tremontes and take my inheritance." And the Lord Ralph, seeing no sign of sorrow, said, "Your father was a great knight." "Ay, once," said Robert, "doubtless, but as I knew him more tree than man." And presently he took horse and rode all night to Tremontes; and when the old man-at-arms would have ridden beside him, and reminded him with a poor smile of some passages of his childhood, Robert said sourly, "Man, I hate my childhood, and will hear no word of it; and you and your fellow-knaves treated me ill; and your kindness was worse than your anger. Ride behind me."

So they rode sadly enough, until at evening, with a great red sunset glowing in the west, and smouldering behind the tree-trunks, he saw the dark tower of Tremontes looking solemnly out above the oaks. Then the man-at-arms asked humbly that he might ride forward and announce the new lord's coming; but Robert forbade him, and rode alone into the court.

He gave his horse to the man-at-arms and walked into the house; in the hall he found a drunken company and much ugly mirth. He surveyed the scene awhile in disgust, for they cried out at first for him to join them, till it came upon them who it was that looked upon them; so they stumbled to their feet and did him obeisance, and slunk out one by one upon some pretence of business, leaving him alone with the old priest, who was heavier and grosser than before. But he had his wits as well as he ever had, and would have told Robert how his father had made a blessed end, with holy oil and sacraments and all due comfort of Mother Church, but Robert cut him short; and after a lonely meal in the great hall, turned to look at such few parchments that there were in the house, and sent for the steward to see how his inheritance stood. It was a miserable tale he had to tell of neglect and thriftlessness; and Robert said very soon that he could only hope to save his estate by living poorly and giving diligence—and that he had no mind to do; so he resolved that if he could find a purchaser, he would sell the home of his fathers, and himself set out into the world he loved, to carve out a fortune, if he might, with his sword.

Among the parchments was one that was closely sealed; it bore a date before his birth; he read it at first listlessly enough, but presently he caught sight of words that made his heart beat faster. It seemed from the script that his father, as a young man, had served for awhile with a great Duke of Spain, the prince of a little kingdom, and that he had even saved his life in battle, and would have been promoted to high honour, but that he had been recalled home to take his inheritance; but the Duke, so said the writing, had given him the iron crown and dagger that the Lord of the Marches wore, and with them the great ruby of the dukedom, that was worth a king's ransom. And the parchment said that it was pledged by the

Duke, by all the most sacred relics of Spain, bones of saints and wood of the True Cross, that should he or any of his heirs come before the Duke with these tokens, the Duke would promote him to chief honour.

Here then was the secret of the iron door and his father's constant fingering of the keys; and this was the plaything of his youth, *The Wound*, as he had called it. Robert bowed his head upon his hands and tried to recollect where he had thrust it last; but though he thought of a score of hiding-places where it might be, he could not remember where it certainly lay. Could he have thrown away by his childish folly a thing which would give him, if he cared to claim it, high honour and great place?—and if he cared not to claim that boon, but only sold the jewel, which was undoubtedly his own, he might be a great lord, among the wealthiest in the land.

Robert sate long in thought in the silent solar, with a candle burning beside him; once or twice his old nurse came in upon him, and longed to kiss him and clasp her child close; but he looked coldly upon her and seemed hardly to remember her.

At last the day began to brighten in the east; and Robert cast himself for awhile upon his father's bed to sleep, and slept a broken sleep. In the morning he first went to the cupboard and found the crown and dagger as he had left them; but though he searched high and low for the jewel, he could not find it in any of the secret places where he used to lay it; and at last he took the crown and dagger in despair, turned adrift the men-at-arms, and left none but the old nurse in the house. The priest asked for some gift or pension that would not leave him destitute, but Robert said, "Go to, you have lived in gluttony and sloth all the years at the expense of my estate; and now that you have nearly beggared me, you ask for more—you are near your end; live cleanly and wisely for a few years, ere you depart to your own place."

"Nay," said the priest whimpering, and with a miserable smile, "but I am old, and it is hard to change."

"So said the carp," quoth Robert with a hard smile, "when they dangled him up with a line out of the moat. Change and adventure are meet for all men. And I look that I do a good deed, when I

restore a recreant shepherd to the fold." The priest went off, crying unworthy tears and cursing the new lord, to try and find a
priest's office if he could; and Robert rode grimly away, back to
his uncle, and told him all the tale.

His uncle sate long in thought, and then said that his resolve
to sell the castle of Tremontes and the estate was, he believed, a
wise one; and it should be his care to find a purchaser. "I myself,"
he said, "have none nearer than yourself to whom to leave my
lands;" and then he advised Robert, if he would try his fortune, to
take the crown and dagger, and to seek out the Duke or his heir,
and to tell him the whole story, and how the precious jewel was
lost.

So Robert rode away to London; and his uncle was sad to see
him go so stonily and sullenly, with a mind so bent upon himself,
and, it seemed, without love for a living thing; and as Robert rode
he pondered; and it seemed to him a useless quest, because he
thought that the giving back of the jewel was part of the terms,
and that the Duke would not promote a man who brought him nothing but a memory of old deeds; and moreover, he thought that the
Duke would not believe the story, but would think that he had the
jewel safe at home, and wished to gain fortune in Spain, and keep
the wealth as well. And as he rode into London, it seemed to him
as though some wise power put it into his heart what he should
do; for he rode by the sign of a maker of rich glass for church windows; and at once a thought darted into his mind; and going in, he
sought out the master of the shop, and told him that he had lost a
jewel from a crown, a jewel of price, and that he was ashamed that
the crown should lack it; and he asked if he could make him a jewel
of glass to set in its place; and he described the jewel, how large it
was and how dull outside, and its fiery heart; and the craftsman
smiled shrewdly and foxily, and told him to return on the third
day, and he should have his will. On the third day he came again;
and the craftsman, opening a box, took from it a jewel so like *The
Wound*, that he thought for a moment that he must have recovered it; so he paid a mighty price for it, and set off light-hearted
for Spain.

After weary wandering, and many strange adventures by sea and land, he rode one day to the Duke's palace gate. It was a great bare house of stone, within a wall, at the end of a little town. It was far larger and greater than he had dreamed; he was stayed at the gate, for he knew as yet but a few words of the language; but he had written on a parchment who he was, and that he desired to see the Duke. And presently there came out a seneschal in haste, and he was led within honourably, and soon he was had into a small room, richly furnished. He was left alone, and the seneschal showed him through which door the Duke would come.

Presently a door opened, and there came in an old shrunken man, in a furred gown, very stately and noble, holding the paper in his hand. Robert did obeisance, but the Duke raised him, and spoke courteously to him in the English tongue, and desired to see his tokens.

Then Robert brought forth the crown and the dagger and the jewel, and the Duke looked at them in silence for awhile, shading his eyes. And then he praised the Lord Marmaduke very nobly, saying that he owed his life to him. And then he told Robert that he would be true to his word, and promote him to honour; but he said that first he must abide with him many days, and go in and out with his knights, and learn the Spanish tongue and the Spanish way of life; so Robert abode with him in great content, and was treated with honour by all, but especially by the Duke, who often sent for him and spoke much of former days.

Then at last there came a day when the Duke sent for him and in the presence of all his lords told them the story and passed the crown and the dagger and the jewel from hand to hand; and the lords eyed the stone curiously and handled it tenderly; and then the Duke said that the knight who could, for the sake of honour, restore a jewel that could buy a county—there was not the like of it in the world, save in the Emperor's crown—was a true knight indeed; and therefore he made Robert Lord of the Marches, put the crown on his head, and a purple robe with a cape of miniver on his shoulders, and commanded that he should be used by all as if of royal birth.

The greatness of his reward was a surprise to Robert, and he had it in his heart to tell the Duke the truth. But the lords passed before him and did obeisance, and he put the good hour aside.

Very soon Robert set out for the Castle of the Marches; and he found it a marvellous house, fit for a king, with wide lands. And there he abode for several years, and did worthily; for he was an excellent knight, and a prudent general; moreover he was just and kind; and the people feared and obeyed his rule, and lived in peace, though none loved Robert; but he made the land prosperous and great, and cleared it of robbers, and raised a mighty revenue for the Duke, who praised him and made him great presents.

One day he heard that the Duke was ill; the next a courier came in haste to summon him to the Duke's presence; he wondered at this; but went with a great retinue. He found the Duke feeble and bent, but with a bright eye; he kissed Robert, like a brother prince, and as they sate alone he opened his heart to him and told him that he had done worthily; he had none of his kin, or none fit to hold his dukedom after him; but that all he desired was that his people should be well ruled, and that he had determined that Robert should succeed him. "There will be envious and grasping hands," he said, "held out—but you are strong and wise, and the people will be content to be ruled by you," and then he showed him a paper that made him a prince in title, and that gave him the Dukedom on his own death.

Now there lived in the Duke's house a wise and learned man named Paul, an alchemist, who knew the courses of the stars and the virtues of plants, and many other secret things; and the Duke delighted much in his conversation, which was ingenious and learned. But Robert heard him vacantly, thinking that such studies were fit only for children. And Paul being old and gentle, loved not Robert, but held that the Duke trusted him overmuch. And one night, when Robert and other lords were sitting with the Duke, Paul being present, the talk turned on the virtues of gems; and Paul, as if making an effort that he had long prepared for, told the Duke of a curious liquor, an *aqua fortis*, that he had distilled, which was a marvellous thing to test the worth of gems, and would tell the true from the false; and the Duke bade him bring the liquor and show him how the spirit worked. And it seemed to Robert that, as Paul spoke, a shadowy hand came from the darkness and clutched at his heart, enveloping him in blackness, so that he sate in a cold dream. And Paul went out, and presently returned bringing a small phial of gold—for the liquor, he said, would eat its way through any baser metal—and in the other hand a little dish of gems. Some of them, he said, were true gems, others of them less precious, and others naught but sparkling glass; and he poured a drop on each; the true gems sparkled unhurt in the clear liquid, the less precious threw off little flakes of impurity, and the glass hissed and melted in the potent venom. And Robert, contrary to his wont, came and stood, sick at heart, feeling the old man's eyes fixed on him with a steady gaze. At last Paul said, "The Prince Robert"—for the Duke had told the lords of the honour he had given him— "seems to wonder more than his wont at these simple toys and tricks; shall not the Duke let us test the great ruby, that its worth may be the better proven? perhaps too it has some small impurity to be purged away, and will shine more bravely, like a noble heart under affliction." And the Duke said, "Yes, let the ruby be brought."

So the lord that had the charge of the Duke's jewels brought a casket, and there in its place lay the great ruby, red as blood. And Robert would have spoken, but the words died upon his tongue, and he saw the shadow of the end.

Then Paul took the ruby and laid it on his dish; and as he raised the phial to pour, he looked at Robert, and said "But perhaps it is shame to treat so great a gem so discourteously?" And the Duke being old and curious said, "Nay, but pour." But then, as Paul raised the phial, the Duke lifted his hand, and said very pleasantly, "Yet after all, I hold not the jewel my own, but the Lord Robert's, who hath so faithfully restored it to me. What will you, my lord?" he said, turning with a smile to Robert. And Robert, looking and smiling very stonily, said, in a voice that he could scarcely command, "Pour, sir, pour!" So Paul poured the liquor.

The great ruby flashed for a moment, and then a thin white steam floated up, while the gem rose in a blood-stained foam, hissing and bubbling. Then there was a silence; and then Robert put his hand to his heart and stood still; the Duke looked at him, and Paul said in his ear, "Now, Lord Robert, play the man!—I knew the secret."

Then Robert rising from his place said that he would ask the Duke's leave to speak to him in private on this matter, and the Duke, coldly but courteously, led the way into an inner room, and there Robert told him all the story. Perhaps a younger man might have been more ready to forgive; but the Duke was old; and when Robert had done the story, he sate looking so aged and broken, that a kind of pity came into Robert's mind, and crushed the pity he felt for himself. But at last the Duke spoke. "You have deceived me," he said, "and I do not know that I can even think that your story is true; you can serve me no longer, for you have done unworthily." And with that he tore the parchment across, and dropped it on the ground, and then made a gesture of dismissal; and Robert rose, hoping that the Duke would yet relent, and said at last, "May I hope that your Grace can say that you forgive me? I do not ask to be restored—but in all other things I have served you well." "No, my Lord Robert," said the Duke at last coldly and severely, "I cannot forgive; for I have trusted one who has deceived me."

So Robert went slowly out of the room through the hall; and no man spoke to him and he spoke to none. Only Paul came to join him, and looked at him awhile, and then said, "Lord Robert, I have been the means of inflicting a heavy blow upon you; but it was not I who struck, but God, to whom I think you give no allegiance." And Robert said, "Nay, Sir Paul, trouble not yourself; you have done as a faithful servant of the Duke should do to a faithless servant; I bear you no malice; as you say, it is not you who strike."

Then the old man said, "Believe me, Lord Robert, that the day will come, and I think it is not far distant, when you will be grateful to the stroke which, at the cost of grievous pain to yourself, has revealed your soul to yourself. All men know the worst that can be known of you; the cup is emptied to the dregs; it is for you to fill it." Then he put out his hand, and Robert grasped it, and went out into the world alone. That night he sent a courier to his castle to say that he would return no more, and that all things were the Duke's; and he sent back to the Duke, by a private messenger, the crown and the dagger; and the Duke mourned over the loss of his trusty servant, but could not forgive him nor hear him spoken of.

Robert only kept for himself the sum of gold with which he had come to the Duke's court; and he travelled into France, for he knew that he would find fighting there, and took service in the army of Burgundy; he was surprised within himself to find how little he cared for the loss of his greatness; indeed he felt that a certain secret heaviness and blackness of spirit had left him, and that he was almost light-hearted; but in one of the first battles he fought in he was stricken from his horse, and trampled under foot. And they took him for tendance to a monastery near the field; and in a few weeks, when he came slowly back to life, he knew that he could fight no more.

Then indeed he fell into a great despair and darkness of spirit. It seemed as though some cruel and secret enemy had struck him blow after blow, and not content with visiting him with shame, had rent from him all that made him even wish to live. But in the monastery lived a wise old monk, with whom he had much talk, and in his weakness told him all his life and his fall. And one day the two sate together in the cloister, on a day in spring, while a bird sang very blithely in a bush that was all pricked with green points and shoots. And the old monk said, "This is a strange tale, Lord Robert, that you have told me; and the wonder grows as I think of it; but it seems to me that God has led you in a wonderful manner; He made you strong and bold and self-sufficient; and then He has taken these things from you, not gently, because you were strong to bear, but very sternly; He has led you through deep waters and yet you live; and He will set you upon the rock that is higher, so that you may serve Him yet."

And then it seemed, in a silence made beautiful by the sweet piping of the bird, that a little flower rose and blossomed in Robert's soul; he saw, in a sudden way that cannot be told in words, that he was indeed in stronger hands than his own; and there came into his mind that in following after strong things, he had missed the thing that was stronger than all—Love, that holds the world in his grasp.

So it came to pass that the Lord Robert became the thing that he had most despised—a monk. And he found here that his courage, which he had thought the strongest thing he had, was yet hardly strong enough to bear the doing of mean and sordid tasks, such as a monk must often do; but it became to him a kind of fierce pleasure to trample on himself, and to do humbly and severely all menial things. He swept the church, he dug in the garden, he fetched and carried burdens, and spared himself in nothing.

But after a time he fell ill; he missed, no doubt, the old activities of life; his days had been full of business and occupation, and though he did not look back—indeed a deep trench seemed to have been dug across his life, and he saw himself across it like a different man, and he could often hardly believe that he was the same—yet it seemed as though some spring had been broken in his spirit. He fell into long sad musings, and waters of bitterness flowed across his soul. The monks thought that he would die, he became so wan and ghost-like; but he never failed in his duty, and though his life stretched before him like a weary road, he knew that it would be long before he reached the end, and that he had many leagues yet to traverse, before the night fell cold on the hills.

Now, there was business to be done for the House in England, and Robert was sent there, the Prior hoping that the change and stir might lighten the load upon his spirit.

It happened at last that he found himself, in the course of his journeyings, not far from Tremontes. His uncle, the Lord Ralph, he heard, was dead, and his lands had gone to the nearest of his kin. He knew nothing of what had befallen Tremontes, but he made enquiries, saying that he had seen the Lord Robert in Spain; he found that there was great curiosity about him; he was plied with questions, and he was forced to speak of himself, as in a strange dream, and to hear the story of his disgrace told with many wild imaginings. It seemed that Ralph had himself undertaken the care

of Tremontes, and had turned it by diligence into a rich estate,
hoping, it was said, to hand it over to the Lord Robert on his return; but that as he had disappeared and made no sign, it was
supposed that he had died fighting, and the Lord Ralph having
died suddenly, Tremontes had passed with the rest of his estate.

Early one summer morning Robert set off across the broad
green flat, and trudged to Tremontes. The country had hardly altered, and it was with a strange thrill of delight that one by one the
familiar landmarks came into view; and at last he saw the castle
itself over the oaks. He had learnt that there was a priest there as
chaplain, a wise and sad man, to whom he bore a letter. Twenty
years had passed since he saw the castle last, but it looked to his
eyes no older; the hens picked and cried in the byre; the sun shone
pleasantly as ever upon the lilied pool and the warm terrace. Robert felt no sadness, but a kind of hunger to be remembered, to be
welcomed, to be received with loving looks. The porter led him in,
up into the familiar hall, where sate a few sober men-at-arms, who
rose and made a seemly obeisance; and he was presently sitting in
a little parlour that opened on the chapel, talking quietly to the
old priest, who seemed glad enough to have his company. Robert
told him that he had known Tremontes in his youth; and after he
had spoken of many indifferent things, he asked that he might withdraw for a little into the chapel, and say a silent prayer for those
who were departed.

The old priest understood him and led the way; and in a moment Robert found himself seated by the little arcade, looking at
the dim figure that hung in the window, where he had sate as a
boy, when the messenger had come to summon him away. How it
all came back to him! The years were obliterated in a flash; he put
out his hand idly to the arcade, where the pillars stood out from
the wall, and his fingers touched a small dusty thing that lay between a pillar and the stones. It was hardly with surprise that he
raised it, and saw that he held the ruby, where he had put it in that
careless hour.

Then there beat upon his mind a great wave of thought, and he
saw how gentle had been the hand that led him, and how surely he

had been guided; he looked into the depth of his soul, and saw the very secret counsels of God. That was an hour full of a strange and marvellous happiness, when he felt like a child leaning against a father's knee. He had no longer any repining or any questioning; but he knelt, full of a mysterious peace, resigning himself utterly into the mighty hands of the Father.

Presently the waning light warned him that the day was turning to the evening; and he came out and spoke to the priest, but with such a solemn and tranquil radiance of mien that the priest said to him, "I thought, brother, when you came to me, that you had a strange thing to tell me; but now you seem like one who has laid his very self down at the foot of the Cross." And Robert smiled and said, "I think I have."

Presently he set off; and a foolish fancy came and fluttered in his mind for a moment, that he ought not to come like a thief and steal so rich a thing away; till he reflected in himself that he had but to speak the word and the whole was his.

The old priest had told him that the Lord of Tremontes, Richard, was a just man, and ruled the estate well and bountifully; that he would have none but honest men to labour for him, and that he was liberal and kind. Just as Robert went out of the gate he met a grave man, in rich but sober attire, riding in, who drew aside to let the monk pass and put off his hat to him. Then it came into Robert's mind to speak to him, and he said, "Do I speak with the Lord Richard of Tremontes?"

"Richard of Parbury, father," said the Lord. "Tremontes is indeed held by me, but I have no lordship here. The Lord Robert of Tremontes may yet be living; we know not if he be alive or dead; and I but hold the estate for him and administer it for him; and if he returns he will find it, I believe, not worse than he left it."

Then Robert made up his mind and said, "Lord Richard, I have a message for you from the Lord Robert—but for your ears alone. I have seen him and know him. You have doubtless heard of his disgrace and his fall; and he will not return. He was but anxious to know that the estate was justly ruled and administered, and he resigns it into your hands."

Then the Lord Richard dismounted from his horse, and bade the monk enter and speak with him at large; but he would not. Then the Lord Richard said, "This is not a light matter, father; a great estate, craving your pardon, cannot thus pass by word of mouth."

"And it shall not," said the monk, "the Lord Robert shall send you due quittance."

Then the Lord Richard said, "Father, be it so, then; but should the Lord Robert return and claim the estate, it is his."

Then the monk said, "He will not return; he is dead to the world." And then he added, for he saw that the Lord Richard was pondering the matter, "I that speak with you am he." Then he blessed the Lord Richard, and departed in haste—and so solemn was his face and manner, that the Lord Richard did not stay him, but went within in wonder and awe.

Then Robert returned to the monastery, with a quiet joy in his heart; and he made a quittance of the estate, and sent it secretly to the Lord Richard by a faithful hand; and when the Lord Richard came in haste to see the monk and speak with him, he had departed for Spain.

Robert journeyed many days and came at last again to the house of the Duke. And he was then admitted, and bidden to dinner; so he sate in the hall that he knew, and no man recognised him in the thin and sunburnt monk that sate and spoke so low and courteously; and afterwards he asked audience of the Duke, who still lived, but was very near his end; and when he was alone with him, he drew out the stone and said, "My lord, your faithful and loving servant has found the ruby and herewith restores it; and he asks your forgiveness, for he loves you truly;" and Robert knelt beside him, and wept, but not for bitterness of heart.

Then said the Duke, speaking low, "My son, I have need to be forgiven and not to forgive." And they had great joy together, and Robert told him all that was in his heart.

"My lord," he said, "God hath led me by a strange path into peace; He saw the evil strength of my heart, and smote me in my pride; and He made me as a little child that He might receive me; and I am His."

And it came that the Duke was sick unto death; and he sent for Robert, who abode in the city, and would have given him the stone; but Robert said with a smile that he would not have it, for he had learnt at least the meaning of one text, that the price of wisdom is above rubies. And he kissed the hand of the Duke.

And the Duke died and was buried; but of Robert's life and death I know no more; but in the High Church, near the altar, is a stone grave, on which are the words "Brother Robert," and underneath the crown of a prince. So I think he lies there, all of him that doth fade.

CERDA

There was once a city of Gaul named Ilitro, a heathen city. It was encircled by a strong wall, with towers and a moat. There was a drawbridge, for carts to enter the city, which was drawn up at night, for the country was often disturbed by warlike bands; beside the great drawbridge was a little bridge, which could be lowered and drawn up as well; the great bridge was hauled up at sundown, and no cart might enter the city after that time; but the little bridge could be lowered till midnight for a traveller, if he was honest.

The tower was kept by a porter named Cerda, a rough, strong man, who had an impediment in his speech, and spake with few; he lived all alone in the tower. There were two rooms; in the lower room were the weights which drew up the bridge, and a wheel which wound up the chains, with another wheel for the smaller bridge, and a fireplace where the porter cooked his food; in the room above, which was approached by a ladder, there was a table and a chair, and a bed of boards with straw upon it, where he slept. The windows were guarded by shutters, and in winter time it was sorely cold in the tower; but the porter heeded it not, for he was a strong and rough man; he had a wild air, and his long shaggy locks fell on his shoulders. But though he spake little and few spoke to him, he had a loving heart full of tender thoughts which he could not put into words. He was fond of flowers and green trees, and would sometimes walk in the woods that came up to the castle wall, in springtime, with a secret joy in the scent of the flowers and their soft bright heads; he liked to watch the wild animals, and the birds had no fear of him, for he fed them often with crumbs and grain; and they would come on his window-ledge and chirp for food. Sometimes a child who passed the bridge would smile at him, and he would smile back and be glad; to some children whom he knew he would shyly give simple presents—carts carved out of wood, or a wooden sword; but he was so rough and uncouth a man that their elders were not pleased that he should speak with them; and indeed most people spoke of him as of one who could be trusted indeed to do hard toil punctually like a beast of burden, but whose mind was not wholly sound, but like that of a dog or ox. But he did his duty so faithfully, and was moreover so strong and fearless, if there was any troublesome comer to deal with, that he was held to be useful in his place. He had no courtesy for grown men, who heeded him no more than if he had been a machine; but he was kind and gentle with women and maidens, and would carry their burdens for them into the city, as far as he might—for he was forbidden to go out of sight of the bridge.

One day, indeed, he had some talk to a grave, quiet man, a traveller, who came like a merchant to the city, and yet seemed to have no business to do. He was indeed a Christian priest, who was on his way to the West; for there were then a few scattered congregations of Christians in Gaul, though the faith was not yet known through the land. And the priest, seeing something wistful in the rude porter's eye, something that seemed dumbly to ask for love, asked him if he prayed; and the porter with a stammering tongue said some words of the gods of the land; but the priest, who loved to let the good seed fall even by the wayside, told him of the Father of all, and of the Divine Son who came to teach the world the truth, and was slain by wicked men.

Cerda felt a strange hope in his heart, half pity and half joy; and the priest told him that any man in any place could speak to the Father when he would, and he repeated to him a prayer that he might say; but Cerda forgot all the prayer except the first two words, *Our Father*, and, indeed, he did not understand the rest. But he would say those words over and over as he went about his

work, and he would add, out of his own mind, a wish that he might
see the Father; for he thought that He might some day come to the
city, to see His sons there—for the priest had told him that all men
were His sons. So the porter kept watch for the Father's coming;
and he hoped that he might know Him if He came.

Now one day there was a great storm of rain and wind. The
wind beat on the tower, and the rain rustled in the moat; and Cerda
at sundown drew up the dripping bridges, and made all safe, knowing that he would not be disturbed again that night. He sat long
that night listening to the wind, which seemed to have a sad and
homeless voice in it, and then he remembered suddenly that he
had not eaten, and he began to prepare his food. He had a little
piece of meat in the house, which a citizen had given him, and
bread, and a few berries which he had gathered in the wood; so he
began to cook the meat; and it was about midnight, and the storm
was fiercer than ever; when in a pause in the gust he thought he
heard a cry out of the wood across the moat. He listened, but it
came not again, and so he fell to his cooking. Then all at once the
wind stopped, and he heard the rain whisper on the wall, when
suddenly came the cry again, a very faint cry, like the crying of a
child. He threw open the shutter of the window that looked to the
wood, and in the glimmering dark, for there was a sickly light from
the moon which laboured among the clouds, he thought he saw a
little figure stand on the edge of the moat. It was dreary enough
outside, but he went to the wheel and let the small bridge down,
and then he went to the little gate and crossed the slippery plank
with care.

There, near the lip of the moat, stood a little child, a boy that
seemed to be about ten years old, all drenched and shivering, with
his face streaming with rain. Cerda did not know the child, but
asked him, as well as he could for his stammering speech, what he
was doing there and what he desired. The child seemed frightened,
and covered his face with his hands; but Cerda drew his hands
away, not unkindly, and felt how cold and wet the little arms were.
Then the child said that he had wandered from the way, and that
seeing a light he had come near, and had found himself on the edge

of the moat, and had cried out in case any one might hear him. Then Cerda asked him again what he was doing; and the child said timidly that he was about his father's business. Cerda was vexed that a father should be so careless of his child, but he could not understand from the child what the business might be.

So at last he said that the child must come into the tower with him, and that he would give him shelter for the night, and that in the morning he would make search for his father. But it was not with a very good grace that he said it, because he was now himself wetted; moreover, he was weary, and would fain have eaten his meal and slept undisturbed. Then the child shrank back from the slippery plank, so Cerda lifted him in his arms and carried him across. Then he pulled up the bridge again and shut the door, but the child seemed ill at ease. So Cerda did what he could to cheer him, wrung the water from his clothes and hair and covered him with a cloak and made him sit by the fire. Then he gave him of his own meat and drink, and brought the berries, bidding him see how fair they were. And the child ate and drank, looking at Cerda with wide open eyes and saying nought.

He looked to Cerda a frail and weakly child, and his wonder and even anger increased at those that had let such a child be about at that hour; and then he saw that the child was weary, so he carried him up the ladder, still wrapped in the cloak, and laid him on his bed and bid him sleep; and then he went down softly to satisfy his own hunger, and was surprised to see that the food was not diminished but rather seemed increased. So Cerda ate and drank, once or twice ascending the ladder to see if the child slept. And when at last he seemed to sleep, then Cerda himself went up and sat in his chair and thought that he would sleep too; but before sleep came upon him he said his words of prayer many times over, and added his further prayer that he might see the Father.

But while he did so it came into his mind how often he had said the same thing, and yet that nothing had happened to bless him; and he thought that the old priest had told him that the Father always listened to the voice of His sons; but then he bethought him that the Father had so many sons, and so wide a land to see to—though he only pictured the world as a few villages and towns like his own, with a greater town called Rome somewhere in the East—that he comforted himself by thinking that the Father had not had time to visit his city, and still less to visit one so humble as himself; and then a fear came into his mind that among the travellers who had passed the Father might have passed and he had not recognised him.

Then at last Cerda slept, his head down upon his breast, and the wind died down outside and left a breathless stillness, save for the drops that fell from the eaves of the tower; and then he dreamed a very strange dream. He thought that he was walking in a wood, and came upon a great open space, down into which descended a wide staircase out of the sky. It was all dark and cloudy at the top, but the clouds were lit with a fierce inner light that touched the edges, as in a winter sunset, with a hue of flame. From the cloud emerged a figure, at first dim, like a wreath of cloud, but slowly defining itself into the shape of a man, who came down slowly and serenely, looking about him as he stepped with a quiet greatness; when he came near the bottom of the ladder he beckoned Cerda to approach, who came trembling; but the other smiled so tenderly that Cerda forgot his fears and fell on his knees at the staircase foot; and the man went down to him and said, "Cerda, thy prayers are heard, and thy patience is noted; and thou shalt indeed see the Father." And as he said the words a great ray of light came from the cloud and seemed to brighten all the place.

Cerda woke with a start, the voice still sounding in his ears; woke to find the room all alight—and he thought for a moment that it was broad day, and that he had for the first time neglected his duty and left the bridge unclosed. But in a moment he saw that it was not the light of day, but a very pure and white radiance, such as the moon makes on the face of a still pool in woods, seen afar from a height. The whole room was lit by it, so that he could see the beams of the roof and the rough stones of the wall. Then he saw that the child had risen from the bed, and that the radiance seemed brightest all about him; it was the same face, but all brightened and glorified; and the child seemed to be clad in a dim white

robe of a soft and cloudlike texture. And then all at once Cerda felt
that he was in the presence of a very high and holy mystery, such
as he had hardly dreamed the world contained, and it came
strangely into his mind, with a shock of awe and almost horror,
that this was the child to whom he had spoken impatiently, whom
he had fed and tended, and whose body he had carried in his arms;
and he fell on his knees and hid his face and could not look on the
child's face.

Then he heard a very low voice that was yet so clear that Cerda
felt it would be heard all through the city, that said, "Cerda, good
and faithful servant of God, thou hast believed and therefore hast
thou seen," and "He that hath seen Me hath seen the Father."

Then there came into Cerda's mind a great rush of beautiful
thoughts; it was as though the tower had burst forth into bloom
and was all filled with lilies and roses. He knew that all men were
sons of the Father, and that the Father waited for them to come to
Him; and he saw that each man's life was a path which led to the
Father, and that the rougher the path was the more surely did it
conduct them; and he saw too, though he could not have said it to
another, that it mattered not how or where a man lived, or how
humble or even hateful his task might be, since the Father knew
best what each of His sons needed, and placed him where he could
best find the way; and he saw, too, that those who seemed to wander in misery or even wickedness, were being secretly drawn to
the Father's heart all the time; all this he saw, and many other
high and holy things which it is not possible for human lips to
speak. But he knew in his heart that a peace was given him which
nothing, not even the heaviest affliction, could ever trouble again.
And then the light died out; and looking up he saw the child once
more, but now very faintly, as though far off but yet near; and then
all was dark. And Cerda slept the sleep of a little child. And in the
morning when he woke, he knew at once that the world was a different place. Hunger, cold, and weariness were but like clouds that
hid the sun for a season; but the vision was the truth. And he went
about his daily toil with so joyful a heart that it seemed as though
his feet were winged.

And that day there came by an old citizen, whom Cerda had heard by report was held to be a Christian; and he looked upon Cerda for a moment in silence, with a kind of wonder in his face. But Cerda could find no words to tell him what had befallen him, till the old man said, "Can it be, Cerda, that you know the truth? for there seems to be something in your face which makes me ask you." And Cerda found words to say that though he knew but little of Christ, yet he believed in Him. "Oh, it matters not," said the other, "what we know *of* Christ, so long as we know *Him*; but you, my brother," he added, "look as you might look if you had seen the Lord face to face." "I think I have," said Cerda. And the old man doubted not, but went away pondering, knowing that the wise and prudent might not know what was revealed unto babes. But no man ever knew why for the rest of his days (for he died as a porter) Cerda slept only in his chair, and never lay down upon his bed; or why, before he closed the little gate, he always knelt for a moment to pray where the feet of the child had stood upon the brink of the moat.

LINUS

In the old days there was a rich city of Asia, Cibyra by name, a prosperous place of wealthy merchants, full of large stone houses, with towers to catch the breeze, cloisters full of shadow and coolness, looking upon garden-closes set with little branching trees, very musical with clear fountains. The land was not yet wholly Christian, but persecution had long ceased, and those in high places called themselves by the Saviour's name; but still there were many who were heathen in all but name, and did not follow the Way, but spoke or thought of the faith as a heavy burden bound on the backs of men. And there was much wickedness in such cities as Cibyra, men and women following the desires of their hearts, and only when sick or tired, or sometimes ashamed, looking fearfully to judgment.

In Cibyra lived a young man called Linus; he was an orphan; his father had been a Greek merchant, struck down in youth by a mysterious disease, already a dying man when his little son was born; he had named him Linus, thinking in his heart of an old sad song, sung by reapers, about a young shepherd who had to suffer death, and had been unwilling to leave the beautiful free life, the woods and hills that he loved. And his mother had approved the name, partly to please the dying man, and partly because the name had been borne by holy men; soon afterwards she, too, had died, leaving her son to the care of her brother, a strict and stern Christian, but with a loving heart; so that Linus had been brought up in simple and faithful ways; and the only thing that had given

33

anxious thoughts to his uncle was that the child's great inheritance had become yearly greater, many streets and houses having
been built on the land which belonged to him. But the boy was
simple and pure, very docile and dutiful, apt to learn, loving beauty
in all things, fond of manly exercise, hating riot and evil talk, generous and noble in body and mind.

Now just when Linus came of age, his uncle had fallen sick and
found himself near his end; he had accustomed Linus to the knowledge of his riches, and had made him understand that his wealth
was not only for show and pleasure, but was to be used generously
and wisely, to help the humble and poor; and this in his last days
was much in his thoughts and often on his lips—though he concealed his coming death from Linus, until at last the boy was roused
at night to take leave of his uncle, who had been both father and
mother to him; and the dying man's last words had been a prayer
for the boy that he might be pure and loving; and then he had sighed
and turning to Linus he took his hand and kissed it, and said, "Remember"; and then with another sigh had died, quietly as he had
lived; and the boy had known what he meant him to keep in mind,
and that it was a charge to him to be careful and generous.

So Linus was left to himself; he was master of a great house
and many servants, and with the revenues of a prince; and when
his grief was a little abated, and memory was more sweet than sad,
he made many plans how to use his wealth; but it is not easy to
spend money wisely, and as yet, though he gave a large sum to the
deacons for the poorer brethren, he had not been able to decide
how to bestow his wealth best, and still his inheritance increased.

Meanwhile his life began to be very full of happiness and pleasure; he loved friendship and merry talk, and music and the sight
of beautiful things, rich houses and fair men and women; and he
had too, besides his wealth and his beauty, much of the fine and
fragrant thing that the Greeks called charm; it was a pleasure to
see him move and speak; in his presence life became a more
honourable and delightful thing, full of far-off echoes and old
dreams, and the charm was the greater because Linus did not know
it himself; all men were kindly and gracious to him, wherever he

went, and so he thought that it was the same for all others; he was modest, and he had been brought up not to turn his thoughts upon himself, but to give others their due, and to show courtesy and respect to all persons, high or low, so that the world was very tender to him; and in the long summer days, with a little business, to make, as it were, a solid core to life, with banquets, and hunting, and military exercises, and the company of the young, the days sped very quickly away, divided one from another by dreamless sleep. And his friends became more and more numerous, and the plans which he had made to use his wealth were put aside for a while. Sometimes he heard a word spoken or saw glances exchanged which somehow cast a little shadow across his mind; but still, men and women, knowing his bringing-up, and awed perhaps by his instinctive purity, put their best side forward for Linus. So that he remained innocent, and thought others so. And when sometimes an old friend of his uncle's said a grave word to him, or warned him against some of those with whom he spent his days, Linus said lightly that he judged no one, and indeed that he had seen nothing to judge.

One evening he found himself at a banquet at the house of a rich man whom for some reason he did not wholly trust. He had hesitated to go, but had put the thought aside, saying to himself that he must not be suspicious. The company had assembled, all being men, and were listening from an open gallery to a concert of lutes and viols, the players being skilfully concealed among the trees of the garden. It was twilight, and the blue sky, with a few bright stars, died into a line of pure green, the sharp tops of the cypresses showing very black against it, and the towers of a neighbouring house looking gravely over.

Somehow Linus did not wholly like the music; it seemed to him as though some bright and yet dangerous beast was walking in the dark alleys of the garden, his eyes sparkling; the music, after a low descant, rose in a delicious wail of sorrow and sank again, and Linus felt something wild and passionate stir in his heart and rise in yearning for he knew not what. He looked round at the guests who sat or stood in little groups, and he felt again that he had not been wise to come. There were several persons there who were not well spoken of, luxurious and effeminate men, whom Linus knew only by repute; but at that moment his host came up and spoke so gently and courteously to Linus, asking him whether he was pleased with the unseen music, that Linus grew ashamed of his secret thoughts.

Presently the banquet was ready, and the guests went in little groups into a large vaulted hall, kept deliciously cool by a fountain, that poured into a marble trough like an altar at the end, with a white statue above it of a boy looking earnestly at the water. At the other end the great doors were open to the garden, and the breeze, heavily laden with the scent of flowers, came wandering in and stirred the flames of the lamps which stood on high stone brackets along the walls. Each side of the room was supported by an arcade of stone built out upon the wall.

Linus lingered behind a little, looking out into the garden, where he heard the soft talk and laughter of the musicians who were dispersing, and in a moment found himself the last to go in, except for a tall thin man, whom Linus knew only by sight and name, and who had the reputation of eccentricity in the town; he was a secret, silent man, tall and lean, with bright dark eyes. He was seen everywhere, but lived alone in a melancholy tower, where he was said to study much and observe the courses of the stars, and it was hinted by some people that he was versed in magical books, though he passed for a Christian. He spoke but little in company, and watched others quietly and gravely, with something of a smile, as one might watch a child at play. But as he belonged to an ancient family, and had a certain fame, he was a welcome guest at many houses.

This man, whose name was Dion, came up to Linus, and with a courteous gesture asked if he might have the honour to place himself next to him— "We have many friends in common," he added; and Linus, who loved to make a new friend, assented; and so they went in together, and took their places side by side about the middle of the great table; on the other side of Linus sat a man, with an uneasy smile, whom he did not know, to whom Linus bowed; at first the conversation was low and fitful; the table was abundantly furnished, and the servants were deft and assiduous; Linus was soon satisfied with meat and drink, which were circulated almost too plentifully; so that he contented himself with refusing the constant proffer of food, kept his full cup untasted, and found pleasure in the talk of Dion, who told him some curious legends.

Soon the talk became louder and more insistent, and frequent laughter broke out in all directions, but Linus felt more and more in a kind of pleasant solitude with his new friend. After a pause in the talk, in which their thoughts seemed to grapple together, Linus took courage, and said that he was surprised to meet Dion in this company. "Yes," said Dion, with a slight smile, "and I confess that I was even more surprised to meet you here; and, moreover, I saw when you came in that you were surprised to be here yourself. You thought that you had travelled a long way from where you began."

At those words, which seemed as though his inmost thoughts had been read, and still more at the glance which accompanied them, Linus felt a strange sensation, almost of fear; and in the silence that followed he heard higher up the table the end of a tale told that seemed to him to be both evil and shameful, and the laugh that followed it brought a blush from his heart to his cheek. "Yes," said Dion, gravely, as though answering a question, "you are right to hate that story, and you feel, I do not doubt, as if it would be well for you to rise and fly such contact. But it would not be well; we must be in the world, but not of it; and if a man can but be sure of keeping his heart clear and bright, he does better to mix with the world; we need not forget that the Master Himself was accused of loving the company of publicans and sinners more than that of the scrupulous Pharisees." These words gave Linus a kind of courage and filled him with wonder, and he looked up at Dion, who was regarding him with dark eyes.

"Yes," went on Dion, "the only thing is that a man should not be deceived by these shows, but should be able to look through and behind them. This room seems bright and solid enough to us; the laughter is loud; it is all very real and true to us; but I think

that you have the power to see further; look in my eyes for a moment and tell me what you see."

Linus looked at Dion's eyes, and all at once he seemed to stand
in a lonely and misty place; it seemed like a hill swept with clouds;
it was but for a moment, and then the bright room and the table
came back; but it swam before his eyes.

"This is very strange," said Linus. "I do not think that I ever
felt this before."

Then Dion said, "Look at the wall there opposite to us, between
the arches, and tell me what you see."

The wall between the arches was a plain wall of stone that gave,
Linus knew, upon the street; he looked for a moment at the wall
and the joints of the masonry. "I see nothing," he said, "but the
wall and the jointed stones."

"Look again," said Dion.

Linus looked again, and suddenly the wall became blurred, as
though a smoke passed over it; then the stones seemed to him to
melt into a kind of mist, which moved this way and that; all at once
the mists drew up, rolling off in ragged fringes, and showed him a
dark room within, plainly furnished with tall presses; in the centre of the room was a table at which a man sat writing in a book, a
large volume, writing busily, his hand moving swiftly and noiselessly over the paper. At the far end of the room was an archway
which seemed to lead into a corridor; but the man never raised his
head. He was an old man with grey hair, clad in a cloudy kind of
gown; his face seemed stern and sad; over his head played a curious radiance, as though from some unseen source, which brightened into two clear centres or points of light over his brows.

While he still wrote, some one whom Linus could not see very
distinctly came quietly into the room through the archway, carrying in his arms another volume like the one in which the man was
writing; the writer never raised his head, but Linus saw that he
was finishing the last page of the book; as he finished he pushed it
aside with something of impatience in his gesture; the other laid
the new volume before him, and the man began at once to write, as

though eager to make up for the moment's interruption; the other took up the finished book, clasped it, and went silently out.

"This is a very strange thing," said Linus faltering. "Who would have supposed there was a room in there? I had thought it gave upon the street."

"There are hidden rooms everywhere," said Dion; "but I see that you are not satisfied; you may go in and look closer; you cannot interrupt him who writes; he has no eyes but for his task—and no one here will notice you."

Linus looked round; it seemed to him indeed as though by some strange attraction the party had been drawn into two groups right and left of him, and that he and Dion were left alone; the merriment was louder and wilder, and frequent peals of laughter indicated to him the telling of some tale—wicked it seemed to him from the glistening eyes and disordered looks of some of the guests; but the laughter seemed to come to him far off as through a veil of water. So he rose from his place and went into the room.

It was very plain and severe; the presses round the room seemed to contain volumes like that in which the man was writing. It was lit with a low radiance of its own, very pure and white. He looked into the door that led into the corridor; it seemed to be brighter in there. He stood waiting, undecided. He looked first at the man who wrote; his hand moved with great rapidity, and his face seemed furrowed and grave; and Linus felt a fear of him, which was increased by the curious light which seemed to well in fountains from his brow, lighting the grey hair, the book, and the strong white hands. He looked back and could see the room he had left. The talk fell on his ear with a dreadful clearness, and the laughter sounded not cheerful, but intolerably hateful and evil; he could see Dion, and in his own place there sat some one half turned away from him, whom he did not recognise, though the form seemed somehow familiar.

While he waited, doubtful as to what he should do, he heard a movement close beside him; and turning saw the messenger who had brought the book, a tall serene-looking man, young of feature, but with a look of age and wisdom about his face. He seemed in some way familiar to him, and this was increased by the half-smiling look which met his own. Then the messenger said in a low distinct tone, but as though sparing of his words, as a man will talk in the presence of one who is at work, and as though answering a question, "Yes, you may look—the book is open to all." And as he said the words he made a little gesture with his hand as though to indicate that he might draw nearer. Linus at once without hesitation went and stood beside the writer and looked upon the book.

For a moment he did not understand, it seemed a record of some talk or other. Then in a moment he saw words which made his cheeks burn, and in another moment it flashed upon him that this was a record of all that was said in the room he had left. The strangeness of the thought scarcely crossed his mind, for he was lost in a kind of terror, a horror of the thought that what was said so lightly and thoughtlessly should be so strictly preserved; he stood for a moment, his eyes fastened on the paper on which the sad syllables shaped themselves, and with his terror there mixed a kind of wild pity for the unhappy people who were talking thus, thinking that each word died as it fell from their lips, and little knew that the record was thus intently made.

He looked up, and at the other side of the writer stood the young man who had bidden him take his place, who made a gesture, laying his finger on his lips as if for silence, while there rang through the hall without the wild laughter which greeted the end of the story—then he motioned him away. As they went softly away together a few paces, Linus looked at him as though to make sure that what he had seen was true; the other gave a mournful motion of the head, saying softly, "Yes! every word;" and added, as if to himself, "every idle word."

Linus stood for a moment as if irresolute; he had an intense longing to go back to the room he had left and tell the guests what he had seen, to silence by any means in his power the talk, and yet half aware that he would not be believed, when the other led him quickly across the room, and pointed to the door that led to the corridor, laying his hand lightly on his arm. Not knowing what he did, and still lost in his miserable doubt, Linus obeyed the gentle touch. They passed through the door and entered a long silent vaulted corridor, with plain round arches; on one side there were presses which Linus knew in himself were full of similar records; on the right were doors, but all closed. They went on to the end; it was all lit with a solemn holy light, the source of which Linus could not see, and the place seemed to grow brighter as they advanced, brighter and cooler—for the air of the room they had left was hot and still.

They went through a door, and Linus found himself in a long large room, with arches open to the daylight. He looked through one of those, and saw a landscape unfamiliar to him and strangely beautiful. It was a great open flat country, full of lawns and thickets and winding streams. It seemed to be uninhabited, and had a quiet peace like a land in which the foot of man had never trodden; far away over the plain he saw a range of blue hills, very beautiful and still, like the hills a man may see in dreams. There were buildings there, for he saw towers and walls, the whole lit with a clear and pearly light, but it was all too distant for him to distinguish anything, and indeed would have been hardly visible but for the surpassing brightness of the air; the breeze that came in was fresh and fragrant, like the breeze of dawn; and far away to the left he saw what looked like the glint of light on a sea or some wide water, where the day seemed to be breaking, and coming up with a tranquil joy.

Linus' heart was so lightened at this sweet place that he only dimly wondered what this strange country was that lay so near the city where he dwelt and yet in which he had never set foot. While he stood there he heard a faint noise of wings, and a bird such as he had never seen appeared flying; but beating its wings and stretching out its feet like a bird coming home, it alighted for a moment on the parapet, and seemed to Linus' eye like a dove, with sparkling lights upon its head and neck, and with a patient eye; but this was only for a moment; as if it had finished its work, it rose again in the air, and in an instant was out of sight; but the next moment, another bird appeared; this was a black bird, strong and even clumsy, but it alighted in the same way on the balustrade, a little further off, and Linus could see its sparkling eye and strong claws. Then came a little bird like a wren, which went as noise-lessly as it came; then several birds all at once. Linus was so much surprised at the sight of these birds that he had no eyes for any-thing else, till his guide touched him on the arm, and he looked up and saw that the room was not unoccupied.

There was a large table of some dark wood in the centre, and by it stood a man who seemed to be reading in a book which lay open on the table, following the lines with his finger; and Linus thought, though he could not see the face, that as he read he wept. And at the same time he knew that this was the master of the house, though how he knew it he could hardly explain, except for the awed and reverent look in the face of his guide; in the presence of the former writer, whom they had just left, his guide had borne him-self, he now reflected, as the son of a house might bear himself in the presence of an old and trusted servant, who was valued more for his honesty than for his courtesy.

But here all was different, and Linus too felt a silent awe steal-ing into his mind, he knew not why, at the sight of the still and gracious figure.

The messenger made a movement with his hand as though Linus were to go forward, so he stepped towards the table; and then he waited, but the man drew a little aside and put the book towards Linus, as though he were to look at it. Linus looked, and saw that it was one of the former books of records; and something of the same wistful sadness came over him at the thought of all the evil words and deeds that were here noted. But now there came a great and wonderful surprise; for, as the man ran his fingers along the lines, they became faint and blurred, and presently the page seemed clean, just as the water dies out of a cloth which is put before a hot fire; it seemed to Linus as though the writing van-ished most speedily when one of the birds lit on the railing; and presently he was sure of this, for each time that a bird came on the ledge the man raised his head a little and seemed to consider—and all the while the dawn brightened over the sea.

Then Linus saw that the hand which moved over the page, a beautiful yet strong hand, was strangely scarred; and at this he caught his breath, for a thought too deep for utterance came into his heart; and then, as though the unasked question was answered, came a clear low voice which said, "These are the wounds with which I was wounded in the house of my friends."

And then, unbidden, but because he could not do otherwise, Linus knelt softly down; and the man, tenderly and gently, as a father might tell a child a secret by slow degrees, fearful that it might be too hard for the tender spirit, turned and looked at him, and Linus felt the eyes sink as it were into his soul, and it seemed to him at that moment that he had said without the need of speech all that had ever been in his heart; he felt himself in one instant understood and cared for, utterly and perfectly, so that he should have no need ever to fear or doubt again; and Linus said softly the only words that came into his mind, the words of one who had doubted and was strengthened, "My Lord and my God."

So he knelt for a moment, and then knew that he was to rise and go, and it seemed to him that the other looked back upon the book with somewhat of a sigh, as one who was content to work, but had waited long.

So Linus went back down the corridor and through the little room, where the man still sat writing, and stepped into the hall again.

The hall seemed very dark and fiery after the radiance of that other morning; the guests were as Linus had left them; Dion sat in his place; and just as Linus came to his own chair, it seemed to him that some one slipped quietly away; and Dion looked at him with a very tender and inquiring gaze. "Yes," said Linus, "I have seen." "And you understand?" said Dion. "Yes," said Linus, "in part—I understand enough."

When Linus looked round the hall again, he was surprised to find that what had distressed and almost terrified him before, the uproar, the evil mirth, the light-hearted wickedness moved him now more with a tender and wondering sorrow; and he asked Dion how it was. "Because," said Dion, "you have seen the end; and you know that though the way is dark and long, we shall arrive." "Yes," he went on, "we shall arrive; there is no doubting that; the Father's heart is wide, and He will bring His sons even from afar."

THE BROTHERS

There was once a great Lord of Yorkshire, the Baron de Benoit, who had two sons named Henry and Christopher. Their mother was long dead; Henry was a bold and careless boy, courageous and fearless, outspoken to every one, yet loving none; fond of the chase, restless, and never weary; but Christopher was a timid and weakly child, with a heart for all; dreaming of great deeds which he feared to do; while Henry dreamed not, but did whatever he undertook, great things or small. Christopher sate much with the old priest, or with the women; when the minstrels played in the hall, his heart was lifted up within him; and he loved to loiter alone in the woods in springtime, to look in the open faces of the flowers, and to listen for the songs of birds. The Baron was a rough good-natured man, who ruled his estates diligently; and he loved Henry well, but Christopher he despised in his heart, and often said that he was a girl spoiled in the making.

Now how different were the boys in character let the following tale witness:

Once the huntsmen caught a wolf, and brought it to the castle yard to make sport; the wolf blinked and snarled in the pen where they put it; and the boys were called to kill it. Christopher bent over to look at it, and thought that the wolf was doubtless wondering why men wished it evil, and was longing for the deep woods and for its warm lair. Henry thrust a spear into Christopher's hand and bade him slay it. The wolf rose at his approach, hobbling on his pinioned feet, hating to die, thought Christopher, among laughter and jests. And he threw the spear down and said, "I will not." "Nay, you dare not," said Henry; and he thrust the spear into the wolf's side; the wolf struggled hard, and as Henry pushed close, tore his hand; but Henry only laughed and thrust again; and then he daubed Christopher's face with the blood that ran from his hand, and said, "Go and tell the maidens that you have slain a wolf in single combat."

But, for all that, Christopher loved his brother exceedingly, and thought him the brightest and goodliest treasure in the world.

There came to stay at the castle an Abbot, a wise and brave man, before whom even the Baron was awed; and he had much talk with Christopher, who opened his heart to him. The Abbot found that he could read, and knew the stories of the saints and the answers of the Mass, and had discernment of good and evil. So the Abbot sought out the Baron, and told him that Christopher would make a very wise priest, and that he was apt to be ruled, and therefore, said he, he will be apt to rule; and he added that he thought that the boy would make a great counsellor, and even bishop; and then the Baron said that Christopher had no courage and endurance. The Abbot replied that he believed he had both, but that they were of a different nature to the courage and endurance of a man-at-arms; that he was of the stuff of which holy men, martyrs and saints, were made; but that it was ill to nurture a dove in the nest of an eagle. So the Baron said that he should take Christopher, and make a priest of him, if the boy would.

Then Christopher was called, and the Baron asked him bluntly whether he would be a priest; and Christopher, seeing the Abbot's kind glance upon him, took courage and said that he would obey his father in all things. But he looked so wan and gentle, and so like his mother, that the Baron put his arm about him and said kindly that he would have him choose for himself, and kissed his cheek. But Christopher burst out weeping and hid his face on his father's shoulder; and then he said, "I will go." And the Abbot said, "Baron, you are a man of war, and yet shall you be proud of this your son; he shall win victories indeed, but in his own field—nay, I doubt not that he will do your house great service and honour."

And so it was arranged that the Abbot, who was on a journey, should return in a week and take the boy.

So Christopher had a week to make his farewells, and he made them faithfully and tenderly, though he thought his heart would break. But the Abbot had told him on parting that God indeed called men, when He would have them to serve Him, and that he too was surely bidden. And Christopher, young though he was, felt that he was like a boat that must battle through a few breakers to reach a quiet haven; and he spake with all and each, and said farewell, until even the roughest were sorry that the boy should go. But the last night was the sorest, for he must part with his brother; the boys slept together in a great bed in a room in the tower; and Christopher dared that night to encircle his brother with his arms, and tell him that he loved him, and that he wished there were something small or great that he could do for him. And Henry, who loved not caresses, said laughing, that he should not need his services for a long time. "But when I am old and weary and have done many deeds of blood, then you may pray for me if you will." Then Christopher would have had him talk awhile, but Henry said he was weary and must sleep, and turned away, adding that he would wake betimes in the morning and that they would talk then. And Christopher lay and heard him breathe softly, and at last, wearied out, he slept. But Henry woke in the dawn, and thinking of a stag that came down to pull the hay from the ricks, and half fearing, too, his brother's tears and sighs, dressed himself quietly and stole away while Christopher slept, thinking that he would return to see him go. And when Christopher woke and found his brother gone, he fell into such a passion of grief that he heeded nothing else, but went through his farewells so stonily and dumbly that the Baron made haste to set him on his journey; and Henry did not return.

So Christopher passed into the holy life, but choosing not to be a priest, he became a monk of the strictest discipline, so that the monks wondered at his holiness. But they at the Castle soon forgot him and thought no more of the frail child.

Then it happened that the Baron rode one day in the sun, and coming home, dismounted, and fell dizzily upon his face; they laid him in his chamber, but he never spoke, only breathed heavily; and that night he died. And Henry, who was now of age, thought but little of his father's death because of the respect that all paid him, and of the wealth and power that thus flowed suddenly into his hands. And he married a fair maiden called the Lady Alice, who bore him a son; and he ruled diligently in his lands, and rode to battle, and lived such a life as he best loved.

But one day there fell upon him a heaviness of limb and a loathing for food; and though they daily tended him, he grew no better; soon he could not even sit upon his horse, but became so pale and wasted that he could hardly rise from his chair. And some thought that a spell was cast upon him, but that mended not matters at all; the king's own leech came to visit him, and shook his head, saying that no art could avail, since the spring of life was somehow broken within him and he must die unless God were good to him and healed him.

Now the Lady Alice feared God, and knew what wonders were wrought by Him at the prayers of saints, so she took counsel with the priests of the Castle, but said no word of it to the Lord Henry, because he jested at sacred things; and the priest told her that three days' journey away was a house of holy monks, where many miracles of healing were wrought, and he advised her to go secretly and ask counsel of the Prior. So under pretence of seeking for another leech, the Lady Alice rode south, and on the third day she came to the place. The monastery stood very solitary in a valley with much wood about it; the walls rose fair and white, with a tall church in the midst, all lit with a heavenly light of evening. And the Lady Alice felt in her burdened heart that God would be gracious and hear her prayers.

They rode to the gate, and Alice asked that she might see the Prior; she would not tell her name, but the porter seeing her attended by two men-at-arms, admitted her; and presently the Lady Alice was had into a small bare room, and in a moment the Prior stood before her. He was an old man, very lean and grim, but with a kindly face; she told him that her husband, a great knight, was sick unto death, but she told him not her name, and the Prior spared to ask her; when she had done her story, the Prior said that there was in the monastery a young monk, Brother Lawrence, of such steadfast life and holiness that his prayers would almost avail to give life to the dead; and that he would dispense him leave, if he were willing to go with her awhile; for the Prior saw that she was a great lady, and he was moved by her grief and purity.

So Brother Lawrence was fetched, and soon stood before them; and the Prior told the lady's tale, and Brother Lawrence said that he would go, if he was permitted. So in the morning they rode away. Then the Lady Alice told him all the tale, saying that the sick man was the Baron de Benoit, and that he loved not God, though he served him faithfully, though knowing not that it was God whom he served. And the monk said, "Ay, and there be many such;" but she wondered that he grew so strangely pale, yet thought that it was his long fasting, and the bitter morning air. Then the monk questioned her very nearly about all her life, saying that in such cases it was needful to know all things, "that our prayers," he said, "beat not in vain against a closed gate." And she told him of all she knew.

Then at last, in a still twilight, they drew near to the Castle, and the lady saw that the monk kept his eyes fixed on the ground, and looked not to left nor right, like a man in a sore conflict; and she knew that he prayed.

That night the monk was laid in a chamber in the tower; and all night his lamp burned, till the dawn came up. And the watchman thought he prayed late; but if they could have seen the monk they would have wondered that he paced softly up and down, looking lovingly about him, the tears welling to his eyes; once he kissed the bedpost of the bed; and then he knelt and wrestled in prayer, until the priest called him to the Mass. And there seemed such a radiance about him, worn and thin though he was, that the priest marvelled to see him.

Then the Lady Alice came to fetch him in a great fearfulness, for she knew that the Lord Henry hated monks; but the monk said to her that she need not fear; and she took comfort.

Then she brought him to the great room where the Baron lay; and she went in, and said, "Henry, I have brought one who works many wonders of healing—and dear husband, be not angry, though he is a monk; for the monks know many things; and perhaps God will be gracious, and give my dear one back to me, to cherish me and our son."

The Lord Henry looked at her very sternly; but the pale and tearful face of his wife, and her loving grief moved him, and he said, "Well, I will see him; and let it testify in how evil a case I am, that monks are brought to my bedside, and I have not even the strength to say them nay." He spoke roughly, but he took the Lady Alice's hand in his own and said to her, "Dear one, make haste. I will not refuse you this, for I think it is the last request that I shall have power to grant—I am past the help of man."

For since the Lady Alice's departure, the Lord Henry had been in very evil case; till then he had hoped; but his sleep had gone from him, and a great blackness came over him, and seemed to part his life, as with a dark chasm, from what lay before him. There in those lonely hours he went through the scenes of his past life; he saw himself a bright and bold boy, and all the joy of his early years came before him, and he saw that his joy had been the greater because he had not known he was more glad than others. He thought of his father and of his frail brother Christopher; and he wished he had been kinder to both; then he had the thought of his wife and his helpless child, and all that might befall them. And he thought, too, of God, whom he must now meet, who seemed to sit like a Judge, in a pavilion of clouds at a ladder's fiery head, with no smile or welcome for him.

So the Lady Alice went out and brought Brother Lawrence to the chamber; and at the door he prayed for strength that he might comfort him that was sick; and Lady Alice pulled the door to and departed; and the two were left alone.

Then Brother Lawrence murmured a Latin salutation, as the custom of his order was; and Henry fixed his eyes, large with sickness, on him, and made a reverence of the head. Then he said, "I wish, sir, I could give you a better welcome; but I am sick, as you see; indeed, I think I am very near my end. The Lady Alice would have me see you, for she says you have wrought wonderful cures. Well, here is a man who is more than willing to be cured; but I am no saint. I believe in God and Holy Church; but—I will speak openly—not much in monks and priests."

"As though," said the monk with a smile, "a man should say 'I believe in food, but not in the eating of it'—yet let that pass, my Lord Baron; I am no foe to plain speaking—it was ever the mark of Christ and the holy saints; but let me ask you first about your disease, for that is my duty now."

Henry was well pleased with the shrewdness of the monk's words; and he answered the Brother's questions about his illness with a good grace. When he had done, the monk shook his head. "I must warn you," he said, "that it is a sore case; but I have known such recover. I would have time to consider; let me abide to-night under your roof, and I will tell you to-morrow what shall be given to me to say;" and the monk made as though he would have withdrawn.

But Henry said, "One question I would ask of you. I had a brother, Christopher by name; he is a monk—but he hath sent me no word of himself for many years—indeed, he may be dead. Can you give me tidings of him?"

The other grew pale to the lips; then he said, as with an effort, "I know your brother, my Lord Baron, but the rules of our order—he is of the same order indeed as myself—are strict, and it is forbidden us to speak of our brethren to those that are without. Be assured, however, that he is alive and well; and perhaps you shall have tidings from himself anon."

Then he went out; and presently the Lady Alice came in to see her husband. Henry seemed to her a little brighter already, and a hope flickered up in her heart. He smiled at her and said, "My Alice, I think well of your monk; he is a shrewd fellow, and knows his trade. I think somewhat better of his kind—he seems to me, indeed, in some way familiar, or reminds me of one that I know; let him be well bestowed, and to-morrow he will tell me, as he said, what he thinks of my case."

But the monk went to the chapel, and there he wrestled sore in prayer; and then he fasted and watched; but at last, wearied out, he fell asleep just before the dawn, and there came a dream to him. He dreamed that he stood in the castle yard, and he had in his hand two pots of flowers, one of lilies and one of roses; and there came to him a tall and strange man, with a look of command in his face, yet full of love; and the monk thought that he turned to the stranger and offered him the flowers, and the man laid his hand upon the roses; but the monk said, "Nay, my lord, rather take the lilies;" and the other said, "The roses are mine and the lilies are mine; one will I take and leave the other awhile; but at thy prayer I will take the lilies first, because thou hast been faithful in a few things." Then the monk gave him the lilies, but with a sore pang; and the other laid his hand upon them, and the lilies withered away. Then the monk said, "And now, my lord, they are not worthy to be given thee," but the other said, "They shall revive and bloom," and then he smiled.

Then the monk awoke, and the dawn came faintly in at the east: and he shivered in his vigil, and fell to pondering on his dream; for he doubted not that it came from God. So, when he had pondered a little, he was amazed and said in his prayer, "Woe is me that I cannot see light." And as he said the words the sun brightened up the sky, and in a moment the monk saw what the Lord would have him to do.

Then, when it was day, he sought the Lady Alice, and she came and stood before him, and he said, "Lady, God will give back your lord to you—for a time; only believe!" Then she fell to weeping for joy, and the monk checked her not, but said, "These be gracious tears." Then he said, "And now I must return in haste; I must not linger." And she prayed him to go with her to the Baron; but he said he must not; but one thing he said he would have her promise, that if it were needful for him to see the Baron, when he should be healed of his disease, he would come to his summons; and the Lady Alice promised and pledged her word. Then he blessed her and departed and rode away, looking neither to left nor right. And the Lady Alice went to her husband, and the Baron said, wondering, that he was better already, and he called for food and ate with appetite; and from that day he revived, climbing back slowly into life again. And there was great rejoicing in the Castle.

And when he was nearly well, and could walk and ride, and his strength increased day by day, giving him exceeding joy, there rode a monk in haste to the Castle, and said to the Lady Alice that Brother Lawrence would see the Baron; and he added that he must not fail to come speedily if he would see him alive, for he was in sore case. Then the Lady Alice asked how it was with him, and the monk said that ever since he had visited the Castle he had been in the chastening of God; his strength ebbed from him day by day. Then the Lady Alice told her husband of his promises, and he said, "Right gladly will I go and see the Brother, for he hath brought me back to life again, and he is a true man."

So the Baron rode away, and as he rode the spring was coming in all the lanes; the trees stood in a cloud of green; the woods were sweet with flowers, and the birds sang loud and clear, and the Baron had such joy in his heart as he had not believed a heart could hold; and he found it in his spirit to thank God for the gift of life restored to him, and as he went he sang softly to himself.

And he came to the house, and because he was a great Baron, the Prior came out to do him honour, and the Baron lighted off his horse and did him great reverence, saying, "Lord Prior, I have lived carelessly and thought little of God and served Him little; but He hath rewarded me though I am unworthy; and now I will serve Him well." Then the Prior rejoiced, and said, "Lord Baron, thou speakest wisely, and the Lord shall increase thee mightily."

Then the Prior led him to the infirmary, for he said that the Brother Lawrence was near to death; and the Baron found him lying in a little bed in a corner of the great room which was all full of light. There stood two monks beside him; but when the Baron entered, Brother Lawrence, who lay in a swoon, raised himself up, and said smiling, "So thou hast come, my brother." And the Baron kneeled down beside him, and said, "Yes, Brother, I have come to show my thanks to you for your prayers and good offices. For God has heard them and given me life." Then Brother Lawrence said, "Give the glory to God, my brother," and the baron said, "Ay, I do that!" and Brother Lawrence smiled and bade the monks depart from him and leave him with the Baron alone. And then Brother Lawrence looked upon him for a while in silence, and his eyes were full of a heavenly light and great joy. And presently he said, "I have a thing that I must tell you, my brother. You asked of me whether I knew your brother Christopher, and I answered you shortly enough, but now I have leave to tell you; and I am he."

Then there was a long silence, and the Baron drew near and kissed him on the cheek.

Then Brother Lawrence said, "And now, dear brother, I will tell you all the truth; for the hand of God is laid upon me, and to-day I must depart;" and then he told him of the vision and interpreted it saying, "The Lord was merciful and let me give my life for thine; and I give it, O how gladly; and I tell you not this for your pity or for your praise, but that you may know that your life is not given you for nought; God had good works prepared for me to walk in, and now must you walk in them—and be not dismayed. He calls you not to the life of prayer; but be loving and just and merciful to the poor and the oppressed; for God has deeds fit for all to do; and though I could have served Him faithfully in the cloister, you will serve Him better in the world; only remember this, that life is lent you, and not given, and you must increase it, that you may give it back more worthily."

Then the Baron was full of heaviness, and said that he could not take life on these terms; that both should live, or that if his brother must die, he would die too. Then Brother Lawrence rebuked him lovingly; and then began to talk of their childish days, saying with a smile, "When I last saw you, dear brother, you promised me that you would talk with me in the morning, and the morning is come now, and you will keep your promise." And then presently he said, "Henry, we are frail things, and it is a pitiful thing that so much of vanity is mingled with our flesh; but I used to think as a child that I would compel you some day to think me brave, and would make you grateful to me for a service done you—and I think of this now and am glad; but now I grow weak and can speak no more; but tell me of your life and of all that I loved in the old days, that I may have you in my mind when I sleep beneath the altar, if God will have one so unworthy to sleep there." And the Baron told him all things, struggling with his tears.

Then said Brother Lawrence: "The hour is come; call my brethren and let me go; He calleth me."

Then the monks came in and made the cross of ashes, and did the rites of death; and Brother Lawrence smiled with closed eyes, but opened them once again upon his brother, who stood to see the end. And presently Brother Lawrence sighed like a weary child and died.

Many years have passed since that day; the Baron is a grey-haired man and has his grandchildren about him; and he has done worthily, knowing that life is lent him for this end. And every year he rides with a man-at-arms or two to stand beside the grave of Christopher, and to renew the vow which he made when his brother died.

THE CLOSED WINDOW

The Tower of Nort stood in a deep angle of the downs; formerly an old road led over the hill, but it is now a green track covered with turf; the later highway choosing rather to cross a low saddle of the ridge, for the sake of the beasts of burden. The tower, originally built to guard the great road, was a plain, strong, thick-walled fortress. To the tower had been added a plain and seemly house, where the young Sir Mark de Nort lived very easily and plentifully. To the south stretched the great wood of Nort, but the Tower stood high on an elbow of the down, sheltered from the north by the great green hills. The villagers had an odd ugly name for the Tower, which they called the Tower of Fear; but the name was falling into disuse, and was only spoken, and that heedlessly, by ancient men, because Sir Mark was vexed to hear it so called. Sir Mark was not yet thirty, and had begun to say that he must marry a wife; but he seemed in no great haste to do so, and loved his easy, lonely life, with plenty of hunting and hawking on the down. With him lived his cousin and heir, Roland Ellice, a heedless good-tempered man, a few years older than Sir Mark; he had come on a visit to Sir Mark, when he first took possession of the Tower; and there had seemed no reason why he should go away; the two suited each other; Sir Mark was sparing of speech, fond of books and of rhymes. Roland was different, loving ease and wine and talk, and finding in Mark a good listener. Mark loved his cousin, and thought it praiseworthy of him to stay and help to cheer so sequestered a house, since there were few neighbours within reach.

And yet Mark was not wholly content with his easy life; there were many days when he asked himself why he should go thus quietly on, day by day, like a stalled ox; still, there appeared no reason why he should do otherwise; there were but few folk on his land, and they were content; yet he sometimes envied them their bondage and their round of daily duties. The only place where he could else have been was with the army, or even with the Court; but Sir Mark was no soldier, and even less of a courtier; he hated tedious gaiety, and it was a time of peace. So because he loved solitude and quiet he lived at home, and sometimes thought himself but half a man; yet was he happy after a sort, but for a kind of little hunger of the heart.

What gave the Tower so dark a name was the memory of old Sir James de Nort, Mark's grand-father, an evil and secret man, who had dwelt at Nort under some strange shadow; he had driven his son from his doors, and lived at the end of his life with his books and his own close thoughts, spying upon the stars and tracing strange figures in books; since his death the old room in the turret top, where he came by his end in a dreadful way, had been closed; it was entered by a turret-door, with a flight of steps from the chamber below. It had four windows, one to each of the winds; but the window which looked upon the down was fastened up, and secured with a great shutter of oak.

One day of heavy rain, Roland, being wearied of doing nothing, and vexed because Mark sat so still in a great chair, reading in a book, said to his cousin at last that he must go and visit the old room, in which he had never set foot. Mark closed his book, and smiling indulgently at Roland's restlessness, rose, stretching himself, and got the key; and together they went up the turret stairs. The key groaned loudly in the lock, and, when the door was thrown back, there appeared a high faded room, with a timbered roof, and with a close, dull smell. Round the walls were presses, with the doors fast; a large oak table, with a chair beside it, stood in the middle. The walls were otherwise bare and rough; the spiders had spun busily over the windows and in the angles. Roland was full of questions, and Mark told him all he had heard of old Sir James and his silent ways, but said that he knew nothing of the disgrace that had seemed to envelop him, or of the reasons why he had so evil a name. Roland said that he thought it a shame that so fair a room should lie so nastily, and pulled one of the casements open, when a sharp gust broke into the room, with so angry a burst of rain, that he closed it again in haste; little by little, as they talked, a shadow began to fall upon their spirits, till Roland declared that there was still a blight upon the place; and Mark told him of the death of old Sir James, who had been found after a day of silence, when he had not set foot outside his chamber, lying on the floor of the room, strangely bedabbled with wet and mud, as though he had come off a difficult journey, speechless, and with a look of anguish on his face; and that he had died soon after they had found him, muttering words that no one understood. Then the two young men drew near to the closed window; the shutters were tightly barred, and across the panels was scrawled in red, in an uncertain hand, the words CLAUDIT ET NEMO APERIT, which Mark explained was the Latin for the text, *He shutteth and none openeth.* And then Mark said that the story went that it was ill for the man that opened the window, and that shut it should remain for him. But Roland girded at him for his want of curiosity, and had laid a hand upon the bar as though to open it, but Mark forbade him urgently. "Nay," said he, "let it remain so—we must not meddle with the will of the dead!" and as he said the word, there came so furious a gust upon the windows that it seemed as though some stormy thing would beat them open; so they left the room together, and presently descending, found the sun struggling through the rain.

But both Mark and Roland were sad and silent all that day; for though they spake not of it, there was a desire in their minds to open the closed window, and to see what would befall; in Roland's mind it was like the desire of a child to peep into what is forbidden; but in Mark's mind a sort of shame to be so bound by an old and weak tale of superstition.

Now it seemed to Mark, for many days, that the visit to the turret-room had brought a kind of shadow down between them. Roland was peevish and ill-at-ease; and ever the longing grew upon

Mark, so strongly that it seemed to him that something drew him to the room, some beckoning of a hand or calling of a voice.

Now one bright and sunshiny morning it happened that Mark was left alone within the house. Roland had ridden out early, not saying where he was bound. And Mark sat, more listlessly than was his wont, and played with the ears of his great dog, that sat with his head upon his master's knee, looking at him with liquid eyes, and doubtless wondering why Mark went not abroad.

Suddenly Sir Mark's eye fell upon the key of the upper room, which lay on the window-ledge where he had thrown it; and the desire to go up and pluck the heart from the little mystery came upon him with a strength that he could not resist; he rose twice and took up the key, and fingering it doubtfully, laid it down again; then suddenly he took it up, and went swiftly into the turret-stair, and up, turning, turning, till his head was dizzy with the bright peeps of the world through the loophole windows. Now all was green, where a window gave on the down; and now it was all clear air and sun, the warm breeze coming pleasantly into the cold stair-way; presently Mark heard the pattering of feet on the stair below, and knew that the old hound had determined to follow him; and he waited a moment at the door, half pleased, in his strange mood, to have the company of a living thing. So when the dog was at his side, he stayed no longer, but opened the door and stepped within the room.

The room, for all its faded look, had a strange air about it, and though he could not say why, Mark felt that he was surely expected. He did not hesitate, but walked to the shutter and considered it for a moment; he heard a sound behind him. It was the old hound who sat with his head aloft, sniffing the air uneasily; Mark called him and held out his hand, but the hound would not move; he wagged his tail as though to acknowledge that he was called, and then he returned to his uneasy quest. Mark watched him for a moment, and saw that the old dog had made up his mind that all was not well in the room, for he lay down, gathering his legs under him, on the threshold, and watched his master with frightened eyes, quivering visibly. Mark, no lighter of heart, and in a kind of fearful haste, pulled the great staple off the shutter and set it on the ground, and then wrenched the shutters back; the space revealed was largely filled by old and dusty webs of spiders, which Mark lightly tore down, using the staple of the shutters to do this; it was with a strange shock of surprise that he saw that the window was dark, or nearly so; it seemed as though there were some further obstacle outside; yet Mark knew that from below the leaded panes of the window were visible. He drew back for a moment, but, unable to restrain his curiosity, wrenched the rusted casement open. But still all was dark without; and there came in a gust of icy wind from outside; it was as though something had passed him swiftly, and he heard the old hound utter a strangled howl; then turning, he saw him spring to his feet with his hair bristling and his teeth bare, and next moment the dog turned and leapt out of the room.

Mark, left alone, tried to curb a tide of horror that swept through his veins; he looked round at the room, flooded with the southerly sunlight, and then he turned again to the dark window, and putting a strong constraint upon himself, leaned out, and saw a thing which bewildered him so strangely that he thought for a moment his senses had deserted him. He looked out on a lonely dim hillside, covered with rocks and stones; the hill came up close to the window, so that he could have jumped down upon it, the wall below seeming to be built into the rocks. It was all dark and silent, like a clouded night, with a faint light coming from whence he could not see. The hill sloped away very steeply from the tower, and he seemed to see a plain beyond, where at the same time he knew that the down ought to lie. In the plain there was a light, like the firelit window of a house; a little below him some shape like a crouching man seemed to run and slip among the stones, as though suddenly surprised, and seeking to escape. Side by side with a deadly fear which began to invade his heart, came an uncontrollable desire to leap down among the rocks; and then it seemed to him that the figure below stood upright, and began to beckon him. There came over him a sense that he was in deadly peril; and, like a man on the edge of a precipice, who has just enough will left to try to escape, he drew himself by main force away from the window, closed it, put the shutters back, replaced the staple, and, his limbs all trembling, crept out of the room, feeling along the walls like a palsied man. He locked the door, and then, his terror overpowering him, he fled down the turret-stairs. Hardly thinking what he did, he came out on the court, and going to the great well that stood in the centre of the yard, he went to it and flung the key down, hearing it clink on the sides as it fell. Even then he dared not re-enter the house, but glanced up and down, gazing about him, while the cloud of fear and horror by insensible degrees dispersed, leaving him weak and melancholy.

Presently Roland returned, full of talk, but broke off to ask if Mark were ill. Mark, with a kind of surliness, an unusual mood for him, denied it somewhat sharply. Roland raised his eyebrows, and said no more, but prattled on. Presently after a silence he said to Mark, "What did you do all the morning?" and it seemed to Mark as though this were accompanied with a spying look. An unreasonable anger seized him. "What does it matter to you what I did?" he said. "May not I do what I like in my own house?"

"Doubtless," said Roland, and sate silent with uplifted brows; then he hummed a tune, and presently went out.

They sate at dinner that evening with long silences, contrary to their wont, though Mark bestirred himself to ask questions. When they were left alone, Mark stretched out his hand to Roland, saying, "Roland, forgive me! I spoke to you this morning in a way of which I am ashamed; we have lived so long together—and yet we came nearer to quarrelling to-day than we have ever done before; and it was my fault."

Roland smiled, and held Mark's hand for a moment. "Oh, I had not given it another thought," he said; "the wonder is that you can bear with an idle fellow as you do." Then they talked for awhile with the pleasant glow of friendliness that two good comrades feel when they have been reconciled. But late in the evening Roland said, "Was there any story, Mark, about your grandfather's leaving any treasure of money behind him?"

The question grated somewhat unpleasantly upon Mark's mood; but he controlled himself and said, "No, none that I know of—except that he found the estate rich and left it poor—and what he did with his revenues no one knows—you had better ask the old men of the village; they know more about the house than I do. But, Roland, forgive me once more if I say that I do not desire Sir James's name to be mentioned between us. I wish we had not entered his room; I do not know how to express it, but it seems to me as though he had sate there, waiting quietly to be summoned, and as though we had troubled him, and—as though he had joined us. I think he was an evil man, close and evil. And there hangs in my mind a verse of Scripture, where Samuel said to the witch, 'Why hast thou disquieted me to bring me up?' Oh," he went on, "I do not know why I talk wildly thus"; for he saw that Roland was looking at him with astonishment, with parted lips; "but a shadow has fallen upon me, and there seems evil abroad."

From that day forward a heaviness lay on the spirit of Mark that could not be scattered. He felt, he said to himself, as though he had meddled light-heartedly with something far deeper and more dangerous than he had supposed—like a child that has aroused some evil beast that slept. He had dark dreams too. The figure that he had seen among the rocks seemed to peep and beckon him, with a mocking smile, over perilous places, where he followed unwilling. But the heavier he grew the lighter-hearted Roland became; he seemed to walk in some bright vision of his own, intent upon a large and gracious design.

One day he came into the hall in the morning, looking so radiant that Mark asked him half enviously what he had to make him so glad. "Glad," said Roland, "oh, I know it! Merry dreams, perhaps. What do you think of a good grave fellow who beckons me on with a brisk smile, and shows me places, wonderful places, under banks and in woodland pits, where riches lie piled together? I am sure that some good fortune is preparing for me, Mark—but you shall share it." Then Mark, seeing in his words a certain likeness, with a difference, to his own dark visions, pressed his lips together and sat looking stonily before him.

At last, one still evening of spring, when the air was intolerably languid and heavy for mankind, but full of sweet promises for trees and hidden peeping things, though a lurid redness of secret thunder had lain all day among the heavy clouds in the plain, the two dined together. Mark had walked alone that day, and had lain upon the turf of the down, fighting against a weariness that seemed to be poisoning the very springs of life within him. But Roland had been brisk and alert, coming and going upon some secret and busy errand, with a fragment of a song upon his lips, like a man preparing to set off for a far country, who is glad to be gone. In the evening, after they had dined, Roland had let his fancy rove in talk. "If we were rich," he said, "how we would transform this old place!"

"It is fair enough for me," said Mark heavily; and Roland had chidden him lightly for his sombre ways, and sketched new plans of life.

Mark, wearied and yet excited, with an intolerable heaviness of spirit, went early to bed, leaving Roland in the hall. After a short and broken sleep, he awoke, and lighting a candle, read idly and gloomily to pass the heavy hours. The house seemed full of strange noises that night. Once or twice came a scraping and a faint hammering in the wall; light footsteps seemed to pass in the turret—but the tower was always full of noises, and Mark heeded them not; at last he fell asleep again, to be suddenly awakened by a strange and desolate crying, that came he knew not whence, but seemed to wail upon the air. The old dog, who slept in Mark's room, heard it too; he was sitting up in a fearful expectancy. Mark rose in haste, and taking the candle, went into the passage that led to Roland's room. It was empty, but a light burned there and showed that the room had not been slept in. Full of a horrible fear, Mark returned, and went in hot haste up the turret steps, fear and anxiety struggling together in his mind. When he reached the top, he found the little door broken forcibly open, and a light within. He cast a haggard look round the room, and then the crying came again, this time very faint and desolate.

Mark cast a shuddering glance at the window; it was wide open and showed a horrible liquid blackness; round the bar in the centre that divided the casements, there was something knotted. He hastened to the window, and saw that it was a rope, which hung heavily. Leaning out he saw that something dangled from the rope below him—and then came the crying again out of the darkness, like the crying of a lost spirit.

He could see as in a bitter dream the outline of the hateful hillside; but there seemed to his disordered fancy to be a tumult of some kind below; pale lights moved about, and he saw a group of forms which scattered like a shoal of fish when he leaned out. He knew that he was looking upon a scene that no mortal eye ought to behold, and it seemed to him at the moment as though he was staring straight into hell.

The rope went down among the rocks and disappeared; but Mark clenched it firmly and using all his strength, which was great, drew it up hand over hand; as he drew it up he secured it in loops round the great oak table; he began to be afraid that his strength would not hold out, and once when he returned to the window after securing a loop, a great hooded thing like a bird flew noiselessly at the window and beat its wings.

Presently he saw that the form which dangled on the rope was clear of the rocks below; it had come up through them, as though they were but smoke; and then his task seemed to him more sore than ever. Inch by painful inch he drew it up, working fiercely and silently; his muscles were tense, and drops stood on his brow, and the veins hammered in his ears; his breath came and went in sharp sobs. At last the form was near enough for him to seize it; he grasped it by the middle and drew Roland, for it was Roland, over the window-sill. His head dangled and drooped from side to side; his face was dark with strangled blood and his limbs hung helpless. Mark drew his knife and cut the rope that was tied under his arms; the helpless limbs sank huddling on the floor; then Mark looked up; at the window a few feet from him was a face, more horrible than he had supposed a human face, if it was human indeed, could be. It was deadly white, and hatred, baffled rage, and a sort of devilish malignity glared from the white set eyes, and the drawn mouth. There was a rush from behind him; the old hound, who had crept up unawares into the room, with a fierce outcry of rage sprang on to the window-sill; Mark heard the scraping of his claws upon the stone. Then the hound leapt through the window, and in a moment there was the sound of a heavy fall outside. At the same instant the darkness seemed to lift and draw up like a cloud; a bank of blackness rose past the window, and left the dark outline of the down, with a sky sown with tranquil stars.

The cloud of fear and horror that hung over Mark lifted too; he felt in some dim way that his adversary was vanquished; he carried Roland down the stairs and laid him on his bed; he roused the household, who looked fearfully at him, and then his own strength failed; he sank upon the floor of his room, and the dark tide of unconsciousness closed over him.

Mark's return to health was slow. One who has looked into the Unknown finds it hard to believe again in the outward shows of life. His first conscious speech was to ask for his hound; they told him that the body of the dog had been found, horribly mangled as though by the teeth of some fierce animal, at the foot of the tower. The dog was buried in the garden, with a slab above him, on which are the words:—

EUGE SERVE BONE ET FIDELIS

A silly priest once said to Mark that it was not meet to write Scripture over the grave of a beast. But Mark said warily that an inscription was for those who read it, to make them humble, and not to increase the pride of what lay below.

When Mark could leave his bed, his first care was to send for builders, and the old tower of Nort was taken down, stone by stone, to the ground, and a fair chapel built on the site; in the wall there was a secret stairway, which led from the top chamber, and came out among the elder-bushes that grew below the tower, and here was found a coffer of gold, which paid for the church; because, until it was found, it was Mark's design to leave the place desolate. Mark is wedded since, and has his children about his knee; those who come to the house see a strange and wan man, who sits at Mark's board, and whom he uses very tenderly; sometimes this man is merry, and tells a long tale of his being beckoned and led by a tall

and handsome person, smiling, down a hillside to fetch gold;
though he can never remember the end of the matter; but about
the springtime he is silent or mutters to himself: and this is Roland;
his spirit seems shut up within him in some close cell, and Mark
prays for his release, but till God call him, he treats him like a dear
brother, and with the reverence due to one who has looked out on
the other side of Death, and who may not say what his eyes beheld.

The Gray Cat

The knight Sir James Leigh lived in a remote valley of the Welsh Hills. The manor house, of rough grey stone, with thick walls and mullioned windows, stood on a rising ground; at its foot ran a little river, through great boulders. There were woods all about; but above the woods, the bare green hills ran smoothly up, so high, that in the winter the sun only peeped above the ridge for an hour or two; beyond the house, the valley wound away into the heart of the hills, and at the end a black peak looked over. The place was very sparsely inhabited; within a close of ancient yew trees stood a little stone church, and a small parsonage smothered in ivy, where an old priest, a cousin of the knight, lived. There were but three farms in the valley, and a rough track led over the hills, little used, except by drovers. At the top of the pass stood a stone cross; and from this point you could see the dark scarred face of the peak to the left, streaked with snow, which did not melt until the summer was far advanced.

Sir James was a silent sad man, in ill-health; he spoke little and bore his troubles bitterly; he was much impoverished, through his own early carelessness, and now so feeble in body that he had small hope of repairing the fortune he had lost. His wife was a wise and loving woman, who, though she found it hard to live happily in so lonely a place with a sickly husband, met her sorrows with a cheerful face, visited her poorer neighbours, and was like a ray of sunlight in the gloomy valley. They had one son, a boy Roderick, now about fifteen; he was a bright and eager child, who was happy

66

enough, taking his life as he found it—and indeed he had known no other. He was taught a little by the priest; but he had no other schooling, for Sir James would spend no money except when he was obliged to do so. Roderick had no playmates, but he never found the time to be heavy; he was fond of long solitary rambles on the hills, being light of foot and strong.

One day he had gone out to fish in the stream, but it was bright and still, and he could catch nothing; so at last he laid his rod aside in a hollow place beneath the bank, and wandered without any certain aim along the stream. Higher and higher he went, till he found, looking about him, that he was as high as the pass; and then it came into his mind to track the stream to its source. The Manor was now out of sight, and there was nothing round him but the high green hills, with here and there a sheep feeding. Once a kite came out and circled slowly in the sun, pouncing like a plummet far down the glen; and still Roderick went onwards till he saw that he was at the top of the lower hills, and that the only thing higher than him was the peak itself. He saw now that the stream ran out of a still black pool some way in front of him, that lay under the very shadow of the dark precipice, and was fed by the snows that melted from the face. It was surrounded by rocks that lay piled in confusion. But the whole place wore an air that was more than desolate; the peak itself had a cruel look, and there was an intent silence, which was only broken, as he gazed, by the sound of rocks falling loudly from the face of the hill and thundering down. The sun warned him that he had gone far enough; and he determined to go homewards, half pleased at his discovery, and half relieved to quit so lonely and grim a spot.

That evening, when he sate with his father and mother at their simple meal, he began to say where he had been. His father heard him with little attention, but when Roderick described the dark pool and the sharp front of the peak he asked him abruptly how near he had gone to the pool. Roderick said that he had seen it from a distance, and then Sir James said somewhat sharply that he must not wander so far, and that he was not to go near that place again. Roderick was surprised at this, for his father as a rule interfered little with what he did; but he did not ask his father the reason, for there was something peevish, even harsh, in his tone. But afterwards, when he went out with his mother, leaving the knight to his own gloomy thoughts, as his will and custom was, his mother said with some urgency, "Roderick, promise me not to go to the pool again; it has an evil name, and is better left to itself." Roderick was eager to know the story of the place, but his mother would not tell him—only she would have him promise; so he promised, but complained that he would rather have had a reason given for his promise; but his mother, smiling and holding his hand, said that it should be enough for him to please her by doing her will. So Roderick gave his promise again, but was not satisfied.

The next day Roderick was walking in the valley and met one of the farmers, a young good-humoured man, who had always been friendly with the boy, and had often been to fish with him; Roderick walked beside him, and told him that he had followed the stream nearly to the pool, when the young farmer, with some seriousness, asked him how near he had been to the water. Roderick was surprised at the same question that his father had asked him being asked again, and told him that he had but seen it from a hill-top near, adding, "But what is amiss with the place, for my father and mother have made me promise not to go there again?"

The young farmer said nothing for a moment, but seemed to reflect; then he said that there were stories about the place, stories that perhaps it was foolish to believe, but he went on to say that it was better to be on the safe side in all things, and that the place had an evil fame. Then Roderick with childish eagerness asked him what the stories were; and little by little the farmer told him. He said that something dwelt near or in the pool, it was not known what, that had an enmity to the life of man; that twice since he was a boy a strange thing had happened there; a young shepherd had come by his death at the pool, and was found lying in the water, strangely battered; that, he said, was long before Roderick was born; then he added, "You remember old Richard the shepherd?" "What!" said Roderick, "the old strange man that used to go about muttering to himself, that the boys threw stones at?"

"Yes," said the farmer, "the very same. Well, he was not always so—I remember him a strong and cheerful man; but once when the sheep had got lost in the hills, he would go to the pool because he thought he heard them calling there, though we prayed him not to go. He came back, indeed, bringing no sheep, but an altered and broken man, as he was thenceforth and as you knew him; he had seen something by the pool, he could not say what, and had had a sore strife to get away." "But what sort of a thing is this?" said Roderick. "Is it a beast or a man, or what?"

"Neither," said the farmer very gravely. "You have heard them read in the church of the evil spirits who dwelt with men, and entered their bodies, and it was sore work even for the Lord Christ to cast them forth; I think it is one of these who has wandered thither; they say he goes not far from the pool, for he cannot abide the cross on the pass, and the church bell gives him pains." And then the farmer looked at Roderick and said, "You know that they ring the bell all night on the feast of All Souls?" "Yes," said Roderick, "I have heard it ring." "Well, on that night alone," said the farmer, "they say that spirits have power upon men, and come abroad to do them hurt; and so they ring the bell, which the spirits cannot listen to—but, young master, it is ill to talk of these things, and Christian men should not even think of them; but as I said, though Satan has but little power over the baptized soul, yet even so, says the priest, he can enter in, if the soul be willing to admit him,— and so I say, avoid the place! it may be that these are silly stories to affright folk, but it is ill to touch pitch; and no good can be got by going to the pool, and perhaps evil;—and now I think I have told you enough and more than enough." For Roderick was looking at him pale and with wide open eyes.

Is it strange that from that day the thing that Roderick most desired was to see the pool and what dwelt there? I think not; when hearts are young and before trouble has laid its heavy hand upon them, the hard and cruel things of life, wounds, blows, agonies, terrors, seen only in the mirrors of another spirit, are but as a curious and lively spectacle that feeds the mind with wonder. The stories to which Roderick had listened in church of men that were haunted by demons seemed to him but as dim and distant experiences on which he would fain look; and the fainter the thought of his promise grew, the stronger grew his desire to see for himself.

In the month of June, when the heart is light, and the smell of the woods is fresh and sharp, Roderick's father and mother were called to go on a journey, to see an ancient friend who was thought to be dying. The night before they set off Roderick had a strange dream; it seemed to him that he wandered over bare hillsides, and came at last to the pool; the peak rose sharp and clear, and the water was very black and still; while he gazed upon it, it seemed to be troubled; the water began to spin round and round, and bubbling waves rose and broke on the surface. Suddenly a hand emerged from the water, and then a head, bright and unwetted, as though the water had no power to touch it. Roderick saw that it was a man of youthful aspect and commanding mien; he waded out to the shore and stood for a moment looking round him; then he beckoned Roderick to approach, looking at him kindly, and spoke to him gently, saying that he had waited for him long. They walked together to the crag, and then, in some way that Roderick could not clearly see, the man opened a door into the mountain, and Roderick saw a glimmering passage within. The air came out laden with a rich and heavy fragrance, and there was a faint sound of distant music in the hill. The man turned and looked upon Roderick as though inviting him to enter; but Roderick shook his head and refused, saying that he was not ready; at which the man stepped inside with a smile, half of pity, and the door was shut.

Then Roderick woke with a start and wished that he had been bold enough to go within the door; the light came in serenely through the window, and he heard the faint piping of awakening birds in the dewy trees. He could not sleep, and presently dressed himself and went down. Soon the household was awake, for the knight was to start betimes; Roderick sate at the early meal with his father and mother. His father was cumbered with the thought of the troublesome journey, and asked many questions about the baggage; so Roderick said little, but felt his mother's eyes dwell

on his face with love. Soon after they rode away; Roderick stood at
the door to see them go, and there was so eager and bright a look
in his face that his mother was somehow troubled, and almost
called him to her to make him repeat his promise, but she feared
that he would feel that she did not trust him, and therefore put the
thought aside; and so they rode away, his mother waving her hand
till they turned the corner by the wood and were out of sight.

Then Roderick began to consider how he would spend the day,
with a half-formed design in his mind; when suddenly the temptation to visit the pool came upon him with a force that he had neither strength nor inclination to resist. So he took his rod, which
might seem to be an excuse, and set off rapidly up the stream. He
was surprised to find how swiftly the hills rose all about him, and
how easily he went; very soon he came to the top; and there lay the
pool in front of him, within the shadow of the peak, that rose behind it very clear and sharp. He hesitated no longer, but ran lightly
down the slope, and next moment he was on the brink of the pool.
It lay before him very bright and pure, like a jewel of sapphire, the
water being of a deep azure blue; he went all round it. There was
no sign of life in the water; at the end nearest the cliff he found a
little cool runnel of water that bubbled into the pool from the cliffs.
No grass grew round about it, and he could see the stones sloping
down and becoming more beautiful the deeper they lay, from the
pure tint of the water.

He looked all around him; the moorland quivered in the bright
hot air, and he could see far away the hills lie like a map, with blue
mountains on the horizon, and small green valleys where men
dwelt. He sate down by the pool, and he had a thought of bathing
in the water; but his courage did not rise to this, because he felt
still as though something sate in the depths that would not show
itself, but might come forth and drag him down; so he sate at last
by the pool, and presently he fell asleep.

When he woke he felt somewhat chilly; the shadow of the peak
had come round, and fell on the water; the place was still as calm
as ever, but looking upon the pool he had an obscure sense as
though he were being watched by an unclosing eye; but he was

thirsting with the heat; so he drew up, in his closed hands, some of the water, which was very cool and sweet; and his drowsiness came upon him, and again he slept.

When next he woke it was with a sense of delicious ease, and the thought that some one who loved him was near him stroking his hand. He looked up, and there close to his side sate very quietly what gave him a shock of surprise. It was a great gray cat, with soft abundant fur, which turned its yellow eyes upon him lazily, purred, and licked his hand; he caressed the cat, which arched its back and seemed pleased to be with him, and presently leapt upon his knee. The soft warmth of the fur against his hands, and the welcoming caresses of this fearless wild creature pleased him greatly; and he sate long in quiet thought, taking care not to disturb the cat, which, whenever he took his hand away, rubbed against him as though to show that it was pleased at his touch. But at last he thought that he must go homewards, for the day began to turn to the west. So he put the cat off his knee and began to walk to the top of the pass, as it was quicker to follow the road. For awhile the cat accompanied him, sometimes rubbing against his leg and sometimes walking in front, but looking round from time to time as though to consult his pleasure.

Roderick began to hope that it would accompany him home, but at a certain place the cat stopped, and would go no farther. Roderick lifted it up, but it leapt from him as if displeased, and at last he left it reluctantly. In a moment he came within sight of the cross in the hilltop, so that he saw the road was near. Often he looked round and saw the great cat regarding him as though it were sorry to be left; till at last he could see it no more.

He went home well pleased, his head full of happy thoughts; he had gone half expecting to see some dreadful thing, but had found instead a creature who seemed to love him.

The next day he went again; and this time he found the cat sitting by the pool; as soon as it saw him, it ran to him with a glad and yearning cry, as though it had feared he would not return; today it seemed brighter and larger to look upon; and he was pleased that when he returned by the stream it followed him much farther, leaping lightly from stone to stone; but at a certain place, where the valley began to turn eastward, just before the little church came in sight, it sate down as before and took its leave of him.

The third day he began to go up the valley again; but while he rested in a little wood that came down to the stream, to his surprise and delight the cat sprang out of a bush, and seemed more than ever glad of his presence. While he sate fondling it, he heard the sound of footsteps coming up the path; but the cat heard the sound too, and as he rose to see who was coming, the cat sprang lightly into a tree beside him and was hidden from his sight. It was the old priest on his way to an upland farm, who spoke fondly to Roderick, and asked him of his father and mother. Roderick told him that they were to return that night, and said that it was too bright to remain indoors and yet too bright to fish; the priest agreed, and after a little more talk rose to go, and as his manner was, holding Roderick by the hand, he blessed him, saying that he was growing a tall boy. When he was gone—and Roderick was ashamed to find how eager he was that the priest should go—he called low to the cat to come back; but the cat came not, and though Roderick searched the tree into which it had sprung, he could find no sign of it, and supposed that it had crept into the wood.

That evening the travellers returned, the knight seeming cheerful, because the vexatious journey was over; but Roderick was half ashamed to think that his mind had been so full of his new plaything that he was hardly glad to see his parents return. Presently his mother said, "You look very bright and happy, dear child," and Roderick, knowing that he spoke falsely, said that he was glad to see them again; his mother smiled and asked him what he had been doing, and he said that he had wandered on the hills, for it was too bright to fish; his mother looked at him for a moment, and he knew in his heart that she wondered if he had kept his promise; but he thought of his secret, and looked at her so straight and full that she asked him no further questions.

The next day he woke feeling sad, because he knew that there would be no chance to go to the pool. He went to and fro with his mother, for she had many little duties to attend to. At last she said,

"What are you thinking of, Roderick? You seem to have little to say to me." She said it laughingly; and Roderick was ashamed, but said that he was only thinking; and so bestirred himself to talk. But late in the day he went a little alone through the wood, and reaching the end of it, looked up to the hill, kissing his hand towards the pool as a greeting to his friend; and as he turned, the cat came swiftly and lovingly out of the wood to him; and he caught it up in his arms and clasped it close, where it lay as if contented.

Then he thought that he would carry it to the house, and say nothing as to where he had found it; but hardly had he moved a step when the cat leapt from him and stood as though angry. And it came into Roderick's mind that the cat was his secret friend, and that their friendship must somehow be unknown; but he loved it even the better for that.

In the weeks that followed, the knight was ill and the lady much at home; from time to time Roderick saw the cat; he could never tell when it would visit him; it came and went unexpectedly, and always in some lonely and secret place. But gradually Roderick began to care for nothing else; his fishing and his riding were forgotten, and he began to plan how he might be alone, so that the cat would come to him. He began to lose his spirits and to be dull without it, and to hate the hours when he could not see it; and all the time it grew or seemed to grow stronger and sleeker; his mother soon began to notice that he was not well; he became thin and listless, but his eyes were large and bright; she asked him more than once if he were well, but he only laughed. Once indeed he had a fright; he had been asleep under a hawthorn in the glen on a hot July day; and waking saw the cat close to him, watching him intently with yellow eyes, as though it were about to spring upon him; but seeing him awake, it came wheedling and fondling him as often before; but he could not forget the look in its eyes, and felt grave and sad.

Then he began to be troubled with dreams; the man whom he had seen in his former dream rising from the pool was often with him—sometimes he led him to pleasant places; but one dream he had, that he was bathing in the pool, and caught his foot between the rocks and could not draw it out. Then he heard a rushing sound, and looking round saw that a great stream of water was plunging heavily into the pool, so that it rose every moment, and was soon up to his chin. Then he saw in his dream that the man sate on the edge of the pool and looked at him with a cold smile, but did not offer to help; till at last when the water touched his lips, the man rose and held up his hand; and the stream ceased to run, and presently his foot came out of the rock easily, and he swam ashore but saw no one.

Then it came to the autumn, and the days grew colder and shorter, and he could not be so much abroad; he felt, too, less and less disposed to stir out, and it now began to be on his mind that he had broken his promise to his mother; and for a week he saw nothing of the cat, though he longed to see it. But one night, as he went to bed, when he had put out his light, he saw that the moon was very bright; and he opened the window and looked out, and saw the gleaming stream and the grey valley; he was turning away, when he heard a light sound of the scratching of claws, and presently the cat sprang upon the window-sill and entered the room. It was now cold and he got into bed, and the cat sprang upon his pillow; and Roderick was so glad that the cat had returned that while he caressed it he talked to it in low tones. Suddenly came a step at the door, and a light beneath it, and his mother with a candle entered the room. She stood for a moment looking, and Roderick became aware that the cat was gone. Then his mother came near, thinking that he was asleep, and he sate up. She said to him, "Dear child, I heard you speaking, and wondered whether you were in a dream," and she looked at him with an anxious gaze. And he said, "Was I speaking, mother? I was asleep and must have spoken in a dream." Then she said, "Roderick, you are not old enough yet to sleep so uneasily—is all well, dear child?" and Roderick, hating to deceive his mother, said, "How should not all be well?" So she kissed him and went quietly away, but Roderick heard her sighing.

Then it came at last to All Souls' Day; and Roderick, going to his bed that night, had a strange dizziness and cried out, and found the room swim round him. Then he got up into his bed, for he thought that he must be ill, and soon fell asleep; and in his sleep he dreamed a dreadful dream. He thought that he lay on the hills beside the pool; and yet he was out of the body, for he could see himself lying there. The pool was very dark, and a cold wind ruffled the waves. And again the water was troubled, and the man stepped out; but behind him came another man, like a hunchback, very swarthy of face, with long thin arms, that looked both strong and evil. Then it seemed as if the first man pointed to Roderick where he lay and said, "You can take him hence, for he is mine now, and I have need of him," adding, "Who could have thought it would be so easy?" and then he smiled very bitterly. And the hunchback went towards himself; and he tried to cry out in warning, and straining woke; and in the chilly dawn he saw the cat sit in his room, but very different from what it had been. It was gaunt and famished, and the fur was all marred; its yellow eyes gleamed horribly, and Roderick saw that it hated him, he knew not why; and such fear came upon him that he screamed out, and as he screamed the cat rose as if furious, twitching its tail and opening its mouth; but he heard steps without, and screamed again, and his mother came in haste into the room, and the cat was gone in a moment, and Roderick held out his hands to his mother, and she soothed and quieted him, and presently with many sobs he told her all the story.

She did not reproach him, nor say a word of his disobedience, the fear was too urgent upon her; she tried to think for a little that it was the sight of some real creature lingering in a mind that was wrought upon by illness; but those were not the days when men preferred to call the strange afflictions of body and spirit, the sad scars that stain the fair works of God, by reasonable names. She did not doubt that by some dreadful hap her own child had some-how crept within the circle of darkness, and she only thought of how to help and rescue him; that he was sorry and that he did not wholly consent was her hope.

So she merely kissed and quieted him, and then she told him that she would return anon and he must rest quietly; but he would not let her leave him, so she stood in the door and called a servant softly. Sir James was long abed, for he had been in ill-health that day, and she gave word that some one must be found at once and go to call the priest, saying that Roderick was ill and she was uneasy. Then she came back to the bed, and holding Roderick's hand she said, that he must try to sleep. Roderick said to her, "Mother, say that you forgive me." To which she only replied, "Dear child, do I not love you better than all the world? Do not think of me now, only ask help of God." So she sate with his hand in both of her own, and presently he fell asleep; but she saw that he was troubled in his dreams, for he groaned and cried out often; and now through the window she heard the soft tolling of the bell of the church, and she knew that a contest must be fought out that night over the child; but after a sore passage of misery, and a bitter questioning as to why one so young and innocent should thus be bound with evil bonds, she found strength to leave the matter in the Father's hands, and to pray with an eager hopefulness.

But the time passed heavily and still the priest did not arrive; and the ghostly terror was so sore on the child that she could bear it no longer and awakened him. And he told her in broken words of the terrible things that had oppressed him; sore fightings and struggles, and a voice in his ear that it was too late, and that he had yielded himself to the evil. And at last there came a quiet footfall on the stair, and the old priest himself entered the room, looking anxious, yet calm, and seeming to bring a holy peace with him.

Then she bade the priest sit down; and so the two sate by the bedside, with the solitary lamp burning in the chamber; and she would have had Roderick tell the tale, but he covered his face with his hands and could not. So she told the tale herself to the priest, saying, "Correct me, Roderick, if I am wrong;" and once or twice the boy corrected her, and added a few words to make the story plain, and then they sate awhile in silence, while the terrified looks of the mother and her son dwelt on the old priest's strongly lined face; yet they found comfort in the smile with which he met them.

At length he said, "Yes, dear lady and dear Roderick, the case is plain enough—the child has yielded himself to some evil power, but not too far, I think; and now must we meet the foe with all our

might. I will abide here with the boy; and, dear lady, you were better in your own chamber, for we know not what will pass; if there
were need I would call you." Then the lady said, "I will do as you
direct me, Father, but I would fain stay." Then he said, "Nay, but
there are things on which a Christian should not look, lest they
should daunt his faith—so go, dear lady, and help us with your
prayers." Then she said, "I will be below; and if you beat your foot
thrice upon the floor, I will come. Roderick, I shall be close at hand;
only be strong, and all shall be well." Then she went softly away.

Then the priest said to Roderick, "And now, dear son, confess
your sin and let me shrive you." So Roderick made confession, and
the priest blessed him: but while he blessed him there came the
angry crying of a cat from somewhere in the room, so that Roderick
shuddered in his bed. Then the priest drew from his robe a little
holy book, and with a reverence laid it under Roderick's hand; and
he himself took his book of prayers and said, "Sleep now, dear son,
fear not." So Roderick closed his eyes, and being very weary slept.
And the old priest in a low whisper said the blessed psalms. And it
came near to midnight; and the place that the priest read was, *Thou
shalt not be afraid for any terror by night, nor for the arrow that
flieth by day; for the pestilence that walketh in darkness, nor for
the sickness that destroyeth in the noonday*; and suddenly there
ran as it were a shiver through his bones, and he knew that the
time was come. He looked at Roderick, who slept wearily on his
bed, and it seemed to him as though suddenly a small and shadowy thing, like a bird, leapt from the boy's mouth and on to the
bed; it was like a wren, only white, with dusky spots upon it; and
the priest held his breath: for now he knew that the soul was out of
the body, and that unless it could return uninjured into the limbs
of the child, nothing could avail the boy; and then he said quietly
in his heart to God that if He so willed He should take the boy's
life, if only his soul could be saved.

Then the priest was aware of a strange and horrible thing; there
sprang softly on to the bed the form of the great gray cat, very lean
and angry, which stood there, as though ready to spring upon the

bird, which hopped hither and thither, as though careless of what might be. The priest cast a glance upon the boy, who lay rigid and pale, his eyes shut, and hardly seeming to breathe, as though dead and prepared for burial. Then the priest signed the cross and said "*In Nomine*"; and as the holy words fell on the air, the cat looked fiercely at the bird, but seemed to shrink into itself; and then it slipped away.

Then the priest's fear was that the bird might stray further outside of his care; and yet he dared not try and wake the boy, for he knew that this was death, if the soul was thrust apart from the body, and if he broke the unseen chain that bound them; so he waited and prayed. And the bird hopped upon the floor; and then presently the priest saw the cat draw near again, and in a stealthy way; and now the priest himself was feeling weary of the strain, for he seemed to be wrestling in spirit with something that was strong and strongly armed. But he signed the cross again and said faintly "*In Nomine*"; and the cat again withdrew.

Then a dreadful drowsiness fell upon the priest, and he thought that he must sleep. Something heavy, leaden-handed, and powerful seemed to be busy in his brain. Meanwhile the bird hopped upon the window-sill and stood as if preparing its wings for a flight. Then the priest beat with his foot upon the floor, for he could no longer battle. In a moment the lady glided in, and seemed as though scared to find the scene of so fierce an encounter so still and quiet. She would have spoken, but the priest signed her to be silent, and pointed to the boy and to the bird; and then she partly understood. So they stood in silence, but the priest's brain grew more numb; though he was aware of a creeping blackness that seemed to overshadow the bird, in the midst of which glared two bright eyes. So with a sudden effort he signed the cross, and said "*In Nomine*" again; and at the same moment the lady held out her hand; and the priest sank down on the floor; but he saw the bird raise its wings for a flight, and just as the dark thing rose, and, as it were, struck open-mouthed, the bird sailed softly through the air, alighted on the lady's hand, and then with a light flutter of wings on to the bed and to the boy's face, and was seen no more; at the same moment the bells stopped in the church and left a sweet silence. The black form shrank and slipped aside, and seemed to fall on the ground; and outside there was a shrill and bitter cry which echoed horribly on the air; and the boy opened his eyes, and smiled; and his mother fell on his neck and kissed him. Then the priest said, "Give God the glory!" and blessed them, and was gone so softly that they knew not when he went; for he had other work to do. Then mother and son had great joy together.

But the priest walked swiftly and sternly through the wood, and to the church; and he dipped a vessel in the stoup of holy water, turning his eyes aside, and wrapped it in a veil of linen. Then he took a lantern in his hand, and with a grave and fixed look on his face he walked sadly up the valley, putting one foot before another, like a man who forced himself to go unwilling. There were strange sounds on the hillside, the crying of sad birds, and the beating of wings, and sometimes a hollow groaning seemed to come down the stream. But the priest took no heed, but went on heavily till he reached the stone cross, where the wind whistled dry in the grass. Then he struck off across the moorland. Presently he came to a rise in the ground; and here, though it was dark, he seemed to see a blacker darkness in the air, where the peak lay.

But beneath the peak he saw a strange sight; for the pool shone with a faint white light, that showed the rocks about it. The priest never turned his head, but walked thither, with his head bent, repeating words to himself, but hardly knowing what he said.

Then he came to the brink; and there he saw a dreadful sight. In the water writhed large and luminous worms, that came sometimes up to the surface, as though to breathe, and sank again. The priest knew well enough that it was a device of Satan's to frighten him; so he delayed not; but setting the lantern down on the ground, he stood. In a moment the lantern was obscured as by the rush of bat-like wings. But the priest took the veil off the vessel; and holding it up in the air, he let the water fall in the pool, saying softly, "Lord, let them be bound!"

But when the holy water touched the lake, there was a strange sight; for the bright worms quivered and fell to the depth of the pool; and a shiver passed over the surface, and the light went out like a flickering lamp. Then there came a foul yelling from the stones; and with a roar like thunder, rocks fell crashing from the face of the peak; and then all was still.

Then the priest sate down and covered his face with his hands, for he was sore spent; but he rose at length, and with grievous pain made his slow way down the valley, and reached the parsonage house at last.

Roderick lay long between life and death; and youth and a quiet mind prevailed.

Long years have passed since that day; all those that I have spoken of are dust. But in the window of the old church hangs a picture in glass which shows Christ standing, with one lying at his feet from whom he had cast out a devil; and on a scroll are the words, DE ABYSSIS · TERRAE · ITERUM · REDUXISTI · ME, the which may be written in English, *Yea, and broughtest me from the deep of the earth again.*

The Hill of Trouble

There was once a great scholar, Gilbert by name, who lived at Cambridge, and was Fellow of St. Peter's College there. He was still young, and yet he had made himself a name for learning, and still more for wisdom, which is a different thing, though the two are often confused. Gilbert was a slender, spare man, but well-knit and well-proportioned. He loved to wear old scholarly garments, but he had that sort of grace in wearing them that made him appear better apparelled than most men in new clothes. His hair was thick and curling, and he had small features clearly cut. His lips were somewhat thin, as though from determined thought. He carried his eyes a little wrinkled up, as though to spare them from the light; but he had a gracious look which he turned on those with whom he spoke; and when he opened his eyes upon you, they were large and clear, as though charged with dreams; and he had a very sweet smile, trustful and gentle, that seemed to take any that spoke with him straight to his heart, and made him many friends. He had the look rather of a courtier than of a priest, and he was merry and cheerful in discourse, so that you might be long with him and not know him to be learned. It may be said that he had no enemies, though he did not conceal his beliefs and thoughts, but stated them so courteously and with such deference to opposite views, that he drew men insensibly to his side. It was thought by many that he ought to go into the world and make a great name for himself. But he loved the quiet College life, the familiar talk with those he knew. He loved the great plenty of books and the discourse of simple and

82

wise men. He loved the fresh bright hours of solitary work, the shady College garden, with its butts and meadows, bordered by ancient walls. He loved to sit at meat in the cool and spacious hall; and he loved too the dark high-roofed College Church, and his own canopied stall with the service-books in due order, the low music of the organ, and the sweet singing of the choir. He was not rich, but his Fellowship gave him all that he desired, together with a certain seemly dignity of life that he truly valued; so that his heart was very full of a simple happiness from day to day, and he thought that he would be more than content to live out his life in the peaceful College that he loved so well.

But he was ambitious too; he was writing a great book full of holy learning; and he had of late somewhat withdrawn himself from the life of the College; he sate longer at his studies and he was seen less often in other Colleges. Ten years he gave himself to finish his task, and he thought that it would bring him renown; but that was only a far-off dream, gilding his studies with a kind of peaceful glory; and indeed he loved the doing of his work better than any reward he might get for it.

One summer he felt he wanted some change of life; the sultry Cambridge air, so dry and low, seemed to him to be heavy and lifeless. He began to dream of fresh mountain breezes, and the sound of leaping streams; so at last he packed his books into a box, and set off a long journey into the hills of the West, to a village where an old friend of his was the priest, who he knew would welcome him.

On the sixth day he arrived at the place; he had enjoyed the journey; much of the time he had ridden, but he often walked, for he was very strong and active of body; he had delighted in seeing the places he had passed through, the churches and the towns and the castles that lay beside the way; he had been pleased with the simple friendly inns, and as his custom was had talked with all travellers that he met. And most of all he had loved, as he drew nearer the West, to see the great green slopes of hills, the black heads of mountains, the steep wooded valleys, where the road lay along streams, that dashed among mossy boulders into still pools.

At last he came to the village which he sought, which lay with its grey church and low stone houses by a bridge, in a deep valley. The vicarage lay a little apart in a pleasant garden; and his friend the Vicar had made him greatly welcome. The Vicar was an old man and somewhat infirm, but he loved the quiet life of the country, and knew all the joys and sorrows of his simple flock. A large chamber was set apart for Gilbert, who ranged his books on a great table, and prepared for much quiet work. The window of the chamber looked down the valley, which was very still. There was no pattering of feet in the road, as there was at Cambridge; the only sounds were the crying of cocks or the bleating of sheep from the hill-pastures, the sound of the wind in the woods, and the falling of water from the hills. So Gilbert was well content.

For the first few days he was somewhat restless; he explored the valley in all directions. The Vicar could not walk much, and only crept to and fro in the town, or to church; and though he sometimes rode to the hills, to see sick folk on upland farms, yet he told Gilbert that he must go his walks alone; and Gilbert was not loth; for as he thus went by himself in the fresh air, a stream of pleasant fancies and gentle thoughts passed lightly through his head, and his work shaped itself in his brain, like a valley seen from a height, where the fields and farms lie out, as if on a map, with the road winding among them that ties them with the world.

One day Gilbert walked alone to a very solitary place among the hills, a valley where the woods grew thickly; the valley was an estuary, where the sea came up blue and fresh twice in the day, covering the wide sandbanks with still water that reflected the face of the sky; in the midst of the valley, joined with the hillside by a chain of low mounds, there rose a large round hill, covered with bushes which grew thickly over the slopes, and among little crags, haunted by hawks and crows. It looked a very solitary, peaceful hill, and he stopped at a farm beside the road to inquire of the way thither, because he was afraid of finding himself unable to cross the streams.

At his knock there came out an ancient man, with whom Gilbert entered into simple travellers' talk of the weather and the road;

Gilbert asked him the name of the place, and the man told him that it was called the Gate of the Old Hollow. Then Gilbert pointing to the hill that lay in the midst, asked him what that was. The old man looked at him for a moment without answering, and then said in a low voice, "That, sir, is the Hill of Trouble." "That is a strange name!" said Gilbert. "Yes," said the old man, "and it is a strange place, where no one ever sets foot—there is a cruel tale about it; there is something that is not well about the place."

Gilbert was surprised to hear the other speak so gravely; but the old man, who was pleased with his company, asked him if he would not rest awhile and eat; and Gilbert said that he would do so gladly, and the more gladly if the other would tell him the story of the place. The old man led him within into a large room, with plain oak furniture, and brought him bread and honey and milk; and Gilbert ate, while the old man told him the legend of the Hill.

He said that long years ago it was a place of heathen worship, and that there stood a circle of stones upon it, where sacrifice was done; and that men, it was said, were slain there with savage rites; and that when the Christian teachers came, and the valley became obedient to the faith, it was forbidden the villagers to go there, and for long years it was desolate; but there had dwelt in the manor-house hard by a knight, fearless and rough, who regarded neither God nor man, who had lately wedded a wife whom he loved beyond anything in the world. And one day there was with the knight a friend who was a soldier, and after dinner, in foolish talk, the knight said that he would go to the Hill, and he made a wager on it. The knight's lady besought him not to go, but he girded on his sword and went laughing. Now at the time, the old man said, there was much fighting in the valley, for the people were not yet subject to the English king, but paid tribute to their own Lords; and the knight had been one that fought the best. What the knight saw on the hill no one ever knew, but he came back at sundown, pale, and like a man that has been strangely scared, looking behind him as though he expected to be followed by something; and from that day he kept his chamber, and would not go abroad, or if he went out, he went fearfully, looking about him; and the English men-at-arms came to the valley, but the knight that had ever been foremost in the fight would not ride out to meet them, but kept his bed. The manor lay off the road, and he ordered a boy to lie in the copse beside the way, and to come up to the house to tell him if any soldiers went by. But a troop of horse came secretly over the hill; and seeing the place lie so solitary and deserted, and being in haste, they came not in, but one of them shot a bolt at a venture; but the knight, it seemed, must have stolen from his bed, and have been peeping through the shutters; for the knight's lady who sate below in sore shame and grief for her husband's cowardice, heard a cry, and coming up found him in his bedgown lying by the window, and a bolt sticking in his brain.

Her grief and misery were so sore at this, that she was for a time nearly mad; they buried the knight in secret in the churchyard; but the lady sate for many days speaking to no one, beating with her hand upon the table and eating little.

One day it seems that she had the thought to go herself to the Hill of Trouble, so she robed herself in haste, and went at early dawn; she went in secret, and came back at noon, smiling to herself, with all her grief gone; and she sate for three days thus with her hands folded, and from her face it was plain that there was joy in her heart; and on the third evening they found her cold and stiff in her chair, dead an hour since, but she was still smiling. And the lands passed to a distant kinsman. And since that day, said the old man, no one had ever set foot on the Hill, except a child not long since that strayed thither, and came back in a great fear, saying that he had seen and spoken with an old man, that had seemed to be angry, but that another person, all in white, had come between them, and had led him by the hand to the right road; it could not be known why the child was frightened, but he said that it was the way the old man looked, and the suddenness with which he came and went; but of the other he had no fear, though he knew him not. "And that, sir, is the tale."

Gilbert was very much astonished at the tale, and though he was not credulous, the story dwelt strongly in his mind. It was now too late to visit the Hill, even if he had wished; and he could not have so vexed the old man as to visit it from his house. He stood for awhile at the gate looking down at it. It was hot and still in the valley. The tide was out and the warm air quivered over the sand-banks. But the Hill had a stillness of its own, as though it guarded a secret, and lay looking out towards the sea. He could see the small crags upon it, in the calm air, and the bushes that grew plentifully all over it, with here and there a little green lawn, or a glade slop-ing down to the green flat in which it stood. The old man was be-side him and said in his shrill piping voice, "You are not thinking of going to the Hill, sir?" "Not now, at all events," said Gilbert, smiling. But the old man said, "Ah, sir, you will not go—there are other things in this world of ours, beside the hills and woods and farms; it would be strange if that were all. The spirits of the dead walk at noonday in the places they have loved; and I have thought that the souls of those who have done wickedness are sometimes bound to a place where they might have done good things, and while they are vexed at all the evil their hands have wrought, they are drawn by a kind of evil habit to do what they chose to do on earth. Perhaps those who are faithful can resist them—but it is ill to tempt them."

Gilbert was surprised at this wise talk from so simple a man; and he said, "How is it that these thoughts come into your mind?" "Oh, sir," said the other, "I am old and live much alone; and these are some of the thoughts that come into my head as I go about my work, but who sends them to me I cannot tell."

Then Gilbert said farewell, and would have paid for his meal, but the old man courteously refused, and said that it was a plea-sure to see a stranger in that lonely place; and that it made him think more kindly of the world to talk so simply with one who was, he was sure, so great a gentleman.

Gilbert smiled, and said he was only a simple scholar; and then he went back to the vicarage house. He told the Vicar of his adven-ture, and the Vicar said he had heard of the Hill, and that there was something strange in the dread which the place inspired. Then Gilbert said, half impatiently, that it was a pity that people were so ridden by needless superstition, and made fears for themselves when there was so much in the world that it was well to fear. But the old Vicar shook his head. "They are children, it is true," he said, "but children, I often think, are nearer to heaven than ourselves, and perhaps have glimpses of things that it is harder for us to see as we get older and more dull."

But Gilbert made up his mind as they talked that he would see the place for himself; and that night he dreamed of wandering over lonely places with a fear upon him of he knew not what. And waking very early, after a restless night, and seeing the day freshly risen, and the dewy brightness of the valley, he put on his clothes in haste, and taking with him a slice of bread from the table, he set out blithely for the Hill, with an eagerness of spirit that he had been used to feel as a child.

He avoided the farm, and took a track that seemed to lead into the valley, which led him up and down through little nooks and pastures, till he came to the base of the Hill. It was all skirted by a low wall of piled stones covered with grey lichens, where the brambles grew freely; but the grass upon the Hill itself had a peculiar richness and luxuriance, as though it was never trodden or crushed underfoot. Gilbert climbed the wall, but the brambles clung to him as though to keep him back; he disentangled them one by one, and in a moment he found himself in a little green glade, among small crags, that seemed to lead to the top of the Hill. He had not gone more than a few paces when the pleasure and excitement died out of his mind, and left him feeling weary and dispirited. But he said to himself that it was his troubled night, and the walk at the unusual hour, and the lack of food; so he took out his bread and ate it as he walked, and presently he came to the top.

Then he suddenly saw that he was at the place described; in front of him stood a tall circle of stones, very grey with age. Some of them were flung down and were covered with bushes, but several of them stood upright. The place was strangely silent; he walked round the circle, and saw that it occupied the top of the Hill; below him were steep crags, and when he looked over he was surprised to see all down the rocks, on ledges, a number of crows that sate silent in the sun. At the motion he made, a number of them, as though surprised to be disturbed, floated off into the air, with loud jangling cries; and a hawk sailed out from the bushes and hung, a brown speck, with trembling wings. Gilbert saw the rich plain at his feet and the winding creek of the sea, and the great hills on left and right, in a blue haze. Then he stepped back, and though he had a feeling that it would be wiser not to go, he put it aside and went boldly into the circle of stones. He stood there for a moment, and then feeling very weary, sate down on the turf, leaning his back against a stone; then came upon him a great drowsiness. He was haunted by a sense that it was not well to sleep there, and that the dreaming mind was an ill defence against the powers of the air—yet he put the thought aside with a certain shame and fell asleep.

He woke with a sudden start some time after; there was a chill in his limbs, not from the air which glowed bright in the steady sun, but a chill of the spirit that made his hair prickle in an unusual way. He raised himself up and looked round him, for he knew by a certain sense that he was not alone; and then he saw leaning against one of the stones and watching him intently, a very old and weary-looking man. The man was pale and troubled; he had a rough cloak such as the peasants wore, the hood of which was pulled over his head; his hair was white and hung about his ears; he had a staff in his hand. But there was a dark look about him, and Gilbert divined in some swift passage of the spirit that he did not wish him well. Gilbert rose to his feet, and at the same moment the old man drew near; and though he looked so old and feeble, Gilbert had the feeling that he was strong and even dangerous. But Gilbert showed no surprise; he doffed his hat to the old man, and said courteously that he hoped he had not wandered to some private place, where he ought not to be. "The heat was great, and I slept unawares," he said. The old man at first made no answer, and then said in a very low and yet clear voice, "Nay, sir, you are welcome. The Hill is free to all; but it has an evil name, I know, and I see but few upon it." Then Gilbert said courteously that he

was but a passer-by, and that he must set off home again, before
the sun was high. And at that the old man said, "Nay, sir, but as
you have come, you will surely wait awhile and speak with me. I
see," he added, "so few of humankind, that my mind and tongue
are alike stiff with disuse; but you can tell me something of your
world—and I," he added, "can tell you something of mine." Then
there came suddenly on Gilbert a great fear, and he looked round
on the tall stones of the circle that seemed to be like a prison. Then
he said, "I am but a simple scholar from Cambridge, and my knowledge of the world is but small; we work," he said, "we write and
read, we talk and eat together, and sometimes we pray." The old
man looked at him with a sudden look, under his brows, as he said
the words; and then he said, "So, sir, you are a priest; and your
faith is a strong one and avails much; but there is a text about the
strong man armed who is overcome of the stronger. And though
the faith you teach is like a fort in an enemy's country, in which
men may dwell safely, yet there is a land outside; and a fort cannot always hold its own." He said this in so evil and menacing a
tone that Gilbert said, "Come, sir, these are wild words; would you
speak scorn of the faith that is the light of God and the victory that
overcometh?" Then the old man said, "Nay, I respect the faith—
and fear it even," he added in a secret tone— "but I have grown up
in a different belief, and the old is better—and this also is a little
stronghold, which holds its own in the midst of foes; but I would
not be disputing," he added—and then with a smile, "Nay, sir, I
know what is in your mind; you like not this place—and you are
right; it is not fit for you to set your holy feet in; but it is mine yet;
and so you must even accept the hospitality of the place; you shall
look thrice in my glass, and see if you like what you shall see." And
he held out to Gilbert a small black shining thing. Gilbert would
have wished to refuse it, but his courtesy bade him take it—and
indeed he did not know if he could have refused the old man, who
looked so sternly upon him. So he took it in his hand. It was a black
polished stone like a sphere, and it was very cold to the touch—so
cold that he would fain have thrown it down; but he dared not. So
he said with such spirit as he could muster, "And what shall I see

beside the stone?—it seems a fair and curious jewel—I cannot give it a name." "Nay," said the old man sharply, "it is not the stone; the stone is naught; but it hides a mystery. You shall see it in the stone."

And Gilbert said, "And what shall I see in the stone?" And the old man said, "What shall be."

So Gilbert looked upon the stone; the sun shone upon it in a bright point of light—and for an instant he saw nothing but the gleaming sides of the ball. But in a moment there came upon him a dizziness like that which comes upon a man who, walking on a hill-top, finds himself on the edge of a precipice. He seemed to look into a great depth, into the dark places of the earth—but in the depth there hung a mist like a curtain. Now while he looked at it he saw a commotion in the mist; and looking closer, he saw that it seemed to be something waving to and fro that drove the mist about; and presently he saw the two arms of a man; and then the mist parted, and he saw the figure of a man standing and waving with his arms, like a man who would fan smoke aside; and the smoke fled from the waving arms and rolled away; and the man stepped aside.

Then Gilbert looked beyond, and he saw a room with a low ceiling and a mullioned window; and he knew it at once for his room in St. Peter's College. There were books on the table; and he saw what seemed like himself, risen to his feet, as though at a sound; and then he saw the door open and a man come in who made an obeisance, and the two seemed to talk together, and presently Gilbert saw the other man pull something from a cloth and put it in his own hands. And the figure of himself seemed to draw near the window to look at the thing; and though it was all very small and distant, yet Gilbert could see that he held in his hands a little figure that seemed a statue. And then the mist rolled in again and all was hid.

He came to himself like a man out of a dream, he had been so intent on what appeared; and he saw the hill-top and the circle of stones, and the old man who stood watching him with a secret smile upon his face. Then Gilbert made as though he would give the stone

back, but before he could speak, the old man pointed to the stone
again—and Gilbert looked again and saw the deep place, and the
cloud, and the man part the cloud.

Then he saw within a garden, and he knew it at once to be the
garden of St. Peter's; it seemed to be summer, for the trees were in
leaf. He saw himself stand, carrying something in his hand, and
looking at a place in the garden wall. There was something on the
wall, a patch of white, but he could not see what it was; and beneath it there stood a small group of men in scholars' dress who
looked upon the wall, but he could not see their faces; but one
whom he recognised as the Master of the College stood with a stick
in his hand, and pointed to the white patch on the wall—and then
something seemed to run by, a cat or dog, and all at once the cloud
flowed in over the picture; and again he came to himself and saw
the hill-top, and the stones, and the old man, who had drawn a
little nearer, and looked at him with a strange smile. And again he
pointed to the stone; and Gilbert looked again and saw the cloud
work very swiftly and part, and the man who swept the clouds off
came forth for an instant, and then was lost to view.

And Gilbert saw a very dark place, with something long and
white, that glimmered faintly, lying in the midst; and he bent down
to look at it, but could not discern what it was. Then he saw in the
darkness which surrounded the glimmering thing some small
threads of dusky white, and some small round things; and he looked
at them long; and presently discerned that the round things were
pebbles, and that the white threads were like the roots of trees;
and then he perceived that he was looking into the earth; and then
with a sickly chill of fear he saw that the long and glimmering thing
was indeed the body of a man, wrapped in grave-clothes from head
to foot. And he could now distinguish—for it grew more distinct—
the sides of a coffin about it, and some worms that moved to and
fro in their dark burrows; but the corpse seemed to shine with a
faint light of its own—and then he could see the wasted feet, and
the thin legs and arms of the body within; the hands were folded
over the breast; and then he looked at the face; and he saw his own
face, only greatly sunk and fallen, with a bandage that tied up the

chin, and leaden eyes; and then the clouds swept in upon it; and
he came to himself like a drowning man, and saw that he was in
the same place; and his first thought was a thrill of joy to know
that he was alive; but then he groaned aloud, and he saw the old
man stand beside him with a very terrible look upon his face, holding out his hand for the stone in silence; so Gilbert gave him back
the stone, and then with a fierce anger said, "Why have you shown
me this? for this is the trickery of hell." And the old man looked at
him very sternly and said, "Why then did you come to this place?
You were not called hither, and they that pry must be punished. A
man who pulls open the door which leads from the present into
the future must not be vexed if he sees the truth—and now, sir," he
added very angrily, "depart hence in haste; you have seen what
you have seen." So Gilbert went slowly from the circle, and very
heavily, and as he stepped outside he looked back. But there was
nothing there but the turf and the grey stones.

Gilbert went slowly down the Hill with a shadow upon him, like
a man who has passed through a sudden danger, or who has had a
sudden glimpse into the dark realities of life. But the whole experience was so strange and dreamlike, so apart from the wholesome
current of his life, that his fears troubled him less than he had supposed; still, a kind of hatred for the quiet valley began to creep
over him, and he found himself sitting long over his books, looking down among the hills, and making no progress. If he was not
silent when in company with the old Vicar, it was because he made
a strong effort, and because his courtesy came to his assistance.
Indeed the old Vicar thought that he had never known Gilbert so
tender or thoughtful as he had been in the last week of his visit.
The truth was that it was an effort to Gilbert to talk about himself,
and he therefore drew the old priest on to talk about the details of
his own life and work. Thus, though Gilbert talked less himself, he
was courteously attentive, so that the old man had a sense that
there had been much pleasant interchange of feeling, whereas he
had contributed the most of the talk himself. Gilbert, too, found a
great comfort in the offices of the Church in these days, and prayed

much that, whatever should befall him, he might learn to rest in the mighty will of God for himself, whatever that will might be.

Soon after this he went back to Cambridge, and there, among his old friends and in his accustomed haunts, the whole impression of the vision on the Hill of Trouble grew faint and indistinct, especially as no incident occurred to revive it. He threw himself into his work, and the book grew under his hands; and he seemed to be more eager to fill his hours than before, and avoided solitary meditation.

Some three years after the date of his vision, there was announced to him by letter the advent of a great scholar to Cambridge, who had read one of Gilbert's books, and was desirous to be introduced to him. Gilbert was sitting one day in his rooms, after a happy quiet morning, when the porter came to the door and announced the scholar. He was a tall eager man, who came forward with great friendliness, and said some courteous words about his pleasure at having met one whom he was so desirous to see. He carried something in his hand, and after the first compliments, said that he had ventured to bring Gilbert a little curiosity that had lately been dug up at Rome, and which he had been fortunate in securing. He drew off a wrapper, and held out to Gilbert a little figure of a Muse, finely sculptured, with an inscription on the pedestal. Gilbert stepped to the window to look at it, and as he did so it flashed across his mind that this was surely the scene that he had observed in the black stone. He stood for a moment with the statue in his hand, with such a strange look in his face, that the new-comer thought for an instant that his gift must have aroused some sad association. But Gilbert recovered himself in a moment and resolutely put the thought out of his mind, praised the statue, and thereupon entered into easy talk.

The great scholar spent some days at Cambridge, and Gilbert was much with him. They talked of learned matters together, but the great scholar said afterwards that though Gilbert was a man of high genius and of great insight into learning, yet he felt in talking with him as though he had some further and deeper preoccupation of thought.

Indeed when Gilbert, by laying of dates together, became aware that it was three years to a day since he had seen the vision in the stone, he was often haunted by the thought of his visit to the Hill. But this lasted only a few days; and he took comfort at the thought that he had seen a further vision in the stone which seemed at least to promise him three more peaceful years of unchanged work, before he need give way to the heaviness that the third vision had caused him. Yet it lay like a dark background in his thoughts.

He kept very much to his work after this event, and became graver and sterner in face, so that his friends thought that his application to study was harmful. But when they spoke of it to Gilbert, he used to say laughingly that nothing but work made life worthy, and that he was making haste; and indeed the great book grew so fast that he was within sight of the end. He had many wrestles within himself, about this time, as to the goodness and providence of God. He argued to himself that he had been led very tenderly beside the waters of comfort, that he had served God as faithfully as he could—and indeed he had little to reproach himself with, though he began to blame himself for living a life that pleased him, and for not going about more in the world helping weak brethren along the way, as the Lord Christ had done. Yet again he said to himself that the great doctors and fathers of the Church had deemed it praiseworthy that a man should devote all the power of his brain to making the divine oracle clear, and that the apostle Paul had spoken of a great diversity of gifts which could be used faithfully in the service of Christ. Still, he reflected that the truest glimpse into the unknown that he had ever received—for he doubted no longer of the truth of the vision—had come to him from one that was, he thought, outside the mercies of God, an unhallowed soul, shut off by his own will and by his wickedness from the fold; and this was a sore burden to him.

At last the book was done; and he went with it to a friend he had at Oxford, a mighty scholar, to talk over some difficult passages. The opinion of the scholar had been cordial and encouraging; he had said that the book was a very great and sound work, useful for doctrine and exhortation, and that many men had given their whole lives to work without achieving such a result. Gilbert had some of the happiness which comes to one who has completed a lengthy task; and though the time drew nigh at which he might expect a further fulfilment of the vision, he was so filled with gratitude at the thought of the great work he had done, that there was little fear or expectation in his mind.

He returned one summer afternoon to Cambridge, and the porter told him that the Master and several of the Fellows were in the garden, and would fain see him on his arrival. So Gilbert, carrying a little bundle which contained his precious book, went out there at once. The Master had caused to be made a new sundial, which he had affixed in such a way to the wall that those whose chambers gave on the garden could read the time of day without waiting to hear the bells.

When Gilbert came out he saw the little group of Fellows standing by the wall, while the Master with a staff pointed out the legend on the dial, which said that the only hours it told were the hours of sunshine. It came upon Gilbert in a moment that this was the second vision, and though two or three of the group saw him and turned to him with pleasant greetings, he stood for a moment lost in the strangeness of the thing. One of them said, "He stands amazed at the novelty of the design;" and as he said the words, an old gray cat that belonged to the College, and lodged somewhere in the roofs, sprang from a bush and ran past him. One of the Fellows said, "Aha, cats do not love change!" and then Gilbert came forward, and greeted his friends; but there lay a cold and terrible thought in the background of his mind, and he could not keep it out of his face; so that one of the Fellows, drawing him aside, asked if he had a good verdict on the book, for he seemed as one that was ill-pleased. And the Master, fearing that Gilbert did not like the dial, came and said to him courteously that he knew it was a new-fangled thing, but that it was useful, and in itself not unpleasant, and that it would soon catch a grace of congruity from the venerable walls around. "But," he added, "if you do not like it, it shall be put in some other place." Then Gilbert bestirred himself and said that he liked the dial very well, so that the Master was content.

But Gilbert, as soon as he was by himself, delivered his mind up to heavy contemplation; the vision had twice fulfilled itself, and it was hardly to be hoped that it would fail the third time. He sent his book to be copied out fair, and when it was gone it was as though he had lost his companion. The hours passed very slowly and drearily; he wrote a paper, to fill the time, of his wishes with regard to what should be done with his books and little property after his death, and was half minded to tear it up again. And then after a few days of purposeless and irresolute waiting, he made up his mind that he must go again to the West, and see his friend the old priest. And though he did not say it to himself in words, yet a purpose slowly shaped itself in his mind that he must at all cost go to the Hill, and learn again what should be, and that thus alone could he break the spell.

He spent a morning in making his farewells; he tried to speak to his friends as usual, but they noticed long afterwards that he had used a special tenderness and wistfulness in all he said; he sate long in his own room, with a great love in his heart for the beautiful and holy peace of the place, and for all the happiness he had known there; and then he prayed very long and earnestly in the chapel, kneeling in his stall; and his heart was somewhat lightened.

Then he set off; but before he mounted his horse he looked very lovingly at the old front of the College, and his servant saw that his eyes were full of tears and that his lips moved; and so Gilbert rode along to the West.

His journey was very different from the same journey taken six years before; he spoke with none, and rode busily, like one who is anxious to see some sad errand through. He found the old Vicar still more infirm and somewhat blind; but the Vicar said that he was very happy to see him, as he himself was near the end of life, and that he could hope for but few years,—adding that it was far different for Gilbert, who, he supposed, would very soon be a Dean with a Cathedral of his own, and would forget his humble friend the old Vicar. But Gilbert put the wit aside, and talked earnestly with the Vicar about the end of life and what might be hereafter. But the old Vicar said solemnly that he knew not, and indeed cared little. But that he would go into the dark like a child holding a loving hand, and would have no need to fear.

That night Gilbert lay in his bed awake, and very strange thoughts passed through his mind, which he strove to quiet by prayers; and so fell asleep; till at last in the dim dawn he awoke. Then after a moment's thought he took a paper and wrote on it, saying that he was gone out and knew not when he would return; but he prayed the Vicar that when he should find the paper, he should at once fall to prayer for him, for there was a sore conflict before him to fight out, both in soul and body, and what would be the issue he knew not. "And if," the end of the writing ran, "I must depart hence, then pray that my passage may be easy, and that I may find the valley bright." And he laid the paper upon the table. Then he dressed himself, and went out alone into the valley, walking swiftly and intently—so intently that when he passed the farm he marked not that the old farmer was sitting in an arbour in the garden, who called shrilly to him; but Gilbert heard not, and the old farmer was too weak to follow; so Gilbert went down to the Hill of Trouble.

It lay, as it had lain six years before, very still and beautiful in the breathless sunshine. The water was in the creek, a streak of sapphire blue; the birds called in the crags, and the bushes and lawns glistened fresh with dew.

But Gilbert, very pale and with his heart beating fast, came to the wall and surmounted it, and went swiftly up the Hill, till he found himself near the stones; then he looked once round upon the hills and the sea, and then with a word of prayer he stepped within the circle.

This time he had not long to wait. As he entered the circle he saw the old man enter from the opposite side and come to meet him, with a strange light of triumph in his eyes. Then Gilbert looked him in the face with a rising horror, and said, "Sir, I have come again; and I doubt the truth of your vision no longer; I have done my work, and I have twice seen the fulfilment—now therefore tell me of my end—that I may be certified how long I have to live. For the shadow of the doubt I cannot bear."

And the old man looked at him with something of compassion and said, "You are young, and you fear the passage hence, knowing not what may be on the other side of the door; but you need not fear. Even I, who have small ground of hope, am ashamed that I feared it so much. But what will you give me if I grant your boon?"

Then Gilbert said, "I have nothing to give."

Then the old man said, "Think once more." Then was there a silence; and Gilbert said;

"Man, I know not what or who thou art; but I think that thou art a lost soul; one thing I can give thee. . . . I will myself intercede for thee before the Throne."

Then the old man looked at him for a moment, and said, "I have waited long . . . and have received no comfort till now;" and then he said, "Wilt thou promise?"

And Gilbert said, "In the name of God, Amen."

Then the old man stretched out his hand and said, "Art thou ready? for the time is come; and thou art called now;" and he touched Gilbert on the breast.

Gilbert looked into the old man's eyes, and seemed to see there an unfathomable sadness, such as he had never seen; but at the touch a pain so fierce and agonising passed through him, that he sank upon the ground and covered his face with his hands.

Just at this time the old priest found the paper; and he divined the truth. So he called his servant and bade him saddle his horse in haste; and then he fell to prayer.

Then he rode down the valley; and though he feared the place, yet he rode to the Hill of Trouble; and though his sight was dim and his limbs feeble, it seemed to him that some one walked beside the horse and guided him; and as he prayed he knew that all was over, and that Gilbert had peace.

He came soon to the place; and there he found Gilbert lying on the turf; and his sight was so dim that it seemed to him as though some one slipped away from Gilbert's side. He put Gilbert on his horse, and held the poor helpless body thereon, but there was so gentle a smile on the face of the dead that he could not fear.

The body of Gilbert lies in the little churchyard; his great book keeps his memory bright; and on the top of the Hill of Trouble stands a little chapel, built out of the stones of the circle; and on the wall, painted at the old priest's charge, is a picture of the Lord Christ, with wounded hands and side, preaching to the disobedient spirits in prison; and they hear him and are glad.

The Light of the Body

It was high noon in the little town of Parbridge; the streets were bright and silent, and the walls of the houses were hot to the touch. The limes in the narrow avenue leading to the west door of the great church of St. Mary stood breathless and still. The ancient church itself looked as if it pondered gravely on what had been and what was to be; and the tall windows of the belfry, with their wooden louvres, seemed to be solemn half-shut eyes. At the south side of the church, connected with it by a wooden cloister, stood a tall house of grey stone. In a room looking out upon the graveyard sate two men. The room had an austere air; its plain whitened walls bore a single picture, so old and dark that it was difficult to see what was represented in it. On some shelves stood a few volumes; near the window was a tall black crucifix of plain wood, the figure white. There was an oak table with writing materials. The floor was paved with squares of wood.

The two men sate close together. One was an old and weather-worn man in a secular dress of dark material; the other a young priest in a cassock, whose pale face, large eyes and wasted hands betokened illness, or the strain of some overmastering thought. It seemed as though they had been holding a grave conversation of strange or sad import, and had fallen into a momentary silence.

The priest was the first to speak. "Well, beloved physician," he said, in a slow and languid voice, though with a half-smile, "I have told you my trouble; and I would have your most frank opinion."

"I hardly know what to say," said the Doctor. "I have prescribed for many years and do not know that I ever heard the like; I must tell you plainly that such things are not written in our medical books."

The priest said nothing, but looked sadly out of the window; presently the Doctor said, "Let me hear the tale from the first beginning, dear Herbert;—it is well to have the whole complete. I would consult with a learned friend of mine about this dark matter, a physician who is more skilled than I am in maladies of the mind—for I think that more ails the mind than the body."

"Well," said the priest a little wearily, "I will tell it you.

"Almost a year ago, on one of the hottest days of the early summer, I went abroad as usual, about noon, to visit Mistress Dennis who was ill. I do not think I felt myself to be unwell, and was full to the brim of little joyous businesses; I stood for a time at the porch to speak with Master Dennis himself, who came in just as I left the house, and I stood uncovered at the door; suddenly the sun stabbed and struck me, as with a scythe, and I saw a whirling blackness before my eyes and staggered. Master Dennis was alarmed, and would have had me go within; but I would not, for I had other work to do; so he led me home; that afternoon I sate over my book; but I could neither read nor think; I was in pain, I remember, and felt that some strange thing had happened to me; I recall, too, rising from my chair, and I am told I fainted and fell.

"Then I remember nothing more but fierce and wild dreams of pain. Sometimes I heard my own voice crying out; at last the pain died away, and left me very weak and sad; but I was still pent up, it seemed to me, in some dark dungeon of the mind, and the view of the room I lay in and the sight of those who visited me only came to me in short glimpses. I am told I babbled strangely; then one morning I came out suddenly, like a man rising from a dive in a pool, and knew that I was myself again; that day was a day of quiet joy; I was weak and silent, but it seemed good to be alive. It was not till the next day that I noticed the thing that I have tried to tell you, that haunts me yet—and I can hardly put it into words.

"It seemed to me that I noticed round about those who came to me a thin veil, as it were of vapour, but it was not dense like smoke or mist; I could see them as well through it as before; it was more like a light that played about them, and it was brightest over the heart and above the brow; at first I thought it was some effect of my weak state, but as I grew stronger I saw it still more clearly.

"And then comes the strangest part of all; the light changed according to the thoughts that were passing in the mind of the person on whom my eyes were set—the thought that it was so came suddenly into my mind and bewildered me; but in a little I was sure of it. I need not give long instances—but I saw, or thought I saw, that when the mind of the man or woman was pure and pitiful, the light was pure and clear, but that when the thoughts were selfish, or covetous, or angry, or unclean, there came a darkness into the light, as when you drop a little ink into clear water. Few came to see me; and I suppose that they were full of pity and perhaps a little love for me in my helpless state, so that the light about them was pure and even; but one day the good dame Ann, who tended me, in stooping to give me drink, thrust a dish off the table, which broke, and spilled its contents, and a dark flush came into the light that was round her for a moment.

"Then too as I got better, and was able to see and speak with my people, there came to me several in trouble of different kinds, and the light was sullen and wavering; one, whose name I will not tell you, came to me with a sin upon his mind, and the vapour was all dark and stained; and so it has been till now; and these last weeks it has been even stranger; because by a kind of practice I have been led to infer what the thoughts in the mind of each person are, at first seeing them. It is true that they have not always told me in words what the light would seem to suggest; but I have good reason to believe that the thoughts are there behind.

"Now," he went on, "this is a sad and dreadful gift, and I do not desire it. It is horrible that the thoughts of men should be made manifest to a man, the thoughts that should be read only by God; and I go to and fro in the world with this cruel horror upon me, and so I am in evil case."

He ceased, as if tired of speaking, and the old Doctor mused, looking on the floor—then he shook his head and said, "My dear friend, I am powerless at present; such a thing has never come to me before—you are as it were in a chamber of life that I have never visited, and I can but stand on the threshold and listen at a closed door." Then he was silent for a little, but presently he said, "This light that you speak of—does it envelop every one?—do you see it about *me* as I speak with you?" "Yes," said Herbert, turning his eyes upon the Doctor, "it is round you, very pure and clean; you are giving all your heart to my story; and it is a good and tender heart. You have not many sorrows except the sorrows of others," and then suddenly Herbert broke off with a vague gesture of the hand and looked at the Doctor with a bewildered look. "Finish what you were saying," said the Doctor with a grave look. "Nay, nay," said Herbert with a sad air, "you have sorrows indeed—the light changes and darkens—but they are not all for yourself."

"This is a strange thing," said the Doctor very seriously— "tell me what you mean."

"Then you must keep from thoughts on your trouble, whatever it is," said Herbert. "I would read no man's secrets; but let this prove to you that I am not speaking of a mere sick fancy—turn not your thoughts on me." Then there was a pause and then Herbert said slowly, "As far as I can read the light, you did a wrong once, long ago, in your youth, and bear the burden of it yet; and you have striven to amend it; and now it is not a selfish fear;"—the priest mused a moment— "How, if the deed has borne fruit in another, for whom you sorrow, for you think that your wrongdoing was the seed of his?"

The Doctor grew pale to the lips, and said in a low voice, "This is a very fearful gift, dear friend. You have indeed laid your finger on the sore spot—it is a thing I have never spoken of to any but God."

Then there was a silence again; and then Herbert said, "But there is another thing of which I have not told you; it is this; you know what I was before my illness—simple, I think, and humble, and with a heart that for all its faults was tender and faithful. Well, with this gift, that has all departed from me; I seem to care neither for man nor God; I see the trouble in another heart, and it moves me not. I feel as if I would not put out a finger to heal another's grief, except that habit has made it hard for me to do otherwise." And then with a sudden burst of passion, "Oh, my heart of stone!" he said.

The Doctor looked at him very sadly and lovingly, and then he rose. "I must be gone," he said, "but by your leave I will consult, without any mention of name, an old friend of mine, the wise physician of whom I spoke; and meanwhile, dear friend, rest and be still. God has sent you a very strange and terrible gift, but He sends not His gifts in vain; and you must see how you may use it for His service."

"Yes, yes, I doubt not," said Herbert wearily— "but the will to serve is gone from me—I would I were sleeping quietly out yonder—the world is poisoned for me, and yet I loved it once."

Then the old physician went away, lost in thought, and Herbert made attempt to address himself to his book, but he could not; he looked back over his life, and saw himself a simple child, very innocent and loving; he saw his eager and clean boyhood, and how the thought had come into his mind to be a priest—it was not for a noble reason, Herbert thought; he had loved the beauty of the dark rich church, the slow and delicate music of the organ, the singing of the choir, the faint sweetness of the incense smoke, the solemn figures of the priests as they moved about the altar—it had been but a love of beauty and solemnity; no desire to save others, and very little love to the Father, though a strange uplifted desire of heart toward the Lord Christ; but as he thought of it now, sitting in the afternoon sunshine, it seemed to him as though he had loved the Saviour more for the beauty of worship which surrounded Him, throned as it were so piteously upon the awful Cross, lifted up, the desire of the world, in all His stainless strength and adorable suffering, to draw souls to Him.

Then he had gone to Oxford, and he thought of his time there, his small bare rooms, the punctual vivid life, so repressed, yet so full of human movement. Herbert had won friends very easily there, and the good fathers had loved him; but all this love, looking back, seemed to him to have been called out not by the lovingness of his own heart, but by a certain unconscious charm, a sweet humility of manner, a readiness to please and be pleased, a desire to do what should win his companion, whoever it might chance to be.

Then he went for a time as a young priest to the cathedral, as a vicar, and there again life had been easy for him; he had gained fame for a sort of easy and pathetic eloquence, that allowed him to make what he spoke of seem beautiful to those who heard it, but now Herbert thought sadly that he had not done this for love of the thoughts of which he spoke, but for the pleasure of arraying them so that they moved and pleased others; and yet he had won some power over souls too, he had himself been so courteous, so gentle, so seeming tender, that others spoke easily to him of their troubles and seemed to find help in his words; then had come the day when the Bishop had sent him to St. Mary's, and there too everything had been as easy to him as before. Yes, that had been the fault all through! he had won by a certain grace what ought to have been won by deep purity and eager desire and great striving.

And this too had at last begun to come home to him; and then he had half despaired of changing himself. He had been like a shallow rippling brook, yet seemed to others like a swift and patient river; and he had prayed very earnestly to God to change his heart; to deepen and widen it, to make it strong and sincere and faithful. And was this, thought Herbert, the terrible answer? was he who had loved ease and beauty on all sides, had loved the surface and the seeming of things, to be thrust violently into the deep places of the human heart, to be shown by a dreadful clearness of vision the stain, the horror, the shadow of the world?

But what was to him the most despairing thought of all was this—and thinking quietly over it, it seemed to him that if this clearness of vision had quickened his zeal to serve, if it had shown him how true and fierce was the battle to be waged in life, and how few men walked in the peace that was so near them that they could have taken it by stretching out their hand—if it had taught him this, had nerved his heart, had sent him speeding into the throng

to heal the secret sorrows that his quickened sight could see, then
the reason of the gift would have been plain to him; but with the
clearer vision had come this deadly apathy, this strange and bitter
loathing for a world where all seemed so sweet outwardly and was
so heavy-hearted within. And Herbert thought of how once as a
child he had seen a beautiful rose-bush just bursting into bloom;
and he had gone near to draw the sweet scent into his nostrils, and
had recognised a dreadful heavy odour below and behind the delicate scent of the roses, and there, when he put the bush aside, was
the swollen body of a dog that had crept into the very heart of the
bush to die, and tainted all the air with the horror of death. He
had hated roses long after, and now it seemed to him that all the
world was like that.

He came suddenly out of his sad reverie with a start; the bell of
the church began to toll for vespers, and he rose up wearily enough
to go. His work, he hardly dared confess to himself, was a heavy
burden to him; of old he had found great peace, day by day, in the
quiet evensong in the dark cool church, the few worshippers, the
gracious pleading of the ancient psalms, so sweet in themselves,
and so fragrant with the incense of immemorial prayer; and he
thought that, besides the actual worshippers, there were round him
a great company of faithful souls, unseen yet none the less present—
all this had been to him a deep refreshment, a draught of the waters
of comfort; but now there was never a gathering when the dark
trouble of thought in other souls was not visibly revealed to him.

He went slowly across the little garden in front of the house;
there by the road grew a few flowers—for Herbert loved to have all
things trim and bright about him. A boy was leaning over the rail
looking at the flowers; and Herbert saw, in the secret light that
hung round the child, the darkening flush that told of the presence of some conscience-stricken wish. The child got hurriedly
down from the rail at the sight of Herbert, who stopped and called
him. "Little one," he said, "come hither." The child stood a moment absorbed, finger on lip, and presently came up to Herbert,
who gathered a few of the flowers and put them into the child's
hands. "Here is a posy for you," he said, "but, dear one, remember

this—the flowers were mine, and you did desire them. God sends us gifts sometimes and sometimes not; when He sends them, it is well to take them gratefully, thus—but if He gives them not, and the voice within says, 'Then will I take them,' we must fly from temptation. Do you understand that, little one?" The child stood considering a moment, and then shyly gave the flowers back. "Ay, that is right," said Herbert, "but you may take them now—God gives them to you!" and he stooped and kissed the child on the forehead.

A few days after the old physician came again to see Herbert, evidently troubled. He told Herbert that he had consulted his friend, who could make nothing of the case. "He said—" he added, and then stopped short. "Nay, I will tell you," he went on, "for in such a matter we may not hesitate. He said that it was a delusion of the mind, not of the eye—and that it was more a case for a priest than for a doctor." "He is right," said Herbert. "I had even thought of that—and I will do what I ought to have done before. I will take my story to my lord the Bishop and I will ask his advice; he is my friend, and he has been a true father to my spirit—and he is a good and holy man as well."

So Herbert wrote to the Bishop, and the Bishop appointed a day to see him. The cathedral city was but a few miles from Parbridge, and Herbert went thither by boat because he was not strong enough to walk. The river ran through a flat country, with distant hills on a far horizon; the clear flowing of the water, the cool weedy bowers and gravelled spaces seen beneath, and the green and glistening rushes that stood up so fresh and strong out of the ripple pleased Herbert's tired mind; he tried much to think what he would say to the Bishop; but he could frame no arguments and thought it best to leave it, and to say what God might put in his mouth to say.

He found the Bishop writing in a little panelled room that gave on a garden. He was in his purple cassock; he rose at Herbert's entrance, and greeted him very kindly. The Bishop's face was smooth and fresh-coloured and lit with a pleasant light of benevolence. He was an active man, and loved little businesses, which he did with all his might. He, like all that knew Herbert, loved him

and found pleasure in his company. So Herbert took what courage
he might—though he saw somewhat that he was both grieved and
surprised to see—and told his story, though his heart was heavy,
and he thought somehow that the Bishop would not understand
him. While he spoke the Bishop's face grew very grave, for he did
not love things out of the common; but he asked him questions
from time to time—and when Herbert said that the trouble had
come upon him after a stroke of the sun, the Bishop's face lightened a little, and he said that the sun at its hottest had great power.

When Herbert had quite finished, the Bishop said courteously
that he thought it was a case for a physician, and Herbert said that
he had himself thought so, but that the doctors could do nothing,
but had sent him back to the priests. Then the Bishop made as
though he would speak, and cleared his throat, but spake nothing.
At last he said, "Dear son, this is a strange and heavy affliction;
but I think it will give way to rest and quiet—and prayer," he added
a little shamefacedly. "These bodies of ours are delicate instruments, and if we work them too hard—as methinks you have done—
they get overstrained in the place in which we drive them; and just
as a scholar who has been disordered dreams of books, and as a
doctor thus afflicted would have grievous fancies of diseases, so
you, my dear son, who have been a very faithful priest, are thus
sadly concerned with the souls of the flock of Christ—and so my
advice is that you go and rest; and if you will, I will send you a
little priest to help you for awhile—or you may travel abroad for a
time, and see fresh things; and, dear son, if there be any narrow-
ness of means, I will myself supply your necessities, and deem the
money well lent to the Lord—and so be comforted!"—and he put
out his hand to bless him.

Herbert was moved by the Bishop's kindness; but he felt that
the Bishop did not see the matter aright, but thought it all a sad
delusion; and he made up his mind to speak. So he said, "Dear
father and my lord, forgive me if I speak yet further—for I am
greatly moved by your kindness, but in this case there is need of
great frankness. It is not indeed as your goodness thinks; indeed
there is no delusion, but a real and yet grievous power of sight—

which I pray God would remove from me—and that as He took the scales off the eyes of the blessed Paul, so I pray that He would put them back on mine. For I see the things I would not, and to me is revealed what ought to be hidden."

Then the Bishop looked a little angered by Herbert's insistence, and said, "Dear son, if this were a gift of God to you, it would be more than He gave even to the blessed Apostles, for we read of no such gift being given to man. Some He made apostles, and some evangelists, but we hear not that He made any to see the very secrets of the soul—such sight is given to God alone—and indeed, dear son, for I will use the same frankness as yourself, it seems to me but a chastening from God. He delivers even those He loves (like the blessed Paul himself, and Austin, and others whom I need not name) to Satan to be buffeted; and though I have myself no fault to find with your ministration, it is plain to me that God is not satisfied, and by His chastening would lead you higher yet."

"But come, for I will ask you a question. This light that you speak of, that plays about the heads (is it so?) of other men, is it always there? Has it, to ask an instance, appeared to you with *me*? I charge you to speak to me with entire freedom in this matter." So Herbert raised his eyes, and looked the Bishop in the face, and said very gravely, "Yes, dear father, it doth appear."

Then the Bishop's face changed a little, and Herbert saw that he was moved; then the Bishop said with a kind of smile, as though he forced himself, "And what is it like?" And Herbert said, looking shamefacedly upon the ground, "Must I answer the question truly?" And the Bishop said, "Yes, upon your vows." Then Herbert said, "Dear father, it is strangely dark and angry." Then the Bishop, knitting his brows, said, "Does it seem so? And how is this a true light? My son, I speak to you plainly; I am a sinner indeed—we are all such—but my whole life is spent in labour for God's Church, and I can truly say that from hour to hour I think not of carnal things, but all my desire is to feed and keep the flock. How dost thou interpret that?" And Herbert, very low, said, "My lord, must I speak?" And the Bishop said, "Yes, upon your vows." Then Herbert said very slowly and sadly, "My lord, I know indeed that your heart is with the work of the Lord, and that you labour abundantly. But can it be—I speak as a faithful son, and sore unwilling—that you have your pleasure in this work, and think of yourself as a profitable servant?"

Then the Bishop looked very blackly upon him and said, "You take too much upon yourself, my son. This is indeed the messenger of Satan that hath you in his grip; but I will pray for you if the Lord will heal you—it may be that there is some dark sin upon your mind; and if so pluck it out of the heart. But we will talk no more; I will only tell you to rest and pray, and think not of these lights and flashes, which are never told of in Holy Church, except in the case of those who are held of evil." And he rose and made a gesture that Herbert should go; so Herbert kissed the Bishop's hand and went very sadly out, for it seemed as though his burden was too great for him to bear.

There followed very sad and weary days when Herbert hardly knew how he could bear the sorrow that pressed upon him. But he preached diligently, and went in and out among his people. And in that time he helped many sad souls and set struggling feet upon the right road, though he knew it not and even cared not.

One day he was walking in the street, and came past a little mean house that lay on the outskirts of the town. There was a small and pitiful garden, sadly disordered, that lay in front of the house. Here there dwelt a wretched man named John, who had done an evil deed in his youth. He had robbed his mother, it was said, a poor and crippled woman, of her little savings; she had struggled hard for her all, but he had beaten her off, and done her violence, and she, between grief and disease, had died. In her last hour she had told the tale; her son had been driven from his employment, and the hearts of all had turned against him. He had left the place, but a few years after he had returned, a man old before his time, with a sore disease upon him, in which all readily saw the wise judgment of God.

He had settled in the little house which had been his mother's before him, and had stood vacant. But none would admit him to their houses or give him work. Occasionally, when labour was short, he had a task given him; but he was slow and feeble, and those that worked with him mocked and derided him. He bore all mockeries patiently and silently, with a kind of hunted look; but none pitied him, and the very children of the street would point at him, call him murderer, and throw stones at him. He would seek at times to do a kindness to the poor and sorrowful by stealth, but his help was often refused even with anger.

Herbert had seen a little sight a few days before that stuck in his mind. He had been passing along the road that led into the country, and had seen some way ahead of him a little child, a girl, with a heavy burden. She had put it down by the wood to rest, when John came suddenly upon her from a lane, where he had been wandering, as his manner was. The girl had seemed frightened, but Herbert, making haste to join them—for he too had a great suspicion of the man—saw him speak gently to her and lift up her burden, and walk on with her. Herbert followed afar off, but gained on the pair, and as he came up heard him speaking to her, and as Herbert thought, telling her a simple story about the birds and flowers. The child was listening half timidly, when from a gate beside the road, which led to the farm to which the child was bound, came out her mother, a tall good-humoured woman, who snatched the burden out of the hands of John, and dusted it over with her apron, as though his touch had polluted it. Then she scolded the child and then fell to rating John with very cruel words.

Herbert came up and from a distance saw John stand very meekly with bowed head; and presently he turned away when the angry woman departed, and Herbert heard him sigh very heavily. He had then half formed a purpose to speak with the man, but he trusted him little, and the old story of his crime chased pity out of Herbert's mind.

Now to-day the sight of the neglected house and wretched garden drew his mind to the outcast; Herbert could not think how the man lived, and his heart smote him for not having tried to comfort him.

So he turned aside and lifted the latch, and went up under an old apple tree that hung over the path, and knocked at the door.

Presently it was opened by John himself, who stood there, a wretched figure of a man, bowed with disease, and his face all ugly and scarred. Herbert, who loved things beautiful, was strangely touched with disgust at the sight of him, but he overcame it, and spoke gently to him, and asked if he might come in and rest awhile.

The man, although he hardly seemed to understand, made way for him, and Herbert entered a room that he thought the meanest and ugliest he had ever seen. The walls were green with mould, and the paved floor was all sunken and cracked. There was no table, nothing but a bench by the fireplace, on which lay coarse roots and the leaves of some bitter herb.

Herbert went on talking quietly about the fine summer and the pleasant season of the year, and sate down upon the bench. And then he had a great surprise. All about the miserable man who stood before him shone the clearest and purest radiance of light he had ever beheld about a human being, gushing in a pure fountain over his head and heart, untouched by the least spot of darkness. It came into Herbert's mind that he had found a man who was very near to God; and so he put all other things aside, and saying that he was truly sorry that he had not sought him out before, asked him in gentle and loving words to tell him all the old sad story. And there, sitting in the mean room, he heard the tale.

John spoke slowly and haltingly, as one who had little use of speech; and the story was far different from what Herbert had believed. The hoard was not that of John's mother, but John's own, which he had entrusted to her. He had asked it of her for a purpose that seemed good enough, to buy a little garden where he thought he could rear fruits and flowers; but she had had the money so long that she considered it to be her own. In telling the story, John laid no blame upon her, but found much to say against himself, and he seemed bowed down with utter contrition that he had ever asked it of her. She had struck him, it seemed, and so his wrath had overmastered him, and he had torn the money from her hands and gone out. Then she had fallen sick, and died before his return, and after that no one had been willing to listen to him. Herbert had asked him what had become of the money, and John told him, with a sort of shame, that he had thrust it into the church-box— "I could not touch the price of blood," he said.

Then Herbert spoke very lovingly to him and tried to comfort him, but John said that he knew himself to be the most miserable of sinners, and that he could not be forgiven, and that he deserved his chastising every whit. And he told Herbert a tale of secret suffering and hunger and cold and weariness, such as had never fallen on Herbert's ears, but all without any thought of pity for himself— indeed, he said, God was very good to him; for He let him live, and even allowed him to take pleasure in the green trees, and the waving grass, and the voices of birds. "And some day," said John, "when I have suffered enough, I think the Father will forgive me, for I am sorry for my sin."

The water stood in Herbert's eyes, but he found some words of comfort, and knelt and prayed with the outcast, telling him that indeed he was forgiven. And he saw a look of joy strike like sunlight across the poor face, when he said that he would not fail to visit him. And he further told him that he should come to the Parsonage next day, and he would give him work to do; and then he shook his hand and departed, a little gladder than he had been for a month.

But on the next day he was bidden early to the cottage; John had been found sitting on the little bench outside his door, cold and dead, with a strange and upturned look almost as though he had seen the heaven opened.

He was buried a few days after; none were found to stand at the grave but Herbert, and the clerk who came unwillingly.

Then, on the next Sunday, Herbert made a little sermon at Evensong and told them all the story of John's life, and his atonement. "My brothers and sisters," he said very softly, making a pause, the silence in the church being breathless below him, "here was a true saint of God among us, and we knew it not. He sinned, though not so grievously as we thought, he suffered grievously, and he took his suffering as meekly as the little child of whom the dear Lord said that of such was the Kingdom. Dear friends, I tell you a truth from my heart; that in the day when we stand, if we are given to stand, beneath the Throne of God, this our poor brother will be nearer to the Throne than any of us, in robes of light, and very close to the Father's heart. May the Father forgive us all, and let us be pitiful and merciful, if by any means we may obtain mercy."

That night, in a dream, it seemed as if some one came suddenly out of a dark place like a grave, and stood before Herbert, exceedingly glorious to behold. How the change had passed upon him Herbert could not tell, for it was John himself, the same, yet transformed into a spirit of purest light. And he smiled upon Herbert and said, "It is even so, dear brother; and now am I comforted in glory—and now that you have seen the truth, the Father would have me visit you to tell you that the trouble laid upon you is departed. Only be true and faithful, and lead souls the nearest way." And in a moment he was gone, but seemed to leave a shining track upon the darkness.

The next morning Herbert awoke with a strange stirring of the heart. He looked abroad from his window, and saw the dew upon the grass, and the quiet trees awakening. And he could hardly contain himself for gladness. When he went to the church, he knew all at once that his sorrow had departed from him, and that he saw no deeper into the heart than other men. The lights that had seemed to shine round others were gone, and his heart was full of love and pity again.

His first visit was to the house of the old physician, who greeted him very kindly; and Herbert with a kind of happy radiance told him that the trouble was departed from him as suddenly as it came; "and," he added, "dear friend, God has shown me marvellous things—I have seen a soul in glory." The old physician's eyes filled with tears and he said, "This is very wonderful and gracious."

The same day came a carriage from the Bishop to fetch Herbert, for the Bishop desired to see him. He went in haste, and was amazed to see that when the carriage came to the door of the Bishop's house, the Bishop himself came out to receive him as though he had waited for him.

The Bishop greeted him very lovingly and took him into his room, and when the door was shut, he said, "Dear son, I sent you from me the other day in bitterness of heart; for you had spoken the truth to me, and I could not bear it; and now I ask your forgiveness; you found as it were the key to my spirit, and flung the door open; and God has shown me that you were right, and that the most secret shrine of my heart, where the fire should burn clearest, was dark and bare. I gave not God the glory, but laid violent hands upon it for myself; and now, if God will, all shall be changed, and I will do my work for God and not for myself, and strive to be humble of heart," and the Bishop's eyes were full of tears. And he held out his hand to Herbert, who took it; and so they sate for a while. Then Herbert said, "Dear father, I will also tell you something. God has taken away from me the terrible gift; also He has shown me the sight of a human spirit, made perfect in suffering and patience; and I am very joyful thereat." So they held sweet converse together, and were very glad at heart.

The Red Camp

It was a sultry summer evening in the old days, when Walter Wyatt came to the house of his forefathers. It was in a quiet valley of Sussex, with the woods standing very steeply on the high hill-sides. Among the woods were pleasant stretches of pasture, and a little stream ran hidden among hazels beside the road; here and there were pits in the woods, where the men of ancient times had dug for iron, pits with small sandstone cliffs, and full to the brim of saplings and woodland plants. Walter rode slowly along, his heart full of a happy content. Though it was the home of his family he had never even seen Restlands—that was the peaceful name of the house. Walter's father had been a younger son, and for many years the elder brother, a morose and selfish man, had lived at Restlands, often vowing that none of his kin should ever set foot in the place, and all out of a native malice and churlishness, which discharged itself upon those that were nearest to him. Walter's father was long dead, and Walter had lived a very quiet homely life with his mother. But one day his uncle had died suddenly and silently, sitting in his chair; and it was found that he had left no will. So that Restlands, with its orchards and woods and its pleas-ant pasture-lands, fell to Walter; and he had ridden down to take possession. He was to set the house in order, for it was much de-cayed in his uncle's time; and in a few weeks his mother was to follow him there.

He turned a corner of the road, and saw in a glance a house that he knew must be his; and a sudden pride and tenderness leapt up within his heart, to think how fair a place he could call his own.

An avenue of limes led from the road to the house, which was built of ancient stone, the roof tiled with the same. The front was low and many-windowed. And Walter, for he was a God-fearing youth, made a prayer in his heart, half of gratitude and half of hope.

He rode up to the front of the house, and saw at once that it was sadly neglected; the grass grew among the paving-stones, and several of the windows were broken. He knocked at the door, and an old serving-man came out, who made an obeisance. Walter sent his horse to the stable; his baggage was already come; and his first task was to visit his new home from room to room. It was a very beautiful solidly built house, finely panelled in old dry wood, and had an abundance of solid oak furniture; there were dark pictures here and there; and that night Walter sate alone at his meat, which was carefully served him by the old serving-man, his head full of pleasant plans for his new life; he slept in the great bedroom, and many times woke wondering where he was; once he crept to the window, and saw the barns, gardens, and orchards lie beneath, and the shadowy woods beyond, all bathed in a cold clear moonlight.

In the morning when he had breakfasted, the lawyer who had charge of his business rode in from the little town hard by to see him; and when Walter's happiness was a little dashed; for though the estate brought in a fair sum, yet it was crippled by a mortgage which lay upon it; and Walter saw that he would have to live sparely for some years before he could have his estate unembarrassed; but this troubled him little, for he was used to a simple life. The lawyer indeed had advised him to sell a little of the land; but Walter was very proud of the old estate, and of the memory that he was the tenth Wyatt that had dwelt there, and he said that before he did that he would wait awhile and see if he could not arrange otherwise. When the lawyer was gone there came in the bailiff, and Walter went with him all over the estate. The garden was greatly overgrown with weeds, and the yew hedges were sprawling all uncut; they went through the byre, where the cattle stood in the straw; they visited the stable and the barn, the granary and the dovecote; and Walter spoke pleasantly with the men that served him; then he went to the ploughland and the pastures, the orchard and the

woodland; and it pleased Walter to walk in the woodpaths, among
the copse and under great branching oaks, and to feel that it was
all his own.

At last they came out on the brow of the hill, and saw Restlands
lie beneath them, with the smoke of a chimney going up into the
quiet air, and the doves wheeling about the cote. The whole valley
was full of westering sunshine, and the country sounds came pleasantly up through the still air.

They stood in a wide open pasture, but in the centre of it rose a
small, dark, and thickly grown square holt of wood, surrounded
by a high green bank of turf, and Walter asked what that was. The
old bailiff looked at him a moment without speaking and then said,
"That is the Red Camp, sir." Walter said pleasantly, "And whose
camp is it?" but it came suddenly into his head that long ago his
father had told him a curious tale about the place, but he could not
remember what the tale was. The old man answering his question
said, "Ah, sir, who can say? perhaps it was the old Romans who
made it, or perhaps older men still; but there was a sore battle
hereabouts." And then he went on in a slow and serious way to tell
him an old tale of how a few warriors had held the place against an
army, and that they had all been put to the sword there; he said
that in former days strange rusted weapons and bones had been
ploughed up in the field, and then he added that the Camp had
ever since been left desolate and that no one cared to set foot within
it; yet for all that it was said that a great treasure lay buried within
it, for that was what the men were guarding, though those that took
the place and slew them could never find it; "and that was all long
ago," he said.

Walter, as the old man spoke, walked softly to the wood and
peered at it over the mound; it was all grown up within, close and
thick, an evil tangle of plants and briars. It was dark and even cold
looking within the wood, though the air lay warm all about it. The
mound was about breast high, and there was a grass-grown trench
all round out of which the earth had been thrown up. It came into
Walter's head that the place had seen strange things. He thought
of it as all rough and newly made, with a palisade round the mound,

with spears and helmets showing over, and a fierce wild multitude
of warriors surging all round; the Romans, if they had been Romans, within, grave and anxious, waiting for help that never came.
All this came into his mind with a pleasant sense of security, as a
man who is at ease looks on a picture of old and sad things, and
finds it minister to his content. Yet the place kept a secret of its
own, Walter felt sure of that. And the treasure, was that there all
the time? buried in some corner of the wood, money lying idle that
might do good things if it could but get forth? So he mused, tapping the bank with his stick. And presently they went on together.
Walter said as they turned away, "I should like to cut the trees
down, and throw the place into the pasture," but the old bailiff said,
"Nay, it is better left alone."

The weeks passed very pleasantly at first; the neighbours came
to see him, and he found that an old name wins friends easily; he
spent much of the day abroad, and he liked to go up to the Red Camp
and see it stand so solitary and dark, with the pleasant valley beneath it. His mother soon came, and they found that with her small
jointure they could indeed live at the place, but that they would
have to live very sparely at first; there must be no horses in the
stable, nor coach to drive abroad; there must be no company at
Restlands for many a year, and Walter saw too that he must not
think awhile of marriage, but that he must give all his savings to
feed the estate.

After awhile, when the first happy sense of possession had gone
off, and then life had settled down into common and familiar ways,
this began to be very irksome to Walter; and what made him feel
even more keenly his fortune was that he made acquaintance with
a squire that lived hard by, who had a daughter Marjory, who
seemed to Walter the fairest and sweetest maiden he had ever seen;
and he began to carry her image about with him; and his heart
beat very sharply in his breast if he set eyes on her unexpectedly;
and she too, seemed to have delight in seeing Walter, and to understand even the thoughts that lay beneath his lightest word. But the
squire was a poor man, and Walter felt bound to crush the thought
of love and marriage down in his heart, until he began to grow

silent and moody; and his mother saw all that was in his heart and
pitied him, but knew not what to do; and Walter began even to
talk of going into the world to seek his fortune; but it was little
more than talk, for he already loved Restlands very deeply.

Now one day when Walter had been dining with the Vicar of
the parish, he met at his table an old and fond man, full of curious
wisdom, who took great delight in all that showed the history of
the old races that had inhabited the land; and he told Walter a
long tale of the digging open of a great barrow or mound upon the
downs, which it seemed had been the grave of a great prince, and
in which they had found a great treasure of gold, cups and plates
and pitchers all of gold, with bars of the same, and many other
curious things. He said that a third of such things by rights belonged to the King; but that the King's Grace had been contented
to take a rich cup or two, and had left the rest in the hands of him
whose land it was. Then the old scholar asked Walter if it were not
true that he had in his own land an ancient fort or stronghold, and
Walter told him of the Red Camp and the story, and the old man
heard him with great attention saying, "Ay, ay," and "Ay, so it would
be," and at the last he said that the story of the treasure was most
likely a true one, for he did not see how it could have grown up
otherwise; and that he did not doubt that it was a great Roman
treasure, perhaps a tribute, gathered in from the people of the land,
who would doubtless have been enraged to lose so much and would
have striven to recover it. "Ay, it is there, sure enough," he said.

Walter offered to go with him to the place; but the old Vicar,
seeing Walter's bright eye, and knowing something of the difficulties, said that the legend was that it would be ill to disturb a thing
that had cost so many warriors their lives; and that a curse would
rest upon one that did disturb it. The old scholar laughed and said
that the curses of the dead, and especially of the heathen dead,
would break no bones—and he went on to say that doubtless there
was a whole hen-roost of curses hidden away in the mound upon
the downs; but that they had hurt not his friend who had opened
it; for he lived very delicately and plentifully off the treasure of
the old prince, who seemed to bear him no grudge for it. "Nay,

doubtless," he said, "if we but knew the truth, I dare say that the old heathen man, pining in some dark room in hell, is glad enough that his treasure should be richly spent by a good Christian gentleman."

They walked together to the place; and the old gentleman talked very learnedly and showed him where the gates and towers of the fort had been—adding to Walter, "And if I were you, Mr. Wyatt, I would have the place cleared and trenched, and would dig the gold out; for it is there as sure as I am a Christian man and a lover of the old days."

Then Walter told his mother of all that had been said; and she had heard of the old tales, and shook her head; indeed when Walter spoke to the old bailiff of his wish to open the place, the old man almost wept; and then, seeing that he prevailed nothing, said suddenly that neither he nor any of the men that dwelt in the village would put out a hand to help for all the gold of England. So Walter rested for awhile; and still his impatience and his hunger grew.

Walter did not decide at once; he turned the matter over in his mind for a week. He spoke no more to the bailiff, who thought he had changed his mind; but all the week the desire grew; and at last it completely overmastered him. He sent for the bailiff and told him he had determined to dig out the Camp; the bailiff looked at him without speaking. Then Walter said laughing that he meant to deal very fairly; that no one should bear a hand in the work who did not do so willingly; but that he should add a little to the wages of every man who worked for him at the Camp while the work was going on. The bailiff shrugged his shoulders and made no reply. Walter went and spoke to each of his men and told them his offer. "I know," he said, "that there is a story about the place, and that you do not wish to touch it; but I will offer a larger wage to every man who works there for me; and I will force no man to do it; but done it shall be; and if my own men will not do it, then I will get strangers to help me." The end of it was that three of his men offered to do the work, and the next day a start was made.

The copse and undergrowth was first cleared, and then the big trees were felled and dragged off the place; then the roots were stubbed up. It was a difficult task, and longer than Walter had thought; and he could not disguise from himself that a strange kind of ill-luck hung about the whole affair. One of his men disabled himself by a cut from an axe; another fell ill; the third, after these two mishaps, came and begged off. Walter replaced them with other workers; and the work proceeded slowly, in spite of Walter's great impatience and haste. He himself was there early and late; the men had it in their minds that they were searching for treasure and were well-nigh as excited as himself; and Walter was for ever afraid that in his absence some rich and valuable thing might be turned up, and perhaps concealed or conveyed away secretly by the finder. But the weeks passed and nothing was found; and it was now a bare and ugly place with miry pools of dirt, great holes where the trees had been; there were cart tracks all over the field in which it lay, the great trunks lay outside the mound, and the undergrowth was piled in stacks. The mound and ditch had all been unturfed; and the mound was daily dug down to the level, every spadeful being shaken loose; and now they came upon some few traces of human use. In the mound was found a short and dinted sword of bronze, of antique shape. A mass of rusted metal was found in a corner, that looked as if it had been armour. In another corner were found some large upright and calcined stones, with abundance of wood-ashes below, that seemed to have been a rude fireplace. And in one part, in a place where there seemed to have been a pit, was a quantity of rotting stuff, that seemed like the remains of bones. Walter himself grew worn and weary, partly with the toil and still more with the deferred hope. And the men too became sullen and ill-affected. It surprised Walter too that more than one of his neighbours spoke with disfavour of what he was doing, as of a thing that was foolish or even wrong. But still he worked on savagely, slept little, and cared not what he ate or drank.

At last the work was nearly over; the place had been all trenched across, and they had come in most places to the hard sandstone, which lay very near the surface. In the afternoon had fallen a heavy drenching shower, so that the men had gone home early, wet and dispirited; and Walter stood, all splashed and stained with mud, sick at heart and heavy, on the edge of the place, and looked very gloomily at the trenches, which lay like an ugly scar on the green hilltop. The sky was full of ragged inky clouds, with fierce lights on the horizon.

As he paced about and looked at the trenches, he saw in one place that it seemed as if the earth was of a different colour at the side of the trench; he stepped inside to look at this, and saw that the digging had laid bare the side of a place like a pit, that seemed to have been dug down through the ground; he bent to examine it, and then saw at the bottom of the trench, washed clear by the rain, something that looked like a stick or a root, that projected a little into the trench; he put his hand down to it, and found it cold and hard and heavy, and in a moment saw that it was a rod of metal that ran into the bank. He took up a spade, and threw the earth away in haste; and presently uncovered the rod. It was a bar, he saw, and very heavy; but examining it closely he saw that there was a stamp of some sort upon it; and then in a moment looking upon a place where the spade had scratched it, he saw that it was a bright yellow metal. It came over him all at once, with a shock that made him faint, that he had stumbled upon some part of the treasure; he put the bar aside, and then, first looking all round to see that none observed him, he dug into the bank. In a moment his spade struck something hard; and he presently uncovered a row of bars that lay close together. He dragged them up one by one, and underneath he found another row, laid crosswise; and another row, and another, till he had uncovered seven rows, making fifty bars in all. Beneath the lowest row his spade slipped on something round and smooth; he uncovered the earth, and presently drew out a brown and sodden skull, which thus lay beneath the treasure. Below that was a mass of softer earth, but out of it came the two thigh-bones of a man.

The sky was now beginning to grow dark; but he dug out the whole of the pit, working into the bank; and he saw that a round hole had been dug straight down from the top, to the sandstone. The bones lay upon the sandstone; but he found other bones at the sides of where the gold had lain; so that it seemed to him as though the gold must have been placed among dead bodies, and have rested among corruption. This was a dim thought that lurked in an ugly way in his mind. But he had now dug out the whole pit, and found nothing else, except a few large blurred copper coins which lay among the bodies. He stood awhile looking at the treasure; but together with the exultation at his discovery there mingled a dark and gloomy oppression of spirit, which he could not explain, which clouded his mind. But presently he came to himself again, and gathering the bones together, he threw them down to the bottom of the pit, as he was minded to conceal his digging from the men. While he did so, it seemed to him that, as he was bending to the pit, something came suddenly behind him and stood at his back, close to him, as though looking over his shoulder. For a moment the horror was so great that he felt the hair of his head prickle and his heart thump within his breast; but he overcame it and turned, and saw nothing but the trenches, and above them the ragged sky; yet he had the thought that something had slipped away. But he set himself doggedly to finish his task; he threw earth into the holes, working in a kind of fury; and twice as he did so, the same feeling came again that there was some one at his back; and twice turning he saw nothing; but the third time, from the West came a sharp thunder-peal; and he had hardly finished his work when the rain fell in a sheet, and splashed in the trenches.

Then he turned to the treasure which lay beside him. He found that he could not carry more than a few of the bars at a time; and he dared not leave the rest uncovered. So he covered them with earth and went stealthily down to the house; and there he got, with much precaution, a barrow from the garden. But the fear of discovery came upon him; and he determined to go into the house and sup as usual, and late at night convey the treasure to the house. For the time, his trove gave him no joy; he could not have believed it would have so weighed on him—he felt more like one who had some guilty secret to conceal, than a man to whom had befallen a great joy.

He went to the house, changed his wet clothes, and came to supper with his mother. To her accustomed questions as to what they had found, he took out the coins and showed them her, saying nothing of the gold, but with a jesting word that these would hardly repay him for his trouble. He could scarcely speak at supper for thinking of what he had found; and every now and then there came upon him a dreadful fear that he had been observed digging, and that even now some thief had stolen back there and was uncovering his hoard. His mother looked at him often, and at last said that he looked very weary; to which he replied with some sharpness, so that she said no more.

Then all at once, near the end of the meal, he had the same dreadful fear that he had felt by the pit. It seemed to him as though some one came near him and stood close behind him, bending over his shoulder; and a kind of icy coldness fell on him. He started and looked quickly round. His mother looked anxiously at him, and said, "What is it, dear Walter?" He made some excuse; but presently feeling that he must be alone, he excused himself and went to his room, where he sate, making pretence to read, till the house should be silent.

Then when all were abed, at an hour after midnight, he forced himself to rise and put on his rough clothes, though a terror lay very sore upon him, and go out to the garden, creeping like a thief. He had with him a lantern; and he carried the barrow on his shoulders for fear that the creaking of the wheel should awake some one; and then stumbling and sweating, and in a great weariness, he went by woodpaths to the hilltop. He came to the place, and having lit his lantern he uncovered the bars, and laid them on the barrow; they were as he had left them. When he had loaded them, the same fear struck him suddenly cold again, of something near him; and he thought for a moment he would have swooned; but sitting down on the barrow in the cool air he presently came to himself. Then he essayed to wheel the barrow in the dark. But he stumbled often, and once upset the barrow and spilled his load. Thus, though fearing discovery, he was forced to light the lantern and set it upon the barrow, and so at last he came to the house; where he disposed the bars at the bottom of a chest of which he had the key, covering them with papers, and then went to bed in a kind of fever, his teeth chattering, till he fell into a wretched sleep which lasted till dawn.

In his sleep he dreamed a fearful dream; he seemed to be sitting on the ground by the Camp, holding the gold in his arms; the Camp, in his dream was as it was before he had cleared it, all grown up with trees. Suddenly out from among the trees there came a man in rusty tarnished armour, with a pale wild face and a little beard, which seemed all clotted with moisture; he held in his hand a pike or spear, and he came swiftly and furiously upon Walter as though he would smite him. But it seemed as though his purpose changed; for standing aside he watched Walter with evil and piercing eyes, so that it seemed to Walter that he would sooner have been smitten. And then he woke, but in anguish, for the man still seemed to stand beside him; until he made a light and saw no one.

He arose feeling broken and ill; but he met his mother with a smile, and told her that he had determined to do what would please her, and work no more at the Camp. And he told the men that he would dig no more, but that they were to level the place and so leave it. And so they did, murmuring sore.

The next week was a very miserable one for Walter; he could not have believed that a man's heart should be so heavy. It seemed to him that he lay, like the poor bones that he had found beneath the treasure, crushed and broken and stifled under the weight of it. He was tempted to do wild things with the gold; to bury it again in the Camp, to drop it into the mud of the pool that lay near the house. In fevered dreams he seemed to row himself in a boat upon a dark sea, and to throw the bars one by one into the water; the reason of this was not only his fear for the treasure itself, but the dreadful sense that he had of being followed by some one, who dogged his footsteps wherever he went. If ever he sate alone, the thing would draw near him and bend above him; he often felt that if he could but look round swiftly enough he would catch a glimpse of the thing, and that nothing that he could see would be so fearful as that which was unseen; and so it came to pass that, as he sate with his mother, though he bore the presence long that he might not startle her, yet after a time of patient agony he could bear it no

more, but looked swiftly behind him; he grew pale and ill, and even
the men of the place noticed how often he turned round as he
walked; till at last he would not even walk abroad, except early
and late when there would be few to see him.

He had sent away his labourers; but once or twice he noticed,
as he went by the Camp, that some one had been digging and grub-
bing in the mire. Sometimes for an hour or two his terrors would
leave him, till he thought that he was wholly cured; but it was like
a cat with a mouse, for he suffered the worse for his respite, till at
last he fell so low that he used to think of stories of men that had
destroyed themselves, and though he knew it to be a terrible sin to
dally with such thoughts, he could not wholly put them from him,
but used to plan in his mind how he could do the deed best, that it
might appear to be an accident. Sometimes he bore his trouble
heavily, but at others he would rage to think that he had been so
happy so short a while ago; and even the love that he bore to
Marjory was darkened and destroyed by the evil thing, and he met
her timid and friendly glances sullenly; his mother was nearly as
miserable as himself, for she knew that something was very grievously amiss, but could not divine what it was. Indeed, she could
do nothing but wish it were otherwise, and pray for her son, for
she knew not where the trouble lay, but thought that he was ill or
even bewitched.

At last, after a day of dreadful gloom, Walter made up his mind
that he would ride to London and see to the disposing of the treasure. He had a thought often in his mind that if he replaced it in
the Camp, he would cease to be troubled; but he could not bring
himself to that; he seemed to himself like a man who had won a
hard victory, and was asked to surrender what he had won.

His intention was to go to an old and wise friend of his father's,
who was a Canon of a Collegiate Church in London, and was much
about the court. So he hid the treasure in a strong cellar and pad-
locked the door; but he took one bar with him to show to his friend.

It was a doleful journey; his horse seemed as dispirited as himself; and his terrors came often upon him, till he was fearful that
he might be thought mad; and indeed what with the load at his

heart and the short and troubled nights he spent, he believed himself that he was not very far from it.

It was with a feeling of relief and safety, like a ship coming into port, that he stayed his horse at the door of the college, which stood in a quiet street of the city. He carried a valise of clothes in which the bar was secured. He had a very friendly greeting from the old Canon, who received him in a little studious parlour full of books. The court was full of pleasant sunshine, and the city outside seemed to make a pleasant and wholesome stir in the air.

But the Canon was very much amazed at Walter's looks; he was used to read the hearts of men in their faces like a wise priest, and he saw in Walter's face a certain desperate look such as he had seen, he said to himself, in the faces of those who had a deadly sin to confess. But it was not his way to make inquisition, and so he talked courteously and easily, and when he found that Walter was inclined to be silent, he filled the silence himself with little talk of the news of the town.

After the meal, which they took in the Canon's room—for Walter said that he would prefer that to dining in the Hall, when the Canon gave him the choice—Walter said that he had a strange story to tell him. The Canon felt no surprise, and being used to strange stories, addressed himself to listen carefully; for he thought that in the most difficult and sad tales of sin the words of the sufferer most often supplied the advice and the way out, if one but listened warily.

He did not interrupt Walter except to ask him a few questions to make the story clear, but his face grew very grave; and at the end he sate some time in silence. Then he said very gently that it was a heavy judgment, but that he must ask Walter one question. "I do not ask you to tell me," he said very courteously, "what it may be; but is there no other thing in which you have displeased God? For these grievous thoughts and fears are sometimes sent as a punishment for sin, and to turn men back to the light."

Then Walter said that he knew of no such sin by which he could have vexed God so exceedingly. "Careless," he said, "I am and have been; and, father, I would tell you anything that was in my heart; I would have no secrets from you—but though I am a sinner, and do not serve God as well as I would, yet I desire to serve Him, and have no sin that is set like a wall between Him and me." He said this so honestly and bravely, looking so full at the priest, that he did not doubt him, and said, "Then, my son, we must look elsewhere for the cause; and though I speak in haste, and without weighing my words, it seems to me that, to speak in parables, you are like a man who has come by chance to a den and carried off for his pleasure the cubs of some forest beast, who returns and finds them gone, and tracks the robber out. The souls of these poor warriors are in some mansion of God, we know not where; if they did faithfully in life they are beaten, as the Scripture says, with few stripes; but they may not enjoy His blessed rest, nor the sweet sleep of the faithful souls who lie beneath the altar and wait for His coming. And now though they cannot slay you, they can do you grievous hurt. The Holy Church hath power indeed over the spirits of evil, the devils that enter into men. But I have not heard that she hath power over the spirits of the dead, and least of all over those that lived and died outside the fold. It seems to me, though I but grope in darkness, that these poor spirits grudge the treasure that they fought and died for to the hands of a man who hath not fought for it. We may think that it is a poor and childish thing to grudge that which one cannot use; but no discourse will make a child think so; and I reckon that these poor souls are as children yet. And it seems to me, speaking foolishly, as though they would not be appeased until you either restored it to them, or used it for their undoubted benefit; but of one thing I am certain, that it must not be used to enrich yourself. But I must ponder over the story, for it is a strange one, and not such as has ever yet come before me."

Then Walter found fresh courage at these wary and wise words, and told him of his impoverished estate and the love he had to Marjory; and the priest smiled, and said that love was the best thing to win in the world. And then he said that as it was now late, they must sleep; and that the night often brought counsel; and so he took Walter to his chamber, a little precise place with a window on the court; and there he left him; but he first knelt down and prayed, and then laid his hand on Walter's head, and blessed him, and commended him to the merciful keeping of God; and Walter slept sweetly, and was scared that night by no dismal dreams; and in the morning the priest took him to the church, and Walter knelt in a little chapel while the old man said his mass, commending therein the burden of Walter's suffering into the merciful hands of God; so that Walter's heart was greatly lightened.

Then after the mass the priest asked Walter of his health, and whether he had suffered any visitation of evil that night; he said "no," and the priest then said that he had pondered long over the story, which was strange and very dark. But he had little doubt now as to what Walter should do. He did not think that the treasure should be replaced now that it was got up, because it was only flying before the evil and not meeting it, but leaving the sad inheritance for some other man. The poor spirit must be laid to rest, and the treasure used for God's glory. "And therefore," he said, "I think that a church must be built, and dedicated to All Souls; and thus your net will be wide enough to catch the sad spirit. And you must buy a little estate for the support of the chaplain thereof, and so shall all be content."

"All but one," said Walter sadly, "for there goes my dream of setting up my own house that tumbles down."

"My son," said the old priest very gravely, "you must not murmur; it will be enough for you if God take away the sore chastening of your spirit; and for the rest, He will provide."

"But there is more behind," he said after a pause. "If you, with an impoverished estate, build a church and endow a priest, there will be questions asked; it will needs be known that you have found a treasure, and it will come, perhaps, to the ears of the King's Grace, and inquisition will be made; so I shall go this morning to a Lord of the Court, an ancient friend of mine, a discreet man; and I will lay the story before him, if you give me leave; and he will advise."

Walter saw that the priest's advice was good; and so he gave him leave; and the priest departed to the Court; but while he was away, as Walter sate sadly over a book, his terrors came upon him with fresh force; the thing drew near him and stood at his shoulder, and he could not dislodge it; it seemed to Walter that it was more malign than ever, and was set upon driving him to some desperate deed; so he rose and paced in the court; but it seemed to move behind him, till he thought he would have gone distraught; but finding the church doors open, he went inside and, in a corner, knelt and prayed, and got some kind of peace; yet he felt all the while as though the presence waited for him at the door, but could not hurt him in the holy shrine; and there Walter made a vow and vowed his life into the hands of God; for he had found the world a harder place than he had thought, and it seemed to him as though he walked among unseen foes. Presently he saw the old priest come into the church, peering about; so Walter rose and came to him; the priest had a contented air, but seemed big with news, and he told Walter that he must go with him at once to the Court. For he had seen the Lord Poynings, that was his friend, who had taken him at once to the king; and the king had heard the story very curiously, and would see Walter himself that day. So Walter fetched the bar of gold and they went at once together; and Walter was full of awe and fear, and asked the priest how he should bear himself; to which the priest said smiling, "As a man, in the presence of a man." And as they went Walter told him that he had been visited by the terror again, but had found peace in the church; and the priest said, "Ay, there is peace to be had there."

They came down to the palace, and were at once admitted; the priest and he were led into a little room, full of books, where a man was writing, a venerable man in a furred gown, with a comely face; this was the Lord Poynings, who greeted Walter very gently but with a secret attention; Walter shewed him the bar of gold, and he looked at it long, and presently there came a page who said that the king was at leisure, and would see Mr. Wyatt.

Walter had hoped that the priest, or at least the Lord Poynings, would accompany him; but the message was for himself alone; so he was led along a high corridor with tall stands of arms. The king had been a great warrior in his manhood, and had won many trophies. They came to a great doorway, where the page knocked; a voice cried within, and the page told Walter he must enter alone.

Walter would fain have asked the page how he should make his obeisance; but there was no time now, for the page opened the door, and Walter went in.

He found himself in a small room, hung with green arras. The king was sitting in a great chair, by a table spread out with parchments. Walter first bowed low and then knelt down; the king motioned him to rise, and then said in a quiet and serene voice, "So, sir, you are the gentleman that has found a treasure and would fain be rid of it again." At these gentle words Walter felt his terrors leave him; the king looked at him with a serious attention; he was a man just passing into age; his head was nearly hairless, and he had a thin face with a long nose, and small lips drawn together. On his head was a loose velvet cap, and he wore his gown furred; round his neck was a jewel, and he had great rings on his forefingers and thumbs.

The king, hardly pausing for an answer, said, "You look ill, Master Wyatt, and little wonder; sit here in a chair and tell me the tale in a few words."

Walter told his story as shortly as he could with the king's kind eye upon him; the king once or twice interrupted him; he took the bar from Walter's hands, and looked upon it, weighing it in his fingers, and saying, "Ay, it is a mighty treasure." Once or twice he made him repeat a few sentences, and heard the story of the thing that stood near him with a visible awe.

At last he said with a smile, "You have told your story well, sir, and plainly; are you a soldier?" When Walter said "no," he said, "It is a noble trade, nevertheless." Then he said, "Well, sir, the treasure is yours, to use as I understand you will use it for the glory of God and for the peace of the poor spirit, which I doubt not is that of a great knight. But I have no desire to be visited of him," and here he crossed himself. "So let it be thus bestowed—and I will cause a quittance to be made out for you from the Crown, which will take no part in the trove. How many bars did you say?" And when Walter said "fifty," the king said, "It is great wealth; and I wish for your sake, sir, that it were not so sad an inheritance." Then he added, "Well, sir, that is the matter; but I would hear the end of this, for I never knew the like; when your church is built and all things are in order, and let it be done speedily, you shall come and visit me again." And then the king said, with a kindly smile, "And as for the maiden of whom I have heard, be not discouraged; for yours is an ancient house, and it must not be extinguished—and so farewell; and remember that your king wishes you happiness;" and he made a sign that Walter should withdraw. So Walter knelt again and kissed the king's ring, and left the chamber.

When Walter came out he seemed to tread on air; the king's gracious kindness moved him very greatly, and loyalty filled his heart to the brim. He found the priest and the Lord Poynings waiting for him; and presently the two left the palace together, and Walter told the priest what the king had said.

The next day he rode back into Sussex; but he was very sorely beset as he rode, and reached home in great misery. But he wasted no time, but rather went to his new task with great eagerness; the foundations of the church were laid, and soon the walls began to rise. Meanwhile Walter had the gold conveyed to the king's Mint; and a message came to him that it would make near upon twenty thousand pounds of gold, a fortune for an earl. So the church was built very massive and great, and a rich estate was bought which would support a college of priests. But Walter's heart was very heavy; for his terrors still came over him from day to day; and he was no nearer settling his own affairs.

Then there began to come to him a sore temptation; he could build his church, and endow his college with lands, and yet he could save something of the treasure to set him free from his own poverty; and day by day this wrought more and more in his mind.

At last one day when he was wandering through the wood, he found himself face to face in the path with Marjory herself; and there was so tender a look in her face that he could no longer resist, so he turned and walked with her, and told her all that was in his heart. "It was all for the love of you," he said, "that I have thus been punished, and now I am no nearer the end;" and then, for he saw that she wept, and that she loved him well, he opened to her his heart, and said that he would keep back part of the treasure, and would save his house, and that they would be wed; and so he kissed her on the lips.

But Marjory was a true-hearted and wise maiden, and loved Walter better than he knew; and she said to him, all trembling for pity, "Dear Walter, it cannot be; this must be given faithfully, because you are the king's servant, and because you must give the spirit back his own, and because you are he that I love the best; and we will wait; for God tells me that it must be so; and He is truer even than love."

So Walter was ashamed; and he threw unworthy thoughts away; and with the last of the money he caused a fair screen to be made, and windows of rich glass; and the money was thus laid out.

Now while the church was in building—and they made all the haste they could—Walter had days when he was very grievously troubled; but it seemed to him a different sort of trouble. In the first place he looked forward confidently to the day when the dark presence would be withdrawn; and a man who can look forward to a certain ending to his pain can stay himself on that; but, besides that, it seemed to him that he was not now beset by a foe, but guarded as it were by a sentinel. There were days when the horror was very great, and when the thing was always near him whether he sate or walked, whether he was alone or in company; and on those days he withdrew himself from men, and there was a dark shadow on his brow. So that there grew up a kind of mystery about him; but, besides that, he learnt things in those bitter hours that are not taught in any school. He learnt to suffer with all the great company of those who bear heavy and unseen burdens, who move in the grip of fears and stumble under the load of dark necessities. He grew more tender and more strong. He found in his hand the key to many hearts. Before this he had cared little about the thoughts of other men; but now he found himself for ever wondering what the inner thoughts of the hearts of others were, and ready if need were to help to lift their load; he had lived before in careless fellowship with light-hearted persons, but now he was rather drawn to the old and wise and sad; and there fell on him some touch of the holy priesthood that falls on all whose sadness is a fruitful sadness, and who instead of yielding to bitter repining would try to make others happier. If he heard of a sorrow or a distress, his thought was no longer how to put it out of his mind as soon as he might, but of how he might lighten it. So his heart grew wider day by day.

And at last the day came when the church was done; it stood, a fair white shrine with a seemly tower, on the hill-top, and a little way from it was the college for the priests. The Bishop came to consecrate it, and the old Canon came from London, and there was a little gathering of neighbours to see the holy work accomplished.

The Bishop blessed the church very tenderly; he was an old infirm man, but he bore his weakness lightly and serenely. He made Walter the night before tell him the story of the treasure, and found much to wonder at in it.

There was no part of the church or its furniture that he did not solemnly bless; and Walter from his place felt a grave joy to see all so fair and seemly. The priests moved from end to end with the Bishop, in their stiff embroidered robes, and there was a holy smell of incense which strove with the sharp scent of the newly-chiselled wood. The Bishop made them a little sermon and spoke much of the gathering into the fold of spirits that had done their work bravely, even if they had not known the Lord Christ on earth.

After all was over, and the guests were departed, the old Canon said that he must return on the morrow to London, and that he had a message for Walter from the king,—who had not failed to ask him how the work went on,—that Walter was to return with him and tell the king of the fulfilment of the design.

That night Walter had a strange dream; he seemed to stand in a dark place all vaulted over, like a cave that stretched far into the earth; he himself stood in the shadow of a rock, and he was aware of some one passing by him. He looked at him, and saw that he was the warrior that he had seen before in his dream, a small pale man, with a short beard, with rusty armour much dinted; he held a spear in his hand, and walked restlessly like a man little content. But while Walter watched him, there seemed to be another person drawing near in the opposite direction. This was a tall man, all in white, who brought with him as he came a strange freshness in the dark place, as of air and light, and the scent of flowers; this one came along in a different fashion, with an assured and yet tender air, as though he was making search for some one to whom his coming would be welcome; so the two met and words passed between them; the warrior stood with his hands clasped upon his spear seeming to drink in what was said—he could not hear the words at first, for they were spoken softly, but the last words he heard were, "And you too are of the number." Then the warrior kneeled down and laid his spear aside, and the other seemed to stoop and bless him, and then went on his way; and the warrior knelt and watched him going with a look in his face as though he had heard wonderful and beautiful news, and could hardly yet believe it; and so holy was the look that Walter felt as though he intruded upon some deep mystery, and moved further into the shadow of the rock; but the warrior rose and came to him where he stood, and looked at him with a half-doubting look, as though he asked pardon, stretching out his hands; and Walter smiled at him, and the other smiled; and at the moment Walter woke in the dawn with a strange joy in his heart, and rising in haste, drew the window curtain aside, and saw the fresh dawn beginning to come in over the woods, and he knew that the burden was lifted from him and that he was free.

In the morning as the old Canon and Walter rode to London, Walter told him the dream; and when he had done, he saw that the old priest was smiling at him with his eyes full of tears, and that he could not speak; so they rode together in that sweet silence which is worth more than many words.

The next day Walter came to see the king: he carried with him a paper to show the king how all had been expended; but he went with no fear, but as though to see a true friend.

The king received him very gladly, and bade Walter tell him all that had been done; so Walter told him, and then speaking very softly told the king the dream; the king mused over the story, and then said, "So he has his heart's desire."

Then there was a silence; and then the king, as though breaking out of a pleasant thought, drew from the table a parchment,
and said to Walter that he had done well and wisely, and therefore
for the trust that he had in him he made him his Sheriff for the
County of Sussex, to which was added a large revenue; and there
was more to come, for the king bade Walter unhook a sword from
the wall, his own sword that he had borne in battle; and therewith
he dubbed him knight, and said to him, "Rise up, Sir Walter Wyatt."
Then before he dismissed him, he said to him that he would see
him every year at the Court; and then with a smile he added, "And
when you next come, I charge you to bring with you my Lady
Wyatt."

And Walter promised this, and kept his word.

The Snake, the Leper, and the Grey Frost

In the heart of the Forest of Seale lay the little village of Birnewood Fratrum, like a lark's nest in a meadow of tall grass. It was approached by green wood-ways, very miry in winter. The folk that lived there were mostly woodmen. There was a little church, the stones of which seemed to have borrowed the hue of the forest, and close beside it a small timbered house, the Parsonage, with a garden of herbs. Those who saw Birnewood in the summer, thought of it as a place where a weary man might rest for ever, in an ancient peace, with the fresh mossy smell of the wood blowing through it, and the dark cool branching covert to muse in on every side. But it was a different place in winter, with ragged clouds rolling overhead and the bare boughs sighing in the desolate gales; though again in a frosty winter evening it would be fair enough, with the red sun sinking over miles of trees.

From the village green a little track led into the forest, and, a furlong or two inside, ended in an open space thickly overgrown with elders, where stood the gaunt skeleton of a ruined tower staring with bare windows at the wayfarer. The story of the tower was sad enough. The last owner, Sir Ralph Birne, was on the wrong side in a rebellion, and died on the scaffold, his lands forfeited to the crown. The tower was left desolate, and piece by piece the villagers carried away all that was useful to them, leaving the shell of a house, though at the time of which I speak the roof still held, and the floors, though rotting fast, still bore the weight of a foot.

139

In the Parsonage lived an old priest, Father John, as he was called, and with him a boy who was held to be his nephew, Ralph by name, now eighteen years of age. The boy was very dear to Father John, who was a wise and loving man. To many it might have seemed a dull life enough, but Ralph had known no other, having come to the Parsonage as a child. Of late indeed Ralph had begun to feel a strange desire grow and stir within him, to see what the world was like outside the forest; such a desire would come on him at early morning, in the fresh spring days, and he would watch some lonely traveller riding slowly to the south with an envious look; though as like as not the wayfarer would be envying the bright boy, with his background of quiet woods. But such fancies only came and went, and he said nothing to the old priest about them, who nevertheless had marked the change for himself with the instinct of love, and would sometimes, as he sate with his breviary, follow the boy about with his eyes, in which the wish to keep him strove with the knowledge that the bird must some day leave the nest.

One summer morning, the old priest shut his book, with the air of a man who has made up his mind in sadness, and asked Ralph to walk with him. They went to the tower, and there, sitting in the ruins, Father John told Ralph the story of the house, which he had often heard before. But now there was so tender and urgent a tone in the priest's voice that Ralph heard him wonderingly; and at last the priest very solemnly, after a silence, said that there was something in his mind that must be told; and he went on to say that Ralph was indeed the heir of the tower; he was the grandson of Sir Ralph, who died upon the scaffold; his father had died abroad, dispossessed of his inheritance; and the priest said that in a few days he himself would set out on a journey, too long deferred, to see a friend of his, a Canon of a neighbouring church, to learn if it were possible that some part of the lands might be restored to Ralph by the king's grace. For the young king that had newly come to the throne was said to be very merciful and just, and punished not the sins of the fathers upon the children; but Father John said that he hardly dared to hope it; and then he bound Ralph to silence; and then after a pause he added, taking one of the boy's hands in his own, "And it is time, dear son, that you should leave this quiet place and make a name for yourself; my days draw to an end; perhaps I have been wrong to keep you here to myself, but I have striven to make you pure and simple, and if I was in fault, why, it has been the fault of love." And the boy threw his arms round the priest's neck and kissed him, seeing that tears trembled in his eyes, and said that he was more than content, and that he should never leave his uncle and the peaceful forest that he loved. But the priest saw an unquiet look in his eye, as of a sleeper awakened, and knew the truth.

A few days after, the priest rode away at sunrise; and Ralph was left alone. In his head ran an old tale, which he had heard from the woodmen, of a great treasure of price, which was hidden somewhere in the tower. Then it came into his mind that there dwelt not far away in the wood an ancient wise man who gave counsel to all who asked for it, and knew the virtues of plants, and the courses of buried springs, and many hidden things beside. Ralph had never been to the house of the wise man, but he knew the direction where it lay; so with the secret in his heart, he made at once for the place. The day was very hot and still, and no birds sang in the wood. Ralph walked swiftly along the soft green road, and came at last upon a little grey house of plaster, with beams of timber, that stood in a clearing near a spring, with a garden of its own; a fragrant smell came from a sprawling bush of box, and the bees hummed busily over the flowers. There was no smoke from the chimney, and the single window that gave on the road, in a gable, looked at him like a dark eye. He went up the path, and stood before the door waiting, when a high thin voice, like an evening wind, called from within, "Come in and fear not, thou that tarriest on the threshold." Ralph, with a strange stirring of the blood at the silver sound of the voice, unlatched the door and entered. He found himself in a low dark room, with a door opposite him; in the roof hung bundles of herbs; there was a large oak table strewn with many things of daily use, and sitting in a chair, with his back to the light, sate a very old thin man, with a frosty beard, clad in a loose grey gown. Over the fireplace hung a large rusty sword; the room was very clean and cool, and the sunlight danced on the ceiling, with the flicker of moving leaves.

"Your name and errand?" said the old man, fixing his grey eyes, like flint stones, upon the boy, not unkindly. "Ralph," said the boy. "Ralph," said the old man, "and why not add Birne to Ralph? that makes a fairer name."

Ralph was so much bewildered at this strange greeting, that he stood confused—at which the old man pointed to a settle, and said, "And now, boy, sit down and speak with me; you are Ralph from Birnewood Parsonage, I know—Father John is doubtless away—he has no love for me, though I know him to be a true man."

Then little by little he unravelled the boy's desire, and the story of the treasure. Then he said, kindly enough, "Yes, it is ever thus— well, lad, I will tell you; and heed my words well. The treasure is there; and you shall indeed find it; but prepare for strange sounds and sights." And as he said this, he took the young hand in his own for a moment and a strange tide of sensation seemed to pass along the boy's veins. "Look in my face," the old man went on, "that I may see that you have faith—for without faith such quests are vain." Ralph raised his eyes to those of the old man, and then a sensation such as he had never felt before came over him; it was like looking from a window into a wide place, full of darkness and wonder.

Then the old man said solemnly, "Child, the time is come—I have waited long for you, and the door is open."

Then he said, with raised hand, "The journey is not long, but it must be done in a waking hour; sleep not on the journey; that first. And of three things beware—the Snake, and the Leper, and the Grey Frost; for these three things have brought death to wiser men than yourself. There," he added, "that is your note of the way; now make the journey, if you have the courage."

"But, sir," said Ralph in perplexity, "you say to me, make the journey; and you tell me not whither to go. And you tell me to beware of three things. How shall I know them to avoid them?"

"You will know them when you have seen them," said the old man sadly, "and that is the most that men can know; and as for the journey, you can start upon it wherever you are, if your heart is pure and strong."

Then Ralph said, trembling, "Father, my heart is pure, I think; but I know not whether I am strong."

Then the old man reached out his hand, and took up a staff that leant by the chair; and from a pocket in his gown he took a small metal thing shaped like a five-pointed star; and he said, "Ralph, here is a staff and a holy thing; and now set forth." So Ralph rose, and took the staff and the star, and made a reverence, and murmured thanks; and then he went to the door by which he had entered; but the old man said, "Nay, it is the other door," and then he bent down his head upon his arms like one who wept.

Ralph went to the other door and opened it; he had thought it led into the wood; but when he opened it, it was dark and cold without; and suddenly with a shock of strange terror he saw that outside was a place like a hill-top, with short strong grass, and clouds sweeping over it. He would have drawn back, but he was ashamed; so he stepped out and closed the door behind him; and then the house was gone in a moment like a dream, and he was alone on the hill, with the wind whistling in his ears.

He waited for a moment in the clutch of a great fear; but he felt he was alive and well, and little by little his fear disappeared and left him eager. He went a few steps forward, and saw that the hill sloped downward, and downward he went, by steep slopes of turf and scattered grey stones. Presently the mist seemed to blow thinner, and through a gap he saw a land spread out below him; and soon he came out of the cloud, and saw a lonely forest country, all unlike his own, for the trees seemed a sort of pine, with red stems, very tall and sombre. He looked round, and presently he saw that a little track below him seemed to lead downward into the pines, so he gained the track; and soon he came down to the wood.

There was no sign as yet of any habitation; he heard the crying of birds, and at one place he saw a number of crows that stood round something white that lay upon the ground, and pecked at it; and he turned not aside, thinking, he knew not why, that there was some evil thing there. But he did not feel alone, and he had a thought which dwelt with him that there were others bound upon the same quest as himself, though he saw nothing of them. Once indeed he thought he saw a man walking swiftly, his face turned away, among the pines; but the trees blotted him from his sight. Then he passed by a great open marsh with reeds and still pools of water, where he wished to rest; but he pushed on the faster, and suddenly, turning a corner, saw that the track led him straight to a large stone house, that stood solitary in the wood. He knew in a moment that this was the end of his journey, and marvelled within himself at the ease of the quest; he went straight up to the house, which seemed all dark and silent, and smote loudly and confidently on the door; some one stirred within, and it was presently opened to him. He thought now that he would be questioned, but the man who opened to him, a grave serving-man, made a motion with his hand, and he went up a flight of stone steps.

As he went up, there came out from a door, as though to meet him with honour, a tall and noble personage, very cheerful and comely, and with a courteous greeting took him into a large room richly furnished; Ralph began to tell his story, but the man made a quiet gesture with his hand as though no explanation was needed, and went at once to a press, which he opened, and brought out from it a small coffer, which seemed heavy, and opened it before him; Ralph could not see clearly what it contained, but he saw the sparkle of gold and what seemed like jewels. The man smiled at him, and as though in reply to a question said, "Yes, this is what you came to seek; and you are well worthy of it; and my lord"—he bowed as he spoke— "is glad to bestow his riches upon one who found the road so easy hither, and who came from so honoured a friend." Then he said very courteously that he would willingly have entertained him, and shown him more of the treasures of the house; "but I know," he added, "that your business requires haste and you would be gone;" and so he conducted him very gently down to the door again, and presently Ralph was standing outside with the precious coffer under his arm, wondering if he were not in a dream; because he had found what he sought so soon, and with so little trouble.

The porter stood at the door, and said in a quiet voice, "The way is to the left, and through the wood." Ralph thanked him, and the porter said, "You know, young sir, of what you are to beware, for the forest has an evil name?" And when Ralph replied that he knew, the porter said that it was well to start betimes, because the way was somewhat long. So Ralph went out along the road, and saw the porter standing at the door for a long time, watching him, he thought, with a kind of tender gaze.

Ralph took the road that led to the left, very light-hearted; it was pleasant under the pines, which had made a soft brown carpet of needles; and the scent of the pine-gum was sharp and sweet. He went for a mile or two thus, while the day darkened above him, and the wind whispered like a falling sea among the branches. At last he came to another great marsh, but a path led down to it from the road, and in the path were strange marks as though some heavy thing had been dragged along, with footprints on either side. Ralph went a few steps down the path, when suddenly an evil smell passed by him; he had been thinking of a picture in one of Father John's books of a man fighting with a dragon, and the brave horned creature, with its red mouth and white teeth, with ribbed wings and bright blue burnished mail, and a tail armed with a sting, had seemed to him a curious and beautiful sight, that a man might well desire to see; the thought of danger was hardly in his heart.

Suddenly he heard below him in the reeds a great routing and splashing; the rushes parted, and he saw a huge and ugly creature, with black oily sides and a red mane of bristles, raise itself up and regard him. Its sides dropped with mud, and its body was wrapped with clinging weeds. But it moved so heavily and slow, and drew itself out on to the bank with such pain, that Ralph saw that there was little danger to one so fleet as himself, if he drew not near. The beast opened its great mouth, and Ralph saw a blue tongue and a pale throat; it regarded him hungrily with small evil eyes; but Ralph sprang backwards, and laughed to see how lumberingly the brute trailed itself along. Its hot and fetid breath made a smoke in the still air; presently it desisted, and as though it desired the coolness, it writhed back into the water again. And Ralph saw that it was only a beast that crept upon its prey by stealth, and that though if he had slept, or bathed in the pool, it might have drawn him in to devour him, yet that one who was wary and active need have no fear; so he went on his way; and blew out great breaths to get the foul watery smell of the monster out of his nostrils.

Suddenly he began to feel weary; he did not know what time of day it was in this strange country, where all was fresh like a dewy morning; he had not seen the sun, though the sky was clear, and he fell to wondering where the light came from; as he wondered, he came to a stone bench by the side of the road where he thought he would sit a little; he would be all the fresher for a timely rest; he sate down, and as though to fill the place with a heavenly peace, he heard at once doves hallooing in the thicket close at hand; while he sate drinking in the charm of the sound, there was a flutter of wings, and a dove alighted close to his feet; it walked about crooning softly, with its nodding neck flashing with delicate colours, and its pink feet running swiftly on the grass. He felt in his pocket and found there a piece of bread which he had taken with him in the morning and had never thought of tasting; he crumbled it for the bird, who fell to picking it eagerly and gratefully, bowing its head as though in courteous acknowledgment. Ralph leant forwards to watch it, and the ground swam before his weary eyes. He sate back for a moment, and then he would have slept, when he saw a small bright thing dart from a crevice of the stone seat on to his knee. He bent forward to look at it, and saw that it was a thing like a lizard, but without legs, of a powdered green, strangely bright. It nestled on his knee in a little coil and watched him with keen eyes. The trustfulness of these wild creatures pleased him wonderfully. Suddenly, very far away and yet near him, he heard the sound of a voice, like a man in prayer; it reminded him, he knew not why, of the Wise Man's voice, and he rose to his feet ashamed of his drowsiness. The little lizard darted from his leg and on to the ground, as though vexed to be disturbed, and he saw it close to his feet. The dove saw it too, and went to it as though inquiringly; the lizard showed no fear, but coiled itself up, and as the dove came close, made a little dart at its breast, and the dove drew back. Ralph was amused at the fearlessness of the little thing, but in a moment saw that something ailed the dove; it moved as though dizzy, and then spread its wings as if for flight, but dropped them again and nestled down on the ground. In a moment its pretty head fell forwards and it lay motionless. Then with a shock of fear Ralph saw that he had been nearly betrayed; that this was the Snake itself of which he had been warned; he struck with his staff at the little venomous thing, which darted forward with a wicked hiss, and Ralph only avoided it with a spring. Then without an instant's thought he turned and ran along the wood-path, chiding himself bitterly for his folly. He had nearly slept; he had only not been stung to death; and he thought of how he would have lain, a stiffening figure, till the crows gathered round him and pulled the flesh from his bones.

After this the way became more toilsome; the track indeed was plain enough, but it was strewn with stones, and little thorny plants grew everywhere, which tripped his feet and sometimes pierced his skin; it grew darker too, as though night were coming on. Presently he came to a clearing in the forest; on a slope to his right hand, he saw a little hut of boughs, with a few poor garden herbs about it. A man was crouched among them, as though he were digging; he was only some thirty paces away; Ralph stopped for a moment, and the man rose up and looked at him. Ralph saw a strangely distorted face under a hairless brow. There were holes where the eyes should have been, and in these the eyes were so deeply sunk that they looked but like pits of shade. Presently the other began to move towards him, waving a large misshapen hand which gleamed with a kind of scurfy whiteness; and he cried out unintelligible words, which seemed half angry, half piteous. Ralph knew that the Leper was before him, and though he loathed to fly before so miserable a wretch, he turned and hurried on into the forest; the creature screamed the louder, and it seemed as though he were asking an alms, but he hobbled so slowly on his thick legs, foully bandaged with rags, that Ralph soon distanced him, and he heard the wretch stop and fall to cursing. This sad and fearful encounter made Ralph sick at heart; but he strove to thank God for another danger escaped, and hastened on.

Gradually he became aware by various signs that he was approaching some inhabited place; all at once he came upon a fair

house in a piece of open ground, that looked to him at first so like
the house of the treasure, that he thought he had come back to it.
But when he looked more closely upon it, he saw that it was not
the same; it was somewhat more meanly built, and had not the
grave and solid air that the other had; presently he heard a sound
of music, like a concert of lutes and trumpets, which came from
the house, and when it ceased there was clapping of hands.

While he doubted whether to draw near, he saw that the door
was opened, and a man, richly dressed and of noble appearance,
came out upon the space in front of the house. He looked about
him with a grave and serene air, like a prince awaiting guests. And
his eyes falling upon Ralph, he beckoned him to draw near. Ralph
at first hesitated. But it seemed to him an unkindly thing to turn
his back upon this gallant gentleman who stood there smiling; so
he drew near. And then the other asked him whither he was bound.
Ralph hardly knew what to reply to this, but the gentleman awaited
not his answer, but said that this was a day of festival, and all were
welcome, and he would have him come in and abide with them.
Ralph excused himself, but the gentleman smiled and said, "I know,
sir, that you are bound upon a journey, as many are that pass this
way; but you carry no burden with you, as is the wont of others."
And then Ralph, with a start of surprise and anguish, remembered
that he had left his coffer on the seat where he had seen the Snake.
He explained his loss to the gentleman, who laughed and said that
this was easily mended, for he would send himself a servant to fetch
it. And then he asked whether he had been in any peril, and when
Ralph told him, he nodded his head gravely, and said it was a great
danger escaped. And then Ralph told him of the Leper, at which
the gentleman grew grave, and said that it was well he had not
stopped to speak with him, for the contagion of that leprosy was
sore and sudden. And then he added, "But while I send to recover
your coffer, you will enter and sit with us; you look weary, and you
shall eat of our meat, for it is good meat that strengtheneth; but
wine," he said, "I will not offer you, though I have it here in abundance, for it weakeneth the knees of those that walk on a journey;
but you shall delight your heart with music, such as the angels love,
and set forth upon your way rejoicing; for indeed it is not late."

And so Ralph was persuaded, and they drew near to the door. Then the gentleman stood aside to let Ralph enter; and Ralph saw within a hall with people feasting, and minstrels in a gallery; but just as he set foot upon the threshold he turned; for it seemed that he was plucked by a hand; and he saw the gentleman, with the smile all faded from his face, and his robe had shifted from his side; and Ralph saw that his side was swollen and bandaged, and then his eye fell upon the gentleman's knee, which was bare, and it was all scurfed and scarred. And he knew that he was in the hands of the Leper himself.

He drew back with a shudder, but the gentleman gathered his robe about him, and said with a sudden sternness, "Nay, it were discourteous to draw back now; and indeed I will compel you to come in." Then Ralph knew that he was betrayed; but he bethought him of the little star that he carried with him, and he took it out and held it before him, and said, "Here is a token that I may not halt." And at that the gentleman's face became evil, and he gnashed with his teeth, and moved towards him, as though to seize him. But Ralph saw that he feared the star. So he went backwards holding it forth; and as the Leper pressed upon him, he touched him with the star; and at that the Leper cried aloud, and ran within the house; and there came forth a waft of doleful music like a dirge for the dead.

Then Ralph went into the wood and stood there awhile in dreadful thought; but it came into his mind that there could be no turning back, and that he must leave his precious coffer behind, "and perhaps," he thought, "the Wise Man will let me adventure again." So he went on with a sad and sober heart, but he thanked God as he went for another danger hardly escaped.

And it grew darker now; so dark that he often turned aside among the trees; till at last he came out on the edge of the forest, and knew that he was near the end. In front of him rose a wide hillside, the top of which was among the clouds; and he could see the track faintly glimmering upwards through the grass; the forest lay like a black wall behind him, and he was now deathly weary of his journey, and could but push one foot before the other.

But for all his weariness he felt that it grew colder as he went higher; he gathered his cloak around him, but the cold began to pierce his veins; so that he knew that he was coming to the Grey Frost, and how to escape from it he knew not. The grass grew crisp with frost, and the tall thistles that grew there snapped as he touched them. By the track there rose in several places tall tussocks of grass, and happening to pass close by one of these, he saw something gleam white amid the grass; so he looked closer upon it, and then his heart grew cold within him, for he saw that the grass grew thick out of the bones of a skeleton, through the white ribs and out of the sightless eyes. And he saw that each of the tussocks marked the grave of a man.

Then he came higher still, and the ground felt like iron below his feet; and over him came a dreadful drowsiness, till his only thought was to lie down and sleep; his breath came out like a white cloud and hung round him, and yet he saw the hill rising in front. Then he marked something lie beside the track; and he saw that it was a man down upon his face, wrapped in a cloak. He tried to lift him up, but the body seemed stiff and cold, and the face was frozen to the ground; and when he raised it the dirt was all hard upon the face. So he left it lying and went on. At last he could go no farther; all was grey and still round him, covered with a bleak hoarfrost. To left and right he saw figures lying, grey and frozen, so that the place was like a battlefield; and still the mountain towered up pitilessly in front; he sank upon his knees and tried to think, but his brain was all benumbed. Then he put his face to the ground, and his breath made a kind of warmth about him, while the cold ate into his limbs; but as he lay he heard a groan, and looking up he saw a figure that lay close to the track rise upon its knees and sink down again.

So Ralph struggled again to his feet with the thought that if he must die he would like to die near another man; and he came up to the figure; and he saw that it was a boy, younger than himself, wrapped in a cloak. His hat had fallen off, and he could see his curls all frosted over a cheek that was smooth and blue with cold. By his side lay a little coffer and a staff, like his own. And Ralph, speaking with difficulty through frozen lips, said, "And what do you here? You are too young to be here." The other turned his face upon him, all drawn with anguish, and said, "Help me, help me; I have lost my way." And Ralph sate down beside him and gathered the boy's body into his arms; and it seemed as though the warmth revived him, for the boy looked gratefully at him and said, "So I am not alone in this dreadful place."

Then Ralph said to him that there was no time to be lost, and that they were near their end. "But it seems to me," he added, "that a little farther up the grass looks greener, as if the cold were not so bitter there; let us try to help each other a few paces farther, if we may avoid death for a little." So they rose slowly and painfully, and now Ralph would lead the boy a step or two on; and then he would lean upon the boy, who seemed to grow stronger, for a pace or two; till suddenly it came into Ralph's mind that the cold was certainly less; and so like two dying men they struggled on, step by step, until the ground grew softer under their feet and the grass darker, and then, looking round, Ralph could see the circle of the Grey Frost below them, all white and hoary in the uncertain light.

Presently they struggled out on to a ridge of the long hill; and here they rested on their staves, and talked for a moment like old friends; and the boy showed Ralph his coffer, and said, "But you have none?" And Ralph shook his head and said, "Nay, I left it on the seat of the Snake." And then Ralph asked him of the Leper's house, and the boy told him that he had seen it indeed, but had feared and made a circuit in the wood, and that he had there seen a fearful sight; for at the back of the Leper's house was a cage, like a kennel of hounds, and in it sate a score of wretched men with their eyes upon the ground, who had wandered from the way; and that he had heard a barking of dogs, and men had come out from the house, but that he had fled through the woods.

While they thus talked together, Ralph saw that hard by them was a rock, and in the rock a hole like a cave; so he said to the boy, "Let us stand awhile out of the wind; and then will we set out again." So the boy consented; and they came to the cave; but Ralph wondered exceedingly to see a door set in the rock-face; and he put out his hand and pulled the door; and it opened; and a voice from within called him by name.

Then in a moment Ralph saw that he was in the house of the Wise Man, who sate in his chair, regarding him with a smile, like a father welcoming a son. All seemed the same; and it was very grateful to Ralph to see the sun warm on the ceiling, and to smell the honeyed air that came in from the garden.

Then he went forward, and fell on his knees and laid the staff and the star down, and would have told the Wise Man his tale; but the Wise Man said, "Went not my heart with thee, my son?"

Then Ralph told him how he had left his treasure, expecting to be chidden. But the Wise Man said, "Heed it not, for thou hast a better treasure in thy heart."

Then Ralph remembered that he had left his companion outside, and asked if he might bring him in; but the Wise Man said, "Nay, he has entered by another way." And presently he bade Ralph return home in peace, and blessed him in a form of words which Ralph could not afterwards remember, but it sounded very sweet. And Ralph asked whether he might come again, but the Wise Man said, "Nay, my son."

Then Ralph went home in wonder; and though the journey had seemed very long, he found that it was still morning in Birnewood.

Then he returned to the Parsonage; and the next day Father John returned, and told him that the lands would be restored to him; and as they talked, Father John said, "My son, what new thing has come to you? for there is a light in your eye that was not lit before." But Ralph could not tell him.

So Ralph became a great knight, and did worthily; and in his hall there hang three pictures in one frame; to the left is a little green snake on a stone bench; to the right a leprous man richly clad; and in the centre a grey mist, with a figure down on its face. And some folk ask Ralph to explain the picture, and he smiles and says it is a vision; but others look at the picture in a strange wonder, and then look in Ralph's face, and he knows that they understand, and that they too have been to the Country of Dreams.

The Temple of Death

It was late in the afternoon of a dark and rainy day when Paullinus left the little village where he had found shelter for the night. The village lay in a great forest country in the heart of Gaul. The scattered folk that inhabited it were mostly heathens, and very strange and secret rites were still celebrated in lonely sanctuaries. Christian teachers, of whom Paullinus was one, travelled alone or in little companies along the great high roads, turning aside to visit the woodland hamlets, and labouring patiently to make the good news of the Word known.

They were mostly unmolested, for they travelled under the powerful name of Romans, and in many places they were kindly received. Paullinus had been for months slowly faring from village to village, without any fixed plan of journeying, but asking his way from place to place, as the Spirit led him. He was a young man, a very faithful Christian, and with a love of adventure and travel which stood him in good stead. He carried a little money, but he had seldom need to use it, for the people were simple and hospitable; he did not try to hold assemblies, for he believed that the Gospel must spread like leaven from quiet heart to quiet heart. Indeed he did not purpose to proclaim the Word, but rather to prepare the way for those that should come after. He was of a strong habit, spare and upright; when he was alone he walked swiftly, looking very eagerly about him. He loved the aspect of the earth, the green branching trees, the wild creatures of the woodland, the voices of birds and the sound of streams. And he had too a great

153

and simple love for his own kind, and though he had little eloquence he had a plentiful command of friendly and shrewd talk, and even better than he loved to speak he loved to listen. He had a sweet and open smile, that drew the hearts of all whom he met to him, especially of the children. And he loved his wandering life in the free air, without the daily cares of settled habit.

He had spent the night with an old and calm man, who had been a warrior in his youth, but who could now do little but attend to his farm. Paullinus had spoken to him of the love of the Father and the tender care that Jesus had to His brothers on earth; the old man had listened courteously, and had said that it sounded fair enough, but that he was too old to change, and must stand in the ancient ways. Paullinus did not press him; his custom was never to do that. In the morning he had gone to and fro in the village, and it was late before he thought of setting out; the old man had pressed him to stay another night, but something in Paullinus' heart had told him that he must not wait, for it seemed to him that there was work to be done. The old man came with him to the edge of the forest, and gave him very particular directions to the village he was bound for, which lay in the heart of the wood. "Of one thing I must advise you," he said. "There is, in the wood, some way off the track, a place to which I would not have you go—it is a temple of one of our gods, a dark place. Be certain, dear sir, to pass it by. No one would go there willingly, save that we are sometimes compelled." He broke off suddenly here and looked about him fearfully; then he went on in a low voice: "It is called the Temple of the Grey Death, and there are rites done there of which I may not speak. I would it were otherwise, but the gods are strong—and the priest is a hard and evil man, who won his office in a terrible way, and shall lose it no less terribly. Oh, go not there, dear stranger;" and he laid his hand upon his arm.

"Dear brother," said Paullinus, "I have no mind to go there—but your words seem to have a dark meaning behind them. What are these rites of which you speak?" But the old man shook his head.

"I may not speak of them," he said, "it is better to be silent."

Then they took a kind leave of each other, and Paullinus said that he would pass again that way to see his friend, "for we are friends, I know." And so he went into the wood. It was a wood of very ancient trees, and the dark leaves roofed over the grassy track making a tunnel. The heavens too grew dark above, and Paullinus heard the drops patter upon the leaves. Generally he loved well enough to walk in the woodways, but here it seemed different. He would have liked a companion. Something sinister and terrible seemed to him to hide within those gloomy avenues, and the feeling grew stronger every moment. But he said to himself some of the simple hymns with which he often cheered his way, and felt again that he was in the hands of God.

Presently he passed a little forest pool that was one of the marks of his way. Upon the further bank he was surprised to see a man sitting, with a rod or spear in his hand, looking upon the water. He was glad to see another man in this solitude, and hailed him cheerfully, asking if he was in the right way. The man looked up at the sound. Paullinus saw that he was of middle age, very strong and muscular—but undoubtedly he had an evil face. He scowled, as though he were vexed to be interrupted, and with an odd and angry gesture of the hand he stepped quickly within the wood and disappeared. Paullinus felt in his mind that the man wished him evil, and went on his way somewhat heavily. And now the sun began to go down and it was darker than ever in the forest; Paullinus came to a place where the road forked, and thinking over his note of the way, struck off to the left, but as he did so he felt a certain misgiving which he could not explain. He now began to hurry, for the light failed every moment, and the colour was soon gone out of the grass beneath his feet, leaving all a dark and indistinguishable brown. Soon the path forked again, and then came a road striking across the one that he had pursued of which he did not think he had been told. He went straight forward, but it was now grown so dark that he could no longer see his way, and stumbled very sadly along the wet path, feeling with his hand for the trees. He thought that he must by this time have gone much further than the distance between the villages, and it was clear to him that he had somehow missed the road.

He at last determined that he would try to return, and went slowly back the way that he had come, till at last the night came down upon him. Then Paullinus was struck with a great fear. There were wolves in those forests he knew, though they lived in the un-visited depths of the wood and came not near the habitations of men unless they were fierce with famine. But he had heard several times a strange snarling cry some way off in the wood, and once or twice he had thought he was being softly followed. So he deter-mined to go no further, but to climb up into a tree, if he could find one, and there to spend an uneasy night.

He felt about for some time, but could discover nothing but small saplings, when he suddenly saw through the trees a light shine, and it came across him that he had stumbled as it were by accident upon the village. So he went forward slowly towards the light—there was no track here—often catching his feet among brambles and low plants, till the gloom lifted somewhat and he felt a freer air, and saw that he was in a clearing in the wood. Then he discerned, in front of him, a space of deeper darkness against the sky, what he thought to be the outline of the roofs of buildings; then the light shone out of a window near the ground; but pres-ently he came to a stop, for he saw the light flash and gleam in the ripples of a water that lay in his path and blocked his way.

Then he called aloud once or twice; something seemed to stir in the house, and presently the light in the window was obscured by the head and shoulders of a man, who pressed to the opening; but there was no answer. Then Paullinus spoke very clearly, and said that he was a Roman, a traveller who had lost his way. Then a harsh voice told him to walk round the water to the left and wait awhile; which Paullinus did.

Soon he heard steps come out of the house and come to the water's edge. Then he heard sounds as though some one were walk-ing on a hollow board—then with a word of warning there fell the end of a plank near him on the bank, and he was bidden to come across. He did so, though the bridge was narrow and he was half afraid of falling; but in a moment he was at the other side, a dark figure beside him. He was bidden to wait again, and the figure went out over the water and seemed to pull in the plank that had served as a bridge; and then the man returned and bade him to come forward. Paullinus followed the figure, and in a moment he could see the dark eaves of a long, low house before him, very rudely but strongly built; then a door was opened showing a lighted room within, and he was bidden to step forward and enter.

He found himself in a large, bare chamber, the walls and ceiling of a dark wood. A pine torch flared and dripped in a socket. There were one or two rough seats and a table spread with a meal. At the end of the room there were some bricks piled for a fireplace with charred ashes and a smouldering log among them, for though it was still summer the nights began to be brisk. On the walls hung some implements; a spade and a hoe, a spear, a sword, some knives and javelins. He that inhabited it seemed to be part a tiller of the soil and part a huntsman; but there were other things of which Paullinus could not guess the use—hooks and pronged forks. There were skins of beasts on the floor, and on the ceiling hung bundles of herbs and dried meats. The air was pungent with pine-smoke. He recognised the man at once as the same that he had seen beside the pool; and he looked to Paullinus even stranger and more dangerous than he had seemed before. He seemed too to be on his guard against some terror, and held in his hand a club, as though he were ready to use it.

Presently he said a few words in a harsh voice: "You are a Roman," he asked; "how may I know it?" "I do not know," said Paullinus, trying to smile, "unless you will believe my word." "What is your business here?" said the man; "are you a merchant?" "No," said Paullinus, "I have no business, I travel, and I talk with those I meet—perhaps I am a teacher—a Christian teacher." At this the man's sternness seemed a little to relax. "Oh, the new faith?" he said, rather contemptuously; "well, I have heard of it—and it will never spread; but I am curious to know what it really is, and you shall tell me of it." But suddenly his angry terrors came upon him again, and he said, with a frown, "But where were you bound, and whence come you?"

Paullinus, with such calmness as he could muster, for he felt himself to be in some danger, he scarcely knew what, mentioned the names of the villages. "Well, you have missed your way," said the man. "Why did you come here to the Temple of Death?" Paullinus had a sudden access of dread at the words. "Is this the Temple?" he said; "it is the place I was bidden to avoid." At this the man gave a fearful kind of smile, like a flash of lightning out of a sombre cloud, and he said, with a certain dark pride, "Ay, there are few that come willingly; but now you must abide with me to-night—unless," he added, with a savage look, "you have a mind to be eaten by wolves." "I will certainly stay," said Paullinus, "I am not afraid—I serve a very mighty God myself, who guards his servants if they guard themselves." "Ay, does He?" said the man, with a flash of anger, "then He must needs be strong;—but I wish you no evil," he added in a moment. "I think you are a brave man, perhaps a good one—I fear you not." "There is no need for you to fear me," said Paullinus, "my God is a God of peace and love—and indeed," he added with a smile, looking at the man's great frame, "I should have thought there was little need for you to fear any one." This last word seemed to dissolve the man's evil mood all at once, for he put away the club he held, in a corner of the room, and bade Paullinus eat and drink, which he did gladly. The meat was a strongly flavoured kind of venison, and there was a rough bread, and a drink that seemed both sweet and strong, and had the taste of summer flowers. He praised the food, and the man said to him, "Ay, I have learnt to suit it to my taste. I live here in much loneliness, and there is none to help me."

After the meal the man asked him to tell him something of the new faith, and Paullinus very willingly told him as simply as he could of the Way of Christ.

The man listened with a sort of gloomy attention. "So it is this," he said at last, "which is taking hold of the world! well, it is pretty enough—a good faith for such as live in ease and security, for women and children in fair houses; but it suits not with these forests. The god who made these great lonely woods, and who dwells in them, is very different,"—he rose and made a strange obeisance as he talked. "He loves death and darkness, and the cries of strong and furious beasts. There is little peace here, for all that the woods are still—and as for love, it is of a brutish sort. Nay, stranger, the gods of these lands are very different; and they demand very different sacrifices. They delight in sharp woes and agonies, in grinding pains, in dripping blood and death-sweats and cries of despair. If these woods were all cut down, and the land ploughed up, and peaceful folk lived here in quiet fields and farms, then perhaps your simple, easy-going God might come and dwell with them—but now, if he came, he would flee in terror."

"Nay," said Paullinus, but somewhat sadly, for the man's words seemed to have a fearful truth about them, "the Father waits long and is kind; the victory of love is slow, but it is sure."

"It is slow enough!" said the man; "these forests have grown here beyond the memory of man, and they will stand long after you and I have been turned to a handful of dust—and so I will serve my gods while I live. But you are weary," he added, "and may sleep; fear not any hurt from me; and as for the way you speak of, well, I will say that I should be content if it had the victory. I am sick at heart of the hard rule of these gods—but I fear them, and will serve them faithfully till I die."

And then he brought some skins of beasts and heaped them in a corner of the room for Paullinus, who lay down gladly, and from mere weariness fell asleep. But the priest sat long before the fire in thought; and twice he went to the door and looked out, as if he were waiting for some tidings.

Once the opening of the door aroused Paullinus; and he saw the dark figure of the priest stand in the doorway, and over his head and shoulders a dark still night, pierced with golden stars; and once again, when he opened the door a second time, the pure gush of air into the close room woke Paullinus from a deep sleep; again he saw the priest stand silent in the door, with his hands clasped behind him; and through the door Paullinus could see the dim ring of dewy woods, that seemed to sleep in quiet dreams; and over the woods a great pale light of dawn that was coming slowly up out of the east.

But Paullinus fell back into sleep again from utter weariness, as a man might dive into a pool. And when at last he opened his eyes, he saw that day was come with an infinite sweetness and freshness; the birds called faintly in the thickets; and the priest was going slowly about his daily task, preparing food; and Paullinus, from where he lay, smiled at him, and the priest smiled back, as though half ashamed, and presently said, "You have slept deeply, sir; and to sleep as you have done shows that a man is brave and innocent."

Then Paullinus rose, and would have helped him, but the man said, "Nay, you are my guest; and besides, I do things in a certain order, as all do who live alone, and I would not have any one to meddle with me." He spoke gruffly, but there was a certain courtesy in his manner.

Presently the priest asked him to come and eat, and they sat together eating in a friendly way. The priest was silent, but Paullinus talked of many things—and at last the priest said, "I thought I loved my loneliness, but it seems that I am pleased to have a companion. I believe," he added, "that I would be content if you would dwell with me." And Paullinus smiled in answer, and said, "Ay, it is not good to live alone."

A little while after Paullinus said that he must set out on his way, and that he was very grateful for so gentle a welcome; but the priest said, "Nay, but you must see the sights of my house and of the temple. Few folk have seen it, and never a foreign man. It is not a merry place," he added, "but it will do to make a traveller's tale."

So he led him to the door, and they went out. Paullinus saw that the house where he had spent the night stood on a little square island, with a deep moat all round it, filled with water; the island was all overgrown with bushes and tall plants, except that in one place there were some pens where sheep and goats were kept; and a path led down to the landing-place where he had crossed it the night before. But what at once seized and held the eyes and mind of Paullinus was the temple. He thought he had never seen so grim a place; it rose above the bushes and above the house. It was of very rough stone, all blank of windows, with a roof of stone; the blocks were very large, and Paullinus wondered how they had been brought there. In front there was a low door, and over it a hideous carving, that seemed to Paullinus to be the work of devils. Apart from the temple, rising among the bushes, stood a rude sculptured figure, with a leering evil face, very roughly but vigorously cut, with an arm raised as though beckoning people to the temple. This figure, of a kind of reddish stone, seemed horrible beyond words to Paullinus. It seemed to him like a servant of Satan, if not Satan himself, frozen into stone.

The priest looked at Paullinus, who could not help showing his horror, with a kind of pride. Then he said, "Will you go further? Will you enter the temple with me, and see what is therein? Perhaps you will after all bow your head to the gods of the forest." And Paullinus said, "Yes, I will go," and he said a silent prayer to the Lord Christ that He would guard him well. Another path paved with stone led from the landing-place to the temple, along which they went slowly; the priest leading. Arrived at the door, the priest made another strange obeisance, lifting his hands slowly above his head and closing his eyes; then he opened the door into the temple itself. There came out a foul and heavy smell that shuddered in the nostrils of Paullinus and left him gasping somewhat for breath. The priest looked at him with a sort of curious wonder, which made Paullinus determine to go further.

The temple itself was large and dark, a sickly light only filtering in through a hole in the roof. The floor was paved, and the roof was supported by great wooden columns, the trunks of large forest trees. The greater part of the building was shut off by a large wooden screen, about the height of a man, close to them, so that they stood in a kind of vestibule. The whole of the building, walls, roof, and floor, had been painted at some time or other a black colour, which was now faded and looked a dark slaty grey. Over the screen in the centre was seen the head of what seemed an image, very great and horrible. The light, which came from an opening immediately above the image, showed a horned and bearded head, misshapen and grotesque. Possibly at another time and place

Paullinus might have smiled at the ugly thing; but here, peering at them over the screen, in the fetid gloom, it froze the blood in his veins.

And now behind the screen were strange sounds as well, a kind of heavy breathing or snorting, and what seemed the scratching of some beast. The priest went up to the screen and opened a sort of panel in it; this was followed by a hoarse and hideous outcry within, half of fear and half of rage. The priest took from an angle of the wall a long pole shod with iron, and leaned within the opening, saying in a stern tone some words that Paullinus did not understand. Presently the noises ceased, and the priest, using a great effort, seemed to pull or push at something with the pole, and there was the sound as of a great gate turning on its hinges. Then he drew his head and arms out, and said to Paullinus, "We may enter." He then threw a door open in the middle of the screen and went in. Paullinus followed.

In front of them stood a great statue on a pedestal; the figure of a thing, half-man half-goat, crouched as though to spring. The smell was still more horrible within, and it became clear to Paullinus that he was in the lair of some ravenous and filthy beast. There lay a mess of bones underneath the statue. To the left, in the wall, there was a strong oaken door, made like a portcullis, which seemed to close the entrance of a den; something seemed to move and stir in the blackness, and Paullinus heard the sound of heavy breathing within. The priest, still holding the pole in his hand, led the way round to the back of the statue. Here, set into the wall, were a number of stone slabs, with what seemed to be a name upon each, rudely carved.

The priest pointed to these and said, "Those are the names of the priests of this shrine. And now," he went on, "I will tell you a thing which is in my mind—I know not why I should wish to say it—but it seems to me that I have a great desire to tell you all and keep nothing back; and I tell you this, though you may turn from me with shame and horror. We have a law that if a man be condemned to death for a certain crime—if he have slain one of his kin—he is bound to a tree in the forest to be devoured piecemeal by the wolves. But if there seem to be cause or excuse for the deed that he has done, then he is allowed to purchase his life on one condition—he may come to this place and slay the priest who serves here, if he can, or himself be slain. And if he slay him he reigns in his stead until he himself be slain. And the rites of this place are these: all of this tribe who may be guilty of the slaying of a man by secret or open violence without due cause are offered here a sacrifice to the god—and that is the task that I have done and must do till I am myself slain. And here in a den dwells a savage beast—I know not its name and its age is very great—that slays and devours the guilty. What wonder if a man's heart grows dark and cruel here; I can only look into my own heart, black as it is, and wonder that it is not blacker. But the gods are good to me, and have not cursed me utterly.

"And now I will tell you that when I saw you by the pool, and when you called to me in the night, I thought that perchance you had come to slay me—and then I saw that you were alone, and not guarded as a prisoner would be; but even then my heart was dark, because the god has had no sacrifice for many a month, and seems to call upon me for a victim—so I had it in my heart to slay you here. And now," he said, "I have opened the door of my heart, and you have seen all that is to be seen."

And then he looked upon Paullinus as if to know his judgment; and Paullinus, turning to the priest, and seeing that in his heart he desired what was better, and abode not willingly in the ways of death, said, "Brother, with all my heart I am sorry for you—and I would have you turn your heart away from these dark and evil gods—who are indeed, I think, the very spirits of hell—and turn to the Father of mercy of whom I spoke, with whom there is forgiveness and love for all His sons, when once they turn to Him and ask His help."

The priest looked very gently at Paullinus as he spoke; but there came a horrible roaring out of the den, and the beast flung himself against the bars as if in rage.

Then the priest said, "For twenty years I have heard no speech like this; for twenty years I have lived with death and done wickedness, and all men turn from me with fear and loathing, and speak not any word to me: I have never looked in a kindly human eye, nor felt the hand of a friend within my own. Judge between me and my sin. I had a brother, an evil man, who made it his pleasure to trouble me. I was stronger than he, and he feared me. I loved a maiden of our tribe, and she loved me; and when my brother knew it he went about to do her a hurt, that it might grieve me. One day she went through the forest alone, and never returned, and I, in madness ranging the wood to find her, found the mangled bones of her body. I knew it by the poor torn hair—she had been devoured by wolves—but burying the bones I saw that the feet were tied together with a cord, and then I knew that some one had bound her by violence and left her to be devoured.

"Then as I returned from burying her, I came upon my brother in a glade of the wood; and he looked upon me with an evil smile, and said, 'Hast thou found her?' And I knew in my heart what he had done, and I slew him where he stood—and then I returned and said what I had done. Then they imprisoned me—for my brother was older than myself, and my enemies said that I had done it to win his inheritance—and at last, after long consulting, they gave me the choice to be devoured of wolves or to become the priest of Death. I chose the latter, because I was mad and hated all mankind. I came to this place at sundown, and my guards left me. I swam the ditch, and knocked at the priest's door; he was an old man and piteous, who abhorred his trade—and there I seized him and slew him with my hands—he was weak and made no resistance—and I flung his body to the beast and carved his name. That is my bitter story—and since then I have lived, accursed and dreaded. These gods are hard taskmasters." He made a wild gesture of the hand and turned his bright eyes upon Paullinus, who stood aghast.

"The tale is told," said the priest. "I who have kept silence all these years have babbled my story to a stranger. Why did I tell you? I thought that with all your talk of mercy and forgiveness you might have a message for my bitter and tired heart—but you shrink from me, and are silent."

"Nay," said Paullinus, "shrink from you!—not so—nay, I cling to you more than ever; come and claim your part in the forgiveness that waits for all—you have suffered, you have repented—and the God whom I serve has comfort and peace for you and for all; His love is wide and deep—claim your share in it." And he took the priest's hand in both of his own.

There was a horrible roaring behind them as they stood: the great beast behind them struck at the bars, but the priest took no heed.

"If I could," he said, with his eyes fixed on Paullinus' face.

"Nay then," said Paullinus, "if you would it is done already, for He reads the very secrets of the heart."

There broke out a loud fierce crashing sound behind them; the great oaken gate heaved and splintered, and a monstrous beast as huge as a horse appeared at the mouth of the den; his small head was laid back on his hairy shoulders, his little eyes gleamed wickedly, and his red mouth opened snarling fiercely. The priest turned, and met the rush of the beast full. In a moment he was flung to the ground with a dreadful rending sound. "Save yourself!" he cried. The huge brute glared, with his foot upon the fallen form, and seemed to hesitate whether to attack his second foe. Paullinus, hardly knowing what he did, seized the great iron-pointed pole, and with a firmness of strength which he had not known himself to possess drove it full into the monster's great throat as it opened its mouth towards him. It made a wild and sickening cry; it raised one foot as though to strike, then it beat the air and struck once at the head of the prostrate form; then, with a gurgling sound, spitting out a flood of hot blood, it collapsed, rolled slowly on one side. Paullinus, watching it intently and still holding the pole, thrust it further in with all his might. It quivered all over, and in a moment lay still. Paullinus made haste to drag the priest out from beneath—but he saw that all was over; the last blow of the beast had battered in the skull—and besides that the body was horribly mangled and crushed. The limbs of the priest were heavy and relaxed; his hands were folded together as though in prayer, and he drew one or two little fluttering breaths, but never opened his eyes.

Paullinus was like one in a dream at this sudden horror; but he kept his senses; once or twice the great beast moved, and drummed on the pavement with a horny paw. So Paullinus drew the prostrate body of the priest outside the screen and closed the door. Then he went with swift steps out of the temple and to the water's edge; he drew up a little water in his hand, looking into the dark and cool moat. Then he came back with a purpose in his mind. He sprinkled the water on the poor mangled brow; and then, choosing the name of the Apostle whom Jesus most loved, he said, "John, I baptize thee, *in nomine*, &c." It was like a prisoner's release; the straining hands relaxed, and with a sigh the new-made Christian presently died. "I doubt I have done right," said Paullinus to himself. "He was coming to the Saviour very swiftly, and I think was at His feet; and if he was not in heart a Christian, the Lord will know when he meets Him in the heavenly places."

When Paullinus went back to the hut he found a rough mattock. First he dug a great hole; the earth was black and soft, and water oozed soon into the depths; then with much painful labour he dragged the great beast thither, and covered him in from the eye of day; and then he toiled to dig a grave for the priest—once he stopped to eat a little food, but he worked with unusual ease and lightness. But the night came down on the forest as he finished the grave—for he did not wish that the priest should lie within the dreadful temple.

Then he went back, very weary but not sad; his terrors and distresses had drawn slowly off from his mind, as he worked in the still afternoon, under the clear sky, all surrounded by woods; the earth seemed like one who had come from a bath, washed through and through by the drench of wholesome rains, and the smell of the woods was sharp and sweet.

Paullinus slept quietly that night, feeling very close to God; but in the morning, when the dawn was coming up, he was awakened by a shouting outside. His sleep had been so deep and still that he hardly knew at first where he was, but it all came swiftly back to him; and then the shouting was repeated. Paullinus rose to his feet and went slowly out.

On the edge of the water, where the causeway crossed it, he saw two men standing, that from their dress seemed to be great chiefs. Behind them, with his hands bound, and attached by a rope held in the hand of one of the chiefs, was a young man of a wild and fierce aspect, in the dress of a serf, a rough tunic and leggings. His head was bare, and he looked around him in dismay, like a beast in a trap. Behind, at the edge of the clearing, stood four soldiers silent, with bows strung and arrows fitted to the string. Over the whole group there seemed to be the shadow of a stern purpose. At the appearance of Paullinus, the two chiefs hurriedly bent together in talk, and looked at him with astonishment. Paullinus came down to the water's edge, when one of the chiefs said, "We have come for the priest; where is he? For he must do his office upon this man, who hath slain one of his kin by stealth."

"It is too late," said Paullinus; "he is dead, and waits for burial."

Then the chiefs seemed again to confer together, and one of them, with a strange reverence, said, "Then you are the new priest of the temple? And yet it seems strange, for you are not of our nation."

"Nay," said Paullinus, "I am a wanderer, a Roman. It was not I who slew him—it was the great beast who lived in the den yonder; and the beast have I slain—but come over and let me tell you all the tale."

So he made haste to put out the bridge, and the two chiefs came over in silence, leaving the prisoner in the hands of the guards who surrounded him. Paullinus led them to the temple, which he could hardly prevail upon them to enter, and showed them the dead body, which was a fearful sight enough; then he showed them the broken gate and the empty den, and then he led them to the mound where the beast lay buried, and offered if they would to uncover the body. "Nay, we would not see him," said the elder chief in a low voice; "it is enough."

Paullinus then led them to the hut and told them the story from beginning to end. The chiefs looked at him with surprise when he told them of the beast's death, and one of them said, "I doubt, sir, you slew him by Roman magic—for he was exceedingly strong, and you look not much of a warrior." "Nay," said Paullinus, smiling, "I doubt he was his own death, as is often the end of evil—he leapt upon the pole: I did but hold it, and the Lord made my hand strong."

When he had done the story the chiefs spoke together a little in a low tone. Then one of them said, "This is a strange tale, sir. And it seems to us that you must be a man whom the gods love, for you stayed here a night with the priest—who was a fierce man and no friend of strangers—and received no hurt. And then you have slain the Hound of Death, unarmed. But we will ask you to go with us, for we cannot decide so grave a matter until we have taken counsel with our tribe. Be assured that you shall be used courteously."

"I will go very willingly," said Paullinus. "My God did indeed send me hither to do a work which He had prepared for me to do, and I would serve His will in all things."

So they first buried the body of the priest in his grave, and then they went together to the village, and messages were sent to the chiefs of the tribe, who came in haste, ten great warriors; and they sat and debated long in low voices. And Paullinus sat without wondering that he could feel so calm, for he knew that he was in jeopardy.

So when they had talked a long while they called Paullinus into the council, and the oldest chief, an ancient warrior with silver hair, much bowed with age, told him that they saw that he was a man favoured of God. "I hide it not from you," he said, "that some of my brethren here would have it that death should be your portion, because you have meddled with sacred and secret things. But I think that it is clear that you have done no wrong, or otherwise you would have been slain; you spoke but now of the God you serve, and we would hear of Him; for now that the priest is dead and the beast dead, we say with reverence that a cloud is lifted from us, and that we have served dark gods too long."

So Paullinus spoke of the Father's love and the coming of the Saviour on to the earth; and when he had finished the chiefs thanked him very courteously, and then they asked him to abide

with them and speak again of the matter. So Paullinus abode there
and made many friends, as his manner was.

Then came a day when the chiefs again held council, and they
told Paullinus that if he would, he should be the priest of the temple
and teach what he would there, and that the temple should be
cleansed; and they said that they would not ask him to be the slayer
of such as had killed a man, for that, they said, seems to belong
rather to a warrior than a priest.

So Paullinus said that he would abide with them, but that he
must first go and be made a priest after his own order; and he departed, but soon returned, and the Temple of Death was made a
Church of Christians.

Paullinus is an old man now; you may see him walk at evening
beside the water, under the shadow of the church. The images have
been broken and defaced; but Paullinus often stops beside a
mound, and thinks of the bones of the great beast that lie whiten-
ing below—and then he stands beside a grave which bears the name
of John, and knows that his brother, that did evil in the days of his
ignorance, but that suffered sore, will be the first to meet him in
the heavenly country, with the light of God about him; "and perhaps," says Paullinus to himself, "he will bear a palm in his hand."

The Tomb of Heiri

In the old days, when the Romans were taking Britain for their own, there lived in Cambria a great prince called Heiri. He was forty summers old; he had long been wed, but had no son to reign after him. Many times had he fought with the Romans, but his tribe had been driven slowly backward to the northern mountains; here for a time he dwelt in some peace, but the Romans crept ever nearer; and Heiri, who was a brave and generous prince and a great warrior, was sore afflicted, seeing the end that must come. He dwelt in a high valley of moorland, where his tribe kept such herds as yet remained to them. Heiri often asked himself in what he and his people had wronged the gods, that they should be thus vexed; for he was, as it seemed, like a wild beast with his back to a wall, fighting with innumerable foes; to the north and east and south and west lay great mountains, and behind them to west and north lay the sea; to south and east the Romans held the land, so that the Cambrians were penned in a corner.

One day heavy news came; a great army of the Romans had come by sea to the estuary in the south. The next day the scouts saw them marching up the pass, like ants, in countless numbers, with a train of baggage; and the day after, when the sun went down, the watch-fires burnt in a long line across the southern moorland, and the sound of the horns the Romans blew came faintly upon the wind; all day the tribesmen drove in their cattle up to the great camp, that lay on a low hill in the centre of the vale. Heiri held a

council with his chiefs, and it was determined that next day they
should give them battle.

That night, when Heiri was sitting in his hut, his beloved wife
beside him, there came to see him the chief priest of the tribe; he
was an old man, hard and cruel, and Heiri loved him not; and he
hated Heiri secretly, being jealous of his power; he came in, his
white priestly robe bound about the waist with a girdle of gold;
and Heiri rose to do him honour, making a sign to his wife that she
should leave them. So she withdrew softly; then the priest sat down.
He asked first of Heiri whether it was determined to fight on the
morrow; and Heiri said that it was so determined. Then the priest
said, "Lord Heiri, to-morrow is the feast of the God of Death; and
he claims a victim, if we are to be victorious." Now Heiri hated the
sacrifice of men, and the priest knew it; and so for a while Heiri
sat in silence, frowning, and beating his foot upon the ground, while
the priest watched him with bright and evil eyes. Then Heiri said,
"To-morrow must many men, both valiant and timid, die; surely
that were enough for the god!" But the priest said, "Nay, my lord,
it is not enough; the law saith that unless a victim should offer
himself, the priests should choose a victim; and the victim must
be goodly; for we are in an evil case." Then Heiri looked at the
priest and said, "Whom have ye chosen?" for he saw that the priests
had named a victim among themselves. So the priest said, "We have
named Nefri—be content."

Now Nefri was a lad of fifteen summers, cousin to Heiri; his
father was long dead, and Heiri loved the boy, who was brave and
gracious, and had hoped in his heart that Nefri would succeed him
as prince of the tribe. Then Heiri was very wroth, and said, "Lord
priest, that may not be; Nefri is next of kin to myself, and will grow
up a mighty warrior; and he shall be chief after me, if the gods
grant him life; look you, to-morrow we shall lose many mighty men;
and it may be that I shall myself fall; for I have been heavy-hearted
for many days, and I think that the gods are calling me—and Nefri
we cannot spare."

Then the priest said, "Lord Heiri, the gods choose whom they
will by the mouth of their priests; it were better that Nefri should

perish than that the people should be lost; and, indeed, the gods
have spoken; for I prayed that the victim should be shown me,
hoping that it might be some common man; but hardly had I done
my prayer, when Nefri came to my hut to bring an offering; and
my heart cried out, 'Arise, for this is he.' The gods have chosen
him, not I; and Nefri must die for the people."

Then Heiri was grievously troubled; for he reverenced the gods
and feared the priests. And he rose up, with anger and holy fear
striving within him; and he said, "Prepare then for the sacrifice;
only tell not Nefri—I myself will bring him—it may be that the gods
will provide another victim." For he hoped within his heart that
the Romans might attack at dawn, so that the sacrifice should tarry.

Then the priest rose up and said, "Lord Heiri, I would it were
otherwise; but we must in all things obey the gods; the sacrifice is
held at dawn, and I will go and set all things in order." So Heiri rose
and bowed to the priest; but he knew in his heart that the priest
sorrowed not, but rather exulted in the victim he had chosen. Then
Heiri sent word that Nefri should come to him, and presently Nefri
came in haste, having risen from his bed, with the warm breath of
sleep about him. And there went as it were a sword through Heiri's
heart, to see the boy so fair and gracious and so full of love and
bravery.

Then Heiri made the boy sit beside him, and embraced him with
his arm; and then he said, "Nefri, I have sent for you in haste, for
there is a thing that I must tell you; to-morrow we fight the Romans, and something tells me in my heart that it will be our last
fight; whether we shall conquer or be conquered I know not, but it
is a day of doom for many—and now hearken. I have prayed many
times in my heart for a son, but no son is given me; but I hoped
that you would reign after me, if indeed there shall be any people
left to rule; and if it so fall out, remember that I spoke with you to-
night, and bade you be brave and just, loving your people and fearing the gods; and forget not that I loved you well."

And Nefri, half in awe and half in eager love for the great prince
his cousin, said, "I will not forget." Then Heiri kissed him on the
cheek and said, "Dear lad, I know it. And now you must sleep, for

there is a sacrifice at dawn, and you must be there with me; but before you sleep—and I would have you sleep here in my hut to-night—pray to the father of the gods to guide and strengthen me—for we are as naught in his hands, and I have a grievous choice to make—a choice between honour and love—and I know not which is the stronger."

Then Heiri spread a bearskin on the floor and bade Nefri sleep, and he himself sat long in thought looking upon the embers. And it was quiet in the hut—only he saw by the firelight the boy's bright eye watching him, till he chid him lovingly, saying, "Sleep, Nefri, sleep." And Heiri himself lay down to sleep, for he knew that a weary day of fighting lay before him.

But the priest went to the other chiefs and spake with each of them, saying that the gods had chosen Nefri for the victim of the sacrifice, but that Heiri would fain forbid it. But the priest did worse than that, for he told many of the tribesmen the same story, and though they were sorry that Nefri should die, yet they feared the gods exceedingly, and did not think to dispute their will.

About an hour before the dawn, when there was a faint light in the air, and the breeze began to blow chill from the hills, and the stars went out one by one, the chiefs began to gather their men; and there was sore discontent in the camp; all night had the rumour spread beside the fires and in the huts that Heiri would resist the will of the gods and save Nefri from death; and many of the soldiers told the chiefs that if this were so they would not fight; so the chiefs assembled in silence before the hut of Heiri, for they feared him greatly, but they feared the gods more, and they had resolved that Nefri should die.

While they stood together Heiri came suddenly out among them. He carried a brand in his hand, which lit up his pale face and bright armour; and he came like a man risen from the dead.

Then the oldest chief, by name Gryf, drew near, and Heiri asked him of the Romans; and the chief said that they were not stirring yet. Then Heiri held up his hand; every now and then came the crying of cocks out of the camp, but in the silence was heard the faint sound of trumpets from the moorland, and Heiri said, "They come."

Then Gryf, the chief, said, "Then must the sacrifice be made in haste," and he turned to Heiri and said, "Lord Heiri, it is rumoured in the camp that Nefri is the chosen victim, but that you seek to save him." And Heiri looked sternly at him and said, "And wherefore are the purposes of the gods revealed? Lo, I will bring Nefri myself to the sacrifice, and we shall see what will befall."

Then the chiefs were glad in their hearts and said, "Lord Heiri, it is well. The ways of the gods are dark, but they rule the lives of men, and who shall say them nay?" And Heiri said, "Ay, they are dark enough."

Then he made order that the scouts should go forth from the camp; and while he yet spake the procession of priests in their white robes passed like ghosts through the huts on their way to the temple. And Heiri said, "We must follow," and he called to Nefri; but the boy did not answer. Then Heiri went within and found him sleeping very softly, with his face upon his hand; and he looked upon him for a moment, and then he put his hand upon his head; and the boy rose up, and Heiri said, "It is time, dear Nefri—and pray still for me, for the gods have not showed me light." So Nefri marvelled, and tried to make a prayer; but he was filled with wonder at the thought of the sacrifice, for he had never been present at a sacrifice before—and he was curious to see a man slain—for the sight of death in those grievous years of battle had lost its terrors even for children. So Nefri rose up; and Heiri smiled upon him and took the boy's hand, and the two went out together.

Then they came with the chiefs through the camp. The precinct of the goddess was at the upper end, to the north; it was a thick grove of alders, through which no eye could pierce; and it was approached by a slanting path so that none could see into the precinct.

So presently they came to the place and entered in; and Heiri felt the boy's hand cold within his own; but it was not fear, for Nefri was fearless, but only eagerness to see what would be done.

They passed inside the precinct; none was allowed to enter except the priests and the chiefs and certain captains. It was a dolorous place in truth. All round ran a wall of high slabs of slate.

At the upper end, on a pedestal, stood the image of the god, a rude and evil piece of handiwork. It was a large and shapeless figure, with hands outspread; in the head of it glared two wide and cruel eyes, painted with paint, red-rimmed and horrible. The pedestal was stained with rusty stains; and at the foot lay a tumbled heap that was like the body of a man, as indeed it was—for the victim was left lying where he fell, until another victim was slain. All around the body sprouted rank grasses out of the paved floor. The priests stood round the image; the chief priest in front holding a bowl and a long thin knife. Two of them held torches which cast a dull glare on the image. The chiefs arranged themselves in lines on each side; and Heiri, still holding Nefri by the hand, walked up to within a few feet of the image, and there stood silent.

Then the chief priest made a sign, and at that two other priests came out with a large box of wood and shovels; and they took the bones of the victim up and laid them in the box, in which they clattered as they fell—and Nefri watched them curiously, but shuddered not; and when the poor broken body was borne away, then Nefri began to look round for the victim, but the priests began a hymn; their loud sad voices rang out very strangely on the chilly air—and the tribesmen without, hearing the sound, trembled for fear and cast themselves upon the ground.

Then there was a silence; and the chief priest came forward, and made signs to Heiri to draw near, and Heiri advanced, and said to Nefri as he did so, "Now, child, be brave." And Nefri looked up at Heiri with parted lips; and then it came suddenly into his mind that he was indeed to be the victim; but he only looked up with a piteous and inquiring glance at Heiri; and Heiri drew him to the pedestal. Then there was a terrible silence, and the hearts of the chiefs beat fast for fear and horror; and some of them turned away their faces, and the tears came to their eyes.

Then the priest raised his knife, while Nefri watched him; but Heiri stepped forward and said, "Lord priest, I have chosen. Hold thy hand. The law saith that a victim must die, and that one may offer himself to die; ye have chosen Nefri, for none has offered himself. But I bid thee hold; for here I offer myself as a victim to the god."

Then there was an awful silence, and the priest looked fiercely and evilly upon Nefri, and made as though he would have smitten him; but Heiri seized the priest's hand in both his own, and with great strength drove the knife into his own breast, stood for a moment, then swayed and fell. And as he lay he said, "My father, I come, the last victim at the shrine;" and then he drew out the knife, sobbed and died. But the chiefs crowded round to look upon him; and Gryf said, "We are undone; our king is dead, and who shall lead us?"

Then he scowled evilly upon the priests, and said, "This is your work, men of blood—and as ye have slain our king, ye shall fight for us to-day, and see if the god will protect you; then, if he saves you, we shall know that you have spoken truly—and if he saves you not then ye are false priests." And the chiefs cried assent; and Gryf, the eldest chief, commanded that weapons should be given them, and that they should be guarded and fight with the vanguard. But Nefri cast himself upon the body of Heiri and wept sore. But while they stood came a scout in terror, and told them that the Romans were indeed advancing. So the temple was emptied in a moment; and Nefri sat by the body of the dead and looked upon it. But the chiefs hastened to the wall of the camp; and it was now day; in the light that fell pale and cold from the eastern hills they saw the Romans creeping across the moor, in black dots and patches, and the sound of the horns drew nearer.

Then they arrayed themselves, and went out in the white morning; and the women watched from the wall. But Heiri's wife was told the tale, and went to the temple, but dared not enter, for no woman might set foot therein; and she wailed sitting at the gate, calling upon Heiri to come forth; but Heiri lay on his back before the image, the blood flowing from his breast, while Nefri held his head upon his knee.

Then went the battle very evilly for the tribe; little by little they were driven back upon the camp; and they were like sheep without a shepherd—and still the chiefs hoped in the help of the god; but the priests were smitten down one by one, and last of all the chief priest fell, his bowels gushing from a wound in his side, and cursed the god and died cursing.

Then the heavens overclouded: blacker and blacker the clouds gathered, with a lurid redness underneath like copper; till a mighty storm fell upon them, just as the Cambrians broke and fled back to the camp, and watched the steady advance of the Roman line, with the eagles bowing and nodding as they swept over the uneven moor.

Then suddenly they were aware of a strange thing. Whence it came they knew not, but suddenly under the camp wall there appeared the figure of a man in armour, on a white horse; it was the form of Heiri as they had often seen him ride forth on his white charger to battle; and behind him seemed to be a troop of dark and shadowy horsemen. Heiri seemed to turn round, and raise his sword in the air, as he had often done in life; and then, with a great rending of the heavens, and a mighty crash of thunder, the troop of horse swept down upon the Roman line. Then came a fearful sound from the moorland; and those who gazed from the wall saw the Romans waver and turn; and in a moment they were in flight, melting away in the moor, as stones that roll from a cliff after a frost; and all men held their breath in silence; for they saw the Romans flying and none to pursue, except that some thought that they saw the white horse ride hither and thither, and the flash of the waving sword of Heiri.

There followed a strange and dreadful night; the list of warriors was called and many were absent; from hour to hour a few wounded men crawled in; and in the morning, seeing that the Romans were not near at hand, they sent out a party with horses to bring in the wounded and the dead; all the priests were among the slain; those of the chiefs that were alive held a meeting and resolved that the camp must now be held, for the Romans would attack the next day; and they sent the women and children, with the herds, away to a secret place in the mountains, all but Heiri's wife, who would not leave the camp.

Then the other chiefs would have made Gryf, the old chief, prince of the tribe; but he refused it, saying that Heiri had wished

Nefri to be chief, and that none but Nefri should succeed. So search
was made for Nefri, and he was found in Heiri's hut with Heiri's
wife; he had stayed beside the body till it grew stiff and cold and
the eyes had glazed; and then he had feared to be alone with it,
and had crept away. So they put a crown upon Nefri's head, and
each of the chiefs in turn knelt before him and kissed his hand;
and Nefri bore himself proudly but gently, as a prince should, rising as each chief approached; and then he was led out before the
people, and they were told that Nefri was prince by the wish of
Heiri; and no one disputed the matter.

Then in the grey dawn a scout came in haste and said that three
Romans were approaching the camp, and that one was a herald;
and the old chief asked Nefri what his will was; and the boy looked
him in the face, and said, "Let them be brought hither." So the
chiefs were again summoned, and the Romans came slowly into
the camp. The herald came in front, and he was followed by an
officer of high rank, as could be seen from his apparel and the
golden trappings of the horse that bore him; and another officer
followed behind; and the herald, who knew something of the Cambrian language, said that this was the Lord Legate himself, and
that he was come to make terms.

The chiefs looked at each other in silence, for they knew that
the Romans must needs have taken the camp that day if they had
assaulted it. The Legate was a young man with a short beard, very
much burnt by the sun, and bearing himself like a great gentleman. He looked about him with a careless and lordly air; and when
they came into the presence of the chiefs, the three dismounted;
and the Legate looked round to see which was the prince; then the
old chief put Nefri forward, and said to the herald, "Here is our
king." And the Legate bowed to Nefri, and looked at him in surprise; and the herald said in the Cambrian language to Nefri that
the Legate was fain to arrange a truce, or indeed a lasting peace, if
that were possible.

Then the old chief said to Nefri, "My lord, ask him wherefore
the Legate has come;" and Nefri asked the herald, and the herald
asked the Legate; then the Legate said, smiling, to the herald, "Tell

him anything but the truth—say that it is our magnanimity;" and then he added in a lower tone, turning to the other officer, "though the truth is that the men will not dare to attack the place after the rout of yesterday;" and the Legate added to the herald, "Say that the Romans respect courage, and have seen that the Cambrians are worthy foes, and we would not press them hard; it is a peaceful land of allies that we desire, and not a land conquered and made desolate." So the herald repeated the words.

Then the old chief bade Nefri say that they must have time to consider, adding that it would not be well to seem eager for peace. Then he said to the other chiefs, "Yet this is our salvation." So they conferred together, and at last it was decided to tell the Legate that they would be friends and allies, but that the boundaries of the land must be respected, and that the Romans must withdraw beyond the boundaries. And this the Legate accepted, and it was determined that all the land that could be seen from the camp should be left to the Cambrians, and that the mountains should be as a wall to them; and this too the Legate approved.

So in the space of an hour the Cambrians were relieved of their foes, and were in peace in their own land. And the Legate was royally entertained; but before he went he asked, through the herald, where the great warrior was who had led the last charge on the day before, for he had taken him to be the prince of the land. Then the old chief said, "He is sick and may not come forth." Then the Legate rode away, and Nefri rode a little way with him to do him honour, and after courteous greetings they departed.

Then the old chief and Nefri talked long together, and they determined what they would do.

Then the people were assembled, and Nefri spoke first, and said that he was young and could not put words together; but he added that the old chief knew his will and would announce it.

Then the old chief stood forward and told the people the story of Heiri's death and how he had died for the people; and then he told them that he had made the priests fight, and that the gods had surely shown that they were false priests, for they were slain, and the gods had not protected them, and that Nefri was prince by the will of Heiri.

And then he said that Heiri with his latest breath had said that he should be the last victim—and that thus it should be; "for Heiri," he said, "has become a god indeed and fought for us, and has conquered the Romans, and, therefore," he said, "the Lord Nefri has decreed that the precinct of the god should not indeed be destroyed—for that were impious; but that a great mound should be raised over the place, and that it should be the tomb of Heiri, and that peaceful offerings should be made there, and that it should be kept as a day of festival; and that Nefri himself should be priest as well as prince, and his successors for ever."

And the people all applauded, for they had dreaded the bloody sacrifices; and the next day and for many days they laboured until over the whole precinct they had raised a mighty mound, burying the image of the god; and for Heiri's body they made a chamber of stone, and they laid him therein, with his face upward to the sky, and made great lamentation over him.

When all things were in order a solemn feast was held; and Nefri on the top of the mound made a sacrifice of fruits and milk, and blessed the people in the name of Heiri; and he made order that to make the place more blessed, all weddings should thenceforth be celebrated upon the mound, so that it should be the precinct of life and not of death. And the people rejoiced.

That night Nefri slept in the hut of Heiri; and at the dead time of darkness, when all was silent in the camp, except for the pacing of the sentry to and fro, Nefri awoke, and saw in the hut the form of Heiri standing, only brighter and fairer than when he lived; and he looked upon Nefri with a smile as though his heart was full of joy; then he came near and said, in a voice like the voice of a distant fall of water, "Nefri, dear child, thou hast done well and wisely; be just and merciful and loving to all; and rule with diligence, and grieve not."

Then Nefri would have asked him of the place wherein his spirit abode, but could not find words; for he was full of wonder, though not afraid. But Heiri smiled again, as though he knew his thoughts, and said, "Ask me not that, for I may not tell; but only this I may tell you, that no man who has lived wisely and bravely need fear the passage; it is but a flying shadow on the path, like a cloud on the hill; and then he stands all at once in a fairer place; neither need he fear that he lays aside with the body the work and labour of life; for he works and labours more abundantly, and his labour is done in joy, without fear or heaviness; and for all such spirits is there high and true labour waiting. Therefore, Nefri, fear not; and though I cannot come to thee again—for thou shalt live and be blest—yet will I surely await thee yonder."

And then there came a darkness, and the form of Heiri seemed to fade gradually away, as though he were withdrawn along some secret path; and there went others with him. And Nefri slept.

And in the morning came Heiri's wife, and said to Nefri that Heiri had stood beside her in the night and comforted her; "and I know," she said, "that he lives and waits for me."

So the land had peace; and Nefri ruled wisely and did justice among the mountains by the sea.

Out of the Sea

It was about ten of the clock on a November morning in the little village of Blea-on-the-Sands. The hamlet was made up of some thirty houses, which clustered together on a low rising ground. The place was very poor, but some old merchant of bygone days had built in a pious mood a large church, which was now too great for the needs of the place; the nave had been unroofed in a heavy gale, and there was no money to repair it, so that it had fallen to decay, and the tower was joined to the choir by roofless walls. This was a sore trial to the old priest, Father Thomas, who had grown grey there; but he had no art in gathering money, which he asked for in a shamefaced way; and the vicarage was a poor one, hardly enough for the old man's needs. So the church lay desolate.

The village stood on what must once have been an island; the little river Reddy, which runs down to the sea, there forking into two channels on the landward side; towards the sea the ground was bare, full of sand-hills covered with a short grass. Towards the land was a small wood of gnarled trees, the boughs of which were all brushed smooth by the gales; looking landward there was the green flat, in which the river ran, rising into low hills; hardly a house was visible save one or two lonely farms; two or three church towers rose above the hills at a long distance away. Indeed Blea was much cut off from the world; there was a bridge over the stream on the west side, but over the other channel was no bridge, so that to fare eastward it was requisite to go in a boat. To seaward there were wide sands, when the tide was out; when it was in, it came up

182

nearly to the end of the village street. The people were mostly fish-ermen, but there were a few farmers and labourers; the boats of the fishermen lay to the east side of the village, near the river chan-nel which gave some draught of water; and the channel was marked out by big black stakes and posts that straggled out over the sands, like awkward leaning figures, to the sea's brim.

Father Thomas lived in a small and ancient brick house near the church, with a little garden of herbs attached. He was a kindly man, much worn by age and weather, with a wise heart, and he loved the quiet life with his small flock. This morning he had come out of his house to look abroad, before he settled down to the making of his sermon. He looked out to sea, and saw with a shadow of sadness the black outline of a wreck that had come ashore a week before, and over which the white waves were now breaking. The wind blew steadily from the north-east, and had a bitter poison-ous chill in it, which it doubtless drew from the fields of the upper ice. The day was dark and over, hung, not with cloud, but with a kind of dreary vapour that shut out the sun. Father Thomas shud-dered at the wind, and drew his patched cloak round him. As he did so, he saw three figures come up to the vicarage gate. It was not a common thing for him to have visitors in the morning, and he saw with surprise that they were old Master John Grimston, the richest man in the place, half farmer and half fisherman, a dark surly old man; his wife, Bridget, a timid and frightened woman, who found life with her harsh husband a difficult business, in spite of their wealth, which, for a place like Blea, was great; and their son Henry, a silly shambling man of forty, who was his father's butt. The three walked silently and heavily, as though they came on a sad errand.

Father Thomas went briskly down to meet them, and greeted them with his accustomed cheerfulness. "And what may I do for you?" he said. Old Master Grimston made a sort of gesture with his head as though his wife should speak; and she said in a low and somewhat husky voice, with a rapid utterance, "We have a matter, Father, we would ask you about—are you at leisure?" Father Thomas said, "Ay, I am ashamed to be not more busy! Let us go

within the house." They did so; and even in the little distance to
the door, the Father thought that his visitors behaved themselves
very strangely. They peered round from left to right, and once or
twice Master Grimston looked sharply behind them, as though they
were followed. They said nothing but "Ay" and "No" to the Father's
talk, and bore themselves like people with a sore fear on their
backs. Father Thomas made up his mind that it was some question
of money, for nothing else was wont to move Master Grimston's
mind. So he had them into his parlour and gave them seats, and
then there was a silence, while the two men continued to look furtively about them, and the goodwife sate with her eyes upon the
priest's face. Father Thomas knew not what to make of this, till
Master Grimston said harshly, "Come, wife, tell the tale and make
an end; we must not take up the Father's time."

"I hardly know how to say it, Father," said Bridget, "but a
strange and evil thing has befallen us; there is something come to
our house, and we know not what it is—but it brings a fear with it."
A sudden paleness came over her face, and she stopped, and the
three exchanged a glance in which terror was visibly written.
Master Grimston looked over his shoulder swiftly, and made as
though to speak, yet only swallowed in his throat; but Henry said
suddenly, in a loud and woeful voice: "It is an evil beast out of the
sea." And then there followed a dreadful silence, while Father Thomas felt a sudden fear leap up in his heart, at the contagion of the
fear that he saw written on the faces round him. But he said with
all the cheerfulness he could muster, "Come, friends, let us not
begin to talk of sea-beasts; we must have the whole tale Mistress
Grimston, I must hear the story—be content—nothing can touch
us here." The three seemed to draw a faint content from his words,
and Bridget began:—

"It was the day of the wreck, Father. John was up betimes, before the dawn; he walked out early to the sands, and Henry with
him—and they were the first to see the wreck—was not that it?" At
these words the father and son seemed to exchange a very swift
and secret look, and both grew pale. "John told me there was a
wreck ashore, and they went presently and roused the rest of the

village; and all that day they were out, saving what could be saved. Two sailors were found, both dead and pitifully battered by the sea, and they were buried, as you know, Father, in the churchyard next day; John came back about dusk and Henry with him, and we sate down to our supper. John was telling me about the wreck, as we sate beside the fire, when Henry, who was sitting apart, rose up and cried out suddenly, 'What is that?'"

She paused for a moment, and Henry, who sate with face blanched, staring at his mother, said, "Ay, did I—it ran past me suddenly." "Yes, but what was it?" said Father Thomas trying to smile; "a dog or cat, methinks." "It was a beast," said Henry slowly, in a trembling voice— "a beast about the bigness of a goat. I never saw the like—yet I did not see it clear; I but felt the air blow, and caught a whiff of it—it was salt like the sea, but with a kind of dead smell behind." "Was that all you saw?" said Father Thomas; "belike you were tired and faint, and the air swam round you suddenly—I have known the like myself when weary."

"Nay, nay," said Henry, "this was not like that—it was a beast, sure enough."

"Ay, and we have seen it since," said Bridget. "At least I have not seen it clearly yet, but I have smelt its odour, and it turns me sick—but John and Henry have seen it often—sometimes it lies and seems to sleep, but it watches us; and again it is merry, and will leap in a corner—and John saw it skip upon the sands near the wreck—did you not, John?" At these words the two men again exchanged a glance, and then old Master Grimston, with a dreadful look in his face, in which great anger seemed to strive with fear, said "Nay, silly woman, it was not near the wreck, it was out to the east." "It matters little," said Father Thomas, who saw well enough this was no light matter. "I never heard the like of it. I will myself come down to your house with a holy book, and see if the thing will meet me. I know not what this is," he went on, "whether it is a vain terror that hath hold of you; but there be spirits of evil in the world, though much fettered by Christ and His Saints—we read of such in Holy Writ—and the sea, too, doubtless hath its monsters; and it may be that one hath wandered out of the waves, like a dog that hath strayed from his home. I dare not say, till I have met it face to face. But God gives no power to such things to hurt those who have a fair conscience."—And here he made a stop, and looked at the three; Bridget sate regarding him with a hope in her face; but the other two sate peering upon the ground; and the priest divined in some secret way that all was not well with them. "But I will come at once," he said rising, "and I will see if I can cast out or bind the thing, whatever it be—for I am in this place as a soldier of the Lord, to fight with works of darkness." He took a clasped book from a table, and lifted up his hat, saying, "Let us set forth." Then he said as they left the room, "Hath it appeared to-day?" "Yes, indeed," said Henry, "and it was ill content. It followed us as though it were angered." "Come," said Father Thomas turning upon him, "you speak thus of a thing, as you might speak of a dog—what is it like?" "Nay," said Henry, "I know not; I can never see it clearly; it is like a speck in the eye—it is never there when you look upon it— it glides away very secretly; it is most like a goat, I think. It seems to be horned, and hairy; but I have seen its eyes, and they were yellow, like a flame."

As he said these words Master Grimston went in haste to the door, and pulled it open as though to breathe the air. The others followed him and went out; but Master Grimston drew the priest aside, and said like a man in a mortal fear, "Look you, Father, all this is true—the thing is a devil—and why it abides with us I know not; but I cannot live so; and unless it be cast out it will slay me— but if money be of avail, I have it in abundance." "Nay," said Father Thomas, "let there be no talk of money—perchance if I can aid you, you may give of your gratitude to God." "Ay, ay," said the old man hurriedly, "that was what I meant—there is money in abundance for God, if he will but set me free."

So they walked very sadly together through the street. There were few folk about; the men and the children were all abroad—a woman or two came to the house doors, and wondered a little to see them pass so solemnly, as though they followed a body to the grave.

Master Grimston's house was the largest in the place. It had a walled garden before it, with a strong door set in the wall. The house stood back from the road, a dark front of brick with gables; behind it the garden sloped nearly to the sands, with wooden barns and warehouses. Master Grimston unlocked the door, and then it seemed that his terrors came over him, for he would have the priest enter first. Father Thomas, with a certain apprehension of which he was ashamed, walked quickly in, and looked about him. The herbage of the garden had mostly died down in the winter, and a tangle of sodden stalks lay over the beds. A flagged path edged with box led up to the house, which seemed to stare at them out of its dark windows with a sort of steady gaze. Master Grimston fastened the door behind them, and they went all together, keeping close one to another, up to the house, the door of which opened upon a big parlour or kitchen, sparely furnished, but very clean and comfortable. Some vessels of metal glittered on a rack. There were chairs, ranged round the open fireplace. There was no sound except that the wind buffeted in the chimney. It looked a quiet and homely place, and Father Thomas grew ashamed of his fears. "Now," said he in his firm voice, "though I am your guest here, I will appoint what shall be done. We will sit here together, and talk as cheerfully as we may, till we have dined. Then, if nothing appears to us,"—and he crossed himself— "I will go round the house, into every room, and see if we can track the thing to its lair: then I will abide with you till evensong; and then I will soon return, and lie here to-night. Even if the thing be wary, and dares not to meet the power of the Church in the day-time, perhaps it will venture out at night; and I will even try a fall with it. So come, good people, and be comforted."

So they sate together; and Father Thomas talked of many things, and told some old legends of saints; and they dined, though without much cheer; and still nothing appeared. Then, after dinner, Father Thomas would view the house. So he took his book up, and they went from room to room. On the ground floor there were several chambers not used, which they entered in turn, but saw nothing; on the upper floor was a large room where Master

Grimston and his wife slept; and a further room for Henry, and a guest-chamber in which the priest was to sleep if need was; and a room where a servant-maid slept. And now the day began to darken and to turn to evening, and Father Thomas felt a shadow grow in his mind. There came into his head a verse of Scripture about a spirit which found a house "empty, swept and garnished," and called his fellows to enter in.

At the end of the passage was a locked door; and Father Thomas said: "This is the last room—let us enter." "Nay, there is no need to do that," said Master Grimston in a kind of haste; "it leads nowhither—it is but a room of stores." "It were a pity to leave it unvisited," said the Father—and as he said the word, there came a kind of stirring from within. "A rat, doubtless," said the Father, striving with a sudden sense of fear; but the pale faces round him told another tale. "Come, Master Grimston, let us be done with this;" said Father Thomas decisively; "the hour of vespers draws nigh." So Master Grimston slowly drew out a key and unlocked the door, and Father Thomas marched in. It was a simple place enough. There were shelves on which various household matters lay, boxes and jars, with twine and cordage. On the ground stood chests. There were some clothes hanging on pegs, and in a corner was a heap of garments, piled up. On one of the chests stood a box of rough deal, and from the corner of it dripped water, which lay in a little pool on the floor. Master Grimston went hurriedly to the box and pushed it further to the wall. As he did so, a kind of sound came from Henry's lips. Father Thomas turned and looked at him; he stood pale and strength-less, his eyes fixed on the corner—at the same moment something dark and shapeless seemed to slip past the group, and there came to the nostrils of Father Thomas a strange sharp smell, as of the sea, only that there was a taint within it, like the smell of corruption.

They all turned and looked at Father Thomas together, as though seeking a comfort from his presence. He, hardly knowing what he did, and in the grasp of a terrible fear, fumbled with his book; and opening it, read the first words that his eye fell upon, which was the place where the Blessed Lord, beset with enemies, said that if He did but pray to His Father, He should send Him forthwith legions of angels to encompass Him. And the verse seemed to the priest so like a message sent instantly from heaven that he was not a little comforted.

But the thing, whatever the reason was, appeared to them no more at that time. Yet the thought of it lay very heavy on Father Thomas's heart. In truth he had not in the bottom of his mind believed that he would see it, but had trusted in his honest life and his sacred calling to protect him. He could hardly speak for some minutes,—moreover the horror of the thing was very great—and seeing him so grave, their terrors were increased, though there was a kind of miserable joy in their minds that some one, and he a man of high repute, should suffer with them.

Then Father Thomas, after a pause—they were now in the parlour—said, speaking very slowly, that they were in a sore affliction of Satan, and that they must withstand him with a good courage— "and look you," he added, turning with a great sternness to the three, "if there be any mortal sin upon your hearts, see that you confess it and be shriven speedily—for while such a thing lies upon the heart, so long hath Satan power to hurt—otherwise have no fear at all."

Then Father Thomas slipped out to the garden, and hearing the bell pulled for vespers, he went to the church, and the three would go with him, because they would not be left alone. So they went together; by this time the street was fuller, and the servant-maid had told tales, so that there was much talk in the place about what was going forward. None spoke with them as they went, but at every corner you might see one check another in talk, and a silence fall upon a group, so that they knew that their terrors were on every tongue. There was but a handful of worshippers in the church, which was dark, save for the light on Father Thomas' book. He read the holy service swiftly and courageously, but his face was very pale and grave in the light of the candle. When the vespers were over, and he had put off his robe, he said that he would go back to his house, and gather what he needed for the night, and that they should wait for him at the churchyard gate. So he strode off to his vicarage. But as he shut to the door, he saw a dark figure come running up the garden; he waited with a fear in his mind, but in a moment he saw that it was Henry, who came up breathless, and said that he must speak with the Father alone. Father Thomas knew that somewhat dark was to be told him. So he led Henry into the parlour and seated himself, and said, "Now, my son, speak boldly." So there was an instant's silence, and Henry slipped on to his knees.

Then in a moment Henry with a sob began to tell his tale. He said that on the day of the wreck his father had roused him very early in the dawn, and had told him to put on his clothes and come silently, for he thought there was a wreck ashore. His father carried a spade in his hand, he knew not then why. They went down to the tide, which was moving out very fast, and left but an inch or two of water on the sands. There was but a little light, but, when they had walked a little, they saw the black hull of a ship before them, on the edge of the deeper water, the waves driving over it; and then all at once they came upon the body of a man lying on his face on the sand. There was no sign of life in him, but he clasped a bag in his hand that was heavy, and the pocket of his coat was full to bulging; and there lay, moreover, some glittering things about him that seemed to be coins. They lifted the body up, and his father stripped the coat off from the man, and then bade Henry dig a hole in the sand, which he presently did, though the sand and water oozed fast into it. Then his father, who had been stooping down, gathering somewhat up from the sand, raised the body up, and laid it in the hole, and bade Henry cover it with the sand. And so he did till it was nearly hidden. Then came a horrible thing; the sand in the hole began to move and stir, and presently a hand was put out with clutching fingers; and Henry had dropped the spade, and said, "There is life in him," but his father seized the spade, and shovelled the sand into the hole with a kind of silent fury, and trampled it over and smoothed it down—and then he gathered up the coat and the bag, and handed Henry the spade. By this time the town was astir, and they saw, very faintly, a man run along the shore eastward; so, making a long circuit to the west, they returned; his father had put the spade away and taken the coat upstairs; and then he went out with Henry, and told all he could find that there was a wreck ashore.

The priest heard the story with a fierce shame and anger, and turning to Henry he said, "But why did you not resist your father, and save the poor sailor?" "I dared not," said Henry shuddering, "though I would have done so if I could; but my father has a power over me, and I am used to obey him." Then said the priest, "This is a dark matter. But you have told the story bravely, and now will I shrive you, my son." So he gave him shrift. Then he said to Henry, "And have you seen aught that would connect the beast that visits you with this thing?" "Ay, that I have," said Henry, "for I watched it with my father skip and leap in the water over the place where the man lies buried." Then the priest said, "Your father must tell me the tale too, and he must make submission to the law." "He will not," said Henry. "Then will I compel him," said the priest. "Not out of my mouth," said Henry, "or he will slay me too." And then the priest said that he was in a strait place, for he could not use the words of confession of one man to convict another of his sin. So he gathered his things in haste, and walked back to the church; but Henry went another way, saying "I made excuse to come away, and said I went elsewhere; but I fear my father much— he sees very deep; and I would not have him suspect me of having made confession."

Then the Father met the other two at the church gate; and they went down to the house in silence, the Father pondering heavily; and at the door Henry joined them, and it seemed to the Father that old Master Grimston regarded him not. So they entered the house in silence, and ate in silence, listening earnestly for any sound. And the Father looked oft on Master Grimston, who ate and drank and said nothing, never raising his eyes. But once the Father saw him laugh secretly to himself, so that the blood came cold in the Father's veins, and he could hardly contain himself from accusing him. Then the Father had them to prayers, and prayed earnestly against the evil, and that they should open their hearts to God, if he would show them why this misery came upon them.

Then they went to bed; and Henry asked that he might lie in the priest's room, which he willingly granted. And so the house was dark, and they made as though they would sleep; but the Father could not sleep, and he heard Henry weeping silently to himself like a little child.

But at last the Father slept—how long he knew not—and suddenly brake out of his sleep with a horror of darkness all about him, and knew that there was some evil thing abroad. So he looked upon the room. He heard Henry mutter heavily in his sleep as though there was a dark terror upon him; and then, in the light of the dying embers, the Father saw a thing rise upon the hearth, as though it had slept there, and woke to stretch itself. And then in the half-light it seemed softly to gambol and play; but whereas when an innocent beast does this in the simple joy of its heart, and seems a fond and pretty sight, the Father thought he had never seen so ugly a sight as the beast gambolling all by itself, as if it could not contain its own dreadful joy; it looked viler and more wicked every moment; then, too, there spread in the room the sharp scent of the sea, with the foul smell underneath it, that gave the Father a deadly sickness; he tried to pray, but no words would come, and he felt indeed that the evil was too strong for him. Presently the beast desisted from its play, and looking wickedly about it, came near to the Father's bed, and seemed to put up its hairy forelegs upon it; he could see its narrow and obscene eyes, which burned with a dull yellow light, and were fixed upon him. And now the Father thought that his end was near, for he could stir neither hand nor foot, and the sweat rained down his brow; but he made a mighty effort, and in a voice which shocked himself, so dry and husky and withal of so loud and screaming a tone it was, he said three holy words. The beast gave a great quiver of rage, but it dropped down on the floor, and in a moment was gone. Then Henry woke, and raising himself on his arm, said somewhat; but there broke out in the house a great outcry and the stamping of feet, which seemed very fearful in the silence of the night. The priest leapt out of his bed all dizzy, and made a light, and ran to the door, and went out, crying whatever words came to his head. The door of Master Grimston's room was open, and a strange and strangling sound came forth; the Father made his way in, and found Master Grimston lying upon the floor, his wife bending over him; he lay still, breathing pitifully, and every now and then a shudder ran through him. In the room there seemed a strange and shadowy tumult going forward; but the Father saw that no time could be lost, and kneeling down beside Master Grimston, he prayed with all his might.

Presently Master Grimston ceased to struggle and lay still, like a man who had come out of a sore conflict. Then he opened his eyes, and the Father stopped his prayers, and looking very hard at him he said, "My son, the time is very short—give God the glory." Then Master Grimston, rolling his haggard eyes upon the group, twice strove to speak and could not; but the third time the Father, bending down his head, heard him say in a thin voice, that seemed to float from a long way off, "I slew him . . . my sin." Then the Father swiftly gave him shrift, and as he said the last word, Master Grimston's head fell over on the side, and the Father said, "He is gone." And Bridget broke out into a terrible cry, and fell upon Henry's neck, who had entered unseen.

Then the Father bade him lead her away, and put the poor body on the bed; as he did so he noticed that the face of the dead man was strangely bruised and battered, as though it had been stamped upon by the hoofs of some beast. Then Father Thomas knelt, and prayed until the light came filtering in through the shutters; and the cocks crowed in the village, and presently it was day. But that night the Father learnt strange secrets, and something of the dark purposes of God was revealed to him.

In the morning there came one to find the priest, and told him that another body had been thrown up on the shore, which was strangely smeared with sand, as though it had been rolled over and over in it; and the Father took order for its burial.

Then the priest had long talk with Bridget and Henry. He found them sitting together, and she held her son's hand and smoothed his hair, as though he had been a little child; and Henry sobbed and wept, but Bridget was very calm. "He hath told me all," she said, "and we have decided that he shall do whatever you bid him; must he be given to justice?" and she looked at the priest very pitifully. "Nay, nay," said the priest. "I hold not Henry to account for the death of the man; it was his father's sin, who hath made heavy atonement—the secret shall be buried in our hearts."

Then Bridget told him how she had waked suddenly out of her sleep, and heard her husband cry out; and that then followed a dreadful kind of struggling, with the scent of the sea over all; and then he had all at once fallen to the ground and she had gone to him—and that then the priest had come.

Then Father Thomas said with tears that God had shown them deep things and visited them very strangely; and they would henceforth live humbly in his sight, showing mercy.

Then lastly he went with Henry to the store-room; and there, in the box that had dripped with water, lay the coat of the dead man, full of money, and the bag of money too; and Henry would have cast it back into the sea, but the priest said that this might not be, but that it should be bestowed plentifully upon shipwrecked mariners unless the heirs should be found. But the ship appeared to be a foreign ship, and no search ever revealed whence the money had come, save that it seemed to have been violently come by.

Master Grimston was found to have left much wealth. But Bridget would sell the house and the land, and it mostly went to rebuild the church to God's glory. Then Bridget and Henry removed to the vicarage and served Father Thomas faithfully, and they guarded their secret. And beside the nave is a little high turret built, where burns a lamp in a lantern at the top, to give light to those at sea.

Now the beast troubled those of whom I write no more; but it is easier to raise up evil than to lay it; and there are those that say that to this day a man or a woman with an evil thought in their hearts may see on a certain evening in November, at the ebb of the tide, a goatlike thing wade in the water, snuffing at the sand, as though it sought but found not. But of this I know nothing.

PAUL THE MINSTREL

I

The old House of Heritage stood just below the downs, in the few meadows that were all that was left of a great estate. The house itself was of stone, very firmly and gravely built; and roofed with thin slabs of stone, small at the roof-ridge, and increasing in size towards the eaves. Inside, there were a few low panelled rooms opening on a large central hall; there was little furniture, and that of a sturdy and solid kind—but the house needed nothing else, and had all the beauty that came of a simple austerity.

Old Mistress Alison, who abode there, was aged and poor. She had but one house-servant, a serious and honest maid, whose only pride was to keep the place sweet, and save her mistress from all care. But Mistress Alison was not to be dismayed by poverty; she was a tranquil and loving woman, who had never married; but who, as if to compensate her for the absence of nearer ties, had a simple and wholesome love of all created things. She was infirm now, but was quite content, when it was fine, to sit for long hours idle for very love, and look about her with a peaceful and smiling air; she prayed much, or rather held a sweet converse in her heart with God; she thought little of her latter end, which she knew could not be long delayed, but was content to leave it in the hands of the Father, sure that He, who had made the world so beautiful and so full of love, would comfort her when she came to enter in at the dark gate.

There was also an old and silent man who looked after the cattle
and the few hens that the household kept; at the back of the house
was a thatched timbered grange, where he laid his tools; but he
spent his time mostly in the garden, which sloped down to the fish-
pond, and was all bordered with box; here was a pleasant homely
scent, on hot days, of the good herbs that shed their rich smell in
the sun; and here the flies, that sate in the leaves, would buzz at
the sound of a footfall, and then be still again, cleaning their hands
together in their busy manner.

The only other member of the quiet household was the boy Paul,
who was distantly akin to Mistress Alison. He had neither father
nor mother, and had lived at Heritage all of his life that he could
remember; he was a slender, serious boy, with delicate features,
and large grey eyes that looked as if they held a secret; but if they
had, it was a secret of his forefathers; for the boy had led a most
quiet and innocent life; he had been taught to read in a fashion,
but he had no schooling; sometimes a neighbouring goodwife would
say to Mistress Alison that the boy should be sent to school, and
Mistress Alison would open her peaceful eyes and say, "Nay, Paul
is not like other boys—he would get all the hurt and none of the
good of school; when there is work for him he will do it—but I am
not for making all toil alike. Paul shall grow up like the lilies of the
field. God made not all things to be busy." And the goodwife would
shake her head and wonder; for it was not easy to answer Mistress
Alison, who indeed was often right in the end.

So Paul grew up as he would; sometimes he would help the old
gardener, when there was work to be done; for he loved to serve
others, and was content with toil if it was sweetened with love; but
often he rambled by himself for hours together; he cared little for
company, because the earth was to him full of wonder and of sweet
sights and sounds. He loved to climb the down, and lie feasting his
eyes on the rich plain, spread out like a map; the farms in their
closes, the villages from which went up the smoke at evening, the
distant blue hills, like the hills of heaven, the winding river, and
the lake that lay in the winter twilight like a shield of silver. He
loved to see the sun flash on the windows of the houses so distant

that they could not themselves be seen, but only sparkled like stars. He loved to loiter on the edge of the steep hanging woods in summer, to listen to the humming of the flies deep in the brake, and to catch a sight of lonely flowers; he loved the scent of the wind blowing softly out of the copse, and he wondered what the trees said to each other, when they stood still and happy in the heat of midday. He loved, too, the silent night, full of stars, when the wood that topped the hill lay black against the sky. The whole world seemed to him to be full of a mysterious and beautiful life of which he could never quite catch the secret; these innocent flowers, these dreaming trees seemed, as it were, to hold him smiling at arm's length, while they guarded their joy from him. The birds and the beasts seemed to him to have less of this quiet joy, for they were fearful and careful, working hard to find a living, and dreading the sight of man; but sometimes in the fragrant eventide the nightingale would say a little of what was in her heart. "Yes," Paul would say to himself, "it is like that."

One other chief delight the boy had; he knew the magic of sound, which spoke to his heart in a way that it speaks to but few; the sounds of the earth gave up their sweets to him; the musical fluting of owls, the liquid notes of the cuckoo, the thin pipe of dancing flies, the mournful creaking of the cider-press, the horn of the oxherd wound far off on the hill, the tinkling of sheep-bells—of all these he knew the notes; and not only these, but the rhythmical swing of the scythes sweeping through the grass, the flails heard through the hot air from the barn, the clinking of the anvil in the village forge, the bubble of the stream through the weir—all these had a tale to tell him. Sometimes, for days together, he would hum to himself a few notes that pleased him by their sweet cadence, and he would string together some simple words to them, and sing them to himself with gentle content. The song of the reapers on the upland, or the rude chanting in the little church had a magical charm for him; and Mistress Alison would hear the boy, in his room overhead, singing softly to himself for very gladness of heart, like a little bird of the dawn, or tapping out some tripping beat of time; when she would wonder and speak to God of what was in her heart.

As Paul grew older—he was now about sixteen—a change came
slowly over his mind; he began to have moods of a silent discontent, a longing for something far away, a desire of he knew not
what. His old dreams began to fade, though they visited him from
time to time; but he began to care less for the silent beautiful life
of the earth, and to take more thought of men. He had never felt
much about himself before; but one day, lying beside a woodland
pool at the feet of the down, he caught a sight of his own face; and
when he smiled at it, it seemed to smile back at him; he began to
wonder what the world was like, and what all the busy people that
lived therein said and thought; he began to wish to have a friend,
that he might tell him what was in his heart—and yet he knew not
what it was that he would say. He began, too, to wonder how people
regarded him—the people who had before been but to him a distant
part of the shows of the world. Once he came in upon Mistress
Alison, who sate talking with a gossip of hers; when he entered,
there was a sudden silence, and a glance passed between the two;
and Paul divined that they had been speaking of himself, and desired to know what they had said.

One day the old gardener, in a more talkative mood than was
his wont, told him a tale of one who had visited the Wishing Well
that lay a few miles away, and, praying for riches, had found the
next day, in digging, an old urn of pottery, full of ancient coins.
Paul was very urgent to know about the well, and the old man told
him that it must be visited at noonday and alone. That he that
would have his wish must throw a gift into the water, and drink of
the well, and then, turning to the sun, must wish his wish aloud.
Paul asked him many more questions, but the old man would say
no more. So Paul determined that he would visit the place for himself.

The next day he set off. He took with him one of his few pos-
sessions, a little silver coin that a parson hard by had given him.
He went his way quickly among the pleasant fields, making towards
the great bulk of Blackdown beacon, where the hills swelled up
into a steep bluff, with a white road, cut in the chalk, winding
steeply up their green smooth sides. It was a fresh morning with a

few white clouds racing merrily overhead, the shadows of which fell every now and then upon the down and ran swiftly over it, like a flood of shade leaping down the sides. There were few people to be seen anywhere; the fields were full of grass, with large daisies and high red sorrel. By midday he was beneath the front of Blackdown, and here he asked at a cottage of a good-natured woman, that was bustling in and out, the way to the well. She answered him very kindly and described the path—it was not many yards away—and then asked where he came from, saying briskly, "And what would you wish for? I should have thought you had all you could desire." "Why, I hardly know;" said Paul smiling. "It seems that I desire a thousand things, and can scarcely give a name to one." "That is ever the way," said the woman, "but the day will come when you will be content with one." Paul did not understand what she meant, but thanked her and went on his way; and wondered that she stood so long looking after him.

At last he came to the spring. It was a pool in a field, ringed round by alders. Paul thought he had never seen a fairer place. There grew a number of great kingcups round the brim, with their flowers like glistening gold, and with cool thick stalks and fresh leaves. Inside the ring of flowers the pool looked strangely deep and black; but looking into it you could see the sand leaping at the bottom in three or four cones; and to the left the water bubbled away in a channel covered with water-plants. Paul could see that there was an abundance of little things at the bottom, half covered with sand—coins, flowers, even little jars—which he knew to be the gifts of wishers. So he flung his own coin in the pool, and saw it slide hither and thither, glancing in the light, till it settled at the dark bottom. Then he dipped and drank, turned to the sun, and closing his eyes, said out loud, "Give me what I desire." And this he repeated three times, to be sure that he was heard. Then he opened his eyes again, and for a moment the place looked different, with a strange grey light. But there was no answer to his prayer in heaven or earth, and the very sky seemed to wear a quiet smile.

Paul waited a little, half expecting some answer; but presently he turned his back upon the pool and walked slowly away; the down lay on one side of him, looking solemn and dark over the trees which grew very plentifully; Paul thought that he would like to walk upon the down; so he went up a little leafy lane that seemed to lead to it. Suddenly, as he passed a small thicket, a voice hailed him; it was a rich and cheerful voice, and it came from under the trees. He turned in the direction of the voice, which seemed to be but a few yards off, and saw, sitting on a green bank under the shade, two figures. One was a man of middle age, dressed lightly as though for travelling, and Paul thought somewhat fantastically. His hat had a flower stuck in the band. But Paul thought little of the dress, because the face of the man attracted him; he was sun-burnt and strong-looking, and Paul at first thought he must be a soldier; he had a short beard, and his hair was grown rather long; his face was deeply lined, but there was something wonderfully good-natured, friendly, and kind about his whole expression. He was smiling, and his smile showed small white teeth; and Paul felt in a moment that he could trust him, and that the man was friendly disposed to himself and all the world; friendly, not in a servile way, as one who wished to please, but in a sort of prodigal, royal way, as one who had great gifts to bestow, and was liberal of them, and looked to be made welcome. The other figure was that of a boy rather older than himself, with a merry ugly face, who in looking at Paul, seemed yet to keep a sidelong and deferential glance at the older man, as though admiring him, and desiring to do as he did in all things.

"Where go you, pretty boy, alone in the noontide?" said the man.

Paul stopped and listened, and for a moment could not answer. Then he said, "I am going to the down, sir, and I have been"—he hesitated for a moment— "I have been to the Wishing Well."

"The Wishing Well?" said the man gravely. "I did not know there was one hereabouts. I thought that every one in this happy valley had been too well content—and what did you wish for, if I may ask?"

Paul was silent and grew red; and then he said, "Oh, just for my heart's desire."

"That is either a very cautious or a very beautiful answer," said the man, "and it gives me a lesson in manners; but will you not sit a little with us in the shade?—and you shall hear a concert of music such as I dare say you shall hardly hear out of France or Italy. Do you practise music, child, the divine gift?"

"I love it a little," said Paul, "but I have no skill."

"Yet you look to me like one who might have skill," said the man; "you have the air of it—you look as though you listened, and as though you dreamed pleasant dreams. But, Jack," he said, turning to his boy, "what shall we give our friend?—shall he have the 'Song of the Rose' first?"

The boy at this word drew a little metal pipe out of his doublet, and put it to his lips; and the man reached out his hand and took up a small lute which lay on the bank beside him. He held up a warning finger to the boy. "Remember," he said, "that you come in at the fifth chord, together with the voice—not before." He struck four simple chords on the lute, very gently, and with a sort of dainty preciseness; and then at the same moment the little pipe and his own voice began; the pipe played a simple descant in quicker time, with two notes to each note of the song, and the man in a brisk and simple way, as it were at the edge of his lips, sang a very sweet little country song, in a quiet homely measure.

There seemed to Paul to be nothing short of magic about it. There was a beautiful restraint about the voice, which gave him a sense both of power and feeling held back; but it brought before him a sudden picture of a garden, and the sweet life of the flowers and little trees, taking what came, sunshine and rain, and just living and smiling, breathing fragrant breath from morning to night, and sleeping a light sleep till they should waken to another tranquil day. He listened as if spellbound. There were but three verses, and though he could not remember the words, it seemed as though the rose spoke and told her dreams.

He could have listened for ever; but the voice made a sudden stop, not prolonging the last note, but keeping very closely to the time; the pipe played a little run, like an echo of the song, the man struck a brisk chord on the lute—and all was over. "Bravely played,

Jack!" said the singer; "no musician could have played it better. You remembered what I told you, to keep each note separate, and have no gliding. This song must trip from beginning to end, like a brisk bird that hops on the grass." Then he turned to Paul and, with a smile, said, "Reverend sir, how does my song please you?"

"I never heard anything more beautiful," said Paul simply. "I cannot say it, but it was like a door opened;" and he looked at the minstrel with intent eyes;— "may I hear it again?" "Boy," said the singer gravely, "I had rather have such a look as you gave me during the song than a golden crown. You will not understand what I say, but you paid me the homage of the pure heart, the best reward that the minstrel desires."

Then he conferred with the other boy in a low tone, and struck a very sad yet strong chord upon his lute; and then, with a grave face, he sang what to Paul seemed like a dirge for a dead hero who had done with mortal things, and whose death seemed more a triumph than a sorrow. When he had sung the first verse, the pipe came softly and sadly in, like the voice of grief that could not be controlled, the weeping of those on whom lay the shadow of loss. To Paul, in a dim way,—for he was but a child—the song seemed the voice of the world, lamenting its noblest, yet triumphing in their greatness, and desirous to follow in their steps. It brought before him all the natural sorrows of death, the call to quit the sweet and pleasant things of the world—a call that could not be denied, and that was in itself indeed stronger and even sweeter than the delights which it bade its listeners leave. And Paul seemed to walk in some stately procession of men far off and ancient, who followed a great king to the grave, and whose hearts were too full of wonder to think yet what they had lost. It was an uplifting sadness; and when the sterner strain came to an end, Paul said very quietly, putting into words the thoughts of his full heart, "I did not think that death could be so beautiful." And the minstrel smiled, but Paul saw that his eyes were full of tears.

Then all at once the minstrel struck the lute swiftly and largely, and sang a song of those that march to victory, not elated nor excited, but strong to dare and to do; and Paul felt his heart beat within him, and he longed to be of the company. After he had sung this to an end, there was a silence, and the minstrel said to Paul, yet as though half speaking to himself, "There, my son, I have given you a specimen of my art; and I think from your look that you might be of the number of those that make these rich jewels that men call songs; and should you try to do so, be mindful of these two things: let them be perfect first. You will make many that are not perfect. In some the soul will be wanting; in others the body, in a manner of speaking, will be amiss; for they are living things, these songs, and he that makes them is a kind of god. Well, if you cannot mend one, throw it aside and think no more of it. Do not save it because it has some gracious touch, for in this are the masters of the craft different from the mere makers of songs. The master will have nothing but what is perfect within and without, while the lesser craftsman will save a poor song for the sake of a fine line or phrase.

"And next, you must do it for the love of your art, and not for the praise it wins you. That is a poisoned wine, of which if you drink, you will never know the pure and high tranquillity of spirit that befits a master. The master may be discouraged and troubled oft, but he must have in his soul a blessed peace, and know the worth and beauty of what he does; for there is nothing nobler than to make beautiful things, and to enlighten the generous heart. Fighting is a fair trade, and though it is noble in much, yet its end is to destroy; but the master of song mars nought, but makes joy;— and that is the end of my sermon for the time. And now," he added briskly, "I must be going, for I have far to fare; but I shall pass by this way again, and shall inquire of your welfare; tell me your name and where you live." So Paul told him, and then added timidly enough that he would fain know how to begin to practise his art. "Silence!" said the minstrel, rather fiercely; "that is an evil and timorous thought. If you are worthy, you will find the way." And so in the hot afternoon he said farewell, and walked lightly off. And Paul stood in wonder and hope, and saw the two figures leave the flat, take to the down, and wind up the steep road, ever grow-ing smaller, till they topped the ridge, where they seemed to stand a moment larger than human; and presently they were lost from view.

So Paul made his way home; and when he pushed the gate of Heritage open, he wondered to think that he could recollect nothing of the road he had traversed. He went up to the house and entered the hall. There sate Mistress Alison, reading in a little book. She closed it as he came in, and looked at him with a smile. Paul went up to her and said, "Mother" (so he was used to call her), "I have heard songs to-day such as I never dreamt of, and I pray you to let me learn the art of making music; I must be a minstrel." "'Must' is a grave word, dear heart," said Mistress Alison, looking somewhat serious; "but let me hear your story first." So Paul told of his meeting with the minstrel. Mistress Alison sate musing a long time, smiling when she met Paul's eye, till he said at last, "Will you not speak, mother?" "I know," she said at last, "whom you have met, dear child—that is Mark, the great minstrel. He travels about the land, for he is a restless man, though the king himself would have him dwell in his court, and make music for him. Yet I have looked for this day, though it has come when I did not expect it. And now I must tell you a story, Paul, in my turn. Many years ago there was a boy like you, and he loved music too and the making of songs, and he grew to great skill therein. But it was at last his ruin, for he got to love riotous company and feasting too well; and so his skill forsook him, as it does those that live not cleanly and nobly. And he married a young wife, having won her by his songs, and a child was born to them. But the minstrel fell sick and presently died, and his last prayer was that his son might not know the temptation of song. And his wife lingered a little, but she soon pined away, for her heart was broken within her; and she too died. And now, Paul, listen, for the truth must be told—you are that child, the son of sorrow and tears. And here you have lived with me all your life; but because the tale was a sad one, I have forborne to tell it you. I have waited and wondered to see whether the gift of the father is given to the son; and sometimes I have thought it might be yours, and sometimes I have doubted. And now, child, we will talk of this no more to-day, for it is ill to decide in haste. Think well over what I have said, and see if it makes a difference in your wishes. I have told you all the tale."

Now the story that Mistress Alison had told him dwelt very much in Paul's mind that night; but it seemed to him strange and far off, and he did not doubt what the end should be. It was as though the sight of the minstrel, his songs and words, had opened a window in his mind, and that he saw out of it a strange and enchanted country, of woods and streams, with a light of evening over it, bounded by far-off hills, all blue and faint, among which some beautiful thing was hidden for him to find; it seemed to call him softly to come; the trees smiled upon him, the voice of the streams bade him make haste—it all waited for him, like a country waiting for its lord to come and take possession.

Then it seemed to him that his soul slipped like a bird from the window, and rising in the air over that magical land, beat its wings softly in the pale heaven; and then like a dove that knows, by some inborn mysterious art, which way its path lies, his spirit paused upon the breeze, and then sailed out across the tree-tops. Whither? Paul knew not. And so at last he slipped into a quiet sleep.

He woke in the morning all of a sudden, with a kind of tranquil joy and purpose; and when he was dressed, and gone into the hall, he found Mistress Alison sitting in her chair beside the table laid for their meal. She was silent and looked troubled, and Paul went up softly to her, and kissed her and said, "I have chosen." She did not need to ask him what he had chosen, but put her arm about him and said, "Then, dear Paul, be content—and we will have one more day together, the last of the old days; and to-morrow shall the new life begin."

So the two passed a long and quiet day together. For to the wise and loving-hearted woman this was the last of sweet days, and her soul went out to the past with a great hunger of love; but she stilled it as was her wont, saying to herself that this dear passage of life had hitherto only been like the clear trickling of a woodland spring, while the love of the Father's heart was as it were a great river of love marching softly to a wide sea, on which river the very world itself floated like a flower-bloom between widening banks.

And indeed if any had watched them that day, it would have seemed that she was the serener; for the thought of the life that lay before him worked like wine in the heart of Paul, and he could only by an effort bring himself back to loving looks and offices of tenderness. They spent the whole day together, for the most part in a peaceful silence; and at last the sun went down, and a cool breeze came up out of the west, laden with scent from miles and miles of grass and flowers, which seemed to bear with it the fragrant breath of myriads of sweet living things.

Then they ate together what was the last meal they were to take thus alone. And at last Mistress Alison would have Paul go to rest. And so she took his hand in hers, and said, "Dear child, the good years are over now; but you will not forget them; only lean upon the Father, for He is very strong; and remember that though the voice of melody is sweet, yet the loving heart is deeper yet." And then Paul suddenly broke out into a passion of weeping, and kissed his old friend on hand and cheek and lips; and then he burst away, ashamed, if the truth be told, that his love was not deeper than he found it to be.

He slept a light sleep that night, his head pillowed on his hand, with many strange dreams ranging through his head. Among other fancies, some sweet, some dark, he heard a delicate passage of melody played, it seemed to him, by three silver-sounding flutes, so delicate that he could hardly contain himself for gladness; but among his sadder dreams was one of a little man habited like a minstrel who played an ugly enchanted kind of melody on a stringed lute, and smiled a treacherous smile at him; Paul woke in a sort of fever of the spirit; and rising from his bed, felt the floor cool to his feet, and drew his curtain aside; in a tender radiance of dawn he saw the barn, deep in shadow, in the little garden; and over them a little wood-end that he knew well by day—a simple place enough—but now it had a sort of magical dreaming air; the mist lay softly about it like the breath of sleep; and the trees, stretching wistfully their leafy arms, seemed to him to be full of silent prayer, or to be hiding within them some divine secret that might not be shown to mortal eyes. He looked long at this; and presently went back to his bed, and shivered in a delicious warmth, while outside, very gradually, came the peaceful stir of morning. A bird or two fluted drowsily in the bushes; then another further away would join his slender song; a cock crew cheerily in a distant grange, and soon it was broad day. Presently the house began to be softly astir; and the faint fragrance of an early kindled fire of wood stole into the room. Then worn out by his long vigil he fell asleep again; and soon waking, knew it to be later than was his wont, and dressed with haste. He came down, and heard voices in the hall; he went in, and there saw Mistress Alison in her chair; and on the hearth, talking gaily and cheerily, stood Mark the minstrel. They made a pause when he came in. Mark extended his hand, which Paul took with a kind of reverence. Then Mistress Alison, with her sweet old smile, said to Paul, "So you made a pilgrimage to the Well of the Heart's Desire, dear Paul? Well, you have your wish, and very soon; for here is a master for you, if you will serve him." "Not a light service, Paul," said Mark gravely, "but a true one. I can take you with me when you may go, for my boy Jack is fallen sick with a stroke of the sun, and must bide at home awhile." They looked at Paul, to see what he would say. "Oh, I will go gladly," he said, "if I may." And then he felt he had not spoken lovingly; so he kissed Mistress Alison, who smiled, but somewhat sadly, and said, "Yes, Paul—I understand."

So when the meal was over, Paul's small baggage was made ready, and he kissed Mistress Alison—and then she said to Mark with a sudden look, "You will take care of him?" "Oh, he shall be safe with me," said Mark, "and if he be apt and faithful, he shall learn his trade, as few can learn it." And then Paul said his good-bye, and walked away with Mark; and his heart was so full of gladness that he stepped out lightly and blithely, and hardly looked back. But at the turn of the road he stopped, while Mark seemed to consider him gravely. The three that were to abide, Mistress Alison, and the maid, and the old gardener, stood at the door and waved their hands; the old house seemed to look fondly out of its windows at him, as though it had a heart; and the very trees seemed to wave him a soft farewell. Paul waved his hand too, and a tear came into his eyes; but he was eager to be gone; and indeed, in his heart, he felt almost jealous of even the gentle grasp of his home upon his heart. And so Mark and Paul set out for the south.

II

Of the life that Paul lived with Mark I must not here tell; but before he grew to full manhood he had learned his art well. Mark was a strict master, but not impatient. The only thing that angered him was carelessness or listlessness; and Paul was an apt and untiring pupil, and learnt so easily and deftly that Mark was often astonished. "How did you learn that?" he said one day suddenly to Paul when the boy was practising on the lute, and played a strange soft cadence, of a kind that Mark had never heard. The boy was startled by the question, for he had not thought that Mark was listening to him. He looked up with a blush and turned his eyes on Mark. "Is it not right?" he said. "I did not learn it; it comes from somewhere in my mind."

Paul learnt to play several instruments, both wind and string. Sometimes he loved one sort the best, sometimes the other. The wind instruments of wood had to him a kind of soft magic, like the voice of a gentle spirit, a spirit that dwelt in lonely unvisited places, and communed more with things of earth than the hearts of men. In the flutes and bassoons seemed to him to dwell the voices of airs that murmured in the thickets, the soft gliding of streams, the crooning of serene birds, the peace of noonday, the welling of clear springs, the beauty of little waves, the bright thoughts of stars. Sometimes in certain modes, they could be sad, but it was the sadness of lonely homeless things, old dreaming spirits of wind and wave, not the sadness of such things as had known love and lost what they had loved, but the melancholy of such forlorn beings as by their nature were shut out from the love that dwells about the firelit hearth and the old roofs of homesteads. It was the sadness of the wind that wails in desolate places, knowing that it is lonely, but not knowing what it desires; or the soft sighing of trees that murmur all together in a forest, dreaming each its own dream, but with no thought of comradeship or desire.

The metal instruments, out of which the cunning breath could draw bright music, seemed to him soulless too in a sort, but shrill and enlivening. These clarions and trumpets spoke to him of brisk morning winds, or the cold sharp plunge of green waves that leap in triumph upon rocks. To such sounds he fancied warriors marching out at morning, with the joy of fight in their hearts, meaning to deal great blows, to slay and be slain, and hardly thinking of what would come after, so sharp and swift an eagerness of spirit held them; but these instruments he loved less.

Best of all he loved the resounding strings that could be twanged by the quill, or swept into a heavenly melody by the finger-tips, or throb beneath the strongly-drawn bow. In all of these lay the secrets of the heart; in these Paul heard speak the bright dreams of the child, the vague hopes of growing boy or girl, the passionate desires of love, the silent loyalty of equal friendship, the dreariness of the dejected spirit, whose hopes have set like the sun smouldering to his fall, the rebellious grief of the heart that loses what it loves, the darkening fears that begin to roll about the ageing mind, like clouds that weep on mountain tops, and the despair of sinners, finding the evil too strong.

Best of all it was when all these instruments could conspire together to weave a sudden dream of beauty that seemed to guard a secret. What was the secret? It seemed so near to Paul sometimes, as if he were like a man very near the edge of some mountain from which he may peep into an unknown valley. Sometimes it was far away. But it was there, he doubted not, though it hid itself. It was like a dance of fairies in a forest glade, which a man could half discern through the screening leaves; but, when he gains the place, he sees nothing but tall flowers with drooping bells, bushes set with buds, large-leaved herbs, all with a silent, secret, smiling air, as though they said, "We have seen, we could tell."

Paul seemed very near this baffling secret at times; in the dewy silence of mornings, just before the sun comes up, when familiar woods and trees stand in a sort of musing happiness; at night when

the sky is thickly sown with stars, or when the moon rises in a soft
hush and silvers the sleeping pool; or when the sun goes down in a
rich pomp, trailing a great glow of splendour with him among
cloudy islands, all flushed with fiery red. When the sun withdrew
himself thus, flying and flaring to the west, behind the boughs of
leafless trees, what was the hidden secret presence that stood there
as it were finger on lip, inviting yet denying? Paul knew within
himself that if he could but say or sing this, the world would never
forget. But he could not yet.

Then, too, Paul learned the magic of words, the melodious ac-
cent of letters, sometimes so sweet, sometimes so harsh; then the
growing phrase, the word that beckons as it were other words to
join it trippingly; the thought that draws the blood to the brain,
and sets the heart beating swiftly—he learned the words that sound
like far-off bells, or that wake a gentle echo in the spirit, the words
that burn into the heart, and make the hearer ashamed of all that
is hard and low. But he learned, too, that the craftsman in words
must not build up his song word by word, as a man fetches bricks
to make a wall; but that he must see the whole thought clear first,
in a kind of divine flash, so that when he turns for words to write
it, he finds them piled to his hand.

All these things Paul learnt, and day by day he suffered all the
sweet surprises and joys of art. There were days that were not so,
when the strings jangled aimlessly, and seemed to have no soul in
them; days when it appeared that the cloud could not lift, as though
light and music together were dead in the world—but these days
were few; and Paul growing active and strong, caring little what
he ate and drank, tasting no wine, because it fevered him at first,
and then left him ill at ease, knowing no evil or luxurious thoughts,
sleeping lightly and hardly, found his spirits very pure and plentiful; or if he was sad, it was a clear sadness that had something
beautiful within it, and dwelt not on any past grossness of his own,
but upon the thought that all beautiful things can but live for a
time, and must then be laid away in the darkness and in the cold.

So Paul grew up knowing neither friendship nor love, only
stirred at the sight of a beautiful face, a shapely hand, or a slender

form; by a grateful wonder for what was so fair; untainted by any desire to master it, or make it his own; living only for his art, and with a sort of blind devotion to Mark, whom he soon excelled, though he knew it not. Mark once said to him, when Paul had made a song of some old forgotten sorrow, "How do you know all this, boy? You have not suffered, you have not lived!" "Oh," said Paul gaily, knowing it to be praise, "my heart tells me it is so."

Paul, too, as he grew to manhood, found himself with a voice that was not loud, but true—a voice that thrilled those who heard it through and through; but it seemed strange that he felt not what he made other men feel; rather his music was like a still pool that can reflect all that is above it, the sombre tree, the birds that fly over, the starry silence of the night, the angry redness of the dawn.

It was on one of his journeys with Mark that the news of Mistress Alison's death reached him. Mark told him very carefully and tenderly, and while he repeated the three or four broken words in which Mistress Alison had tried to send a last message to Paul—for the end had come very suddenly—Mark himself found his voice falter, and his eyes fill with tears. Paul had, at that sight, cried a little; but his life at the House of Heritage seemed to have faded swiftly out of his thoughts; he was living very intently in the present, scaling, as it were, day by day, with earnest effort, the steep ladder of song. He thought a little upon Mistress Alison, and on all her love and goodness: but it was with a tranquil sorrow, and not with the grief and pain of loss. Mark was very gentle with him for awhile; and this indeed did shame Paul a little, to find himself being used so lovingly for a sorrow which he was hardly feeling. But he said to himself that sorrow must come unbidden, and that it was no sorrow that was made with labour and intention. He was a little angered with himself for his dulness—but then song was so beautiful, that he could think of nothing else; he was dazzled.

A little while after, Mark asked him whether, as they were near at hand, he would turn aside to see Mistress Alison's grave. And Paul said, "No; I would rather feel it were all as it used to be!"— and then seeing that Mark looked surprised and almost grieved,

Paul, with the gentle hypocrisy of childhood, said, "I cannot bear it yet," which made Mark silent, and he said no more, but used Paul more gently than ever.

One day Mark said to him, very gravely, as if he had long been pondering the matter, "It is time for me to take another pupil, Paul. I have taught you all I know; indeed you have learned far more than I can teach." Then he told him that he had arranged all things meetly. That there was a certain Duke who lacked a minstrel, and that Paul should go and abide with him. That he should have his room at the castle, and should be held in great honour, making music only when he would. And then Mark would have added some words of love, for he loved Paul as a son. But Paul seemed to have no hunger in his heart, no thought of the days they had spent together; so Mark said them not. But he added very gently, "And one thing, Paul, I must tell you. You will be a great master—indeed you are so already—and I can tell you nothing about the art that you do not know. But one thing I will tell you—that you have a human heart within you that is not yet awake: and when it awakes, it will be very strong; so that a great combat, I think, lies before you. See that it overcome you not!" And Paul said wondering, "Oh, I have a heart, but it is altogether given to song." And so Mark was silent.

Then Paul went to the Duke's Castle of Wresting and abode with him year after year. Here, too, he made no friend; he was gracious with all, and of a lofty courtesy, so that he was had in reverence; and he made such music that the tears would come into the eyes of those who heard him, and they would look at each other, and wonder how Paul could thus tell the secret hopes of the heart. There were many women in the castle, great ladies, young maidens, and those that attended on them. Some of these would have proffered love to Paul, but their glances fell before a certain cold, virginal, almost affronted look, that he turned to meet any smile or gesture that seemed to hold in it any personal claim, or to offer any gift but that of an equal and serene friendship. As a maiden of the castle once said, provoked by his coldness, "Sir Paul seems to have everything to say to all of us, but nothing to any one of us." He was kind

to all with a sort of great and distant courtesy that was too secure
even to condescend. And so the years passed away.

III

It was nearly noon at the Castle of Wresting, and the whole
house was deserted, for the Duke had ridden out at daybreak to
the hunt; and all that could find a horse to ride had gone with him;
and, for it was not far afield, all else that could walk had gone afoot.
So bright and cheerful a day was it that the Duchess had sent out
her pavilion to be pitched in a lawn in the wood, and the Duke
with his friends were to dine there; none were left in the castle
save a few of the elder serving-maids, and the old porter, who was
lame. About midday, however, it seemed that one had been left;
for Paul, now a tall man, strongly built and comely, yet with a somewhat dreamful air, as though he pondered difficult things within
himself, and a troubled brow, under which looked out large and
gentle eyes, came with a quick step down a stairway. He turned
neither to right nor left, but passed through the porter's lodge. Here
the road from the town came up into the castle on the left, cut
steeply in the hill, and you could see the red roofs laid out like a
map beneath, with the church and the bridge; to the right ran a
little terrace under the wall. Paul came through the lodge, nodding gravely to the porter, who returned his salute with a kind of
reverence; then he walked on to the terrace, and stood for a moment leaning against the low wall that bounded it; below him lay
for miles the great wood of Wresting, now all ablaze with the brave
gold of autumn leaves; here was a great tract of beeches all rusty
red; there was the pale gold of elms. The forest lay in the plain,
here and there broken by clearings or open glades; in one or two
places could be seen the roofs of villages, with the tower of a church
rising gravely among trees. On the horizon ran a blue line of downs,
pure and fine above the fretted gold of the forest. The air was very
still, with a fresh sparkle in it, and the sun shone bright in a cloud-
less heaven; it was a day when the heaviest heart grows light, and
when it seems the bravest thing that can be designed to be alive.

Once or twice, as Paul leaned to look, there came from the wood, very far away, the faint notes of a horn; he smiled to hear it, and it seemed as though some merry thought came into his head, for he beat cheerfully with his fingers on the parapet. Presently he seemed to bethink himself, and then walked briskly to the end of the terrace, where was a little door in the wall; he pushed this open, and found himself at the head of a flight of stone steps, with low walls on either hand, that ran turning and twisting according to the slope of the hill, down into the wood.

Paul went lightly down the steps; once or twice he turned and looked up at the grey walls and towers of the castle, rising from the steep green turf at their foot, above the great leafless trees—for the trees on the slope lost their leaves first in the wind. The sight pleased him, for he smiled again. Then he stood for a moment, lower down, to watch the great limbs and roots of a huge beech that seemed to cling to the slope for fear of slipping downwards. He came presently to a little tower at the bottom that guarded the steps. The door was locked; he knocked, and there came out an old woman with a merry wrinkled face, who opened it for him with a key, saying, "Do you go to the hunt, Sir Paul?" "Nay," he said smiling, "only to walk a little alone in the wood." "To make music, perhaps?" said the old woman shyly. "Perhaps," said Paul smiling, "if the music come—but it will not always come for the wishing."

As Paul walked in the deep places of the wood, little by little his fresh holiday mood died away, and there crept upon him a shadow of thought that had of late been no stranger to him. He asked himself, with some bitterness, what his life was tending to. There was no loss of skill in his art; indeed it was easier to him than ever; he had a rich and prodigal store of music in him, music both of word and sound, that came at his call. But the zest was leaving him. He had attained to his utmost desire, and in his art there was nothing more to conquer. But as he looked round about him and saw all the beautiful chains of love multiplying themselves about those among whom he lived, he began to wonder whether he was not after all missing life itself. He saw children born, he saw them growing up; then they, too, found their own path of love, they married, or were given in marriage; presently they had children of their own; and even death itself, that carried well-loved souls into the dark world, seemed to forge new chains of faith and loyalty. All this he could say and did say in his music. He knew it, he divined it by some magical instinct; he could put into words and sounds the secrets that others could not utter—and there his art stopped. It could not bring him within the charmed circle—nay, it seemed to him that it was even like a fence that kept him outside. He looked forward to a time when his art of itself must fade, when other minstrels should arise with new secrets of power; and what would become of him then?

He had by this time walked very far into the wood, and as he came down through a little rise, covered with leafy thickets, he saw before him a green track, that wound away among the trees. He followed it listlessly. The track led him through a beech wood; the smooth and shapely stems, that stood free of undergrowth, thickly roofed over by firm and glossy autumn foliage, with the rusty fallen floor of last year's leaves underfoot, brought back to him his delight in the sweet and fresh world—so beautiful whatever the restless human heart desired in its presence.

He became presently aware that he was approaching some dwelling, he knew not what; and then the trees grew thinner; and in a minute he was out in a little forest clearing, where stood, in a small and seemly garden, inclosed with hedges and low walls and a moat, a forest lodge, a long low ancient building, ending in a stone tower.

The place had a singular charm. The ancient battlemented house, overgrown with ivy, the walls green and grey with lichens, seemed to have sprung as naturally out of the soil as the trees among which it stood, and to have become one with the place. He lingered for a moment on the edge of the moat, looking at a little tower that rose out of the pool, mirrored softly in the open spaces of the water, among the lily-leaves. The whole place seemed to have a wonderful peace about it; there was no sound but the whisper of leaves, and the doves crooning, in their high branching fastnesses, a song of peace.

As Paul stood thus and looked upon the garden, a door opened, and there came out a lady, not old, but well advanced in years, with a shrewd and kindly face; and then Paul felt a sort of shame within him, for standing and spying at what was not his own; and he would have hurried away, but the lady waved her hand to him with a courtly air, as though inviting him to approach. So he came forward, and crossing the moat by a little bridge that was hard by, he met her at the gate. He doffed his hat, and said a few words asking pardon for thus intruding on a private place, but she gave him a swift smile and said, "Sir Paul, no more of this—you are known to me, though you know me not. I have been at the Duke's as a guest; I have heard you sing—indeed," she added smiling, "I have been honoured by having been made known to the prince of musical men—but he hath forgotten my poor self; I am the Lady Beckwith, who welcomes you to her poor house—the Isle of Thorns, as they call it—and will deem it an honour that you should set foot therein; though I think that you came not for my sake."

"Alas, madam, no," said Paul smiling too. "I did but walk solitary in the forest; I am lacking in courtesy, I fear; I knew not that there was a house here, but it pleased me to see it lie like a jewel in the wood."

"You knew not it was here, or you would have shunned it!" said the Lady Beckwith with a smile. "Well, I live here solitary enough with my daughters—my husband is long since dead—but to-day we must have a guest—you will enter and tarry with us a little?"

"Yes, very willingly," said Paul, who, like many men that care not much for company, was tenderly courteous when there was no escape. So after some further passages of courtesy, they went within.

The Lady Beckwith led him into a fair tapestried room, and bade him be seated, while she went to call upon her servants to make ready refreshments for him. Paul seated himself in an oak chair and looked around him. The place was but scantily furnished, but Paul had pleasure in looking upon the old solid furniture, which reminded him of the House of Heritage and of his far-off boyhood. He was pleased, too, with the tapestry, which represented a wood of walnut-trees, and a man that sate looking upon a stream as though he listened; and then Paul discerned the figure of a brave bird wrought among the leaves, that seemed to sing; while he looked, he heard the faint sound in a room above of some one moving; then a lute was touched, and then there rose a soft voice, very pure and clear, that sang a short song of long sweet notes, with a descant on the lute, ending in a high drawn-out note, that went to Paul's heart like wine poured forth, and seemed to fill the room with a kind of delicate fragrance.

Presently the Lady Beckwith returned; and they sate and talked awhile, till there came suddenly into the room a maiden that seemed to Paul like a rose; she came almost eagerly forward; and Paul knew in his mind that it was she that had sung; and there passed through his heart a feeling he had never known before; it was as though it were a string that thrilled with a kind of delicious pain at being bidden by the touch of a finger to utter its voice.

"This is my daughter Margaret;" said the Lady Beckwith; "she knows your fame in song, but she has never had the fortune to hear you sing, and she loves song herself."

"And does more than love it," said Paul almost tremblingly, feeling the eyes of the maiden set upon his face; "for I heard but now a lute touched, and a voice that sang a melody I know not, as few that I know could have sung it."

The maiden stood smiling at him, and then Paul saw that she carried a lute in her hand; and she said eagerly, "Will you not sing to us, Sir Paul?"

"Nay," said the Lady Beckwith smiling, "but this is beyond courtesy! It is to ask a prince to our house, and beg for the jewels that he wears."

The maiden blushed rosy red, and put the lute by; but Paul stretched out his hand for it. "I will sing most willingly," he said. "What is my life for, but to make music for those who would hear?"

He touched a few chords to see that the lute was well tuned; and the lute obeyed his touch like a living thing; and then Paul sang a song of spring-time that made the hearts of the pair dance with joy. When he had finished, he smiled, meeting the smiles of both; and said, "And now we will have a sad song—for those are ever the sweetest—joy needs not to be made sweet."

So he sang a sorrowful song that he had made one winter day, when he had found the body of a little bird that had died of the frost and the hard silence of the unfriendly earth—a song of sweet things broken and good times gone by; and before he had finished he had brought the tears to the eyes of the pair. The Lady Beckwith brushed them aside—but the girl sate watching him, her hands together, and a kind of worship in her face, with the bright tears trembling on her cheeks. And Paul thought he had never seen a fairer thing; but wishing to dry the tears he made a little merry song, like the song of gnats that dance up and down in the sun, and love their silly play—so that the two smiled again.

Then they thanked him very urgently, and Margaret said, "If only dear Helen could hear this"; and the Lady Beckwith said, "Helen is my other daughter, and she lies abed, and may not come forth."

Then they put food before him; and they ate together, Margaret serving him with meat and wine; and Paul would have forbidden it, but the Lady Beckwith said, "That is the way of our house—and you are our guest and must be content—for Margaret loves to serve you." The girl said little, but as she moved about softly and deftly, with the fragrance of youth about her, Paul had a desire to draw her to him, that made him ashamed and ill at ease. So the hours sped swiftly. The maiden talked little, but the Lady Beckwith had much matter for little speech; she asked Paul many questions, and told him something of her own life, and how, while the good Sir Harry, her husband, lived, she had been much with the world, but now lived a quiet life, "Like a wrinkled apple-tree behind a house," she added with a smile, "guarding my fruit, till it be plucked from the bough." And she went on to say that though she had feared, when she entered the quiet life, the days would hang heavy, yet there never seemed time enough for all the small businesses that she was fain to do.

When the day began to fall, and the shadows of the trees out of the forest began to draw nearer across the lawn, Paul rose and said, "Come, I will sing you a song of farewell and thanks for this day of pleasure," and he made them a cheerful ditty; and so took his leave, the Lady Beckwith saying that they would speak of his visit for many days—and that she hoped that if his fancy led him again through the wood, he would come to them; "For you will find an open door, and a warm hearth, and friends who look for you." So Paul went, and walked through the low red sunset with a secret joy in his heart; and never had he sung so merrily as he sang that night in the hall of the Duke; so that the Duke said smiling that they must often go a-hunting, and leave Sir Paul behind, for that seemed to fill him to the brim with divine melody.

Now Paul that night, before he laid him down to sleep, stood awhile, and made a prayer in his heart. It must be said that as a child he had prayed night and morning, in simple words that Mistress Alison had taught him, but in the years when he was with Mark the custom had died away; for Mark prayed not, and indeed had almost an enmity to churches and to priests, saying that they made men bound who would otherwise be free; and he had said to Paul once that he prayed the best who lived nobly and generously, and made most perfect whatever gift he had; who was kind and courteous, and used all men the same, whether old or young, great or little; adding, "That is my creed, and not the creed of the priests—but I would not have you take it from me thus—a man may not borrow the secret of another's heart, and wear it for his own. All faiths are good that make a man live cleanly and lovingly and laboriously; and just as all men like not the same music, so all men are not suited with the same faith; we all tend to the same place, but by different ways; and each man should find the nearest way for him." Paul, after that, had followed his own heart in the matter; and it led him not wholly in the way of the priests, but not against them, as it led Mark. Paul took some delight in the ordered solemnities of the Church, the dark coolness of the arched aisles, the holy smell—he felt there the nearer to God. And to be near to

God was what Paul desired; but he gave up praying at formal seasons, and spoke with God in his heart, as a man might speak to his
friend, whenever he was moved to speak; he asked His aid before
the making of a song; he told Him when he was disheartened, or
when he desired what he ought not; he spoke to Him when he had
done anything of which he was ashamed; and he told Him of his
dreams and of his joys. Sometimes he would speak thus for half a
day together, and feel a quiet comfort, like a strong arm round him;
but sometimes he would be silent for a long while.

Now this night he spoke in his heart to God, and told him of
the sweet and beautiful hope that had come to him, and asked Him
to make known to him whether it was His will that he should put
forth his hand, and gather the flower of the wood—for he could
not even in his secret heart bring himself that night to speak, even
to God, directly about the maiden; but, in a kind of soft reverence,
he used gentle similitudes. And then he leaned from his window,
and strove to send his spirit out like a bird over the sleeping wood,
to light upon the tower; and then his thought leapt further, and he
seemed to see the glimmering maiden chamber where she slept,
breathing evenly. But even in thought this seemed to him too near,
as though the vision were lacking in that awful reverence, which is
the herald of love. So he thought that his spirit should sit, like a
white bird, on the battlement, and send out a quiet song.

And then he fell asleep, and slept dreamlessly till the day came
in through the casements; when he sprang up, and joy darted into
his heart, as when a servitor fills a cup to the brim with rosy and
bubbling wine.

Now that day, and the next, and for several days, Paul thought
of little else but the house in the wood and the maiden that dwelt
there. Even while he read or wrote, pictures would flash before his
eye. He saw Margaret stand before him, with the lute in her hand;
or he would see her as she had moved about serving him, or he
would see her as she had sate to hear him sing, or as she had stood
at the door as he went forth—and all with a sweet hunger of the
heart; till it seemed to him that this was the only true thing that
the world held, and he would be amazed that he had missed it for

so long. That he was in the same world with her; that the air that
passed over the house in the wood was presently borne to the castle;
that they two looked upon the same sky, and the same stars—this
was all to him like a delicate madness that wrought within his brain.
And yet he could not bring himself to go thither. The greater his
longing the more he felt unable to go without a cause; and yet the
thought that there might be other men that visited the Lady
Beckwith, and had more of the courtly and desirable arts of life
than he, was like a bitter draught—and so the days went on; and
never had he made richer music; it seemed to rush from his brain
like the water of a full spring.

A few days after, there was a feast at the castle and many were
bidden; and Paul thought in his heart that the Lady Beckwith would
perhaps be there. So he made a very tender song of love to sing,
the song of a heart that loves and dares not fully speak.

When the hour drew on for the banquet, he attired himself with
a care which he half despised, and when the great bell of the castle
rang, he went down his turret stairs with a light step. The custom
was for the guests to assemble in the great hall of the castle; but
they of the Duke's household, of whom Paul was one, gathered in a
little chamber off the hall. Then, when the Duke and Duchess with
their children came from their rooms, they passed through this
chamber into the hall, the household following. When the Duke
entered the hall, the minstrels in the gallery played a merry tune,
and the guests stood up; then the Duke would go to his place and
bow to the guests, the household moving to their places; then the
music would cease, and the choir sang a grace, all standing. Paul's
place was an honourable one, but he sate with his back to the hall;
and this night, as soon as he entered the hall, and while the grace
was sung, he searched with his eyes up and down the great tables,
but he could not see her whom he desired to see, and the joy died
out of his heart. Now though the Lords and Knights of the castle
honoured Paul because he was honoured by the Duke, they had
little ease with him; so to-night, when Paul took his place, a Knight
that sate next him, a shrewd and somewhat malicious man, who
loved the talk of the Court, and turned all things into a jest, said

"How now, Sir Paul? You entered to-night full of joy; but now you are like one that had expected to see a welcome guest and saw him not." Then Paul was vexed that his thoughts should be so easily read, and said with a forced smile, "Nay, Sir Edwin, we musical men are the slaves of our moods; there would be no music else; we have not the bold and stubborn hearts of warriors born." And at this there was a smile, for Sir Edwin was not held to be foremost in war-like exercise. But having thus said, Paul never dared turn his head. And the banquet seemed a tedious and hateful thing to him.

But at last it wore to an end, and healths had been drunk, and grace was sung; and then they withdrew to the Presence Chamber, where the Duke and Duchess sate upon chairs of state under a canopy, and the guests sate down on seats and benches. And presently the Duke sent courteous word to Paul that if he would sing they would gladly hear him. So Paul rose in his place and made obeisance, and then moved to a dais which was set at the end of the chamber; and a page brought him his lute. But Paul first made a signal to the musicians who were set aloft in a gallery, and they played a low descant; and Paul sang them a war-song with all his might, his voice ringing through the room. Then, as the voice made an end, there was a short silence, such as those who have sung or spoken from a full heart best love to hear—for each such moment of silence is like a rich jewel of praise—and then a loud cry of applause, which was hushed in a moment because of the presence of the Duke.

Then Paul made a bow, and stood carelessly regarding the crowd; for from long use he felt no uneasiness to stand before many eyes; and just as he fell to touching his lute, his eye fell on a group in a corner; the Lady Beckwith sate there, and beside her Margaret; behind whom sate a young Knight, Sir Richard de Benoit by name, the fairest and goodliest of all in the castle, whom Paul loved well; and he leaned over and said some words in the maiden's ear, who looked round shyly at him with a little smile.

Then Paul put out all his art, as though to recover a thing that he had nearly lost. He struck a sweet chord on the lute, and the talk all died away and left an utter silence; and Paul, looking at

but one face, and as though he spoke but to one ear, sang his song
of love. It was like a spell of magic; men and women turned to each
other and felt the love of their youth rise in their hearts as sweet
as ever. The Duke where he sate laid a hand upon the Duchess'
hand and smiled. They that were old, and had lost what they loved,
were moved to weeping—and the young men and maidens looked
upon the ground, or at the singer, and felt the hot blood rise in
their cheeks. And Paul, exulting in his heart, felt that he swayed
the souls of those that heard him, as the wind sways a field of wheat,
that bends all one way before it. Then again came the silence, when
the voice ceased; a silence into which the last chords of the lute
sank, like stones dropped into a still water. And Paul bowed again,
and stepped down from the dais—and then with slow steps he
moved to where the Lady Beckwith sate, and bowing to her, took
the chair beside her.

Then came a tumbler and played many agile tricks before them;
and then a company of mummers, with the heads of birds and
beasts, danced and sported. But the Lady Beckwith said, "Sir Paul,
I will tell you a tale. A bird of the forest alighted at our window-sill
some days ago, and sang very sweetly to us—and we spread crumbs
and made it a little feast; and it seemed to trust us, but presently it
spread its wings and flew away, and it comes not again. Tell us,
what shall we do to tempt the wild bird back?" And Paul, smiling
in her face, said, "Oh, madam, the bird will return; but he leads,
maybe, a toilsome life, gathering berries, and doing small businesses. The birds, which seem so free, live a life of labour; and
they may not always follow their hearts. But be sure that your bird
knows his friends; and some day, when he has opportunity, he will
alight again. To him his songs seem but a small gift, a shallow twittering that can hardly please." "Nay," said the Lady Beckwith, "but
this was a nightingale that knew the power of song, and could touch
all hearts except his own; and thus, finding love so simple a thing
to win, doubtless holds it light." "Nay," said Paul, "he holds it not
light; it is too heavy for him; he knows it too well to trifle with it."

Then finding that the rest were silent, they two were silent. And
so they held broken discourse; and ever the young Knight spoke in

Margaret's ear, so that Paul was much distraught, but dared not seem to intervene, or to speak with the maiden, when he had held aloof so long.

Presently the Lady Beckwith said she had a boon to ask, and that she would drop her parables. And she said that her daughter Helen, that was sick, had been very envious of them, because she had not heard his songs, but only a soft echo of them through the chamber floor. "And perhaps, Sir Paul," she said, "if you will not come for friendship, you will come for mercy; and sing to my poor child, who has but few joys, a song or twain." Then Paul's heart danced within him, and he said, "I will come to-morrow." And soon after that the Duke went out and the guests dispersed; and then Paul greeted the Lady Margaret, and said a few words to her; but he could not please himself in what he said; and that night he slept little, partly for thinking of what he might have said: but still more for thinking that he would see her on the morrow.

So when the morning came, Paul went very swiftly through the forest to the Isle of Thorns. It was now turning fast to winter, and the trees had shed their leaves. The forest was all soft and brown, and the sky was a pearly grey sheet of high cloud; but a joy as of spring was in Paul's heart, and he smiled and sang as he went, though he fell at times into sudden silences of wonder and delight. When he arrived, the Lady Beckwith greeted him very lovingly, and presently led him into a small chamber that seemed to be an oratory. Here was a little altar very seemly draped, with stools for kneeling, and a chair or two. Near the altar, at the side, was a little door in the wall behind a hanging; the Lady Beckwith pulled the hanging aside, and bade Paul to follow; he found himself in a small arched recess, lit by a single window of coloured glass, that was screened from a larger room, of which it was a part, by a curtain. The Lady Beckwith bade Paul be seated, and passed beyond the curtain for an instant. The room within seemed dark, but there came from it a waft of the fragrance of flowers; and Paul heard low voices talking together, and knew that Margaret spake; in a moment she appeared at the entrance, and greeted him with a very sweet and simple smile, but laid her finger on her lips; and so slipped back into the room again, but left Paul's heart beating strangely and fiercely. Then the Lady Beckwith returned, and said in a whisper to Paul that it was a day of suffering for Helen, and that she could not bear the light. So she seated herself near him, and Paul touched his lute, and sang songs, five or six, gentle songs of happy untroubled things, like the voices of streams that murmur to themselves when the woods are all asleep; and between the songs he spoke not, but played airily and wistfully upon his lute; and for all that it seemed so simple, he had never put more art into what he played and sang. And at last he made the music die away to a very soft close, like an evening wind that rustles away across a woodland, and moves to the shining west. And looking at the Lady Beckwith, he saw that she had passed, on the wings of song, into old forgotten dreams, and sate smiling to herself, her eyes brimming with tears. And then he rose, and saying that he would not be tedious, put the lute aside, and they went out quietly together. And the Lady Beckwith took his hand in both her own and said, "Sir Paul, you are a great magician—I could not believe that you could have so charmed an old and sad-hearted woman. You have the key of the door of the land of dreams; and think not that I am ungrateful; that you, for whose songs princes contend in vain, should deign to come and sing to a maiden that is sick—how shall I repay it?" "Oh, I am richly repaid," said Paul, "the guerdon of the singer is the incense of a glad heart—and you may give me a little love if you can, for I am a lonely man." Then they smiled at each other, the smile that makes a compact without words.

Then they went down together, and there was a simple meal set out; and they ate together like old and secure friends, speaking little; but the Lady Beckwith told him somewhat of her daughter Helen, how she had been fair and strong till her fifteenth year; and that since that time, for five weary years, she had suffered under a strange and wasting disease that nothing could amend. "But she is patient and cheerful beneath it, or I think my heart would break;—but I know," she added, and her mouth quivered as she spoke, "that she can hardly see another spring, and I would have her last days to be sweet. I doubt not," she went on, "the good and wise purposes of God, and I think that he often sends his bright angels to comfort her—for she is never sad—and when you sing as you sang just now, I seem to understand, and my heart says that it is well."

While they spoke the Lady Margaret came into the room, with a sudden radiance; and coming to Paul she kneeled down beside him, and kissed his hand suddenly, and said, "Helen thanks you, and I thank you, Sir Paul, for giving her such joy as you could hardly believe."

There came a kind of mist over Paul's eyes, to feel the touch of the lips that he loved so well upon his hand; but at the same time it appeared to him like a kind of sin that he who seemed to himself, in that moment, so stained and hard, should have reverence done him by one so pure. So he raised her up, and said, "Nay, this is not meet"; and he would have said many other words that rushed together in his mind, but he could not frame them right. But presently the Lady Beckwith excused herself and went; and then Paul for a sweet hour sate, and talked low and softly to the maiden, and threw such worship into his voice that she was amazed. But he said no word of love. And she told him of their simple life, and how her sister suffered. And then Paul feared to stay longer, and went with a mighty and tumultuous joy in his heart.

Then for many days Paul went thus to the Isle of Thorns—and the Lady Margaret threw aside her fear of him, and would greet him like a brother. Sometimes he would find her waiting for him at the gate, and then the air was suddenly full of a holy radiance. And the Lady Beckwith, too, began to use him like a son; but the Lady Helen he never saw—only once or twice he heard her soft voice speak in the dark room. And Paul made new songs for her, but all the time it was for Margaret that he sang.

And they at the castle wondered why Sir Paul, who used formerly to sit so much in his chamber, now went so much abroad. But he guarded his secret, and they knew not whither he went; only he saw once, from looks that passed between two of the maidens, that they spoke of him; and this in times past might have made him ashamed, but now his heart was too high, and he cared not.

There came a day when Paul, finding himself alone with the Lady Beckwith, opened his heart suddenly to her; but he was checked, as it were, by a sudden hand, for there came into her face a sad and troubled look, as though she blamed herself for something. Then she said to him, faltering, that she knew not what to say, for she could not read her daughter's heart— "and I think, Sir Paul," she added, "that she hath no thought of love—love of the sort of which you speak. Nay, the maiden loves you well, like a dear brother; she smiles at your approach, and runs to meet you when she hears your step at the door"; and then seeing a look of pain and terror in the face of Paul, she said, "Nay, dear Paul, I know not. God knows how gladly I would have it so, but hearts are very strangely made; yet you shall speak if you will, and I will give you my prayers." And then she stooped to Paul, and kissed his brow, and said, "There is a mother's kiss, for you are the son of my heart, whatever befall."

So presently the maiden came in, and Paul asked her to walk a little with him in the garden, and she went smiling; and then he could find no words at all to tell her what was in his heart, till she said, laughing, that he looked strangely, and that it seemed he had nought to say. So Paul took her hand, and told her all his love; and she looked upon him, smiling very quietly, neither trembling nor amazed, and said that she would be his wife if so he willed it, and that it was a great honour; "and then," she added, "you need not go from us, but you can sing to Helen every day." Then he kissed her; and there came into his heart a great wave of tenderness, and he thanked God very humbly for so great a gift. Yet he somehow felt in his heart that he was not yet content, and that this was not how he had thought it would fall out; but he also told himself that he would yet win the maiden's closer love, for he saw that she loved not as he loved. Then after a little talk they went together and told the Lady Beckwith, and she blessed them; but Paul could see that neither was she content, but that she looked at Margaret with a questioning and wondering look.

Then there followed very sweet days. It was soon in the springtime of the year; the earth was awaking softly from her long sleep, and was by gentle degrees arraying herself for her summer pomp. The primroses put out yellow stars about the tree roots; the hyacinths carpeted the woods with blue, and sent their sweet breath down the glade; and Paul felt strange desires stir in his heart, and rise like birds upon the air; and when he walked with the Lady Margaret among the copses, or rested awhile upon green banks, where the birds sang hidden in the thickets, his heart made continual melody, and rose in a stream of praise to God. But they spoke little of love; at times Paul would try to say something of what was in his mind; but the Lady Margaret heard him, sedately smiling, as though she were pleased that she could give him this joy, but as though she understood not what he said. She loved to hear of Paul's life, and the places he had visited. And Paul, for all his joy, felt that in his love he was, as it were, voyaging on a strange and fair sea alone, and as though the maiden stood upon the shore and waved her hand to him. When he kissed her or took her hand in his own, she yielded to him gently and lovingly, like a child; and it was then that Paul felt most alone. But none the less was he happy, and day after day was lit for him with a golden light.

IV

One day there came a messenger for Paul, and brought him news that made him wonder: the House of Heritage had fallen, on Mistress Alison's death, to a distant kinsman of her own and of his. This man, who was without wife or child, had lived there solitary, and it seemed that he was now dead; and he had left in his will that if Sir Paul should wish to redeem the house and land for a price, he should have the first choice to do so, seeing his boyhood had been spent there. Now Paul was rich, for he had received many great gifts and had spent little; and there came into his heart a great and loving desire to possess the old house. He told the Lady Beckwith and Margaret of this, and they both advised him to go and see it. So Paul asked leave of the Duke, and told him his business. Then the Duke said very graciously that Paul had served him well, and that he would buy the house at his own charges, and give

it to Paul as a gift; but he added that this was a gift for past service, and that he would in no way bind Paul; but he hoped that
Paul would still abide in the castle, at least for a part of the year,
and make music for them. "For indeed," said the Duke very royally, "it were not meet that so divine a power should be buried in a
rustic grange, but it should abide where it can give delight. Indeed,
Sir Paul, it is not only delight! but through your music there flows
a certain holy and ennobling grace into the hearts of all who attentively hear you, and tames our wild and brutish natures into something worthier and more seemly." Then Paul thanked the Duke very
tenderly, and said that he would not leave him.

So Paul journeyed alone with an old man-at-arms, whom the
Duke sent with him for his honour and security; and when he arrived at the place, he lodged at the inn. He found the House of
Heritage very desolate, inhabited only by the ancient maid of Mistress Alison, now grown old and infirm. So Paul purchased the
house and land at the Duke's charges, and caused it to be repaired,
within and without, and hired a gardener to dress and keep the
ground. He was very impatient to be gone, but the matter could
not be speedily settled; and though he desired to return to Wresting, and to see Margaret, of whom he thought night and day, yet
he found a great spring of tenderness rise up in his heart at the
sight of the old rooms, in which little had been changed. The
thought of his lonely and innocent boyhood came back to him, and
he visited all his ancient haunts, the fields, the wood, and the down.
He thought much, too, of Mistress Alison and her wise and gracious ways; indeed, sitting alone, as he often did in the old room
at evening, it seemed to him almost as though she sate and watched
him, and was pleased to know that he was famous, and happy in
his love; so that it appeared to him as though she gave him a bene-
diction from some far-off and holy place, where she abode and was
well satisfied.

Then at last he was able to return; but he had been nearly six
weeks away. He had moved into the house and lived there; and it
had filled him with a kind of solemn happiness to picture how he
would some day, when he was free, live there with Margaret for

his wife; and perhaps there would be children too, making the house sweet with their laughter and innocent games—children who should look at him with eyes like their mother's. Long hours would pass thus while he sate holding a book or his lute between his hands, the time streaming past in a happy tide of thoughts.

But the last night was sad, for he had gone early to his bed, as he was to start betimes in the morning; and he dreamed that he had gone through the wood to the Isle of Thorns, and had seen the house stand empty and shuttered close, with no signs of life about it. In his dream he went and beat upon the door, and heard his knocks echo in the hall; and just as he was about to beat again, it was opened to him by an old small woman, that looked thin and sad, with grey hair and many wrinkles, whom he did not know. He had thrust past her, though she seemed to have wished to stay him; and pushing on, had found Margaret sitting in the hall, who had looked up at him, and then covered her face with her hands, and he had seen a look of anguish upon her face. Then the dream had slipped from him, and he dreamed again that he was in a lonely place, a bleak mountain-top, with a wide plain spread out beneath; and he had watched the flight of two white birds, which seemed to rise from the rocks near him, and fly swiftly away, beating their wings in the waste of air.

He woke troubled, and found the dawn peeping through the chinks of the shutter; and soon he heard the tramping of horses without, and knew that he must rise and go. And the thought of the dream dwelt heavily with him; but presently, riding in the cool air, it seemed to him that his fears were foolish; and his love came back to him, so that he said the name Margaret over many times to himself, like a charm, and sent his thoughts forward, imagining how Margaret, newly risen, would be moving about the quiet house, perhaps expecting him. And then he sang a little to himself, and was pleased to see the old man-at-arms smile wearily as he rode beside him.

Three days after he rode into the Castle of Wresting at sundown, and was greeted very lovingly; the Duke would not let him sing that night, though Paul said he was willing; but after dinner he asked him many questions of how he had fared. And Paul hoped that he might have heard some talk of the Lady Margaret. But none spoke of her, and he dared not ask. One thing that he noticed was that at dinner the young Sir Richard de Benoit sate opposite him, looking very pale; and Paul, more than once, looking up suddenly, saw that the Knight was regarding him very fixedly, as though he were questioning of somewhat; and that each time Sir Richard dropped his eyes as though he were ashamed. After dinner was over, and Paul had been discharged by the Duke, he had gone back into the hall to see if he could have speech of Sir Richard, and ask if anything ailed him; but he found him not.

Then on the morrow, as soon as he might, he made haste to go down to the Isle of Thorns. As he was crossing a glade, not far from the house, he saw to his surprise, far down the glade, a figure riding on a horse, who seemed for a moment to be Sir Richard himself. He stood awhile to consider, and then, going down the glade, he cried out to him. Sir Richard, who was on a white horse, drew rein, and turned with his hand upon the loins of the horse; and then he turned again, and, urging the horse forward, disappeared within the wood. There came, as it were, a chill into Paul's heart that he should be thus unkindly used; and he vexed his brain to think in what he could have offended the Knight; but he quickly returned to his thoughts of love; so he made haste, and soon came down to the place.

Now, when he came near, he thought for a moment of his dream; and shrank back from stepping out of the trees at the corner whence he could see the house; but chiding himself for his vain terrors, he went swiftly out, and saw the house stand as before, with the trees all delicate green behind it, and the smoke ascending quietly from the chimneys.

Then he made haste; and—for he was now used to enter unbidden—went straight into the house; the hall and the parlours were all empty; so that he called upon the servants; an old serving-maid came forth, and then Paul knew in a moment that all was not well. He looked at her for a moment, and a question seemed to be choked in his throat; and then he said swiftly, "Is the Lady Beckwith within?" The old serving-maid said gravely, "She is with the Lady Helen, who is very sick." Then Sir Paul bade her tell the Lady Beckwith that he was in the house; and as he stood waiting, there came a kind of shame into his heart, that what he had heard was so much less than what he had for an instant feared; and while he strove to be more truly sorry, the Lady Beckwith stood before him, very pale. She began to speak at once, and in a low and hurried voice told him of Helen's illness, and how that there was little to hope; and then she put her hand on Paul's arm, and said, "My son, why did you leave us?" adding hastily, "Nay, it could not have been otherwise." And Paul, looking upon her face, divined in some sudden way that she had not told him all that was in her mind. So he said, "Dear mother, you know the cause of that—but tell me all, for I see there is more behind." Then the Lady Beckwith put her face in her hands, and saying, "Yes, dear Paul, there is more," fell to weeping secretly. While they thus stood together—and Paul was aware of a deadly fear that clutched at his heart and made all his limbs weak— the Lady Margaret came suddenly into the room, looking so pale and worn that Paul for a moment did not recognise her. But he put out his arms, and took a step towards her; then he saw that she had not known he was in the house; for she turned first red and then very pale, and stepped backwards; and it went to Paul's heart like the stabbing of a sharp knife, that she looked at him with a look in which there was shame mingled with a certain fear.

Now while Paul stood amazed and almost stupefied with what he saw, the Lady Beckwith said quickly and almost sternly to Margaret, "Go back to Helen—she may not be left alone." Margaret slipped from the room; and the Lady Beckwith pointed swiftly to a chair, and herself sate down. Then she said, "Dear Paul, I have dreaded this moment and the sight of you for some days—and though I should wish to take thought of what I am to say to you, and to say it carefully, it makes an ill matter worse to dally with it—so I will even tell you at once. You must know that some three days after you left us, the young Knight Sir Richard de Benoit fell from his horse, when riding in the wood hard by this house, and was grievously hurt by the fall. They carried him in here and we tended him. I had much upon my hands, for dear Helen was in great suffering; and so it fell out that Margaret was often with the Knight—who, indeed, is a noble and generous youth, very pure and innocent of heart—and oh, Paul, though it pierces my heart to say it, he loves her—and I think that she loves him too. It is a strange and terrible thing, this love! it is like the sword that the Lord Christ said that He came to bring on earth, for it divides loving households that were else at one together; and now I must say more— the maiden knew not before what love was; she had read of it in the old books; and when you came into this quiet house, bringing with you all the magic of song, and the might of a gentle and noble spirit, and offered her love, she took it gladly and sweetly, not knowing what it was that you gave; but I have watched my child from her youth up, and the love that she gave you was the love that she would have given to a brother—she admired you and reverenced you. She knew that maidens were asked and given in marriage, and she took your love, as a child might take a rich jewel, and love the giver of it. And, indeed, she would have wedded you, and might have learned to love you in the other way. But God willed it otherwise; and seeing the young Knight, it was as though a door was opened in her spirit, and she came out into another place. I am sure that no word of love has passed between them; but it has leaped from heart to heart like a swift fire; and all this I saw too late; but seeing it, I told Sir Richard how matters stood; and he is an honourable youth; for from that moment he sought how he might be taken hence, and made reasons to see no more of the maid. But his misery I could see; and she is no less miserable; for she has a very pure and simple spirit, and has fought a hard conflict with herself; yet will she hold to her word.

"And now, dear Paul, judge between us, for the matter lies in your hands. She is yours, if you claim her; but her heart cannot be yours awhile, though you may win it yet. It is true that both knights and maidens have wedded, loving another; yet they have learned to love each other, and have lived comfortably and happily; but

whether, knowing what I have been forced to tell you, you can be
content that things should be as before, I know not."

Then the Lady Beckwith made a pause, and beat her hands together, watching Paul's face; Paul sate very still and pale, all the
light gone out of his eyes, with his lips pressed close together. And
at the sight of him the tears came into the Lady Beckwith's eyes,
and she could not stay them. And Paul, looking darkly on her, strove
to pity her, but could not; and clasping the arms of his chair, said
hoarsely, "I cannot let her go." So they sate awhile in silence; and
then Paul rose and said, "Dear lady, you have done well to tell me
this—I know deep down in my heart what a brave and noble thing
you have done: but I cannot yet believe it—I will see the Lady Margaret and question her of the matter." Then the lady said, "Nay,
dear Paul, you will not—you think that you would do so; but you
could not speak with her face to face of such a matter, and she
could not answer you. You must think of it alone, and to-morrow
you must tell me what you decide; and whichever way you decide
it, I will help you as far as I can." And then she said, "You will pity
me a little, dear Paul, for I had rather have had a hand cut off than
have spoken with you thus." And these simple words brought Paul
a little to himself, and he rose from his place and kissed the Lady
Beckwith's hand, and said, "Dear mother, you have done well; but
my sorrow is greater than I can bear," And at that the Lady
Beckwith wept afresh; but Paul went out in a stony silence, hardly
knowing what he did.

Then it seemed to Paul as though he went down into deep waters
indeed, which passed cold and silent, in horror and bitterness, over
his soul. He did not contend or cry out; but he knew that the light
had fallen out of his life, and had left him dark and dead.

So he went slowly back to the castle through the wood, hating
his life and all that he was; once or twice he felt a kind of passion
rise within him, and he said to himself, "She is pledged to me, and
she shall be mine." And then there smote upon him the thought
that in thinking thus he was rather brute than man. And he fell at
last into an agony of prayer that God would lead him to the light,
and show him what he should do. When he reached the castle he

put a strong constraint upon himself; he went down to the hall; he
even sang; but it was like a dream; he seemed to be out of the body,
and as it were to see himself standing, and to hear the words falling from his own lips. The Duke courteously praised him, and said
that he was well content to hear his minstrel again.

As he left the hall, he passed through a little anteroom, that
was hung with arras, on the way to his chamber; and there he saw
sitting on a bench, close to the door that led to the turret stair, the
young Knight, Sir Richard; and there rose in his heart a passion of
anger, so strong that he felt as though a hand were laid upon his
heart, crushing it. And he stood still, and looked upon the Knight,
who raised so pale and haggard a face upon him, that Paul, in spite
of his own misery, saw before him a soul as much or more vexed
than his own; and then the anger died out of his heart, and left in
him only the sense of the bitter fellowship of suffering; the Knight
rose to his feet, and they stood for a moment looking at each other;
and then the Knight said, pale to the lips, "Sir Paul, we are glad to
welcome you back—I have heard of the Duke's gift, and rejoice that
your inheritance should thus return to you." And Paul bowed and
said, "Ay, it is a great gift; but it seems that in finding it I have lost
a greater." And then, seeing the Knight grow paler still, if that were
possible, he said, "Sir Richard, let me tell you a parable; there was
a little bird of the wood that came to my window, and made me
glad—so that I thought of no other thing but my wild bird, that
trusted me: and while I was absent, one hath whispered it away,
and it will not return." And Sir Richard said, "Nay, Sir Paul, you
are in this unjust. What if the wild bird hath seen its mate? And,
for you know not the other side of the parable, its mate hath hid
itself in the wood, and the wild bird will return to you, if you bid it
come."

Then Sir Paul, knowing that the Knight had done worthily and
like a true knight, said, "Sir Richard, I am unjust; but you will pardon me, for my heart is very sore." And so Paul passed on to his
chamber; and that night was a very bitter one, for he went down
into the sad valley into which men must needs descend, and he

saw no light there. And once in the night he rose dry-eyed and fevered from his bed, and twitching the curtain aside, saw the forest
lie sleeping in the cold light of the moon; and his thought went out
to the Isle of Thorns, and he saw the four hearts that were made
desolate; and he questioned in his heart why God had made the
hard and grievous thing that men call love.

Then he went back and fell into a sort of weary sleep; and waking therefrom, he felt a strange and terrible blackness seize upon
his spirit, so that he could hear his own heart beat furious and thick
in the darkness; and he prayed that God would release him from
the prison of the world. But while he lay, he heard the feet of a
horse clatter on the pavement, it being now near the dawn; and
presently there came a page fumbling to the door, who bore a letter from the Lady Beckwith, and it ran;—

> "*I would not write to you thus, dear Paul, un-
> less my need were urgent; but the dear Helen is
> near her end, and has prayed me many times that,
> if it were possible, you should come and sing to
> her—for she fears to go into the dark, and says that
> your voice can give her strength and hope. Now if
> it be possible, come; but if you say nay to my mes-
> senger, I shall well understand it. But the dear one
> hath done you no hurt, and for the love of the God
> who made us, come and comfort us—from her who
> loves you as a son, these.*"

Then Paul when he had read, pondered for awhile; and then he
said to the page, "Say that I will come." So he arrayed himself with
haste, and went swiftly through the silent wood, looking neither
to left or to right, but only to the path at his feet. And presently he
came to the Isle of Thorns; it lay in a sort of low silver mist, the
house pushing through it, as a rock out of the sea. And then a
sudden chill came over Paul, and the very marrow of his bones
shuddered; for he knew in his heart that this was nothing but the
presaging of death; and he thought that the dreadful angel stood

waiting at the door, and that presently the spirit of one that lay within must arise, leaving the poor body behind, and go with the angel.

In the high chamber where Helen lay burnt a light behind a curtain; and Paul saw a form pass slowly to and fro. And he would fain have pitied the two who must lose her whom they loved; but there passed over his spirit a sort of bitter wind; and he could feel no pity for any soul but his own, and his heart was dry as dust; he felt in his mind nothing but a kind of dumb wonder as to why he had troubled himself to come.

There must have been, he saw, a servant bidden to await his coming, because, as his feet sounded on the flags, the door was opened to him; and in a moment he was within the hall. At the well-known sights and scents of the place, the scene of his greatest happiness, the old aching came back into his stony heart, and grief, that was like a sharp sword, thrust through him. Suddenly, as he stood, a door opened, and Margaret came into the hall; she saw him in a moment; and he divined that she had not known he was within, but had meant only to pass through; for she stopped short as though irresolute, and looked at him with a wild and imploring gaze, like a forest thing caught in a trap.

In a moment there flowed into Paul's heart a great pity and tenderness, and a strength so wonderful that he knew it was not his own, but the immortal strength of God. And he stepped forward, forgetting all his own pain and misery, and said, "Margaret, dear one, dear sister, what is the shadow that hath fallen between us at this time? I would not," he went on, "speak of ourselves at such an hour as this; but I see that there is somewhat—we minstrels have a power to look in the heart of those we love—and I think it is this—that you can love me, dear one, as a brother, and not as a lover. Well, I am content, and so it shall be. I love you too well, little one, to desire any love but what you can give me—so brother and sister we will be." Then he saw a light come into her face, and she murmured words of sorrow that he could not hear; but he put his arm about her as a brother might, and kissed her cheek. And then she put her hands upon his shoulder, and her face upon them, and broke out into a passion of weeping. And Paul, saying "Even so," kissed and comforted her, as one might comfort a child, till she looked up, as if to inquire somewhat of him. And he said smiling, "So this is my dear sister indeed—yes, I will be content with that—and now take me to the dear Helen, that I may see if my art can comfort her." Then it was very sweet to Paul's sore heart that she drew her arm within his own and led him up from the room. Then there came in haste the Lady Beckwith down to meet them, with a look of pain upon her face; and Paul said, still smiling, "We are brother and sister henceforth." Then the Lady Beckwith smiled too out of her grief and said, "Oh, it is well."

Then they passed together through the oratory and entered the chamber of death. And then Paul saw a heavenly sight. The room was a large one, dim and dark. In a chair near the fire, all in white, sate a maiden like a lily—so frail and delicate that she seemed like a pure spirit, not a thing of earth. She sate with a hand upraised between her and the fire; and when Paul came in, she looked at him with a smile in which appeared nothing but a noble patience, as though she had waited long; but she did not speak. Then they drew a chair for Paul, and he took his lute, and sang soft and low, a song of one who sinks into sweet dreams, when the sounds of day are hushed—and presently he made an end. Then she made a sign that Paul should approach, and he went to her, and kneeled beside her, and kissed her hand. And Margaret came out of the dark, and put her hand on Paul's shoulder saying, "This is our brother." And Helen smiled in Paul's face—and something, a kind of heavenly peace and love, seemed to pass from her eyes and settle in Paul's heart; and it was told him in that hour, he knew not how, that this was his bride whom he had loved, and that he had loved Margaret for her sake; and that moment seemed to Paul to be worth all his life that had gone before, and all that should go after. So he knelt in the silence; and then in a moment, he knew not where or whence, the whole air seemed full of a heavenly music about them, such music as he had never dreamed of, the very soul and essence of the music of earth. But Helen laid her head back, and, smiling still, she died. And Paul laid her hand down.

Then without a word he rose, and went from the chamber; and he stepped out into the garden, and paced there wondering; he saw the trees stand silent in their sleep, and the flowers like stars in their dewy beds. And he knew that God was very near him; he put all his burdens and sorrows, his art, and all himself within the mighty hands; and he knew that he could never doubt again of the eternal goodness and the faithful tender love of the Father. And all the while the dawn slowly brightened over the wood, and came up very slowly and graciously out of the east. Then Paul gave word that he must return to the castle, but would come back soon. And as he mounted the steps, he saw that there was a man pacing on the terrace above, and knew that it was the Knight Richard, whom he sought. So he went up on the terrace, and there he saw the young Knight looking out over the forest; Paul went softly up to him and laid his hand upon his shoulder, and the Knight turned upon him a haggard and restless eye. Then Paul said, "Sir Richard, I come from the Isle of Thorns—but I have more to say to you. You are a noble Knight and have done very worthily—and I yield to you with all my heart the dear Margaret, for we are brother and sister, and nought else, now and henceforth." Then Sir Richard, as though he hardly heard him aright, stood looking upon his face; and Paul took his hand very gently in both his own, and said, "Yes, it is even so— and we will be brothers too." Then he went within the castle—and lying down in his chamber he slept peacefully like a little child.

V

Many years have passed since that day. First Sir Richard wedded the Lady Margaret, and dwelt at the Isle of Thorns. A boy was born to them, whom they named Paul, and a daughter whom they called Helen. And Paul was much with them, and had great content. He made, men said, sweeter music than ever he had done, in those days. Then the Duke died; and Paul, though his skill failed not, and though the King himself would have had him to his Court, went back to the House of Heritage, and there dwelt alone, a grave and kindly man, very simple of speech, and loving to walk and sit alone. And Sir Richard and the Lady Margaret bought an estate hard by and dwelt there.

Now Paul would make no more music, save that he sometimes played a little on the lute for the pleasure of the Lady Margaret; but he took into his house a boy whom he taught the art; and when he was trained and gone into the world, to make music of his own, Paul took another—so that as the years went on, he had sent out a number of his disciples to be minstrels; so his art was not lost; and one of these, who was a very gracious child named Percival, he loved better than the rest, because he saw in him that he had a love for the art more than for all the rewards of art. And once when they sate together, the boy Percival said, "Dear sir, may I ask you a question?" "A dozen, if it be your will," said Paul, smiling; "but, dear child, I know not if I can answer it." Then the boy said, "Why do you not make more music, dear sir? for it seems to me like a well that holds its waters close and deep, and will not give them forth." Then Paul said smiling, "Nay, I have given men music of the best. But there are two reasons why I make no more; and I will tell you them, if you can understand them. The first is that many years ago I heard a music that shamed me; and that sealed the well." Then the boy said musing, "Tell me the name of the musician, dear Sir Paul, for I have heard that you were ever the first." Then Paul said, "Nay, I know not the name of the maker of it." Then the boy said smiling, "Then, dear sir, it must have been the music of the angels." And Paul said, "Ay, it was that." Then the boy was silent, and sate in awe, while Paul mused, touching his lute softly. Then he roused himself and said, "And the second reason, dear child, is this. There comes a time to all that *make*—whether it be books or music or pictures—when they can make no new thing, but go on in the old manner, working with the fingers of age the dreams of youth. And to me this seems as it were a profane and unholy thing, that a man should use so divine an art thus unworthily; it is as though a host should set stale wine before his guests, and put into it some drug which should deceive their taste; and I think that those who do this do it for two reasons: either they hanker for the praise thereof, and cannot do without the honour—and that is unworthy—

or they do it because they have formed the habit of it, and have nought to fill their vacant hours—and that is unworthy too. So hearing the divine music of which I spoke but now, I knew that I could attain no further; and that there was a sweet plenty of music in the hand of God, and that he would give it as men needed it; but that my own work was done. For each man must decide for himself when to make an end. And further, dear child, mark this! The peril for us and for all that follow art is to grow so much absorbed in our handiwork, so vain of it, that we think there is nought else in the world. Into that error I fell, and therein abode. But we are in this world like little children at school. God has many fair things to teach us, but we grow to love our play, and to think of nought else, so that the holy lessons fall on unheeding ears; but now I have put aside my play, and sit awhile listening to the voice of God, and to all that He may teach me; and the lesson is hard to spell; but I wait upon Him humbly and quietly, till He call me hence. And now we have talked enough, and we will go back to our music; and you shall play me that passage over, for you played it not deftly enough before."

Now it happened that a few days later Paul in his sleep dreamed a dream; and when he woke, he could scarce contain his joy; and the boy Percival, seeing him in the morning, marvelled at the radiance that appeared in his face; and a little later Paul bade him go across the fields to the Lady Margaret's house, and to bid her come to him, if she would, for he had something that he must tell her, and he might not go abroad. So Percival told the Lady Margaret; and she wondered at the message, and asked if Sir Paul was sick. And the boy said, "No, I never saw him so full of joy—so that I am afraid."

Then the Lady Margaret went to the House of Heritage; and Paul came to greet her at the door, and brought her in, and sate for awhile in silence, looking on her face. The Lady Margaret was now a very comely and sedate lady, and had held her son's child in her arms; and Paul was a grey-haired man; yet in his eyes she was still the maiden he had known. Then Paul, speaking very softly, said, "Dear Margaret, I have bidden you come hither, for I think I am called hence; and when I depart, and I know not when it may be, I would close my eyes in the dear house where I was nurtured." Then she looked at him with a sudden fear, but he went on, "Dear one, I have dreamed very oft of late of Helen—she stands smiling in a glory, and looks upon me. But this last night I saw more. I know not if I slept or waked, but I heard a high and heavenly music; and then I saw Helen stand, but she stood not alone; she held by the hand a child, who smiled upon me; and the child was like herself; but I presently discerned that the child had a look of myself as well; and she loosed the child's hand from her own, and the child ran to me and kissed me; and Helen seemed to beckon me; and then I passed into sleep again. But now I see the truth. The love that I bear her hath begotten, I think, a child of the spirit that hath never known a mortal birth; and the twain wait for me." And Margaret, knowing not what to say, but feeling that he had seen somewhat high and heavenly, sate in silence; and presently Paul, breaking out of a muse, began to talk of the sweet days of their youth, and of the tender mercies of God. But while he spoke, he suddenly broke off, and held up his hand; and there came a waft of music upon the air. And Paul smiled like a tired child, and lay back in his chair; and as he did so a string of the lute that lay beside him broke with a sweet sharp sound. And the Lady Margaret fell upon her knees beside him, and took his hand; and then she seemed to see a cloudy gate, and two that stood together—a fair woman and a child; and up to the gate, out of a cloud, came swiftly a man, like one that reaches his home at last; and the three went in at the gate together, hand in hand;—and then the music came once again, and died upon the air.

Renatus

Renatus was a Prince of Saxony that was but newly come to his princedom; his father had died while he was a boy, and the realm had been administered by his father's brother, a Duke of high courage and prudence. The Duke was deeply anxious for the fate of the princedom and his nephew's fortunes, for they lived in troubled times; the Barons of the province were strong and haughty men, with little care for the Prince, and no thought of obedience; each of them lived in his castle, upon a small realm of his own; the people were much discontented with the rule of the Barons, and the Duke saw plainly enough that if a prince could arise who could win the confidence of the people, the Barons would have but little power left. Thus his care was so to bring up the Prince Renatus that he should understand how hard a task was before him; but the boy, though quick of apprehension, was fond of pleasure and amusement, and soon wearied of grave instructions; so the Duke did not persist overmuch, but strove to make the little Prince love him and confide in him, hoping that, when the day of trial came, he might be apt to ask advice rather than act hastily and perhaps foolishly; but yet in this the Duke had not perfectly succeeded, as he was by nature grave and austere, and even his face seemed to have in it a sort of rebuke for lively and light-minded persons. Still the Prince, though he was not at ease with the Duke, trusted him exceedingly, and thought him wise and good, even more than the Duke imagined.

The days had been full of feasting and pageants, and Renatus was greatly excited and eager at finding himself in so great a place. He had borne himself with much courtesy and dignity in his receiving of embassies and such compliments; he had, too, besides the sweet gifts of youth and beauty, a natural affectionateness, which led him to wish to please those about him; and the Duke's heart was full of love and admiration for the graceful boy, though there lay in the back of his mind a shadow of fear; and this grew very dark when he saw two of the most turbulent Barons speaking together in a corner, with sidelong glances at the Prince, at one of the Court assemblies, and divined that they thought the boy would be but a pretty puppet in their hands.

The custom was that the Prince, on the eve of his enthroning, should watch for two hours alone in the chapel of the castle, from eleven to one at night, and should there consecrate himself to God; the guests of the evening were departed; and a few minutes before eleven the Duke sate with the Prince in a little room off the chapel, waiting till it was time for the Prince to enter the building. Renatus was in armour, as the custom was, with a white robe over all. He sate restlessly in a chair, and there was a mischievous and dancing light of pleasure in his eye, that made the Duke doubly grave. The Duke, after some discourse of other matters, made a pause; and then, saying that it was the last time that he should take the privilege of guardianship—to offer advice unless it were sought—said: "And now, Renatus, you know that I love you as a dear son; and I would have you remember that all these things are but shows, and that there sits behind them a grave and holy presence of duty; these pomps are but the signs that you are truly the Prince of this land; and you must use your power well, and to God's glory; for it is He that makes us to be what we are, and truly calls us thereto." Renatus heard him with a sort of courteous impatience, and then, with a smile, said: "Yes, dear uncle, I know it; but the shows are very brave; and you will forgive me if my head is full of them just now. Presently, when the pageants are all over, I shall settle down to be a sober prince enough. I think you do not trust me wholly in the

matter—but I would not seem ungrateful," he added rather hastily, seeing the gravity in the Duke's face— "for indeed you have
been as a true father to me."

The Duke said no more at that time, for he cared not to give
untimely advice, and a moment after, a bell began to toll in the
silence, and the chaplain came habited to conduct the Prince to
his chapel. So they went the three of them together.

It was dark and still within the church; in front of the altar-
steps were set a faldstool and a chair, where the Duke might pray,
or sit if he were weary; two tall wax lights stood beside, and lit up
the crimson cloth and the gold fringes, so that it seemed like a rare
flower blossoming in the dark. A single light, in a silver lamp hung
by a silver chain, burnt before the altar; all else was dim; but they
could see the dark stalls of the choir, with their carven canopies,
over which hung the banners of old knights, that moved softly to
and fro; beyond were the pillars of the aisles, glimmering faintly
in a row. The roof and windows were dark, save where here and
there a rib of stone or a tracery stood out very rich and dim. All
about there was a kind of holy smell, of wood and carven stone
and incense-smoke.

The chaplain knelt beneath the altar; and the Prince knelt down
at the faldstool, the Duke beside him on the floor. And just as the
old bell of the castle tolled the hour, and died away in a soft hum
of sound, as sweet as honey, the chaplain said an ancient prayer,
the purport of which was that the Christian must watch and pray;
that only the pure heart might see God; and asking that the Prince
might be blest with wisdom, as the Emperor Solomon was, to do
according to the will of the Father.

Then the chaplain and the Duke withdrew; but as the Duke rose
up, he laid his hand on the Prince's head and said, "God be with
you, dear son, and open your eyes." And Renatus looked up at him
and smiled.

Then the Duke went back to the little room, and prayed abundantly. It was arranged that he should wait there until the Prince's
vigil was over, when he would go to attend him forth; and so the
Prince was left by himself.

For a time Renatus prayed, gathering up the strength of his mind to pray earnestly; but other thoughts kept creeping in, like children peeping and beckoning from a door. So he rose up after a little, and looked about him; and something of the solemnity of the night and the place came into his mind.

Then, after a while, he sate, his armour clinking lightly as he moved; and wrapping his robe about him—for it grew chill in the church—he thought of what had been and what should be. The time flew fast; and presently Renatus heard the great bell ring the hour of midnight; so he knelt and prayed again, with all his might, that God would bless him and open his eyes.

Then he rose again to his feet; and now the moon was risen and made a very pure and tender radiance through one of the high windows; and Renatus looking about him, was conscious of a thrill of fear that passed through him, as though there were some great presence near him in the gloom; then his eyes fell on a little door on his right, opposite to the door by which they had entered, which he knew led out into the castle court; but underneath the door, between it and the sill, there gleamed a line of very golden light, such as might come from a fire without. The Prince had no foolish terrors, as he was by nature courageous, and the holy place that he was in made him feel secure. But the light, which now began to grow in clearness, and to stream, like a rippling flow of brightness, into the church, surprised him exceedingly. So he rose up and went to the little door, expecting that he would find it closed; but it opened to his hand.

He had thought to see the dark court of the castle as he had often seen it, with its tall chimneys and battlements, and with lights in the windows. But to his amazement he saw that he was on the edge of a vast and dizzy space, so vast that he had not thought there could be anything in the world so great. The church and he seemed to float together in the space, for the solid earth was all gone—and it came into his head that the great building in which he stood, so fair and high, was no larger than a mote that swims in the strong beams of the sun. The space was all misty and dim at first, but over it hung a light like the light of dawn, that seemed to gush from a place in the cloud, near at hand and yet leagues away. Then as his sight became more used to the place, he saw that it was all sloping upwards and downwards, and built up of great steps or stairs, that ran across the space and were lost at last in cloud; and that the light came from the head of the steps. Then with a sudden shock of surprise he saw that there were persons kneeling on the steps; and every moment his sight became clearer and clearer, so that he could see the persons nearest to him, their robes and hands, and even the very lineaments of their faces.

Very near him there were three figures kneeling, not together in a group, but with some space between them. And, in some way that he could not explain, he felt that all the three were unconscious both of each other and of himself.

Looking intently upon them, he saw that they were kings, in royal robes. The nearest to him was an ancient man, with white hair; he knelt very upright and strong; his face was like parchment, with heavy lines, but his eyes glowed like a fire. Renatus thought he had never seen so proud a look. He had an air of command, and Renatus seemed to know that he had been a warrior in his youth. In his hands he held a crown of fine golden work, filled with jewels of great rarity and price; and the king held the crown as though he knew its worth; he seemed, as it were, to be proffering it, but as a gift of mighty value, the worthiest thing that he had to offer.

On a step below him at a little distance knelt the second; he was a younger man, in the prime of life; he had the look more of a student than a warrior, of one who was busied in many affairs, and who pondered earnestly over high matters of policy and state. He had a wiser face than the older man, but his brow was drawn by lines, as though he had often doubted of himself and others; and he had a crown in one hand, which he held a little irresolutely, as though he half loved it, and were yet half wearied of it; as though he was fain to lay it down, and yet not wholly glad to part with it.

Then Renatus turned a little to the third; and he was more richly apparelled than the others; his hands were clasped in prayer; and by his knee there lay a splendid diadem, an Emperor's crown, with few jewels, but each the price of a kingdom. And Renatus saw that he was very young, scarce older than himself; and that he had the most beautiful face he had ever seen, with large soft eyes, clear-cut features, and a mouth that looked both pure and strong; but in his face there was such a passion of holiness and surrender, that Renatus fell to wondering what it was that a man could so adore. He was the only one of the three who looked, as it were, rapt out of himself; and the crown lay beside him as if he had forgotten its very existence.

Then there came upon the air a great sound of jubilant and tender music like the voice of silver trumpets—and the cloud began to lift and draw up on every side, and revealed at last, very far off and very high, yet strangely near and clear, a Throne at the head of the steps. But Renatus dared not look thereon, for he felt that the time was not come; but he saw, as it were reflected in the eyes of the kings, that they looked upon a sight of awful splendour and mystery. Then he saw that the two that still held their crowns laid them down upon the ground with a sort of fearful haste, as though they were constrained; but the youngest of the kings smiled, as though he were satisfied beyond his dearest wish.

Then Renatus felt that somewhat was to be done too bright and holy for a mortal eye to behold, and so he drew back and softly closed the door; and it was a pain to find himself within the dark church again; it was as though he had lost the sight of something that a man might desire above all things to see—but he dared look no longer; and the music came again, but this time more urgently, in a storm of sound.

Then Renatus went back to his place, that seemed to him very small and humble beside what he had seen outside. And all the pride was emptied out of his heart, for he knew that he had looked upon the truth, and that it was wider than he had dreamed; and then he knelt and prayed that God would keep him humble and diligent and brave; but then he grew ashamed of his prayer, for he remembered that, after all, he was but still praying for himself; and he had a thought of the young Emperor's face, and he knew that there was something deeper and better still than humility and diligence and courage; what it was he knew not; but he thought that he had been, as it were, asking God for those fair things, like flower-blooms or jewels, which a man may wear for his own pride; but that they must rather rise and blossom, like plants out of a rich soil. So he ended by praying that God would empty him of all unworthy thoughts, and fill him full of that good and great thing, which, in the Gospel story, Martha went near to miss, but Mary certainly divined.

That was a blessed hour, to the thought of which Renatus afterwards often turned in darker and more weary days. But it drew swiftly to an end, and as he knelt, the bell beat one, and his vigil was over.

Presently the Duke came to attend him back; and Renatus could not speak of the vision, but only told the Duke that he had seen a wonderful thing, and he added a few words of grateful love, holding the Duke's hand close in his own.

On the next day, before Renatus came to be enthroned, the Barons came to do him homage; and Renatus, asking God to give him words that he might say what was in his heart, spoke to them, the Duke standing by; he said that he well knew that it appeared strange that one so young as himself should receive the homage of those who were older and wiser and more strong, adding: "But I believe that I am truly called, under God, to rule this land for the welfare of all that dwell therein, and I will rule it with diligence. Nay—for it is not well that a land should have many masters—I purpose that none shall rule it but myself, under God." And at that the Barons looked upon one another, but Renatus, leaning a little forward, with his hand upon his sword-hilt, said: "I think, my Lords, that there be some here that are saying to themselves, *He hath learnt his lesson well*, and I hope that it may be seen that it is so—but it is God and not man who hath put it into my heart to say this; it is from Him that I receive this throne. Counsel will I ask, and that gladly; but remembering the account that I must one day make, I will rule this realm for the welfare of the people thereof, and I will have all men do their parts; so see that your homage be of the heart and not of the lips, for it is to God that you make it, and not to me, who am indeed unworthy; but He that hath set me in this place will strengthen my hands. I have spoken this," he said, "not willingly; but I would have no one mistake my purpose in the matter."

Then the Barons came silently to do obeisance; and so Renatus came to his own; but more of him I must not here say, save that he ruled his realm wisely and well, and ever gave God the glory.

The Isles of Sunset

About midway between the two horns of the bay, the Isles of Sunset pierced the sea. There was deep blue water all around them, and the sharp and fretted pinnacles of rock rose steeply up to heaven. The top of the largest was blunt, and covered with a little carpet of grass and sea-herbs. The rest were nought but cruel spires, on which no foot but that of sea-birds could go. At one place there was a small creek, into which a boat might be thrust, but only when the sea was calm; and near the top of the rock, just over this, was the dark mouth of a little cave.

The bay in which the Isles lay was quite deserted; the moorland came to the edge of the cliffs, and through a steep and rocky ravine, the sides of which were overgrown with ferns and low trees, all brushed landward by the fierce winds, a stream fell hoarsely to the sea, through deep rockpools. The only living things there were the wild birds, the moorfowl in the heather, hawks that built in the rock face, and pigeons that made their nest in hollow places. Sometimes a stag pacing slowly on the cliff-top would look over, but that was seldom.

Yet on these desolate and fearful rocks there dwelt a man, a hermit named David. He had grown up as a fisher-boy in the neighbouring village—an awkward silent boy with large eyes which looked as though they were full of inward dreams. The people of the place were Christians after a sort, though it was but seldom that a priest came near them; and then only by sea, for there was no road to the place. But David as a boy had heard a little of the

251

Lord Christ, and of the bitter sacrifice he made for men; and there
grew up in his heart a great desire to serve Him, and he prayed
much in his heart to the Lord, that he would show him what he
might do. He had no parents living. His mother was long dead,
and his father had been drowned at sea. He lived in the house of
his uncle, a poor fisherman with an angry temper, where he fared
very hardly; for there were many mouths to feed, and the worst
fell to the least akin. But he grew up handy and active, with strong
limbs and a sure head; and he was well worth his victual, for he
was a good fisherman, patient of wind and rain; and he could scale
the cliff in places where none other dared go, and bring down the
eggs and feathers of the sea-birds. So they had much use of him,
and gave him but little love in return. When he was free of work,
the boy loved to wander alone, and he would lie on the heather in
the warm sun, with his face to the ground, drinking in the fragrant
breath of the earth, and praying earnestly in his heart to the Lord,
who had made the earth so fair and the sea so terrible. When he
came to man's estate, he had thoughts of making a home of his
own, but his uncle seemed to need him—so he lingered on, doing
as he was bid, very silent, but full of his own thoughts, and sure
that the Lord would call him when he had need of him; one by one
the children of the family grew up and went their ways; then his
uncle's wife died, and then at last one day, when he was out fishing with his uncle, there came a squall and they beat for home. But
the boat was overset and his uncle was drowned; and David himself was cast ashore in a wonderful manner, and found himself all
alone.

Now while he doubted what he should do, he dreamed a dream
that wrought powerfully in his mind. He thought that he was walking in the dusk beside the sea, which was running very high, when
he saw a light drawing near to him over the waves. It was not like
the light of a lantern, but a diffused and pale light, like the moon
labouring in a cloud. The sea began to abate its violence, and then
David saw a figure coming to him, walking, it seemed, upon the
water as upon dry land, sometimes lower, sometimes higher, as
the waves ran high or low. He stopped in a great wonder to watch

the approach of the figure, and he saw that it was that of a young man, going very slowly and tranquilly, and looking about him with a gentle and smiling air of command. All about him was a light, the source of which David could not see, but he seemed like a man walking in the light of an open window, when all around is dark. As he came near, David saw that he was clad in a rough tunic of some dark stuff, which was girt up with a girdle at the waist. His head and his feet were bare. Yet though he seemed but poorly clad, he had the carriage of a great prince, whose power none would willingly question. But the strangest thing was that the sea grew calm before his feet, and though the wind was blowing fiercely, yet it did not stir the hair, which fell somewhat long on his shoulders, or so much as ruffle his robe. And then there came into David's head a verse of Scripture where it says, "*What manner of man is this that even the winds and the sea obey him?*" And then the answer came suddenly into David's mind, and he knelt down where he was upon the beach, and waited in a great and silent awe; and presently that One drew near, and in some way that David did not understand, for he used no form of speech, his eyes made question of David's soul, and seemed to read its depths. And then at last He spoke in words that He had before used to a fisherman beside another sea, and said very softly, "Follow Me." But He said not how He should be followed; and presently He seemed to depart in a shining track across the sea, till the light that went with Him sank like a star upon the verge. Then in his dream David was troubled, and knew not how to follow; till he thought that it might be given him, as it was given once to Peter, to walk dry-shod over the depth; but when he set foot upon the water there broke so furious a wave at him, that he knew not how to follow. So he went back and kneeled upon the sand, and said aloud in his doubt, "What shall I do, Lord?" and as the words sounded on his tongue he awoke.

Then all that day he pondered how he should find the Lord; for he knew that though he had a hope in his heart, and though he leaned much upon God, yet he had not wholly found him yet. God was sometimes with him and near to him, but sometimes far withdrawn; and then, for he was a very simple man, he said in himself,

"I will give myself wholly to the search for my Lord. I will live solitary, and I will fix my mind upon Him"; for he thought within himself that his hard life, and the cares of the household in which he had dwelt, had been what had perhaps kept him outside; and therefore he thought that God had taken these cares away from him. And so he made up his mind.

Then he cast about where he had best dwell; and he thought of the Isles of Sunset as a lonely place, where he might live and not be disturbed. There was the little cave high up in the rock-face, looking towards the land, to which he had once scrambled up. This would give him shelter; and there were moreover some small patches of earth, near the base of the rock, where he could grow a few herbs and a little corn. He had some money of his own, which would keep him until his garden was grown up; and he could fish, he thought, from the rocks, and find shell-fish and other creatures of the sea, which would give him meat.

So the next day he bought a few tools that he thought he would need, and rowed all over when it was dusk. He put his small stores in a cave by the water's edge. The day after, he went and made a few farewells; he told no one where he was going; but it pleased him to find a little love for him in the hearts of some. One parting was a strangely sore one: there was an old and poor woman that lived very meanly in the place, who had an only granddaughter, a little maid. These two he loved very much, and had often done them small kindnesses. He kept this good-bye to the last, and went to the house after sundown. The old woman bade him sit down, and asked him what he meant to do, now that he was alone. "I am going away, mother," he said gently. The child, hearing this, came over the room from where she sate, and said to him, "No, David, do not go away." "Yes, dear child," he said, "I must even go." Then she said, "But where will you go? May I not come to see you sometimes?" and she put her small arms round his neck, and laid her cheek to his. Then David's heart was very full of love, and he said smiling, and with his arm round the child, "Dear one, I must not say where I am going—and it is a rough place, too, not fit for such tender little folk as you; but, if I can, I will come again and see you." Then the old grandmother, looking upon him very gravely, said, "Tell me what is in your mind." But he said, "Nay, mother, do not ask me; I am going to a place that is near and yet far; and I am going to seek for one whom I know not and yet know; and the way is long and dark." Then she forbore to ask him more, and fell to pondering sadly; so after they had sate awhile, he rose up and loosed the child's arms from him, kissing her; and the tears stood in his eyes; and he thought in himself that God was very wise; for if he had had a home of his own, and children whom he loved, he could never have found it in his heart to leave them. So he went out.

Then he climbed up the steep path that led to the downs, and so to the bay where the Isles lay. And just as he reached the top, the moon ran out from a long bank of cloud; and he saw the village lie beneath him, very peaceful in the moonlight; there were lights in some of the windows; the roofs were silvered in the clear radiance of the moon, and the shadows lay dark between. He could see the little streets, every inch of which he knew, and the port below. He could see the coast stretch away to the east, headland after headland, growing fainter; and the great spaces of the sea, with the moon glittering on the waves. There was a holy and solemn peace about it all; and though his life had not been a happy one there, he knew in a flash that the place was very dear to his heart, and he said a prayer to God, that he would guard and cherish the village and those that dwelt there. Then he turned, and went on to the downs; and presently descended by a steep path to the sea, through the thickets. He took off his clothes, and tied them in a pack on his back; and then he stepped quietly into the bright water, which lapped very softly against the shore, a little wave every now and then falling gently, followed by a long rustling of the water on the sand, and a silence till the next wave fell. He waded on till he could swim, and then struck out to where the Isles stood, all sharp and bright in the moon. He swam with long quiet strokes, hearing the water ripple past; and soon the great crags loomed out above him, and he heard the waves fall among their rocky coves. At last he felt the ground beneath his feet; and coming out of the water he

dressed himself, and then—for he would not venture on the cliffs
in the uncertain light—gathering up some dried weeds of the sea,
he made a pillow for his head and slept, in a wonderful peace of
mind, until the moon set; and not long after there came a pale light
over the sea in the east, brightening slowly, until at last the sun,
like a fiery ball, broke upwards from the sea; and it was day.

Now when David awoke in the broad daylight, he found himself full of a great joy and peace. He seemed, as it were, to have
leaped over a wide ditch, and to see the world across it. Now he
was alone with God, and he had put all the old, mean, hateful life
away from him. It did not even so much as peep into his mind that
he would have to endure many hardships of body, rain, and chilly
winds, a bed of rock, and fare both hard and scanty. This was not
what had troubled him in the old days. What had vexed his heart
had been unclean words and deeds, greediness, hardness, cruel
taunts, the lack of love, and the meanness and baseness of the petty
life. All that was behind him now; he felt free and strong, and while
he moved about to spy out his new kingdom, he sang loudly to himself a song of praise. The place pleased him mightily; over his head
ran up the cliff with its stony precipices and dizzy ledges. The lower
rocks all fringed with weeds, like sea-beasts with rough hair, stood
out black from the deep blue water that lay round the rocks. He
loved to hear the heavy plunge of the great waves around his bas-
tions, the thin cries of the sea-birds that sailed about the precipice, or that lit on their airy perches. Everywhere was a brisk sharp
scent of the sea, and the fresh breeze, most unlike the close sour
smell of the little houses. He felt himself free and strong and clean,
and he thought of all the things he would say to God in the pleasant solitude, and how he would hear the low and far-off voice of
the Father speaking gently with his soul.

His first care was to find the cave that was to shelter him. He
spent the day in climbing very carefully and lightly all over the
face of the rock. Never had he known his hand so strong, or his
head so sure. He sate for a time on a little ledge, to which he had
climbed on the crag face, and he feasted his eyes upon the sight of
the great cliffs of the mainland that ran opposite him, to left and

right, in a wide half-circle. His eyes dwelt with pleasure upon the high sloping shoulders of rock, on which the sun now shone very peacefully, the strip of moorland at the top, the brushwood growing in the sloping coves, the clean shingle at the base of the rocks, and the blue sky over all. That was the world as God had made it, and as He intended it to be; it was only men who made it evil, huddling together in their small and filthy dens, so intent on their little ugly lives, their food and drink and wicked ways.

Presently he found the cave-mouth, and noted in his mind the best way thither. The cave seemed to him a very sweet place; the mouth was all fringed with little ferns; inside it was dry and clean; and in a few hours he had disposed all his small goods within it. There was a low slope, on one side of the rocks, where the fern grew plentifully. He gathered great armfuls of the dry red stalks, and made himself a rustling bed. So the day wore pleasantly away. One of his cares was to find water; but here it seemed that God blessed him very instantly, for he found a place near the sea, where a little spring soaked cool out of the rock, with a pleasant carpet of moss and yellow flowers. He found, too, some beds of shell-fish, which he saw would give him food and bait for his fishing. So about sundown he cast a line from the end of the rocks and presently caught a fish, a ling, which lives round rocky shores. This he broiled at a small fire of driftwood, for he had brought tinder with him; and it pleased him to think of the meal that the Apostles took with the risen Christ, a meal which He had made for them, and to which He Himself called them; for that, too, was a broiled fish, and eaten by the edge of the sea. Also he ate a little of the bread he had brought with him; and with it some of a brisk juicy herb, called samphire, that sprouted richly in the cliff, which gave his meat an aromatic savour; and with a drink of fresh spring water he dined well, and was content; then he climbed within the cave, and fell asleep to the sound of the wind buffeting in the cliff, and the fall of great waves on the sea beaches.

Now I might make a book of all the things that David saw and did on the islands, but they were mostly simple and humble things. He fared very hard, but though he often wondered how he would find food for the next day, it always came to him; and he kept his health in a way which seemed to him to be marvellous; indeed he seemed to himself to be both stronger in body and lighter in spirit than he had even been before. He both saw and heard things that he could not explain. There were sounds the nature of which he could not divine; on certain days there was a far-off booming, even when the waves seemed still; at times, too, there was a low musical note in the air, like the throbbing of a tense string of metal; once or twice he heard a sound like soft singing, and wondered in his heart what creature of the sea it might be that uttered it. On stormy nights there were sad moans and cries, and he often thought that there were strange and unseen creatures about him, who hid themselves from sight, but whose voices he certainly heard; but he was never afraid. One night he saw a very beautiful thing; it had been a still day, but there was an anxious sound in the wind which he knew portended a storm; he was strangely restless on such days, and woke many times in the night: at last he could bear the silence of the cave no more, and went out, descending swiftly by the rocks, the path over which he could have now followed blindfold, down to the edge of the sea. Then he saw that the waves that beat against the rock were all luminous, as though lit with an inner light; suddenly, far below, how deep he knew not, he saw a great shoal of fish, some of them very large, coming softly round the rocks; the water, as it touched their blunt snouts, burst as it were into soft flame, and showed every twinkle of their fins and every beat of their tails. The shoal came swiftly round the rocks, swimming intently, and it seemed as though there was no end of them. But at last the crowd grew thinner and then ceased; but he could still see the water rippling all radiant in the great sea-pools, showing the motion of broad ribbons of seaweed that swayed to and fro, and lighting up odd horned beasts that stirred upon the ledges. From that day forth he was often filled with a silent wonder at all the sleepless life that moved beneath the vast waters, and that knew nothing of the little human lives that fretted themselves out in the thin air above. That day was to him like the opening of a door into the vast heart of God.

But for all his happiness, the thought weighed upon him, day after day, of all the grief and unhappiness that there was about him. A dying bird that he found in a pool, and that rolled its filmy eye upon him in fear, as if to ask why he must disturb it in its last sad languid hour, the terror in which so many of the small fish abode—he saw once, when the sea was clear, a big fish dart like a dark shadow, with open mouth and gleaming eye, on a little shoal of fishes that sported joyfully in the sun; they scattered in haste, but they had lost their fellows—all this made him ponder; but most of all there weighed on his heart the thought of the world he had left, of how men spoke evil of each other, and did each other hurt; of children whose lot was to be beaten and cursed for no fault, but to please the cruel temper of a master; of patient women, who had so much to bear—so that sometimes he had dark thoughts of why God made the world so fair, and then left so much that was amiss, like a foul stream that makes a clear pool turbid. And there came into his head a horror of taking the lives of creatures for his own use—the shell-worm that writhed as he pulled it from the shell; the bright fish that came up struggling and gasping from the water, and that fought under his hand—and at last he made up his mind that he would take no more life, though how he would live he knew not; and as for the world of men, he became very desirous to help a little as best he could; and there being at this time a wreck in the bay, when a boat and all on board were lost, he thought that he would wish, if he could, to keep a fire lit on dark nights, so that ships that passed should see that there was a dwelling there, and so keep farther away from the dangerous rocks.

By this time it had become known in the country where he was— his figure had been seen several times from the cliffs; and one day there had come a boat, with some of those that knew him, to the island. He had no wish to mix again with men; but neither did he desire to avoid them, if it was God's will that they should come. So he came down courteously, and spoke with the master of the boat, who asked him very curiously of his life and all that he did. David told him all; and when the master asked him why he had thus fled away from the world, David said simply that he had done so that he might pray to God in peace. Then the master said that there were many waking hours in the day, and he knew not what there might be to say prayers about, "for," he said, "you have no book to make prayers out of, like the priests, and you have no store of good-sounding words with which to catch the ear of God." Then David said that he prayed to God to guard all things great and small, and to help himself along the steep road to heaven. Then the master wondered very much, and said that a man must please himself, and no doubt it was a holy work. Then he asked a little shame-facedly for David to pray for him, that he might be kept safe from shipwreck, and have good fortune for fishing, to which David replied, "Oh, I do that already."

Before the master went away, and he stayed not long, he asked David how he lived, and offered him food. And David being then in a strait—for he had lately vowed to take no life, said gladly that he would have anything they could give him. So the master gave him some victual. And it happened, just at this time, that some of the boats from the village had a wonderful escape from a storm, and through that season they caught fish in abundance; so it was soon noised abroad that this was all because of David's prayers; and after that he never had need of food, for they brought him many little presents, such as eggs, fruit, and bread—for he would take no meat—giving them into his hands when he was on the lower rocks, or leaving them on a ledge in the cove when he was aloft. And as, when the fish were plenteous, they gave him food in grati-tude, and when fish were scarce, they gave it him even more abun-dantly that they might have his prayers, David was never in lack; in all of which he saw the wonderful hand of God working for him.

Now David pondered very much how he might keep a light aloft on dangerous nights.

His first thought was to find a sheltered place among the rocks to seaward, where his fire could burn and not be extinguished by the wind; but, though he climbed all about the rocks, he could find no place to his mind. One day, however, he was in the furthest re-cess of his cave, when he felt that among the rocks a little thin wind blew constantly from one corner; and feeling about with his hands, he found that it came out of a small crack in the rocks. The stone above it seemed to be loose; and he perceived after a while that the end of the cave must be very near to the seaward face of the crag, and that the cave ran right through the rock, and was only kept from opening on the outer side by a thin barrier of stone; so after several attempts, using all his strength, he worked the stone loose; and then with a great effort, he thrust the stone out; it fell with a great noise, leaping among the crags, and at last plunging into the sea. The wind rushed in through the gap; then he saw that he had, as it were, a small window looking out to sea, so small that he could not pass through it, but large enough to let a light shine forth, if there were a light set there; but though it seemed again to him like the guiding hand of God, he could not devise how he should shelter the light within from the wind. Indeed the hole made the cave a far less habitable place for himself, for the wind whistled very shrewdly through; he found it easy enough to stop the gap with an old fisherman's coat—but then the light was hidden from view. So he tried a further plan; he dug a hole in the earth at the top of the cliff, and then made a bed of dry sand at the bottom of it; and he piled up dry seaweed and wood within, thinking that if he lit his beacon there, it might be sheltered from the wind, and would burn fiercely enough to throw up the flame above the top of the pit. He saw that heavy rain would extinguish his fire; but the nights were most dangerous when it blew too strongly for rain to fall. So one night, when the wind blew strongly from the sea, he laid wood in order, which he had gathered on the land, and conveyed with many toilsome journeys over to the island. Then he lighted the pile, but it was as he feared; the wind blew fiercely over the top, and drove the flames downward, so that the pit glowed with a fierce heat; and sometimes a lighted brand was caught up and whirled over the cliffs; but he saw plainly enough that the light would not show out at sea. He was very sad at this, and at last went heavily down to his cave, not knowing what he should do; and pondering long before he slept, he could see no way out.

In the morning he went up to the cliff-top again, and turned his steps to the pit. The fire had burned itself out, but the sides were still warm to the touch; all the ashes had been blown by the force of the wind out of the hole; but he saw some bright things lie in the sand, which he could not wholly understand, till he pulled them out and examined them carefully. They were like smooth tubes and lumps of a clear stuff, like molten crystal or frozen honey, full of bubbles and stains, but still strangely transparent; and then, though he saw that these must in some way have proceeded from the burning of the fire, he felt as though they must have been sent to him for some wise reason. He turned them over and over, and held them up to the light. It came suddenly into his mind how he would use these heavenly crystals; he would make, he thought, a frame of wood, and set these jewels in the frame. Then he would set this in the hole of his cave, and burn a light behind; and the light would thus show over the sea, and not be extinguished.

So this after much labour he did; he fitted all the clear pieces into the frame, and he fixed the frame very firm in the hole with wooden wedges. Then he pushed clay into the cracks between the edges of the frame and the stone. Then he told some of those who came to him that he had need of oil for a purpose, and they brought it him in abundance, and wicks for a lamp; and these he set in an earthen bowl filled with oil, and on a dark night, when all was finished, he lit his lamp; and then clambered out on the furthest rocks of the island, and saw his light burn in the rocks, not clearly, indeed, but like an eye of glimmering fire. Then he was very glad at heart, and he told the fishermen how he had found means to set a light among the cliffs, and that he would burn it on dark and stormy nights, so that they might see the light and avoid the danger. The tidings soon spread, and they thought it a very magical and holy device; but did not doubt that the knowledge of it was given to David by God.

So David was in great happiness. For he knew that the Father had answered his prayer, and allowed him, however little, to help the seafaring folk.

He made other things after that; he put up a doorway with a door of wood in the entering of the cave; he made, too, a little boat that he might go to and fro to the land without swimming. And now, having no care to provide food, for they brought it him in abundance, he turned his mind to many small things. He made a holy carving in the cave, of Christ upon the cross—and he carved around it a number of creatures, not men only but birds and beasts, looking to the Cross, for he thought that the beasts also should have their joy in the great offering. His fame spread abroad; and there came a priest to see him, who abode with him for some days, prayed with him, and taught him much of the faith. The priest gave him a book, and showed him the letters; but David, though he longed to read what was within, could not hold the letters in his head.

He tamed, too, the wild birds of the rock, so that they came to his call; one was a gull, which became so fearless that it would come to his cave, and sit silent on a rock, watching him while he worked. He kept a fish, too, in a pool of the rocks, that would rise to the edge when he approached.

But all this time he went not near to the village; for his solitude had become very dear to him, and he prayed continually; and at evening and morning and midday he would sing praises to God, simple words that he had made.

One morning he awoke in the cave, and as he bestirred himself he thought in his heart of all his happiness. It was a still morning, but the sky was overcast. Suddenly he heard voices below him; and thinking that he was needed, he descended the rocks quickly, and came down a little way from a group of sailors who were standing on the shore; there was a boat drawn up on the sand, and near at hand there lay at anchor a small ship, that seemed to be of a foreign gear, and larger than he was wont to see. He came somewhat suddenly upon the group, and they seemed, as it were, to be amazed to see a man there. He went smilingly towards them, but as he did so there came into his heart a feeling of danger, he knew not what; and he thought that it would be better to retire up the rocks to his cave, and wait till the men had withdrawn—for it was not likely that they would visit him there, or that even if they saw the way thither, they would adventure it, as it was steep and dangerous. But he put the thought away and came up to them. They seemed to be conferring together in low voices, and the nearer that he drew, the less he liked their look. He spoke to them, but they seemed not to understand, and answered him back very roughly in a tongue he did not understand. But presently they put one forward, an old man, who had some words of English, who asked him what he did there. He tried to explain that he lived on the island, but the old man shook his head, evidently not believing that there could be one living in so bare a place. Then the men conferred again together, and presently the old man asked him, in his broken speech, whether he would take service on the ship with them. David said, smiling, that he would not, for he had other work to do; and the old man seemed to try and persuade him, saying that it was a good service; that they lived a free life, wandering where they would; but that they had lost men lately, and were hardly enough to sail the ship.

Then it came into David's mind that he had fallen in with pirates. They were not often seen in these parts, for there was little enough that they could get, the folk being all poor, and small traffic passing that way. And then, for he saw the group beginning to gather round him, he made a prayer in his heart that he should be delivered from the evil, and made proffer to the men of the little stores that he had. The old man shook his head, and spoke with the others, who now seemed to be growing angry and impatient; and then he said to David that they had need of him to help to sail the ship, and that he must come whether he would or no. David cast a glance round to see if he could escape up the rocks; but the men were all about him, and seeing in his eye that he thought of flight, they laid hands upon him. David resisted with all his might, but they overpowered him in a moment, bound his hands and feet, and cast him with much force into their boat. Then David was sorely disheartened; but he waited, committing his soul to God. While he waited, he saw a strange thing; on the beach there lay a box, tightly corded; the men raised this up very gently, and with difficulty, as it seemed to be heavy. Then they carried it up above the tide-mark; and, making a hole among the loose stones, they buried it very carefully, casting stones over it. Then one of them with a chisel made a mark on the cliff behind, to show where the box lay—and then, first looking carefully out to sea, they came into the boat, and rowed off to the ship, which seemed almost deserted; paying no more heed to David than if he had been a log of wood.

The old man who understood English steered the boat; and David tried to say some words to him, to ask that he should be released; but the old man only shook his head; and at last bade David be silent with great anger. They rowed slowly out, and David could see the great rocks, that had now been his home so long, rising, still and peaceful, in the morning light. Every rock and cranny was known to him. There was the place where, when he first came, he was used to fish. There was the cliff-top where he had made his fire; he could even see his little window in the front of the rocks, and he thought with grief that it would be dark and silent henceforth. But he thought that he was somehow in the hand of God; and that though to be dragged away from his home seemed grievous, there must be some task to which the Father would presently set him, even if it were to go down to death; and though the cords that bound him were now very painful, and his heart was full of sorrow, yet David felt a kind of peace in his spirit which showed him that God was still with him.

When they got to the ship, there arose a dispute among the men as to whether they should run out to sea before it was dark, or whether they should lie where they were; there was but little wind, so they made up their minds to stay. David himself thought from the look of the sky that there was strong weather brewing. The old man who spoke English asked him what he thought, and he told him that there would be wind. He seemed to be disposed to believe David; but the men were tired, and it was decided to stay.

They had unbound David that he might go on board; and the pain in his hands and feet was very great when the bonds were unloosed; and when he was on board they bound him again, but not so tightly, and led him down into a cabin, close and dirty, where a foul and smoky lamp burnt. They bade him sit in a corner. The low ill-smelling place was very grievous to David, and he thought with a sore heart of his clean cold cave, and his bed of fern. The

men seemed to take no further heed of him, and went about preparing a meal. There seemed to be little friendliness among them;
they spoke shortly and scowled upon each other; and David divined that there had been some dispute aboard, and that they were
ill-content. There was little discipline, the men going and coming
when they would.

Before long a meal was prepared; some sort of a stew with a
rich strong smell, that seemed very gross and foul to David, who
had been used so long to his simple fare. The men came in and
took from the dish what they desired; and a large jar was opened,
which from its fierce smell seemed to contain a hot and fiery spirit;
and that it was so David could easily discern, from the flushed faces
and louder talk of the men, which soon became mingled with a
gross merriment. The old man brought a mess of the food to David,
who shook his head smiling. Then the other, with more kindness
than David had expected, asked if he would have bread; and fetched
him a large piece, unbinding his hands for a little, that he might
eat. Then he offered him some of the spirit; but David asked for
water, which the old man gave him, binding his hands after he had
drunk, with a certain gentleness.

Presently the old man, after he too had eaten, came and sate
down beside David; and in his broken talk seemed to wish to win
him, if he could, to join them more willingly. He spoke of the pleasant life they lived, and of the wealth that they made, though he
said not how they came by it. He told him that he had seen some of
it hidden that day, which they had done for greater security, so
that, if the ship should be cast away, the men might have some of
their spoil waiting for them; and David understood from him,
though he had but few words to explain it, that it had been that
which had caused a strife among them. For they had come by the
treasure very hardly, and they had lost some of the crew in so doing it—and some of the men had desired to share it, and have done
with the sea for ever; but that it had been decided to make another
voyage first.

Then David said very gently that he did not desire to join them,
for he was a man of peace; and he told him of his lonely life, and

how he made a light to keep ships off the dangerous coast; and at that the old man looked at him with a fixed air, and nodded his head as though he had himself heard of the matter, or at least seen the light—all this David told him, speaking slowly as to a child; but it seemed as though every minute the remembrance of the language came more and more back to the old man.

But at last the man shook his head, and said that he was sorry so peaceful a life must come to an end. But, indeed, David must go with them whether he would or no; and that they would be good comrades yet; and he should have his share of whatever they got. And then he left David and went on to the deck.

Then there fell a great despair upon David; and at the same time the crew, excited by the drink they had taken, for they drained the jar, began to dispute among themselves, and to struggle and fight; and one of them espied David, and they gathered round and mocked him. They mocked at his dress, his face, his hair, which had grown somewhat long. And one of them in particular seemed most urgent, speaking long to the others, and pointing at David from time to time, while the others fell into a great laughter. Then they fell to plucking his hair, and even to beating him—and they tried to force the spirit into his mouth, but he kept his teeth clenched; and the very smell of the fiery stuff made his brain sick. But he could nor stir hand or foot; and presently there came into his mind a great blackness of anger, so that he seemed to be in the very grip of the evil one; and he knew in his heart that if he had been unbound, he would have slain one or more of them; for his heart beat thick, and there came a strange redness into his sight, and he gnashed his teeth for rage; at which they mocked him the more. But at last the old man came down into the cabin, and when he saw what they were at, he spoke very angrily to them, stamping his foot; and it seemed as though he alone had any authority, for they left off ill-using David, and went from him one by one.

Then, after a while they began to nod in their places; one or two of them cast themselves into beds made in the wall; others fell on the floor, and slept like beasts; and at last they all slept; and last of all the old man came in again, bearing a lamp, and looked

round the room in a sort of angry disgust. Then he said a word to
David, and opening a door went on into a cabin beyond, closing
the door behind him.

Then, in the low light of the smoking lamp, and in the hot and
reeking room, with the foul breathing of the sleepers round him,
David spent a very dreadful hour. He had never in the old days
seen so ill a scene; and it was to him, exhausted by pain and by
rage, as if a dark thing came behind him, and whispered in his secret ear that God regarded not men at all, and that the evil was
stronger than the good, and prevailed. He tried to put the thought
away; but it came all the more instantly, that what he had seen
could not be, if God had indeed power to rule. It was not only the
scene itself, but the thought of what these men were, and the black
things they had doubtless done, the deeds of murder, cruelty, and
lust that were written plainly on all their faces; all these came like
dark shadows and gathered about him.

David stirred a little to ease himself of his pain and stiffness;
and his foot struck against a thing. He looked down, and saw in
the shadow of the table a knife lying, which had fallen from some
man's belt. A thought of desperate joy came into his mind. He bent
himself down with his bound hands, and he contrived to gather up
the knife. Then, very swiftly and deftly, he thrust the haft between
his knees; then he worked the rope that bound his hands to and
fro over the blade; the rope parted, and the blood came back into
his numbed fingers with a terrible pain. But David heeded it not,
and stooping down, he cut the cord that bound his feet; then he
rose softly, and sate down again; for the blood, returning to his
limbs, made him feel he could not stand yet awhile. All was still in
the cabin, except for the slow breathing of those that slept; save
that every now and then one of the sleepers broke into a stifled
cry, and muttered words, or stirred in his sleep.

Presently David felt that he could walk. He pondered for a
moment whether he should take the knife, if he were suddenly attacked; but he resisted the thought, and left the knife lying on the
ground.

Then stepping lightly among the sleepers, he moved like a shadow to the door; very carefully he stepped; and at each movement or muttered word he stopped and caught his breath. Suddenly one of the men rose up, leaning on his arm, and looked at him with a stupid stare; but David stood still, waiting, with his heart fit to break within his breast, till the man lay down again. Then David was at the door. The cabin occupied half the ship to the bows; the rest was undecked, with high bulwarks; a rough ladder of steps led to the gangway. David stood for a moment in the shadow of the door; but there seemed no one on the watch without. The pure air and the fresh smell of the sea came to his senses like a breath of heaven. He stepped swiftly over a coil of rope; then up the ladder, and plunged noiselessly into the sea.

He swam a few strokes very strongly; and then he looked about him. The night was as dark as pitch. He could see a dim light from the ship behind him; the water rose and fell in a slow heavy swell; but which way the land lay he could not tell. But he said to himself that it was better to drown and be certainly with God, than in the den of robbers he had left. So he turned himself round in the water, trying to remember where the shore lay, but it was all dark, both the sky and sea, with a pitchy blackness; only the lights of the ship glimmered towards him like little bright paths across the heaving tide.

Suddenly there came a thing so wonderful that David could hardly believe he saw truly; a bright eye of light, as it were, opened upon him in the dark, far off, and hung high in the heavens, like a quiet star. The radiance of it was like the moon, cold and clear. And though David could not at first divine whence it came, he did not doubt in his heart that it was there to guide him; so he struck out towards it, with long silent strokes. He swam for a long time, the light shining softly over the water, and seeming to rise higher over his head, while the glimmering of the ship's lights grew fainter and more murky behind him. Then he became aware that he was drawing near to the land; great dark shapes loomed up over his head, and he heard the soft beating of waves before him. Then he could see too, as he looked upon the light, that there was a glimmer around it; and he saw that it came from the edges and faces of rocks that were lit up by the radiance. So he swam more softly; and presently his foot struck a rock covered with weed; so he put his feet down, waded in cautiously, and pulling himself up by the hands found himself on a rocky shore, and knew that it was his own island.

Then the light above him, as though it had but waited for his safety to be secured, died softly away, like the moon gliding into a cloud. David wondered very much at this, and cast about in his mind how it might be; but his heart seemed to tell him that there was some holy and beautiful thing on the island very near to him. He could hardly contain himself for gladness; and he thought that God had doubtless given him this day of misery and terror, partly that he might value his peace truly, and partly that he might feel that he had it not of right, but by the gracious disposition of the Father.

So he climbed very softly and swiftly to the cave; and entered it with a great gladness; and then he became aware of a great awe in his mind. There was somewhat there, that he could not see with his eyes, but which was more real and present than anything he had ever known; the cave seemed to shine with a faint and tender gleam that was dying away by slow degrees; as though the roof and walls had been charged with a peaceful light, which still rayed about them, though the radiance that had fed it was withdrawn. He took off his dripping clothes, and wrapped himself in his old sea-cloak. But he did not think of sleep, or even of prayer; he only sate still on his bed of fern, with his eyes open in the darkness, drinking in the strong and solemn peace which seemed to abide there. David never had known such a feeling, and he was never to know it again so fully; but for the time he seemed to sit at the foot of God, satisfied. While he thus sate, a great wind sprang up outside and thundered in the rocks; fiercer and fiercer it blew, and soon there followed it the loud crying of the sea, as the great waters began to heave and rage. Then David bestirred himself to light and trim his lamp, and set it in the window as a warning to ships. And when he had done this he felt a great and sudden weariness, and he laid

himself down; and sleep closed over him at once, as the sea closes
over a stone that is flung into it.

Once in the night he woke, with the roar of the storm in his
ears, and wondered that he had slept through it. He had been
through many stormy nights, but he had never heard the like of
this. The wind blew with a steady roar, like a flood of thunder
outpoured; in the midst of if, the great waves, hurled upon the
rocks, uttered their voices; and between he heard the hiss of the
water, as it rushed downwards from the cliff face. In the midst of
all came a sharp and sudden wailing cry; and then he began to
wonder what the poor ship was doing, which he thought of as riding
furiously at her anchor, with the drunken crew, and the old man
with his sad and solemn face, who seemed so different from his
unruly followers, and yet was not ashamed to rule over them and
draw profit from their evil deeds. In spite of the ill they had tried
to do him, he felt a great pity for them in his heart; but this was
but for a moment, for sleep closed over him again, and drew him
down into forgetfulness.

When David woke in the morning, the gale had died away, but
the sky wept from low and ragged clouds, as if ashamed and sullen
at the wrath of the day before. Water trickled in the cracks of the
rock; and when David peered abroad, he looked into the thin drift-
ing clouds. He had a great content in his heart, but the awe and
the strange peace of the night had somehow diminished.

He began to reflect upon the light that he had seen from the
sea. It was not his lamp that had given out such light, for it was
clear and thin, while the light his own lamp gave was angry and
red. Moreover, when he had lighted the lamp before the storm, it
was standing idle, not in the window-place, but on the rock-shelf
where he had set it. Then he knew that some great and holy mystery had been wrought for him that night, and that he had been
very tenderly used.

Presently he descended the cliff, and went out upon the seaward side. The waves still rose angrily under the grey sky, but were
fast abating. He saw in a moment that the shore was full of wreck-
age: there were spars and timbers everywhere, and all the litter of

a ship. Some of the timbers were flung so high upon the rocks that he saw how great the violence of the storm had been. He walked along, and in a minute he came upon the body of a man lying on his face, strangely battered.

Then he saw another body, and yet another. He lifted them up, but there was no sign of life in them; and he recognised with a great sadness that they were the pirates who had dragged him from his home. He had for a moment one evil thought in his mind, a kind of triumph in his heart that God had saved him from his enemies, and delivered them over to death; but he knew that it was a wicked thought, and thrust it from him; at last at the end of the rocks he found the old captain himself. There was a kind of majesty about him, even in death, as he lay looking up at the sky, with one arm flung across his breast, and the other arm outstretched beside him. Then he saw the ribs of the ship itself stick up among the rocks, and he wondered to find the hull so broken and ruinous.

His next care was that the poor bodies should have burial. So about midday he took his boat from its shelter, and rowed across to the land; and then, with a strange fear of the heart, he climbed the cliff, and walked down slowly to the village, which he had thought in his heart he would never have seen again.

The wind had now driven the clouds out of the sky, and the sun came out with a strong white light, the light that shines from the sky when the earth has been washed clean by rain. It sparkled brightly in the little drops that hung like jewels in the grass and bushes. It was with a great throb of the heart that David came out upon the end of the down, and saw the village beneath him. It looked as though no change had passed over it, but as though its life must have stood still, since he left it; then there came tears into David's eyes at the thought of the old hard life he had lived there, and how God had since filled his cup so full of peace; so with many thoughts in his heart he came slowly down the path to the town. He first met two children whom he did not know; he spoke to them, but they looked for a moment in terror at his face; his hair and beard were long, and he was all tanned by the sun; but he spoke softly to them, and presently they came to him and

were persuaded to tell their names. They were the children, David
thought, of a young lad whom he had known as a boy; and presently, as the manner of children is when they have laid aside fear,
they told him many small things, their ages and their doings, and
other little affairs which seem so big to a child; and then they would
take his hands and lead him to the village, while David smiled to
be so lovingly attended. He was surprised, when he entered the
street, to see how curiously he was regarded. Even men and women,
that he had known, would hardly speak with him, but did him reverence. The children would lead him to their house first; and so he
went thither, not unwilling. When they were at the place, he found
with a gentle wonder that it was even the house where he had himself dwelt. He went in, and found the mother of the children within,
one whom he had known as a girl. She greeted him with the same
reverence as the rest; so that he at last took courage, and asked
her why it should not be as it had been before. And then he learned
from her talk, with a strange surprise, that it was thought that he
was a very holy man, much visited by God, who not only had been
shown how, by a kind of magical secret, to save ships from falling
on that deadly coast, but as one whose prayers availed to guard
and keep the whole place safe. He tried to show her that this was
not so, and that he was a simple person in great need of holiness;
but he saw that she only thought him the holier for his humility,
so he was ashamed to say more.

Then he went to the chief man in the village, and told him
wherefore he had come—that there was a wreck on the shore of
the islands, and that there were bodies that must be buried. One
more visit he paid, and that was to the little maiden whom he had
seen the last when he went away. She was now nearly grown to a
woman, and her grandmother was very old and weak, and near her
end. David went there alone, and said that he had returned as he
had promised; but he found that the child had much lost her remembrance of him, and could hardly see the friend she had known
in the strong and wild-looking figure that he had become. He talked
a little quietly; the old grandmother, who could not move from her
chair, was easier with him, and asked him, looking curiously upon

him, whether he had found that of which he went in search. "Nay, mother," he said, "not found; but I am like a man whose feet are set in the way, and who sees the city gate across the fields." Then she smiled at him and said, "But I am near the gate." Then he told her that he often thought of her, and made mention of her in his prayers; and so rose to go; but she asked him to bless her, which David did very tenderly, and kissed her and departed; but he went heavily; because he feared to be regarded as he was now regarded; and he thought in his heart that he would never return again, but dwell alone in his cave with God. For the world troubled him; and the voices of the children, and the looks of those that he had known before seemed to lay soft hands about his heart, and draw him back into the world.

The same day he returned to the cave; and the boats came out and took the bodies away, and they were laid in the burying-ground.

Then the next day many returned to clear away the wreck; and David came not out of his cave while they did this; for it went to his heart to see the joy with which they gathered what had meant the death of so many men. They asked him what they should leave for him, and he answered, "Nothing—only a piece of plain wood, for a purpose." So when evening came they had removed all; and the island, that had rung all day with shouts and talk and the feet of men, was silent again; but before they went, David said that he had a great desire to see a priest, if a message could be sent; and this they undertook to do. But David was very heavy-hearted for many days, for it seemed to him that the sight of the world had put all the peace out of his heart; and his prayers came hollow and dry.

A few days after there came a boat to the rock; the sea was running somewhat high, and they had much ado to make a landing. David went down to the water's edge, and saw that besides the fishermen, whom he knew, there was a little wizened man in a priest's dress, that seemed bewildered by the moving of the boat and the tossing of the big waves with their heaving crests, that broke upon the rocks with a heavy sound. At last they got the boat into the creek, and the little priest came nimbly ashore, but not without a wetting. The fishermen said that they would return in the evening, and fetch the priest away.

He looked a frail man, and David could not discern whether he were young or old; and he felt a pity for a man who was so unhandy, and who seemed to be so scared of the sea. But the priest came up to him and took his hand. "I have heard much of you, my brother," he said, "and I have desired to see you—but this sea of yours is a strange and wild monster, and I trust it not,—though indeed it is God's handiwork. Yet King David, your patron, was of the same mind, I think, and wrote in one of his wise psalms how it made the heart to melt within him." David looked at him with much attention as he spoke, and there was something in the priest's eye, a kind of hidden fire, joined with a wise mirth, that made him, all of a sudden, feel like a child before him. So he said, "Where will your holiness sit? It is cold here in the wind; I have a dwelling in the rocks, but it is hard to come by except for winged fowl, and for men like myself who have been used to the precipices."

"Well, show the way, brother," said the priest cheerfully, "and I will adventure my best." So David showed him the way up the crags, and went slowly in front of him, that he might help him up; but the priest climbed like a cat, looking blithely about him, and had no need of help, though he was encumbered with his robe.

When they were got there, the priest looked curiously about him, and presently knelt down before the carving, and said a little prayer to himself.

Then he questioned David about his life, asking questions briskly, as though he were accustomed to command; and David felt more and more every moment that he was as a child before this masterful and wary man. He told him of his early life, and of his visions, and of his desire to know God, and of the light that he set in the rocks; and then he told him of his adventure with the pirates, not forgetting the treasure. The priest heard him with great attention, and said presently that he had done well, and that God was with him. Then he asked him how he would have the treasure bestowed, and David said that he had no design in his mind. "Then that shall be my care," said the priest, "and I doubt not that the Lord hath sent it us, that there may be a church in this lonely place."

And then, turning to David with a wonderful and piercing look, he said, "And this peace of spirit that you speak of, that you came here to seek, tell me truly, brother, have you found it?"

Then David looked upon the ground a little and said, "Dear sir, I know not; I am indeed strangely happy in this lonely place; but to speak all the truth, I feel like a man who lingers at a gate, and who hears the sound of joy and melody within, which rejoices his heart, but he is not yet admitted. No," he went on, "I have not found the way. The Father is indeed very near me, and I am certain of His love—but there is still a barrier between me and His Heart."

Then the priest bowed his head awhile in thought, but said nothing for a long space; and then David said, "Dear sir, advise me." Then the priest looked at him with a clear gaze, and said, "Shall I advise you, O my brother?" And David said "Yes, dear sir." Then the priest said, "Indeed, my brother, I see in your life the gracious hand of God. He did redeem you, and he planted in your heart a true seed of peace. You have lived here a holy and an innocent life; but he withholds from you his best gift, because you are not willing to be utterly led by him. There have been in ancient days many such souls, who have fled from the wickedness of the world, and have spent themselves in prayer and penance, and have done a holy work—for indeed there are many victories that may be won by prayer. But indeed, dear brother, I think that God's will for you is that this lonely life of yours should have an end. I think that you have herein followed your own pleasure overmuch; and I believe that God would now have you go back to the world, and work for him therein. You have a great power with this simple folk; but they are as sheep without a shepherd, and must be fed, and none but you can now feed them. You will bethink you of the visit that the Lord Christ paid to the Sisters of Bethany; Martha laboured much to please Him, but she laboured for her own pleasing too; and Mary it was that had the good part, because she thought not of herself but of the Lord. And now, dear brother, I would have you do what will be very grievous to you. I would have you go back to your native place, and there abide to labour for God; you may come hither at seasons, and be alone with God, and that will refresh you; but you are now, methinks, like a man who has found a great treasure, and who speaks no word of it to others, and neither uses it himself, but only looks upon it and is glad."

Then David was very sad at the priest's words, knowing that he spoke the truth. But the priest said, "Now we will speak no more of this awhile; and I would not have you do it, unless your heart consents thereto; only be strong." And then he asked if he might have somewhat to eat; and David brought him his simple fare; so they ate together, and while they ate, it came into David's mind that this was certainly the way. All that afternoon they sate, while the wind rustled without, and the sea made a noise; and then the priest said they would go and look at the treasure, because it was near evening, and he must return. So they went down together, and drew the rocks off from the box. It was a box of wood, tightly corded, and they undid it, and found within a great store of gold and silver pieces, which the priest reckoned up, and said that it would be abundant for a church.

Then they saw the boat approach; and the priest blessed David, and David thanked him with tears, for showing him the truth; and the priest said, "Not so, my brother; I did but show you what is in your own heart, for God puts such truth in the heart of all of us as we can bear; but sometimes we keep it like a sword in its scabbard, until the bright and sharp thing, that might have wrought great deeds, be all rusted and blunted."

And then the priest departed, taking with him the box of gold, and David was left alone.

David was very heavy-hearted when he was left alone on the island. He knew that the priest had spoken the truth, but he loved his solitary life, and the silence of the cave, the free air and the sun, and the lonely current of his own thoughts. The sun went slowly down over the waters in a great splendour of light and colour, so that the clouds in the sky seemed like purple islands floating in a golden sea; David sitting in his cave thought with a kind of terror of the small and close houses of the village, the sound of feet, and talk of men and women. At last he fell asleep; and in his sleep he dreamed that he was in a great garden. He looked about him with pleasure, and he presently saw a gardener moving about at his work. He went in that direction, and he saw that the man, who was old and had a very wise and tender face, was setting out some young trees in a piece of ground. He planted them carefully with deft hands, and he smiled to himself as he worked, as though he was full of joyful thoughts. David wished in his heart to go and speak with him, but something held him back. Presently the gardener went away, and while he was absent, another man, of a secret aspect, came swiftly into the place, peering about him. His glance passed David by, and David knew that he was in some way unseen. The man looked all about him in a furtive haste, and then plucked up one of the trees, which seemed to David to be already growing and shooting out small leaves and buds. The man smoothed down the ground where he drew it out, and then went very quickly away. David would have wished to stop him, but he could not. Then the old gardener came back, and looked long at the place whence the tree had been drawn. Then he sighed to himself, and cast a swift look in the direction in which the man had fled. He had brought other trees with him, but he did not plant one in the empty space, but left it bare. Then David felt that he must follow the other, and so he did. He found him very speedily, but it was outside the garden, in a rough place, where thorny bushes and wild plants grew thickly. The other had cleared a little space among them, and here he set the tree; but he planted it ill and hastily, as though he was afraid of being disturbed; and then he departed secretly. David stood and watched the tree a little. It seemed at first to begin to grow again as it had done before, but presently something ailed it and it drooped. Then David saw the thorny bushes near it begin to stretch out their arms about it, and the wild herbs round about sprang up swiftly, and soon the tree was choked by them, and hardly appeared above the brake. David began to be sorry for the tree, which still kept some life in it, and struggled as it were feebly to put out its boughs above the thicket. While he stood he saw the old gardener approaching, and as he approached he carefully considered the ground. When he saw the tree, he smiled, and drew it out carefully, and went back to the garden, and David followed him; he planted it again tenderly in the ground; and the tree which had looked so drooping and feeble began at once to put forth leaves and flowers. The gardener smiled again, and then for the first time looked upon David. His eyes were deep and grave like a still water; and he smiled as one might who shares a secret with another. And then of a sudden David awoke, and found the light of dawn creeping into the cave; and he fell to considering the dream, and in a moment knew that it was sent for his learning. So he hesitated no longer, but gave up his will to God.

It was a sad hour for David nevertheless; he walked softly about the cave, and he put aside what he would take with him, and it seemed to him that he was, as it were, uprooting a tree that had grown deep; he tied up what he would take with him, but he left some things behind, for he thought that he might return. And then he kneeled down and prayed, the tears running over his face; and lastly he rose and kissed the cold wall of the cave; at the door he saw the gull that had been with him so oft, and he scattered some crumbs for it, and while the bird fell to picking the crumbs, David descended the rock swiftly, not having the heart to look about him; and then he put his things in the boat, and rowed swiftly and silently to the shore, looking back at the great rocks, which stood up all bright and clear in the fresh light of the dawn, with the waves breaking softly at their feet.

David had no fixed plan in his mind, as he rowed across to the land. He only thought that it was right for him to return, and to take up his part in the old life again. He did not dare to look before him, but simply put, as it were, his hand in the hand of God, and hoped to be led forward. He was soon at the shore, and he pulled his boat up on the land, and left it lying in a little cave that opened upon the beach; then he shouldered his pack, and went slowly, with even strides, across the hill and down to the village. He met no one on the way, and the street seemed deserted. He made his way to the house of the old woman who was his friend; he put his small pack at the door and entered. The little house was quite silent. But he heard a sound of weeping; when he came into the outer room, he saw the maiden sitting in a chair with her face bowed on the table. He called to her by name; she lifted her head and looked at him for a moment and then rose up and came to him, as a child comes to be comforted. He saw at once that some grievous thing had happened; and presently with sobs and tears she told him that her grandmother had died a few days before, that she had been that day buried, and that she knew not what she was to do; there seemed more behind; and David at last made out that she was asked in marriage by a young fisherman whom she did not love, and she knew not how else to live. And then he said that he was come back and would not depart from her, and that she should be a daughter to him.

Now of the rest of the life of David I must not here speak; he lived in the village, and he did his part; a little chapel was built in the place with the money of the pirates; and David went in and out among the folk of the place, and drew many to the love of God; he went once back to the cave, but he abode not long there; but of one thing I will tell, and that is of a piece of carving that David did, working little by little in the long winter nights at the piece of wood that came from the pirate ship. The carving is of a man standing on the shore of the sea, and holding up a lantern in his hand, and on the sea is carved a ship. And David calls his carving "The Light of the World." At the top of it is a scroll, with the words thereon, "He shall send down from on high to fetch me, and shall take me out of many waters." And beneath is another scroll on which is graven, "Thou also shalt light my candle; the Lord my God shall make my darkness to be light."

The Slype House

In the town of Garchester, close to St. Peter's Church, and near the river, stood a dark old house called the Slype House, from a narrow passage of that name that ran close to it, down to a bridge over the stream. The house showed a front of mouldering and discoloured stone to the street, pierced by small windows, like a monastery; and indeed, it was formerly inhabited by a college of priests who had served the Church. It abutted at one angle upon the aisle of the church, and there was a casement window that looked out from a room in the house, formerly the infirmary, into the aisle; it had been so built that any priest that was sick might hear the Mass from his bed, without descending into the church. Behind the house lay a little garden, closely grown up with trees and tall weeds, that ran down to the stream. In the wall that gave on the water, was a small door that admitted to an old timbered bridge that crossed the stream, and had a barred gate on the further side, which was rarely seen open; though if a man had watched attentively he might sometimes have seen a small lean person, much bowed and with a halting gait, slip out very quietly about dusk, and walk, with his eyes cast down, among the shadowy byways.

The name of the man who thus dwelt in the Slype House, as it appeared in the roll of burgesses, was Anthony Purvis. He was of an ancient family, and had inherited wealth. A word must be said of his childhood and youth. He was a sickly child, an only son, his father a man of substance, who lived very easily in the country; his mother had died when he was quite a child, and this sorrow had been borne very heavily by his father, who had loved her tenderly, and after her death had become morose and sullen, withdrawing himself from all company and exercise, and brooding angrily over his loss, as though God had determined to vex him. He had never cared much for the child, who had been peevish and fretful; and the boy's presence had done little but remind him of the wife he had lost; so that the child had lived alone, nourishing his own fancies, and reading much in a library of curious books that was in the house. The boy's health had been too tender for him to go to school; but when he was eighteen, he seemed stronger, and his father sent him to a university, more for the sake of being relieved of the boy's presence than for his good. And there, being unused to the society of his equals, he had been much flouted and despised for his feeble frame; till a certain bitter ambition sprang up in his mind, like a poisonous flower, to gain power and make himself a name; and he had determined that as he could not be loved he might still be feared; so he bided his time in bitterness, making great progress in his studies; then, when those days were over, he departed eagerly, and sought and obtained his father's leave to betake himself to a university of Italy, where he fell into somewhat evil hands; for he made a friendship with an old doctor of the college, who feared not God and thought ill of man, and spent all his time in dark researches into the evil secrets of nature, the study of poisons that have enmity to the life of man, and many other hidden works of darkness, such as intercourse with spirits of evil, and the black influences that lie in wait for the soul; and he found Anthony an apt pupil. There he lived for some years till he was nearly thirty, seldom visiting his home, and writing but formal letters to his father, who supplied him gladly with a small revenue, so long as he kept apart and troubled him not.

Then his father had died, and Anthony came home to take up his inheritance, which was a plentiful one; he sold his land, and visiting the town of Garchester, by chance, for it lay near his home, he had lighted upon the Slype House, which lay very desolate and gloomy; and as he needed a large place for his instruments and devices, he had bought the house, and had now lived there for twenty years in great loneliness, but not ill-content.

To serve him he had none but a man and his wife, who were quiet and simple people and asked no questions; the wife cooked his meals, and kept the rooms, where he slept and read, clean and neat; the man moved his machines for him, and arranged his phials and instruments, having a light touch and a serviceable memory.

The door of the house that gave on the street opened into a hall; to the right was a kitchen, and a pair of rooms where the man and his wife lived. On the left was a large room running through the house; the windows on to the street were walled up, and the windows at the back looked—on the garden, the trees of which grew close to the casements, making the room dark, and in a breeze rustling their leaves or leafless branches against the panes. In this room Anthony had a furnace with bellows, the smoke of which discharged itself into the chimney; and here he did much of his work, making mechanical toys, as a clock to measure the speed of wind or water, a little chariot that ran a few yards by itself, a puppet that moved its arms and laughed—and other things that had wiled away his idle hours; the room was filled up with dark lumber, in a sort of order that would have looked to a stranger like disorder, but so that Anthony could lay his hand on all that he needed. From the hall, which was paved with stone, went up the stairs, very strong and broad, of massive oak; under which was a postern that gave on the garden; on the floor above was a room where Anthony slept, which again had its windows to the street boarded up, for he was a light sleeper, and the morning sounds of the awakening city disturbed him.

The room was hung with a dark arras, sprinkled with red flowers; he slept in a great bed with black curtains to shut out all light; the windows looked into the garden; but on the left of the bed, which stood with its head to the street, was an alcove, behind the hangings, containing the window that gave on the church. On the same floor were three other rooms; in one of these, looking on the garden, Anthony had his meals. It was a plain panelled room. Next was a room where he read, filled with books, also looking on the

garden; and next to that was a little room of which he alone had
the key. This room he kept locked, and no one set foot in it but
himself. There was one more room on this floor, set apart for a
guest who never came, with a great bed and a press of oak. And
that looked on the street. Above, there was a row of plain plastered rooms, in which stood furniture for which Anthony had no
use, and many crates in which his machines and phials came to
him; this floor was seldom visited, except by the man, who sometimes came to put a box there; and the spiders had it to themselves;
except for a little room where stood an optic glass through which
on clear nights Anthony sometimes looked at the moon and stars,
if there was any odd misadventure among them, such as an eclipse;
or when a fiery-tailed comet went his way silently in the heavens,
coming from none might say whence and going none knew whither,
on some strange errand of God.

Anthony had but two friends who ever came to see him. One
was an old physician who had ceased to practise his trade, which
indeed was never abundant, and who would sometimes drink a
glass of wine with Anthony, and engage in curious talk of men's
bodies and diseases, or look at one of Anthony's toys. Anthony had
come to know him by having called him in to cure some ailment,
which needed a surgical knife; and that had made a kind of friendship between them; but Anthony had little need thereafter to consult him about his health, which indeed was now settled enough,
though he had but little vigour; and he knew enough of drugs to
cure himself when he was ill. The other friend was a foolish priest
of the college, that made belief to be a student but was none, who
thought Anthony a very wise and mighty person, and listened with
open mouth and eyes to all that he said or showed him. This priest,
who was fond of wonders, had introduced himself to Anthony by
making believe to borrow a volume of him; and then had grown
proud of the acquaintance, and bragged greatly of it to his friends,
mixing up much that was fanciful with a little that was true. But
the result was that gossip spread wide about Anthony, and he was
held in the town to be a very fearful person, who could do strange

mischief if he had a mind to; Anthony never cared to walk abroad, for he was of a shy habit, and disliked to meet the eyes of his fellows; but if he did go about, men began to look curiously after him as he went by, shook their heads and talked together with a dark pleasure, while children fled before his face and women feared him; all of which pleased Anthony mightily, if the truth were told; for at the bottom of his restless and eager spirit lay a deep vanity unseen, like a lake in woods; he hungered not indeed for fame, but for repute—*monstrari digito*, as the poet has it; and he cared little in what repute he was held, so long as men thought him great and marvellous; and as he could not win renown by brave deeds and words, he was rejoiced to win it by keeping up a certain darkness and mystery about his ways and doings; and this was very dear to him, so that when the silly priest called him Seer and Wizard, he frowned and looked sideways; but he laughed in his heart and was glad.

Now, when Anthony was near his fiftieth year, there fell on him a heaviness of spirit which daily increased upon him. He began to question of his end and what lay beyond. He had always made pretence to mock at religion, and had grown to believe that in death the soul was extinguished like a burnt-out flame. He began, too, to question of his life and what he had done. He had made a few toys, he had filled vacant hours, and he had gained an ugly kind of fame— and this was all. Was he so certain, he began to think, after all, that death was the end? Were there not, perhaps, in the vast house of God, rooms and chambers beyond that in which he was set for awhile to pace to and fro? About this time he began to read in a Bible that had lain dusty and unopened on a shelf. It was his mother's book, and he found therein many little tokens of her presence. Here was a verse underlined; at some gracious passages the page was much fingered and worn; in one place there were stains that looked like the mark of tears; then again, in one page, there was a small tress of hair, golden hair, tied in a paper with a name across it, that seemed to be the name of a little sister of his mother's that died a child; and again there were a few withered flowers, like little sad ghosts, stuck through a paper on which was written his

father's name—the name of the sad, harsh, silent man whom Anthony had feared with all his heart. Had those two, indeed, on some
day of summer, walked to and fro, or sate in some woodland corner, whispering sweet words of love together? Anthony felt a sudden hunger of the heart for a woman's love, for tender words to
soothe his sadness, for the laughter and kisses of children—and he
began to ransack his mind for memories of his mother; he could
remember being pressed to her heart one morning when she lay
abed, with her fragrant hair falling about him. The worst was that
he must bear his sorrow alone, for there were none to whom he
could talk of such things. The doctor was as dry as an old bunch of
herbs, and as for the priest, Anthony was ashamed to show anything but contempt and pride in his presence.

For relief he began to turn to a branch of his studies that he
had long disused; this was a fearful commerce with the unseen
spirits. Anthony could remember having practised some experi-
ments of this kind with the old Italian doctor; but he remembered
them with a kind of disgust, for they seemed to him but a sort of
deadly juggling; and such dark things as he had seen seemed like a
dangerous sport with unclean and coltish beings, more brute-like
than human. Yet now he read in his curious books with care, and
studied the tales of necromancers, who had indeed seemed to have
some power over the souls of men departed. But the old books gave
him but little faith, and a kind of angry disgust at the things at-
tempted. And he began to think that the horror in which such men
as made these books abode, was not more than the dark shadow
cast on the mirror of the soul by their own desperate imaginings
and timorous excursions.

One day, a Sunday, he was strangely sad and heavy; he could
settle to nothing, but threw book after book aside, and when he
turned to some work of construction, his hand seemed to have lost
its cunning. It was a grey and sullen day in October; a warm wet
wind came buffeting up from the West, and roared in the chimneys and eaves of the old house. The shrubs in the garden plucked
themselves hither and thither as though in pain. Anthony walked
to and fro after his midday meal, which he had eaten hastily and

without savour; at last, as though with a sudden resolution, he went to a secret cabinet and got out a key; and with it he went to the door of the little room that was ever locked.

He stopped at the threshold for a while, looking hither and thither; and then he suddenly unlocked it and went in, closing and locking it behind him. The room was as dark as night, but Anthony going softly, his hands before him, went to a corner and got a tinder-box which lay there, and made a flame.

A small dark room appeared, hung with a black tapestry; the window was heavily shuttered and curtained; in the centre of the room stood what looked like a small altar, painted black; the floor was all bare, but with white marks upon it, half effaced. Anthony looked about the room, glancing sidelong, as though in some kind of doubt; his breath went and came quickly, and he looked paler than was his wont.

Presently, as though reassured by the silence and calm of the place, he went to a tall press that stood in a corner, which he opened, and took from it certain things—a dish of metal, some small leathern bags, a large lump of chalk, and a book. He laid all but the chalk down on the altar, and then opening the book, read in it a little; and then he went with the chalk and drew certain marks upon the floor, first making a circle, which he went over again and again with anxious care; at times he went back and peeped into the book as though uncertain. Then he opened the bags, which seemed to hold certain kinds of powder, this dusty, that in grains; he ran them through his hands, and then poured a little of each into his dish, and mixed them with his hands. Then he stopped and looked about him. Then he walked to a place in the wall on the further side of the altar from the door, and drew the arras carefully aside, disclosing a little alcove in the wall; into this he looked fearfully, as though he was afraid of what he might see.

In the alcove, which was all in black, appeared a small shelf, that stood but a little way out from the wall. Upon it, gleaming very white against the black, stood the skull of a man, and on either side of the skull were the bones of a man's hand. It looked to him, as he gazed on it with a sort of curious disgust, as though a dead man had come up to the surface of a black tide, and was preparing presently to leap out. On either side stood two long silver candlesticks, very dark with disuse; but instead of holding candles, they were fitted at the top with flat metal dishes; and in these he poured some of his powders, mixing them as before with his fingers. Between the candlesticks and behind the skull was an old and dark picture, at which he gazed for a time, holding his taper on high. The picture represented a man fleeing in a kind of furious haste from a wood, his hands spread wide, and his eyes staring out of the picture; behind him everywhere was the wood, above which was a star in the sky—and out of the wood leaned a strange pale horned thing, very dim. The horror in the man's face was skilfully painted, and Anthony felt a shudder pass through his veins. He knew not what the picture meant; it had been given to him by the old Italian, who had smiled a wicked smile when he gave it, and told him that it had a very great virtue. When Anthony had asked him of the subject of the picture, the old Italian had said, "Oh, it is as appears; he hath been where he ought not, and he hath seen somewhat he doth not like." When Anthony would fain have known more, and especially what the thing was that leaned out of the wood, the old Italian had smiled cruelly and said, "Know you not? Well, you will know some day when you have seen him;" and never a word more would he say.

When Anthony had put all things in order, he opened the book at a certain place, and laid it upon the altar; and then it seemed as though his courage failed him, for he drew the curtain again over the alcove, unlocked the door, set the tinder-box and the candle back in their place, and softly left the room.

He was very restless all the evening. He took down books from the shelves, turned them over, and put them back again. He addressed himself to some unfinished work, but soon threw it aside; he paced up and down, and spent a long time, with his hands clasped behind him, looking out into the desolate garden, where a still, red sunset burnt behind the leafless trees. He was like a man who has made up his mind to a grave decision, and shrinks back upon the brink. When his food was served he could hardly touch it, and he drank no wine as his custom was to do, but only water, saying to himself that his head must be clear. But in the evening he went to his bedroom, and searched for something in a press there; he found at last what he was searching for, and unfolded a long black robe, looking gloomily upon it, as though it aroused unwelcome thoughts; while he was pondering, he heard a hum of music behind the arras; he put the robe down, and stepped through the hangings, and stood awhile in the little oriel that looked down into the church. Vespers were proceeding; he saw the holy lights dimly through the dusty panes, and heard the low preluding of the organ; then, solemn and slow, rose the sound of a chanted psalm on the air; he carefully unfastened the casement which opened inward and unclosed it, standing for a while to listen, while the air, fragrant with incense smoke, drew into the room along the vaulted roof. There were but a few worshippers in the church, who stood below him; two lights burnt stilly upon the altar, and he saw distinctly the thin hands of a priest who held a book close to his face. He had not set foot within a church for many years, and the sight and sound drew his mind back to his childhood's days. At last with a sigh he put the window to very softly, and went to his study, where he made pretence to read, till the hour came when he was wont to retire to his bed. He sent his servant away, but instead of lying down, he sate, looking upon a parchment, which he held in his hand, while the bells of the city slowly told out the creeping hours.

At last, a few minutes before midnight, he rose from his place; the house was now all silent, and without the night was very still, as though all things slept tranquilly. He opened the press and took from it the black robe, and put it round him, so that it covered him from head to foot, and then gathered up the parchment, and the key of the locked room, and went softly out, and so came to the door. This he undid with a kind of secret and awestruck haste, locking it behind him. Once inside the room, he wrestled awhile with a strong aversion to what was in his mind to do, and stood for a moment, listening intently, as though he expected to hear some sound. But the room was still, except for the faint biting of some small creature in the wainscot.

Then with a swift motion he took up the tinder-box and made a light; he drew aside the curtain that hid the alcove; he put fire to the powder in the candlesticks, which at first spluttered, and then swiftly kindling sent up a thick smoky flame, fragrant with drugs, burning hotly and red. Then he came back to the altar; cast a swift glance round him to see that all was ready; put fire to the powder on the altar, and in a low and inward voice began to recite words from the book, and from the parchment which he held in his hand; once or twice he glanced fearfully at the skull, and the hands which gleamed luridly through the smoke; the figures in the picture wavered in the heat; and now the powders began to burn clear, and throw up a steady light; and still he read, sometimes turning a page, until at last he made an end; and drawing something from a silver box which lay beside the book, he dropped it in the flame, and looked straight before him to see what might befall. The thing that fell in the flame burned up brightly, with a little leaping of sparks, but soon it died down; and there was a long silence, in the room, a breathless silence, which, to Anthony's disordered mind, was not like the silence of emptiness, but such silence as may be heard when unseen things are crowding quietly to a closed door, expecting it to be opened, and as it were holding each other back.

Suddenly, between him and the picture, appeared for a moment a pale light, as of moonlight, and then with a horror which words cannot attain to describe, Anthony saw a face hang in the air a few feet from him, that looked in his own eyes with a sort of intent fury, as though to spring upon him if he turned either to the right hand or to the left. His knees tottered beneath him, and a sweat of icy coldness sprang on his brow; there followed a sound like no sound that Anthony had ever dreamed of hearing; a sound that was near and yet remote, a sound that was low and yet charged with power, like the groaning of a voice in grievous pain and anger, that strives to be free and yet is helpless. And then Anthony knew that he had indeed opened the door that looks into the other world, and that a deadly thing that held him in enmity had looked out. His reeling brain still told him that he was safe where he was, but that he must not step or fall outside the circle; but how he should resist the power of the wicked face he knew not. He tried to frame a prayer in his heart; but there swept such a fury of hatred across the face that he dared not. So he closed his eyes and stood dizzily waiting to fall, and knowing that if he fell it was the end.

Suddenly, as he stood with closed eyes, he felt the horror of the spell relax; he opened his eyes again, and saw that the face died out upon the air, becoming first white and then thin, like the husk that stands on a rush when a fly draws itself from its skin, and floats away into the sunshine.

Then there fell a low and sweet music upon the air, like a concert of flutes and harps, very far away. And then suddenly, in a sweet clear radiance, the face of his mother, as she lived in his mind, appeared in the space, and looked at him with a kind of heavenly love; then beside the face appeared two thin hands which seemed to wave a blessing towards him, which flowed like healing into his soul.

The relief from the horror, and the flood of tenderness that came into his heart, made him reckless. The tears came into his eyes, not in a rising film, but a flood hot and large. He took a step forwards round the altar; but as he did so, the vision disappeared, the lights shot up into a flare and went out; the house seemed to be suddenly shaken; in the darkness he heard the rattle of bones, and the clash of metal, and Anthony fell all his length upon the ground and lay as one dead.

But while he thus lay, there came to him in some secret cell of the mind a dreadful vision, which he could only dimly remember afterwards with a fitful horror. He thought that he was walking in the cloister of some great house or college, a cool place, with a pleasant garden in the court. He paced up and down, and each time that he did so, he paused a little before a great door at the end, a huge blind portal, with much carving about it, which he somehow knew he was forbidden to enter. Nevertheless, each time that he came to it, he felt a strong wish, that constantly increased, to set foot therein. Now in the dream there fell on him a certain heaviness, and the shadow of a cloud fell over the court, and struck the sunshine out of it. And at last he made up his mind that he would enter. He pushed the door open with much difficulty, and found himself in a long blank passage, very damp and chilly, but with a glimmering light; he walked a few paces down it. The flags underfoot were slimy, and the walls streamed with damp. He then thought that he would return; but the great door was closed behind him, and he could not open it. This made him very fearful; and while he considered what he should do, he saw a tall and angry-looking man approaching very swiftly down the passage. As he turned to face him, the other came straight to him, and asked him very sternly what he did there; to which Anthony replied that he had found the door open. To which the other replied that it was fast now, and that he must go forward. He seized Anthony as he spoke by the arm, and urged him down the passage. Anthony would fain have resisted, but he felt like a child in the grip of a giant, and went forward in great terror and perplexity. Presently they came to a door in the side of the wall, and as they passed it, there stepped out an ugly shadowy thing, the nature of which he could not clearly discern, and marched softly behind them. Soon they came to a turn in the passage, and in a moment the way stopped on the brink of a dark well, that seemed to go down a long way into the earth, and out of which came a cold fetid air, with a hollow sound like a complaining voice. Anthony drew back as far as he could from the pit, and set his back to the wall, his companion letting go of him. But he could not go backward, for the thing behind him was in the passage, and barred the way, creeping slowly nearer. Then Anthony was in a great agony of mind, and waited for the end.

But while he waited, there came some one very softly down the passage and drew near; and the other, who had led him to the place, waited, as though ill-pleased to be interrupted; it was too murky for Anthony to see the new-comer, but he knew in some way that he was a friend. The stranger came up to them, and spoke in a low voice to the man who had drawn Anthony thither, as though pleading for something; and the man answered angrily, but yet with a certain dark respect, and seemed to argue that he was acting in his right, and might not be interfered with. Anthony could not hear what they said, they spoke so low, but he guessed the sense, and knew that it was himself of whom they discoursed, and listened with a fearful wonder to see which would prevail. The end soon came, for the tall man, who had brought him there, broke out into a great storm of passion; and Anthony heard him say, "He hath yielded himself to his own will; and he is mine here; so let us make an end." Then the stranger seemed to consider; and then with a quiet courage, and in a soft and silvery voice like that of a child, said, "I would that you would have yielded to my prayer; but as you will not, I have no choice." And he took his hand from under the cloak that wrapped him, and held something out; then there came a great roaring out of the pit, and a zigzag flame flickered in the dark. Then in a moment the tall man and the shadow were gone; Anthony could not see whither they went, and he would have thanked the stranger; but the other put his finger to his lip as though to order silence, and pointed to the way he had come, saying, "Make haste and go back; for they will return anon with others; you know not how dear it hath cost me." Anthony could see the stranger's face in the gloom, and he was surprised to see it so youthful; but he saw also that tears stood in the eyes of the stranger, and that something dark like blood trickled down his brow; yet he looked very lovingly at him. So Anthony made haste to go back, and found the door ajar; but as he reached it, he heard a horrible din behind him, of cries and screams; and it was with a sense of gratitude, that he could not put into words, but which filled all his heart, that he found himself back in the cloister again. And then the vision all fled away, and with a shock coming to himself, he found that he was lying in his own room; and then he knew that a battle had been fought out over his soul, and that the evil had not prevailed.

He was cold and aching in every limb; the room was silent and dark, with the heavy smell of the burnt drugs all about it. Anthony crept to the door, and opened it; locked it again, and made his way in the dark very feebly to his bed-chamber; he had just the strength to get into his bed, and then all his life seemed to ebb from him, and he lay, and thought that he was dying. Presently from without there came the crying of cocks, and a bell beat the hour of four;

and after that, in his vigil of weakness, it was strange to see the light glimmer in the crevices, and to hear the awakening birds that in the garden bushes took up, one after another, their slender piping song, till all the choir cried together.

But Anthony felt a strange peace in his heart; and he had a sense, though he could not say why, that it was as once in his childhood, when he was ill, and his mother had sate softly by him while he slept.

So he waited, and in spite of his mortal weakness that was a blessed hour.

When his man came to rouse him in the morning, Anthony said that he believed that he was very ill, that he had had a fall, and that the old doctor must be fetched to him. The man looked so strangely upon him, that Anthony knew that he had some fear upon his mind. Presently the doctor was brought, and Anthony answered such questions as were put to him, in a faint voice, saying, "I was late at my work, and I slipped and fell." The doctor, who looked troubled, gave directions; and when he went away he heard his man behind the door asking the doctor about the strange storm in the night, that had seemed like an earthquake, or as if a thunderbolt had struck the house. But the doctor said very gruffly, "It is no time to talk thus, when your master is sick to death." But Anthony knew in himself that he would not die yet.

It was long ere he was restored to a measure of health; and indeed he never rightly recovered the use of his limbs; the doctor held that he had suffered some stroke of palsy; at which Anthony smiled a little, and made no answer.

When he was well enough to creep to and fro, he went sadly to the dark room, and with much pain and weakness carried the furniture out of it. The picture he cut in pieces and burnt; and the candles and dishes, with the book, he cast into a deep pool in the stream; the bones he buried in the earth; the hangings he stored away for his own funeral.

Anthony never entered his workroom again; but day after day he sate in his chair, and read a little, but mostly in the Bible; he made a friend of a very wise old priest, to whom he opened all his heart, and to whom he conveyed much money to be bestowed on the poor; there was a great calm in his spirit, which was soon written in his face, in spite of his pain, for he often suffered sorely; but he told the priest that something, he knew not certainly what, seemed to dwell by him, waiting patiently for his coming; and so Anthony awaited his end.

THE TROTH OF THE SWORD

Sir Hugh was weary, for he had ridden far and fast that day, and ridden warily too, by bypaths and green forest roads, for the country was much harried by robbers at that time, under the grim chief that went by the name of the Red Hound: he was an outlaw that had been a knight; but for his cruelty and his blackness of heart and his pitiless wickedness he had been driven from his stronghold into the forest, where he lived a hunted life, rending hitherto all that were sent against him, a terror in the land; writing his anger upon broken churches and charred farmsteads. Sparing none but the children whom he took to serve him, and maidens to please himself and his men.

But Sir Hugh had been safe enough; for the Red Hound was out northwards; and Sir Hugh was gallantly attended by a troop of jingling horse, that went swiftly before and behind him, while he rode in the midst, silent as was his wont, his eyes dwelling wistfully upon the green and lonely places of the forest, the bright faces of the flowers, and the woodland things that slipped away into the brake. For all his deeds of might—and Hugh though young in years was old in valour—he had a deep desire for peace and the fair and beautiful arts of life. He could sing tuneably to the lute; and he loved the delicate things of earth with a love of which he spoke to none.

At last they struck out of the forest into a firmer road; and here was a wall by the wayside and a towered gate; but the wood climbed steeply within. At the gate they halted, and presently Sir Hugh was admitted. The road within was paved with stone, and led to the left; and here Sir Hugh dismounted, and saying that he would stretch his limbs, left his horse to be led by the page that rode beside him, giving him a smiling glance, which had made the boy a willing and loving servant. The troop rode off among the copses; and Sir Hugh, taught by the porter, took a grassy path that led steeply through the wood to the right, the porter telling him that he would be the first at the castle gate; for the path was steep and direct, while the road wound at an easier slope, to the top of the hill where the Castle stood.

Sir Hugh unlaced his helmet, for the day had been still and hot. He was a very gracious youth to behold. His face was beardless and clean-cut. His skin was as the skin of a child, for he had lived a pure life, eating and drinking sparingly. Another might have been mocked for this; but Sir Hugh was so gallant a fighter, so courteous, so loving, that he was let to please himself. His eyes were large and quiet; his hair rippled into short brown curls. He had no signs of travel, save a little dust upon his brow; and this he washed off at a rill that fell clear through the wood, dripping from the rocks. And so he went up easily, and glancing about him. The oak-copse interlaced its boughs above his head; the sun had lately set, and there was a soft twilight in the forest. In the pale sky floated a few dark clouds, with rims of fire caught from the sinking sun; sometimes the wood was all about him, with close undergrowth and grassy paths. Sometimes he saw a pile of rocks, all overgrown with moss, indistinct in the gloom. Sometimes he saw a dell where a stream went murmuring down, hidden in climbing plants; sometimes a little lawn would open in the heart of the chase, where a deer stood to graze, leaping lightly into the brake at the sight of him.

He came very suddenly to the end of the path. Through the interlaced leaves of the copse a great bulk loomed up, that seemed strangely high and dark; the wood ended, and he saw the Castle before him, with its turrets and battlements showing black against the green sky; a light or two burnt with a fiery redness in some of the high windows.

He stepped out on to the wide platform of the Castle, and saw before him the wooded ridges of the lower hills, with light veils of mist lying among them, that had a golden hue from the setting sun; beyond, rose the shadowy shapes of mountains, that seemed to guard a sweet and solemn secret of peace in their midst. As he looked round, his troop rode briskly out of the wood, with a sudden clatter, and a sharp ringing of weapons, as they came out upon the paved space; and presently a warder looked out, and the great doors of the Castle were opened to them.

Sir Hugh bore with him a letter of great import. The Lord whom he served, the Earl Fitz-Simon, was a man of haughty strength and great pride. His Countess was lately dead, and he had no son to bear his name. He was old and grizzled and brought a terror about with him. He was as powerful indeed as the King himself, of whom the Earl spoke scornfully, without concealment, doing him a scanty homage when they met. Sir Hugh was of distant kin to him, and had been brought up in his Castle; and the Earl went as near loving him as he had ever gone, wishing that he had him as his son, and indeed desiring that he should have the Earldom after him if he had no heir of his own, and marry his only daughter, a grim maiden. And Hugh loved the Earl very faithfully, giving him the worship of a son.

On the day before the Earl had sent for him; and Hugh had stood beside him as he sate and wrote in silence, watching his great bony hand and his knotted brow, bristled with stiff hair. Presently the Earl had thrown down his pen, and exclaiming that he was but an ill clerk, had smiled pleasantly upon Hugh, telling him in a few sour words that he meant to take another wife, and that his choice had fallen upon the Lady Mary, the daughter of the Lord Bigod (whose Castle it was that Sir Hugh now approached). "A goodly maiden, apt to bear strong children to my body." And as he said this he made a pause, and watched Hugh narrowly to see how he took the news, and whether he had hoped for the Earldom after him. But Hugh had given him an open smile in return, and said that he wished him much happiness, and heirs to rule after him. And the Earl had nodded well-pleased, knowing that Hugh had spoken what was in his heart, and that no other man that he knew would have so wished in Hugh's place; and then the Earl had sworn a coarse oath or two, saying that he was old and spent, and if he did not beget an heir, Hugh should come after him; but that if he did beget a man-child, then that Hugh should have the guarding of him after he himself was gone. And then he did up his letter roughly, splashed wax upon it, and pricked it with a signet; and bade Hugh ride in haste with a score of troopers, saying, "And I trust you with this because you do not turn your eyes aside to vanity, as the priests say, and care nothing for the looks of maidens; therefore you will be a safe messenger; and you will put my ring (he gave it him) upon the Lady Mary's finger before the priest, and kiss her on the lips if you have a mind; and bid her ride within the week to the wedding; and stay not for the Lord Bigod, for he is more maid than man, and will not willingly let his daughter go; but will fear to keep her from my behest."

And then he beat his hand on Hugh's shoulder, as his manner was when he was pleased; and then to Hugh's surprise bent and kissed his cheek, as a man might kiss his son, and then, as if ashamed, frowned upon him, and said "with haste!"—and in an hour Hugh was gone.

Now when they entered the Castle, which had a great court within, full of galleries, there was a great stir of people to see them; the horses were led away to the stables; the troopers passed into the guard room; and an old seneschal with a white staff asked Hugh courteously of his business, and then led him up a flight of steps, and into a long dark room, hung with a faded green arras.

Here sate a pale thin man at a table, looking upon a book, in a velvet gown; the seneschal cried out Hugh's name, who made an obeisance, and then advancing, put the letter in the hands of the Lord Bigod, saying, "From the Earl Fitz-Simon; these." Then the Lord Bigod rent the paper, looking curiously upon it; and read therein. Hugh observed him closely; he looked more like a priest than a knight, but there was something very sweet and noble about his air, and he looked as a man might look who had known both sorrow and thought, and wished well to all the world. The Lord

Bigod read the letter, and then grew somewhat pale; then he read it again, and walked to the window, turning it in his hands. He stood so long, holding the letter behind him, and looking out, that Hugh saw that he was wrestling in mind and ill-at-ease. Then he turned, and said very courteously to Hugh, though his voice trembled somewhat, "Know you what is within this letter?" And Hugh said, "Yea, sir." And the Lord Bigod said, "It is a great matter." And then, after another long silence, the Lord Bigod turned to the seneschal who waited at the door, and said, "See that Sir Hugh be well bestowed:" and then with an inclination of the head to Sir Hugh he added, "I will think hereon, and you shall hear my words to-morrow." Hugh turned and followed the seneschal out; and he felt a great pity for the kind Lord whom he had left, for he saw that he was in great sadness of mind and perplexity. The seneschal asked Hugh if he would join the knights, but Hugh said he was weary and would rest. So the seneschal led him to a spacious chamber, from which Hugh could see the tree-tops of the forest, and the mountains very black, with a great orange glow of sunset behind; food was served him, and his page came to him, to do off his armour. And presently, seeing that the page was very weary, he bade him lie down to sleep; so the page lay down upon a little bed that was in a turret opening on the room; and soon after Sir Hugh himself lay down upon a great pillared bed, made of oak, and hung with tapestries. But he could not sleep, but lay wearily gazing at the glimmering window and hearing the breathing of the boy in the turret hard by, till at last he too fell asleep.

The morning came with a great brightness and freshness, with the hoarse cries of the jackdaws that lived in the ledges of the tower; Sir Hugh dressed himself carefully and noiselessly, not to wake the page, who still slept deeply; then he stood beside the boy's bed; the boy stretched out his arms in slumber and then awoke, ashamed to be later than his master, and to find him apparelled.

Presently the seneschal came, and led Hugh to the Hall, where were the two sons of the Lord Bigod, with a large company of knights, that stood up at his appearing, and did him great honour;

and then came a message for him to go to the Lord Bigod. Hugh saw at once that he was very weary and had not slept; the letter lay on the table beside him; and he said to Hugh that he had given the letter great thought, and that it was a very honourable behest: "And herewith I accept it for the Lady Mary," he said stammeringly, "who will do as my daughter and as the chosen of the honourable Earl should do." Then he was silent for a space, presently adding, "I have not told my daughter the tidings yet; I will tell her; and then you shall have speech with her; but I would," he added, "that there was not such haste in the matter; for a maiden is a tender thing and merits tender usage; do you think, sir"—and here he looked anxiously upon Hugh— "do you think that the Earl will consent to a longer delay, that the maiden may grow accustomed to the thought? She has as yet spoken to no man but myself and her brothers, and though she is fearless and of a high spirit"—he broke off suddenly, and then with a wistful glance at Sir Hugh, added, "Will the Earl delay awhile?" Sir Hugh felt a great pity for the man who stood so anxiously before him, but he hardened his heart and said, "I think that the Earl will not delay his purpose: he is swift to do his will." A great cloud of sadness came down on the Lord Bigod's face, and he said very low, "That is a good way, the way of a great warrior—so be it then, sir," and he softly withdrew, asking Hugh to wait for him.

Then fell a long silence; and Hugh, looking upon the folded letter on the table, felt it to be a cruel thing; but he never wavered in loyalty to the Earl, and thought to himself that the longer the maiden waited the more would she perchance be terrified; that great men must wed as they would—and other things with which he sought to excuse what seemed a harsh deed.

Suddenly he heard a footstep; a door opened; and the Lord Bigod appeared, leading a maiden into the room, who encircled his arm with her hands. She was tall and slender, apparelled all in white, with a girdle of gold. She was very pale, but bore herself with a gentle and simple grace; and there fell upon Hugh a thought that he cast from him as it were with both his hands. He had never

known love, and his heart was as pure as snow; the maidens that
he had seen had appeared to him but as distant visions of tenderness and grace, stirring in his heart nothing but a sort of brotherly
compassion for things so delicate and frail, and unfit for the hard
world in which men must live. But at the sight of the Lady Mary,
her great eyes, in which there seemed a trace of swimming tears,
he felt suddenly a deep passionate hunger of the heart, as though
a sweet and deep mystery, lying far-off, had been brought suddenly
near to him. Was this love, that great power of which the poets
sung; the power which had lost kingdoms and wrought the destruc-
tion of men? He feared it was so indeed. He felt as a poor man
might, who had lived in pinching want, and had suddenly found a
great treasure of gold, at the stroke of a mattock in his field. One
glance passed between them; and it seemed as though some other
thing had passed; as though their souls had leapt together. Then
he dropped his eyes and stood waiting, while a faint fragrance
seemed to pass upon the air. Then the Lord Bigod said very gravely,
"Sir Hugh, I have told the Lady Mary of your errand; and she will
do the bidding of the Earl in every point. To-day we will make
preparation; to-morrow shall the betrothal be; and on the third
day the Lady Mary shall ride with you; and now I will leave you
together for awhile; for the Lady Mary would ask you many things,
and you will be courteous and tell her all." Then he kissed his
daughter, and led her to a chair before the table, and motioned to
Sir Hugh to be seated at the table-side; and then he went out of
the room in haste.

Then the Lady Mary began to speak in a low clear voice that
had no trembling in it; but her hands that were clasped together
on the table trembled; and Hugh took courage, and told her of the
greatness of the Earl and his high courage, praising him generously and nobly; he spoke of the Earl's daughter, and of the kins-
folk that abode there; and of the priest of the Castle, and of the
knights; and of the Castle itself, and its great woodland chase; and
the Lady Mary heard him attentively, her eyes fixed upon his face,
and her lips parted. And then she asked him one or two questions,
but broke off, and said, "Sir Hugh, you will know that all this is

very new and strange to me; but it is not the newness and strangeness that is most in my heart; but it is the thought of what I leave behind, this house and my kin; and my father who is above all things dear to me—for I know no other place but this, and no other faces have I seen." Then Sir Hugh felt his whole heart melted within him at the sight both of her grief and of her high courage. And the thought that she should thus pass in all her stainless grace to the harsh embrace of the old and grim Earl, came like a horror into his heart; but he only said, "Lady, I have dwelt all my life with the Earl and he has ever used me gently and graciously, and he is as a father to me; I know that men fear him; yet I can but say that he has a true heart full of wisdom and might." And the Lady Mary smiled faintly, and said, "I will be sure it is so indeed." And so she rose, and presently withdrew.

The day passed like a swift dream for Sir Hugh. He could think of nothing but the Lady Mary, with a strange leaping of the heart; that she was in the Castle above him, hidden somewhere like a flower in the dark walls; that he would stand before her to plight his Lord's troth; that he would ride with her through the forest; and that he would have her near him through the months, when she was wedded to the Earl—all this was a secret and urgent joy to him; not that he thought ever to win her love—such a traitorous imagining never even crossed his mind—but he thought that she would be as a sweet sister to him, whom he would guard as he could from every shadow of care; the thought of her sadness, and of her fear of the Earl worked strongly in his heart; but he saw no way out of that; and indeed believed, or tried to believe in his heart, that she would love the Earl for his might, and that he would love her for her grace, and that so all would be well.

The next day he rose very early, and was soon summoned to the chapel. There were few present; there seemed indeed, from soft movements and whisperings, to be ladies in a gallery beside the altar, but they were hidden in a lattice. The sons of the Lord Bigod were there, looking full of joyful excitement; other lords and knights sate within the chapel, and an old priest, in stiff vestments, with a worn and patient face, knelt by the altar, his lips moving as

in prayer. Presently the Lord Bigod came in, as pale as death and
sore troubled, and with him walked the Lady Mary, who seemed to
bring the very peace of God with her. She was pale, but clear of
complexion, and with a great brightness in her eyes, as of one
whose will was strong. Then Hugh drew near to the altar, and
plighted the Earl's troth to her, putting the great ring, with its ruby
as red as blood, upon her finger. He noticed, as he waited to put
the ring upon her hand, that a ray of light from the window darted
through the signet, and cast a light, like a drop of blood, upon the
maiden's white palm; and then the voice of the priest, raised softly
in blessing, fell upon his ear with a tender hope; and at the end he
knelt down very gently, and kissed the Lady Mary's hand in token
of fealty; and the thought of the Earl's jest about bidding him to
kiss her on the lips came like a shameful thought into his mind.

Then the day passed slowly and sadly; but he saw not the Lady
Mary save once, when, as he walked in the wood, trying to cool his
hot brain with the quiet, he saw her stand on a balcony looking out
over the forest with an infinite and patient sadness of air, as of
one that bade farewell.

And again the sun went down, and the night passed; and at daybreak he heard the clatter of horsehoofs in the court, the jingling
of the stirrups, and the voices of his troop, who made merry adieux
to their new comrades.

Then he came down himself; and saw beside his horse a smaller
horse richly caparisoned; then in a moment, very swiftly, came the
Lady Mary down the stairs, with the Lord Bigod and her brothers;
she kissed her brothers, who looked smilingly at her; and then her
father, hanging for a moment on his neck, and whispering a word
into his ear; and Hugh could see the Lord Bigod's face working, as
he restrained his tears, in anguish of heart. Then she smiled palely
upon Hugh; her father lifted her to her horse; and they rode out
with a great waving of handkerchiefs and crying of farewells, the
bell of the Castle ringing as sweet as honey in the tower.

They rode all day in the green forest, with a troop in front and
a troop behind. The air was cool and fresh, and the sun lay sweetly

upon the glades and woodpaths. All things seemed to rejoice together; the birds sang out of their simple joy, and the doves cooed,
hidden in the heart of great green trees; and the joy of being with
the maiden outweighed all other thoughts in the mind of Sir Hugh.
Sometimes they were silent, and sometimes they talked softly together like brother and sister. What pleased him best was that she
seemed to have put all care and anxiety away from her mind; once
or twice, after a silence, he saw a tear glisten on her cheek; but she
spoke, with no show of courage, but as though she had formed a
purpose, and would take whatever befel her with a gentle tranquillity. The little services that he was enabled to do her seemed to
him like a treasure that he laid up for the days to come; and the
love which he felt in his heart had no shadow in it; it was simply as
the worship of a pure spirit for the most delicate and beautiful thing
that the world could hold.

At last the sun set when they were yet some miles from the
Earl's Castle; and while Hugh was still counting up the minutes
that remained to him, he saw the troop in front come to a halt; and
presently one of them rode back, and told him with an uneasy air
that there was a great smoke in the wood to the left; and that they
thought they were not far from the haunts of the Red Hound. But
Hugh said lightly, not to terrify the maiden, that the Red Hound
was far to the north; to which the trooper replied with a downcast
look, "It was so said, sir." "Ride on then warily!" said Hugh—and
he bade the troop behind come up nearer. The Lady Mary presently asked him what the matter was; and though by this time a
dreadful anxiety had sprung into Hugh's mind, he told her who
the Red Hound was, and she replied that she had heard of him;
but seeing that he was somewhat troubled she forbore to speak
more of that, but pointed out to him a little tuft of red flowers that
grew daintily in the crevice of a rock beside the path. He turned to
look at it; and suddenly became aware that something, he could
not clearly say what, had slipped away at that moment from the
bushes beside the road; the thought came into his mind that this
was a spy set to watch them; and so he bade the men draw their
swords, and close about them in a ring.

They were now in the thickest of the wood. The green road in which they were riding dipped down to a low marshy place, where a stream soaked through the path. The rock, which seemed like a little pinnacle, rose sharply on their left clear of the bushes: all else was forest, except that a little path or clearing led up to the left, among the trees. There was an utter stillness in the air, which was all full of a golden light. The swords came merrily out of the scabbards with a sudden clang. The troopers closed in about them; but then, with a sudden dark rush out of the wood, there swept down the clearing a number of horsemen, roughly clad with leather cuirasses and gaiters, all armed with long pointed spears. It seemed as though they must have been ambushed there against them, they came on with such suddenness.

In a moment there was a scene of fierce confusion; swords flashed high; there were groans and shouts; a trooper, pierced by a lance, fell writhing at their feet; one of the enemy, cut down by a sword blow, fell to the earth and crouched there, blood dripping from his head and shoulder; but the armoured troopers, well drilled and trained, would have prevailed, had not a flight of arrows sung with a sharp rattle out of the thicket, and four of the men behind him fell, two of them instantly slain, and two grievously wounded. The riderless horses, wounded too, rushed snorting down the road, and another troop of men on foot poured out of the forest behind them.

In the middle of the enemies' lancers rode a tall man, red-haired and scowling, with yet something of a knightly air. Hugh recognised him at once as none other than the Red Hound himself, whom he had seen long ago before the days of his outlawry. He did not join in the fight, but sate on his horse a little apart, shouting a command from moment to moment.

Hugh cast a swift glance round; the men on foot were yet some little way off, running down the road; the troopers in front had pushed the lancemen a little way up the clearing; and Hugh determined to attempt a desperate rush with the Lady Mary up the road: desperate indeed it was, but he saw that if he could but get clear of the fight, there were none that could follow, except perhaps the chief himself; Hugh leant across his horse's neck; the Lady Mary sate still and silent, like the daughter of a line of knights, looking at the combat with a steady and unblenching look. He laid his hand on her bridle rein, and she turned and looked in his eyes; and he saw that therein which made him glad in the midst of the dangers—though he was too much accustomed to battle to have fear for himself—it was as a man, that had been long voyaging, might see, in a clear dawn, the cliffs of his home across the leaping seas.

He pointed, and said a word in her ear; she glanced at him, nodded, and drew up her rein; but at that moment his horse gave a short upward jerk, and then fell grovelling on his knees, an arrow sticking in his side, close to Sir Hugh's knee. He flung his foot clear, and leapt to the Lady's side; and then in a moment he saw that the battle was gone against him past mending. Another flight of arrows sang from the thicket, and four of the troopers in the glade fell from their horses, and the lancers, who were drawing back, pressed down upon them. Then Sir Hugh signed swiftly to the Lady that she should ride clear; but in that moment the Lady's horse fell too. Sir Hugh caught her in his arms, and dragged her free of the horse, tearing her gown by the knee, for the arrow that had slain the horse had pierced through the Lady's garment, though without wounding her. Then he saw that they were very hard beset, and that there was no way out; so he hastened to the rock, laid his hands upon a little ledge about as high as his head; leapt up, set his sword beside him, and then, stooping down, drew the Lady up beside him. Then he shouted to his men to come back to the rock; there were but a handful left; but they drew back slowly, and made a little ring about the base of the rock, while the others drew slowly in around them, but halted at a little distance, fearing the flashing swords.

The Red Hound himself stood near at hand; Hugh heard him shout his commands aloud, and heard him say that they should save the girl alive, and take the Knight captive if they could—and the Lady Mary heard it too, for she turned to Sir Hugh, and with a sudden look of entreaty, said, "Hugh, I must not fall into his hands." He looked at her smiling, and said, "Nay, dear, you shall not."

And then Hugh saw that it was indeed the end, and that his death was at hand; he had seen men in abundance die, and had often wondered how it was that death should come to him at the last. But now, instead of fear, there came to him a sort of fierce joy that he should die with her whom he was now not ashamed to love; and in the midst of the shouting and the tumult, he had a sudden vision of himself and her wandering away, two happy spirits, hand in hand, from the place of their passion.

And now the last of his troopers had fallen. Then the Lady Mary drew close to him, and said, "Is it time?" And he said, "Yes, dear, it is the time; fear nought—you will feel nothing—and you will wait for me, for I shall follow you close. And now, dear one, turn your face from me lest it unman me—there is nought to fear." So she smiled again, and he kissed her on the lips, and she turned from him; and he struck one stroke with his sword; she quivered once, and sinking down moved no more.

Then Sir Hugh prayed a prayer; and looking upon his sword, off which the blood now dripped, he poised it in his hand like a lance. The spearmen had closed in to the rock. But Hugh hurled his sword point foremost at the Red Hound, and saw it sink through his skull, till the hilt clattered on his brow; and then he cast one look upon the Lady; and, as a man might enter the gates of his home, he leapt very joyfully down among the spears.

THE WAVING OF THE SWORD

The things that are set down here happened in the ancient days when there was sore fighting in the land; the king, who was an unjust man, fighting to maintain his realm, and the barons fighting for the law; and the end was not far off, for the king was driven backwards to the sea, and at last could go no further; so he gathered all the troops that he might in a strong fort that lay in the midst of the downs, where the hills dipped to the plain to let the river pass through; and the barons drew slowly in upon him, through the forest in the plain. Beyond the downs lay the sea, and there in a little port was gathered the king's navy, that if the last fight went ill with him, as indeed he feared it would, he might fly for safety to another land.

Now in a house below the down, a few miles from the king's stronghold, dwelt a knight that was neither old nor young, and his name was Sir Henry Strange. He lived alone and peevishly, and he did neither good nor evil. He had no skill in fighting, but neither had he skill in peaceful arts. He had tried many things and wearied of all. He had but a small estate, which was grown less by foolish waste. He could have made it into a rich heritage, for his land was good. But he had no patience with his men, and confused them by his orders, which he would not see carried out. Sometimes he would fell timber, and then leave it to rot in the wood; or he would plough a field, and sow it not. At one time he had a fancy to be a minstrel, but he had not patience to attain to skill; he would write a ballad and leave it undone; or he would begin to carve a figure of wood, and toss it aside; sometimes he would train a dog or a horse; but he would so rage if the beast, being puzzled for all its goodwill, made mistakes, that it grew frightened of him—for nothing can be well learnt except through love and trust. He would sometimes think that he should have been a monk, and that under hard discipline he would have fared better—and indeed this was so, for he had abundant aptitude. He was alone in the world, for he had come into his estate when young; but he had had no patience to win him a wife. At first, indeed, his life had not been an unhappy one, for he was often visited by small joyful thoughts, which made him glad; and he took much pleasure, on sunshiny days, in the brave sights and sounds of the world. But such delights had grown less; and he was now a tired and restless man of forty years, who lay long abed and went not much abroad; and was for ever telling himself how happy he would be if this or that were otherwise. Far down in his heart he despised himself, and wondered how God had come to make so ill-contented a thing; but that was a chamber in his mind that he visited not often; but rather took pleasure in the thought of his skill and deftness, and his fitness for the many things he might have done.

And now in the war he had come to a pass. He would not join himself to the king, because the king was an evil man, and he liked not evil; yet he loved not rebellion, and feared for his safety if the king had the upper hand; but it was still more that he had grown idle and soft-hearted, and feared the hard faring and brisk jesting of the camp. Yet even so the thought of the war lay heavy on his heart, and he wondered how men, whose lives were so short upon the goodly earth, should find it in their hearts to slay and be slain for such shadowy things as command and dominion; and he thought he would have made a song on that thought, but he did not.

And now the fighting had come very near him; and he had let some of his men go to join the king, but he went not himself, saying that he was sick, and might not go abroad.

He stood on a day, at this time, by a little wall that enclosed his garden-ground. It was in the early summer; the trees had put on their fresh green, and glistened in the still air, and the meadows were deep with grass, on the top of which seemed to float unnumbered yellow flowers. In and out the swallows passed, hunting for the flies that danced above the grass; and he stood, knowing how fair the earth was, and yet sick at heart, wondering why he could not be as a careless bird, that hunts its meat all day in the sun, and at evening sings a song of praise among the thickets.

Over the trees ran the great down with its smooth green sides, as far as the eye could see. The heat winked on its velvety bluffs, and it seemed to him, as it had often seemed before, like a great beast lying there in a dream, with a cloth of green cast over its huge limbs.

He was a tall lean man, somewhat stooping. His face had a certain beauty; his hair and beard were dark and curling; he had large eyes that looked sadly out from under heavy lids. His mouth was small, and had a very sweet smile when he was pleased; but his brow was puckered together as though he pondered; his hands were thin and delicate, and there was something almost womanly about his whole air.

Presently he walked into the little lane that bordered his garden. He heard the sound of wheels coming slowly along the white chalky road; he waited to look, and saw a sad sight. In the cart was a truss of hay, and sunk upon it sate a man, his face down on his breast, deadly pale; as the cart moved, he swayed a little from side to side. The driver of the cart walked beside, sullenly and slowly; and by him walked a girl, just grown a woman, as pale as death, looking at the man that sate in the cart with a look of terror and love; sometimes she would take his helpless hand, and murmur a word; but the man heeded not, and sate lost in his pain. As they passed him he could see a great bandage on the man's chest that was red with blood. He asked the waggoner what this was, and he told him that it was a young man of the country-side that had been hurt in a fight; he was but newly married, and it was thought he could not live. The cart had stopped, and the woman pulled a little cup out of a jug of water that stood in the straw, and put it to the wounded man's lips, who opened his eyes, all dark and dazed with pain, but with no look of recognition in them, and drank greedily, sinking back into his sick dream again. The girl put the cup back, and clasped her hands over her eyes, and then across her breast with a low moan, as though her heart would break. The tears came into Sir Henry's eyes; and fumbling in his pockets he took out some coins and gave them to the woman, with a kind word. "Let him be well bestowed," he said. The woman took the coins, hardly heeding him; and presently the cart started again, a shoot of pain darting across the wounded man's face as the wheels grated on the stones.

Sir Henry stood long looking after them; and it came into his heart that war was a foul and evil thing; though he half envied the poor soul that had fought his best, and was now sinking into the shadow of death.

While he thus lingered there sprang into his mind a thought that made him suddenly grow erect.

He walked swiftly along the lane with its high hedges and tall elms. The lane was at the foot of the down, but raised a little above the plain, so that he could see the rich woodland with its rolling lines, and far away the faint line of the Northern hills. It was very still, and there seemed not a care in the great world; it seemed all peace and happy quiet life; yet the rumbling of the cart-wheels which he still heard at a distance, now low and now loud, told him of the sorrow that lay hidden under those dreaming woods; was it all thus? And then he thought of the great armies that were so near, and of all the death they meant to deal each other. And yet God sat throned aloft watching all things, he thought, with a calm and quiet eye, waiting, waiting. But for what? Was His heart indeed pitiful and loving, as His priests said? and did He hold in His hand, for those that passed into the forgetful gate, some secret of joyful peace that would all in a moment make amends?

He stopped beside a little stile—there, in front of him, over the tops of an orchard, the trees of which were all laden with white and rosy flowers, lay a small high-shouldered church, with a low steeple of wood. The little windows of the tower seemed to regard him as with dark sad eyes. He went by a path along the orchard edge, and entered the churchyard, full of old graves, among which grew long tumbled grass. He thought with a throb, that was almost of joy, of all those that had laid down their weary bones there in the dust, husband by wife, child by mother. They were waiting too, and how quietly! It was all over for them, the trouble and the joy alike; and for a moment the death that all dread seemed to him like a simple and natural thing, the one thing certain. There at length they slept, a quiet sleep, waiting for the dawn, if dawn there were.

He crossed the churchyard and entered the church; the coolness and the dark and the ancient holy smell was sweet after the brightness and the heat outside. Every line of the place was familiar to him from his childhood. He walked slowly up the little aisle and passed within the screen. The chancel was very dark, only lighted by two or three deep-set windows. He made a reverence and then drew near to the altar.

All the furniture of the church was most simple and old; but over the altar there was a long unusual-looking shelf; he went up to it, and stood for awhile gazing upon it. Along the shelf lay a rude and ancient sword of a simple design, in a painted scabbard of wood; and over it was a board with a legend painted on it.

The legend was in an old form of French words, long since disused in the land. But it said:

Unsheathe me and die thyself, but the battle shall be stayed.

He had known the look of the sword, and the words on the board from a child. The tale was that there had been in days long past a great battle on the hill, and that the general of one of the armies had been told, in a dream or vision, that if he should himself be slain, then should his men have the victory; but that if he lived through the battle, then should his men be worsted. Now before the armies met, while they stood and looked upon each other, the general, so said the tale, had gone out suddenly and alone, with his sword bare in his hand, and his head uncovered; and that as he advanced, one of his foes had drawn a bow and pierced him through the brain, so that he fell in his blood between the armies; and that then a kind of fury had fallen upon his men to avenge his death, and they routed the foe with a mighty slaughter. But the sword had been set in the church with this legend above it; and there it had lain many a year.

So Sir Henry disengaged the sword from its place very tenderly and carefully. It had been there so long that it was all covered with dust; and then, holding it in his hands, he knelt down and made a prayer in his heart that he might have strength for what he had a mind to do; and then he walked softly down the church, looking about him with a sort of secret tenderness, as though he were bidding it all farewell; his own father and mother were buried in the church; and he stopped for awhile beside their grave, and then, holding the sword by his side—for he wished it not to be seen of any—he went back to his house, and put the sword away in a great chest, that no one might know where it was laid.

Then he tarried not, but went softly out; and all that afternoon he walked about his own lands, every acre of them; for he did not think to see them again; and his mind went back to the old days; he had not thought that all could be so full of little memories. In this place he remembered being set on a horse by his father, who held him very lovingly and safely while he led the great beast about; he remembered how proud he had been, and how he had fancied himself a mighty warrior. On this little pond, with all its reeds and waterlilies, he had sailed a boat on a summer day, his mother sitting near under a tree to see that he had no danger; and thus it was everywhere; till, as he walked in the silent afternoon, he could almost have believed that there were others that walked with him unseen, to left and right; for at every place some little memory roused itself, as the flies that rise buzzing from the leaves when you walk in an alley, until he felt like a child again, with all the years before him.

Then he came to the house again, and did the same for every room. He left one room for the last, a room where dwelt an old and simple woman that had nursed him; she was very frail and aged now, and went not much abroad, but sate and did little businesses; and it was ever a delight to her if he asked her to do some small task for him. He found her sitting, smiling for pleasure that he should come to her thus; and he kissed her, and sate beside her for awhile, and they talked a little of the childish days, for he was still ever a child to her. Then he rose to leave her, and she asked him, as was her wont, if there was anything that she could do for him, for it shamed her, she said, to sit and idle, when she had been so busy once, and when there was still so much to do. And he said, "No, dear nurse, there is nothing at this time." And he hesitated for an instant, and then said, "There is indeed one thing; I have a business to do to-night, that is hard and difficult; and I do not know what the end will be; will you say a prayer for your boy to-night, that he may be strong?" She looked at him quickly and was silent; and then she said, "Yes, dear child, but I ever do that—and I have no skill to make new prayers—but I will say my prayer over and over if that will avail." And he said, smiling at her, though the tears were in his eyes, "Yes, it will avail," and so he kissed her and went away, while she fell to her prayers.

Now the day had all this while grown stiller and hotter, till there was not a breath stirring; and now out to the eastwards there came on an angry blackness in the sky, with a pale redness beneath it, where the thunder dwelt. Sir Henry sate down, for he was weary of his walking, and in a little he fell asleep; his thoughts still ran upon the sword, for he dreamed that he had it with him in a wood that he knew not, that was dark with the shade of leaves; and he hung the sword upon a tree, and went on, to win out of the wood if he could, for it seemed very close and heavy in the forest; sometimes through the trees he saw a space of open ground, with ferns glistening in the sun; but he could not find the end of the wood; so he came back in his dream to where he had left the sword; and while he stood watching it, he saw that something dark gathered at the scabbard end, and presently fell with a little sound among the leaves. Then with a shock of terror he saw that it was blood; and he feared to take the sword back; but looking downwards he perceived that where the blood had fallen, there were red flowers growing among the leaves of a rare beauty, which seemed to be born of the blood. So he gathered a handful, and wreathed the sword with them; and then came a gladness into his mind, with which he

316   A. C. BENSON

awoke, and found it evening; he came back to himself with a kind of terror, and a fear darted into his breast; the windows were open, and there came in a scent of flowers; and he felt a great love for the beautiful earth, and for his quiet life; and he looked at the chest; and there came into his mind a strong desire to take the sword out, and lay it back in the church, and let things be as they had been; and so he sate and mused.

Presently his old serving-man came in and told him he had set his supper; so Henry went into the parlour, and made some pretence to be about to eat; sending the old man away, who babbled a little to him of the war, of the barons' army that drew nearer, and of how the king was sore bested. When he was gone Sir Henry ate a little bread and drank a sup of wine; and then he rose up, like one who had made up his mind. He went to the chest and drew out the sword; and then he went softly out of the house, and presently walking swiftly he came out on the down.

It was now nearly dusk; the sky lay clear and still, fading into a sort of delicate green, but all the west was shrouded in a dim blackness, the cloud being spread out, like a great dark bird winging its way slowly up the sky. Then far down in the west there leapt, as it were, interlacing streams of fire out of the cloud, and then followed a low rolling of thunder.

But all the while he mounted the down, up a little track that gleamed white in the grass; and now he could see the huge plain, with a few lights twinkling out of farms; far down to the west there was a little redness of light, and he thought that this was doubtless where the army of the barons lay; but he seemed to himself to have neither wonder nor fear left in his mind; he only went like one that had a task to perform; and soon he came to the top.

Here all was bare, save for some bushes of furze that grew blackly in the gloom; he stepped through them, and he came at last to where a great mound stood, that was held to be the highest place in all the down, a mound that marked the place of a battle, or that was perhaps the burying-place of some old tribe—for it was called the Barrow of the Seven Kings.

He came quickly to the mound, and went to the top; and then he laid the sword upon the turf by him, and kneeled down; once again came a great outpouring of fire from heaven in the west, and a peal of thunder followed hard upon it; and indeed the storm was near at hand; he could see the great wings of the cloud moving now, and a few large drops splashed in the grass about him, and one fell upon his brow.

And now a great fear fell upon Henry of he knew not what. He seemed to himself to be in the presence of some vast and fearful thing, that was passing swiftly by; and yet seemed, for all its haste, to have espied him, and to have been, as it were, stayed by him; there came into his mind a recollection of how he had once, on a summer's day, joined the mowers in one of the fields, and had mowed a few swathes with them for the pleasure of seeing the rich seeded grass fall before the gleaming scythe. At one of his strokes, he remembered, he had uncovered a little field-mouse, that sate in the naked field, its high covert having been swept bare from above it, and watched him with bright eyes of fear, while he debated whether he should crush it; he had done so, he remembered, carelessly, with his foot, and now he wished that he had spared it, for it was even so that he himself felt.

So to strengthen himself in his purpose, he made a prayer aloud, though it was a thing that in his idle life he had much foregone; and he said:

"Lord God, if Thou indeed hearest and seest me, make me strong to do what I have a mind to do; I have lived foolishly and for myself, and I have little to give. I have despised life, and it is as an empty husk to me. I have put love away from me, and my heart is dry; I have had friends and I have wearied of them. I have profited nothing; I have wasted my strength in foolish dreams of pleasure, and I have not found it. I am as a weed that cumbers the fair earth."

Then he stayed for a moment, for he was afraid; for it seemed to him as though somewhat stood near to listen. Then he said again:—

"But, Lord, I do indeed love my fellow men a little; and I would have the waste of life stayed. It is a pitiful thing that I have to offer, but it is all that I have left—an empty life, which yet I love. I will not promise, Lord, to yield my life to the service of men, for I love my ease too well, and I should not keep my word—so I offer my life freely into Thy hand, and let it avail that which it may avail."

Then the blackness seemed to gather all about him, and he felt with his hand in the turf and found the sword; then he drew the scabbard off, and flung it down beside him, and he raised the sword in his hands.

Then it seemed as though the heavens opened above him, but he saw not the fire, nor heard the shouting of the thunder that followed; he fell on his face in the turf without a sound and moved no more.

Now it happened that about the time that he unsheathed the sword, it came into the heart of the king to send a herald to the barons; for he saw the host spread out below him on the plain, and he feared to meet them; and the barons, too, were weary of fighting; and the king bound himself by a great oath to uphold the law of the realm, and so the land had peace.

The next day came a troop of men-at-arms along the hill; and they wondered exceedingly to see a man lie on the mound with a sword in his hand unsheathed, and partly molten. He lay stiff and cold, but they could not tell how he came by his death, and they knew not what he had done for the land; his hand was so tightly clenched upon the sword, that they took it not out, but they buried him there upon the hill-top, very near the sky, and passed on; and no man knew what had become of him. But God, who made him and had need of him, knoweth.

Stories by 'B'

Jamesian scholar Rosemary Pardoe uncovered seven forgotten ghost tales by 'B' published in the *Magdalene College Magazine* between 1911 and 1914. It is believed that A. C. Benson is the likely author.

The Strange Case of Mr. Naylor

There is, or there used to be, in the College Library at Magdalene, a fine copy of that well-known curiosity of literature, the *Psychomachia* of Matthaeus Grondoburgensis (Kronberg?). The sub-title is long and complex—*De gesticulationibus Daemonum*, etc. It is full of all sorts of miscellaneous absurdities, charms, incantations, magical formulae, and so forth. The copy, as I remember it, was a fine one, on thick, wrinkled paper, with large margins, and in a yellow parchment binding, with the arms and coronet of some French Count, I fancy, on the title. I used to prowl about in the library in those days, and take down all sorts of books; this was in a bottom shelf in the inner room, under the window, I think.

When I pulled it out, a few scraps of closely-written paper fell out of the book. In examining the place where they had been lying, it seemed as if at some time or other, two pages must have been fastened together at the top and side, because the margins were discoloured, and that the loose sheets had been pushed in at the bottom. The paste, or whatever it was, had perished. On the previous page there comes the famous incantation *Quam bonus*, etc., "for the relief of the spirits of distressed and scrupulous scholars."

The written papers seemed to be a rough diary, and to have been cut out of a book. The date, I should imagine, the earlier part of the eighteenth century. The writing began in the middle of a sentence. I will give a few extracts before I make any comment:

"spite of ye Ill News from home, I contrived to
enjoy myself fairly, with Gibbs and Lestrange. When
they were gone, I drank the end of my Posset, which
was cold and sweet, and pulled my curtain aside before going to bed. Looking across ye Pondyard [the
former name of the Garden]—it was a fine, moonlight night—I saw ye Figure of a Man, I knew not
whom, stand in a long black coat, under ye Terrace,
just where ye Caslamon [?] Bushes grow thickly. He
seemed to hold something white in his hand, and to
consider it attentively. I wondered very much at this,
but believing it to be a falling Shadow of a Tree or
what not, I thought no more of it at that time."

Then follow several brief entries such as "Saw ye Man again, as
fixed as ever. I do not much like this."

The writer seems to have become somewhat anxious about the
sight, and to have consulted one of his friends.

"Got Gibbs to look with me at ye Figure, which I
saw plain enough, and asked him if he saw anything.
He said 'Nothing that I can see,' and looked at me so
strangely that I begged him to promise to say nothing of it. I wish I had not spoken with him, for he
chatters. He said he would not speak of it."

The sight of the figure seems to have affected the writer's spirits, and he began to consider it in some way as a warning sent to
him. A long entry of rather morbid self-examination follows. Then
there comes a statement connecting the pages with the *Psychomachia*.

"Got ye *Psych.* out of ye library and read much
in it. God deliver me, how troubled I am."

A night or two later he took a decisive step.

"Begged ye key of ye Terrace from old Rigg, and though much afraid, walked to ye place, & saw what amazed me strangely. The man was there, but ye Blackness of his Cloathes seemed to be dispersed as I approached. Yet I saw what he held in his hand, and it was a small white Bone. Coming closer, I saw a horrid sight, which vexes me extreamly to remember. A face, very pale, with holes where eyes and mouth should be, hung in ye air. Yet on coming quite close, it was gone of a sudden."

Then follows a curious entry:

"Came to-day on some strange writing in ye *Psych.*, ye Footsteps, it seemed, of one who had been before me. In one place was *'Feci. Kal. Mart. Jno. Naylor,'* at another *'Computavi et feci.'* But what displeased me most was to find a note about ye Bone, which is too ill to set down here."

The last reference no doubt is to a disgusting form of incantation which may be found in a foot note on p.342 of the *Psychomachia*. The writer made up his mind to consult the Tutor of the College.

"I went to Dr Summers, and with much discomfort told him of ye sight. He was kind and cheerful, and advised me against Suppers and Smoaking, and to less reading. Then I asked him if there was ever a Master of ye College called Naylor; at which he turned and looked very oddly upon me for a minute, holding a Book in his hand, and answered to my surprise that he would ask ye Master, which seemed to me no answer."

He appears to have prosecuted further enquiries.

    "To-day as I cd perform no work, I talked with old Rigg about Mr. Naylor. He was not a Fellow, but a Member who lived in ye College and was much given to study. He dyed by ye Terrace, having fallen in a Fitt. There was much ado to prevent an Inquest, yet was it prevented."

Then follows:

    "Ye Master sent for me and advised me not to studdy so late. He said no more, but seemed vexed."

The end of the story is not complete. The writer seems to have got entirely unhinged by his experience, and to have become able to discern the figure, even on dark nights. "The Bone seemed to burn with a lowish light, and to send out sparks."

He finally consulted a Parson, unnamed, who lived in the town, perhaps the incumbent of St Giles. "Told ye Parson all ye story and he said he could deliver me."

    "We went together to ye Copped-Hall Field, and so through ye Gate to ye Terrace, where he left me, bidding me to fall to prayer. Then he went forwards, and I heard him speak in a loud voice, when I was suddenly delivered from my Fear, God be praised! He came back pale and trembling, and I noticed that he sweated much. Later he had me to ye Parsonage, where I spoke freely to him, and purpose to amend. He told me that it was a sore Business, and that this kind went not out but by . . ."

The MS ends at this point. It is hopeless to conjecture with any certainty what the facts are. There is the recorded burial of a Mr. Naylor in the St Giles' Register "of Magdalen Coll. M.A.". But whether the writer of the diary, who was evidently an undergraduate, had been prosecuting studies into occult matters, before the apparition occurred, what the 'ill news' were, whether the sight was a mere figment of his imagination, or whether it was a species of psychical obsession, it is impossible to say. I confess that the brevity and simplicity of the entries gives the story a strong sense of verisimilitude, and it is perhaps just as well that it is impossible to investigate the matter further. I remember that I myself, after finishing the pages, was seized with a sort of horror at the whole business. I did just turn a few further leaves of the *Psychomachia*, and saw a few more of Mr. Naylor's neat annotations; though it seemed to me that as the book went on a kind of agitation crept into the notes, both in their substance and in their calligraphy. Beyond that I could not go; and what is become of the old volume I do not care to enquire. I replaced it in its dusty corner beneath the window, shutting the MS in among the pages. I should like to have destroyed the record and the book as well, and I hope with all my heart that someone at once more sensible and independent than myself may have lighted on it all and committed book and diary alike to the cleansing fire!

When the Door is Shut

When the houses in Magdalene Street, beyond the Old Lodge, were recently being demolished, the clearing away of some flimsy lath-and-plaster accretions revealed a large solid chimney-stack of brick, of Tudor workmanship, with some pleasantly designed buttressing and chamfering, indicating that it was a portion of a substantial mansion. It stood a little way North of the new building, a few yards inside the wall. Beyond the chimney-stack, up the slope towards St Giles' Church, a fragment of ancient wall was discernible, with the base of a mullioned window, and further North still an old doorway. These were undoubtedly the remains of Copped Hall, a house of some size, which stood detached in a little close, called The Green Peele, with an avenue of lime-trees running East towards the Pond-yard, now the Fellows' Garden. The houses on the Chesterton road abutted on the close and overlooked it. It was the property of the College, was partially demolished at the end of the eighteenth century, and became merged in the street. I have no doubt in my own mind that the doorway was the scene of two tragedies which took place in the eighteenth century.

The first incident is purely traditional, but there is an unmistakable allusion to the second event in that curious book, *Things Fleshly and Ghostly*, by Thomas Peck, in the chapter entitled "Of Foul and Lubberly Insecution." The incident is clumsily and obscurely hinted at, and Peck evidently took pains to avoid identification. But there is a singular entry in one of the College record

326

books, which makes the story somewhat plainer. This entry is entitled "Concerning the death of Mr. Richard Mauleverer," and contains a few facts, leanly told, with notes of a conversation. The record is written in the first person, and is signed "Jno Bellamy, Fellow of Magdalene College"; it seems to have been inscribed in the book on the day of Mr. Mauleverer's funeral. Out of these two records I have pieced together the story as far as I can, just bridging one or two gaps by supplying obvious inferences, and I will tell it as a connected narrative, without undue citations.

Mr. Richard Mauleverer came of a good Worcestershire family, and was born in 1705. He entered Magdalene in 1723, as a commoner, where he did not waste much time in study; in 1726, by private influence, he was elected a Bye Fellow on the Spendluffe foundation, on taking his degree. He did not reside very long, and soon after, succeeded to some landed property; nothing is known of his movements until 1756, when he reappeared at Cambridge, and took a lease of Copped Hall; he was then a man of means and kept riding-horses. He was a bachelor, and lived at Copped Hall with a manservant and an old housekeeper. He was cordially received by the Fellows, the Master, Thomas Chapman, being apparently a distant connection; his chief crony, however, was John Bellamy, Wray Fellow, who had been a contemporary of Mauleverer's, and was a man of convivial habits. If Mr. Bellamy had never been seen drunk, it was equally certain that he had seldom been seen what is ordinarily called sober; but he was a civil, witty man, given to harmless expletives, a good raconteur, and excellent company when he was free of the gout, to which he was a martyr. Mauleverer usually dined in Hall at two o'clock dinner, after his morning ride, and spent the afternoon in the combination room. He was a strong and hearty man, of scanty discourse, good humoured enough, but very stubborn when he had once made up his mind.

The front door of Copped Hall was in the street, and admitted you to a small paved hall lighted by two slits of windows on either side of the door. To left and right were two parlours running through the house; behind the hall, entered by a door opposite the front door, was a small study, where Mr. Mauleverer mostly sat. The room had two windows, with a considerable space between them, looking out on the lime avenue. The fireplace was on the right, and to the left was a door which communicated with the garden by a short passage, which seemed to have been taken out of the room. If you went out into the avenue and looked back at the house, you saw the two windows of the study, with a bedroom above it with three windows; between the two windows of the study, and under the centre window of the bedroom, was a curious projection of brick like a large flat buttress.

Mr. Mauleverer found the room dark when the summer foliage was out; he got into his head that a window had been stopped up in the centre, and on tapping about the panelling of the room he found that the space between the windows sounded hollow. So he had the panelling removed. In the space an archway appeared, with a strong nail-studded oak door, which had been very elaborately fastened up; the interstices had been plastered; but what at once attracted Mr. Mauleverer's attention were two broad strips of lead, one nailed from the top of the door to the bottom, and one across the door halfway up, on which were traced some curious geometrical figures. Mr. Mauleverer had the external buttress taken down, and the outer side of the door appeared, with similar strips of lead affixed. He decided to have the door reopened, and the lead was torn away.

It seems that the same day on which this was done, Mr. Mauleverer received a note from an old Fellow of Jesus, Mr. Hinde. He went to see him, but soon afterwards returned, asked for the strips of lead, and took them away with him, after which they were never seen again intact. He came back apparently rather troubled; and it seems that the same evening he told Mr. Bellamy a confused story, related to him by Mr. Hinde, of a murder that had been done at Copped Hall some seventy years before. The circumstances were obscure. But it is clear that a woman living at Copped Hall with her husband, a drunken brute, had been attacked by him in the garden, had fled to the house, and had endeavoured to close the door; the ruffian had burst it open, and killed her with an axe, for which he was very properly hanged at Huntingdon. Mr. Hinde, he said, had urgently advised him to have the door closed up again, but that he said he would not do, for it was a convenience.

The first day that the door was opened a curious event happened; a bird flew in at the open door, as if chased by a hawk, with a loud out-cry, and was killed against a mirror in the room, making an ugly splash of blood on the glass, and cracking the mirror; a week later a very inexplicable thing occurred. Mr. Mauleverer opening the door one evening saw something looking round one of the jambs, and perceived that it was a little ape, with white teeth and large eyes; it looked wickedly at him, and tried to dodge into the house; but Mr. Mauleverer was too quick for it, and straddled across the threshold; the little creature ran quickly to the nearest lime-tree, climbed up the trunk, and Mr. Mauleverer could not discover where it was, though he heard it hiss and chatter in the branches. It was thought that it was one of a pair of apes kept by Dr. Long, Master of Pembroke Hall. Mr. Mauleverer went across to Pembroke to see if it was so, but saw the two apes snug enough, and found little comfort in the sight.

A week later Mr. Mauleverer had a strange conversation with Mr. Bellamy in the latter's room. He told Mr. Bellamy that he had awaked at night, and he had heard something moving about in the room below, the dining parlour. He had gone down, and he had there seen and smelt something "which sickened him." "What was it?" said Mr. Bellamy. "I do not know," said Mr. Mauleverer. Then, after a pause, he said, "I do not know, but I reckon it must have been a bear!" "God-a-mercy!" said Mr. Bellamy, putting down a tankard which he was raising to his lips, "Why a bear?" "Well," said Mr. Mauleverer, slowly and painfully, "it was about that bigness and very heavy; it shuffled to and fro; it put its foot softly and lumberingly to the ground, and then there fell a little clattering of claws upon the boards, as it pushed forwards." "God-a-mercy!" said Mr. Bellamy again. "Yes, and worse than that," said Mr. Mauleverer, as though finding some relief in the telling, "it smelt strong and rank like some great hairy beast, and when I came near it puffed its hot breath upon me—Faugh!" said Mr. Mauleverer, with a kind of sickness upon him, and he took up his tankard and drank. Mr. Bellamy sat musing, and then said, "I have heard of a man— indeed he was own uncle to myself—who saw snakes when no snakes were there; but that was under—under somewhat different circumstances; and I do not think he smelled them!" "I have had enough of it," said Mr. Mauleverer suddenly, in a fury; "I will not have quadrupeds, with birds and feathered fowl, to make free of my house and garden. By God, I will not!" "I would not!" said Mr. Bellamy, "but how did the matter end?" "The beast shuffled away," said Mr. Mauleverer, "through the hall, into the study, and was hidden from my sight; the door stood open into the garden, though I am sure I closed it over-night." "I think I would tell the Mayor," said Mr. Bellamy soothingly; and here the notes come to an end.

A week later—it was always on Saturday nights that the events had occurred—Mr. Mauleverer did not dine in hall, but was busy all day in his study, the door being bolted. He had seen Mr. Hinde again in the morning. The manservant was puzzled, because there came a smell from the study of something boiling. Mr. Mauleverer ate a poor meal in haste, and went back to his study at nightfall, and the servant said that his hands were dirty and discoloured.

Late that night the servant was awaked by a sudden outcry in the garden. It was a moonlight night; he got hastily up and went to the window. He saw Mr. Mauleverer flying, as for his life, into the house, screaming horribly aloud. After him ran something big and dusky. Mr. Mauleverer got to the door, slipped in, closed it, and there was a silence of a minute or two while the creature sniffed about the door. Then came a great crash; the servant fled down-stairs, and came into the study in great haste. He saw that the door was wide open, and a table had been overset. He made a light, and found Mr. Mauleverer lying, his feet to the door, with a great gash on his forehead, quite dead. There was nothing else inside the room. When the body was examined, the inside of the hands were found all white, as if with chalk; and a lump of chalk was found broken on the carpet. In the orchard was found a little firebucket lying in the grass in the avenue, which seemed to have been bitten and spurned; there were some cinders hereabouts, and some lumps of what appeared to have been molten lead.

The only other thing of note in the room was that on the inner side of the door was found scrawled very hurriedly in chalk some words in Greek which appeared to be:

rusai hemas apo tou . . .

But at the end of the last letter there was a great line, as if the door had been dashed in on the hand of the writer.

Mr. Hinde died on the following day in his rooms at Jesus, of a stroke of palsy. He had been heavily affected by the news of the death, and it was thought to have hastened his end.

There was an inquest held, and the verdict given was that Mr. Mauleverer died of a fall, occasioned by a sudden stroke of apoplexy. I daresay he did! After the apoplexy, the fall, But what did the apoplexy follow after? I hope with all my heart that Mr. Mauleverer was knocked senseless by the blow, when the door was stove in.

The Strange Fate of Mr. Peach

The Rev. Francis Leadbetter, M.A., was Bursar of Magdalene in 1786, a tall, lean, shrunken man, who walked lamely, with a long pointed nose that always looked frozen in the hottest weather; a man of incredible feebleness of digestion, which caused him to prefer a basin of hot bread and milk in his rooms to the pleasant combination-room suppers of toasted cheese, washed down with a tankard of spiced ale; but for all that, and perhaps because of that, a serious and God-fearing man, a staunch friend and a civil companion, much respected and indeed not a little loved by those who knew him, in spite of his stiff and precise talk. Those who met Mr. Leadbetter for the first time were apt to think him a kill-joy, with a taste for canting talk; he was apt to speak much of mercies and favours vouchsafed to him by Providence; his ill-health was a mercy, his shuffling gait was another mercy, because, as he was careful to explain, the first kept him from riotous company— "the tents of Kedar"—to which he had a strong inclination in his youth; while the second kept him from a youthful passion for field sports, and especially shooting, "in which soul-destroying pursuit," said Mr. Leadbetter, "I might easily have wasted many precious hours, which have accordingly been spent in reviewing, and indeed in improving, the somewhat declining revenue of the College." But even so, there was an ironical twinkle in Mr. Leadbetter's sunken eye, as he spoke thus, which inclined one to recognise a merrier spirit within; and those who came to know him had a way of using his friendship, valuing his good opinion, and consulting him about their private affairs, on which he was ready to spend much care and trouble.

Mr. Leadbetter was sitting one forenoon with an old friend of his, Mr. Burton, Steward of St John's College, who had rooms over the front gateway of the College. The chamber in which they sate had windows east and west, and four little doors in the corners communicating with the four turrets of the gateway. The room was entered by one of these, by a little staircase; another led up to Mr. Burton's bedroom. They were talking business together, and Mr. Burton, having occasion to refer to a ledger, went into another of the little doors and disappeared from view for a moment. He was presently followed by Mr. Leadbetter, who was a highly inquisitive man. "What do you in there, Mr. Burton?" he said. "It is in here that I keep my ledgers," said the muffled voice of Mr. Burton within. "Is it permitted to a curious soul to enter?" said Mr. Leadbetter. "I have a most singular desire, doubtless an unregenerate one, to see the other side of all doorways." "By all means, dear Sir," said Mr. Burton. Mr. Leadbetter accordingly stepped in under the low-browed door and found himself in a very curious scene. There were some plain shelves in the lower part of the place, which was lighted by a little peephole, above which ran up to the top of the turret a tube of rough brickwork, with the dried plaster oozing from the joints.

"A singular place, upon my word!" said Mr. Leadbetter, "it seems a sad waste of useful space: a strange formality to build a costly turret, and leave it to ledgers and spiders; now a man might do worse than keep doves here; or if one needed long rods for any purpose, they might be securely stacked away—fishing-rods, for instance, or busby-brooms."

Mr. Burton laughed, and said he had no use for rods, and as for doves, he did not desire to have them hallooing in the wall when he wanted to sleep.

"You are right," said Mr. Leadbetter, "they would be ill company; but I love to design a use for all useless things; and it would be a mercy for me to have so kindly a place in my rooms at

Magdalene; boxes might be drawn up with a pulley therein and finely bestowed."

Presently they came out and sate down to their work again, till Mr. Leadbetter rose to go. "I am expecting a visitor to-day or to-morrow," he said. "You will remember Mr. Peach, once a Fellow of my College and now Vicar of Steeple Ashton? He is riding to Cambridge to stay a few days with me. I look forward to much improving talk with him; he is, alas, of a convivial turn, but he is a serious man at bottom; his heart is right; and when he has fulfilled his desire for secular talk, we sit together and enquire into the state of our souls in a very blessed manner! Oh, the holiness of his discourse, even when he is full of meat! His friendship is indeed a favour!" Mr. Burton laughed, not very pleasantly. "Oh, I know the man," he said, "and I do not respect him; we had, indeed, a private feud of some standing; he called me by hard names; I was the guardian of a young man, cousin to Mr. Peach, who died; and a part of his fortune went to Mr. Peach himself. Whether he was disaffected at not receiving more, or whether out of mere over-bearingness, I do not know—but he must needs accuse me of mis-managing and neglecting the affair, when I had not only spent much time over it, but, indeed, had it not been for me, the estate would have been utterly wrecked through a dishonest lawyer. Mr. Peach was most ungentlemanly; and when I explained to him the business with such patience as I could muster, he said that I might, indeed, prove on paper that I was not exactly a rogue; but that I was morally, if just not criminally, responsible for the wastage!"

"Tut, tut!" said Mr. Leadbetter, "that was rough usage; but poor Peach is a sharp-tempered man, and not circumspect in his speech. I doubt that he meant no harm, and would make amends, if he knew how! I knew there had been passages between you, and I would make you at peace with him, if I could."

"No, no!" said Mr. Burton, in much wrath. "He meant what he said. We parted in anger, and I told him that if I had evidence that he spoke ill of me to others, I would have the whole matter out in open court and expose him for a bully and a slanderer; we parted in enmity; and I have no tenderness for him; he is a bad-hearted man, sir; and it is you who are too fond and simple!"

"Oh, fie, Mr. Burton, to speak so!" said Mr. Leadbetter. "A Christian must be ready to forgive, else he is not forgiven; it ill beseems us to speak ill of another, when we are all poor sinners together."

"Eh?" said Mr. Burton. "I can have no objection to your saying so, if you wish; though some sinners are poorer than others, it seems to me! but if your judgment is true, as well may be, let us take it for granted, and leave Mr. Peach alone."

"I cannot quit it at that!" said Mr. Leadbetter. "I would have you to forgive him."

"But I will not!" said Mr. Burton. "Hark ye, dear sir; I have no quarrel with you; but I will not meet Peach in friendship; and if there is any risk of meeting him in the street, I will not go abroad while he is in Cambridge."

"This is very wrong!" said Mr. Leadbetter, "and I shall hope you may come to a better mind. Mr. Peach will be with me this afternoon—he is riding from Hitchin—I had hoped you would have consented to meet him, and let bygones be!"

"God in heaven!" said Mr. Burton, "I will not be thus baited. I will not meet Peach. The man stinks in my nostrils; he is a low rascal, with a vile tongue; if I met him, it would go hard with me not to take a stick to him."

Mr. Leadbetter said nothing, and presently sighed; and with a shake of the head, made his adieu.

Mr. Leadbetter went back to his rooms, and spent the afternoon in reading a good book, and in thinking sadly over Mr. Burton's words. Indeed, one of the reasons why he had invited Mr. Peach to Cambridge was to try to reconcile his old friends. He did not go to dinner, but ate a little mess of fish; at about six o'clock his servant arrived with some hot dishes, which he disposed before the fire. This was to be Mr. Peach's supper. To these were added a magnum of claret and a bottle of sound port. Mr. Leadbetter was very solicitous that all should be good and plentiful, and walked with the servant to an adjoining set of rooms, where

Mr. Peach was to be lodged, to see that the fire was burning well. He then dismissed the servant, asking him to come in again later and to see that Mr. Peach's luggage was unpacked. "I am expecting him," he said, "at any moment; he will be ready for his supper at once, and he will retire early to rest, for he will be tired with his long journey."

The servant went away; and Mr. Leadbetter sate long by the fire, turning the dishes and wine, so that they should be well warmed. At eight Mr. Peach had not come, and Mr. Leadbetter went to the gate and looked up and down the street; it had turned very foggy after sunset, and the road was so full of mist that he could hardly see the houses opposite; the passers-by came suddenly upon him out of the white vapour; the porter had seen no one; the servant arrived, and Mr. Leadbetter sent him away again, asking him to return at nine; but at nine, Mr. Peach had not arrived. "He will have cast a shoe, perhaps," said Mr. Leadbetter, "and as the fog is so close, he may decide to spend the night on the road. I would not suppose that anything untoward has occurred. You need not return; I will await him until midnight, and we will make shift for ourselves. It will be a pleasure for me to unpack a valise!" and Mr. Leadbetter thought to himself that he would like to see what another man carried in his luggage.

But at about ten o'clock Mr. Leadbetter became strangely uneasy. His hair prickled, and he started once or twice, believing that some one had entered the room; once he thought he heard himself called, and he went out and stood in the court. "I am strangely nervous!" he said to himself, "it must be the slice of hung beef I ate at breakfast. I mistrusted its effect at the time, and I am justly punished for my greediness; oh, my poor malicious heart! the wages of sin are indeed paid in ready money!"

At midnight Mr. Leadbetter went out to the gate and gave directions that the porter should remain up for a little. But he had given up Mr. Peach for the night; he went back to his room, made up the fire, and once more disposed the dishes and the wine. Then he ate a crust of bread, made a long prayer for all who travel by land or by water, and so to bed.

In the night Mr. Leadbetter had a very dreadful dream. He thought that he looked into a dark place, with a faint and glimmering light; and then he saw that he was inside of a tower of brick, very like the turret in Mr. Burton's rooms; but at the bottom of it was a curious dimness like a transparent mist. A little light, like that of a lantern, moved about high above him, in the cap of the turret, and something dark shifted to and fro. But when he got more used to the darkness, he saw something that shocked him woefully, and made his mouth seem suddenly dry from fear; this was the figure of a man who seemed to be naked and struggling; he had blood on his face and shoulders; he waved his hands to and fro as if dizzy, and then in a hollow and choked voice he called once upon the name of God, and twice he cried in an agonised tone: "Help, for God's sake, help!" Then something seemed to fall heavily and strike him, so that he sank down and settled upon himself, and moved no more.

Mr. Leadbetter woke with a start and a cry, and found himself sick and faint, and in a deadly anguish, with the sweat running down upon him. He did not know who or what he had seen. The only thing he was sure of was the place, and that was Mr. Burton's turret. Little by little his disorder abated, and he perceived that it was only a nightmare fancy, caused perhaps by diet, and by his talk with Mr. Burton, which had displeased him, and his long waiting for Mr. Peach. And he saw that his distempered fancy had but woven into his dream the unusual sight of the day, the little bare brick turret. He could not, however, sleep, and read long in his Bible; then at last he rose in the dawn, and betook himself to the Chapel service, where he got a little comfort. But all that day, Mr. Peach did not come.

The next day Mr. Leadbetter became very much concerned about Mr. Peach. He sent off an express to Hitchin, to the inn where he knew that Mr. Peach would have lain. Then he himself took a little carriage, and rode out along the road, enquiring at the villages; and here he got his first news. He found that a man who answered in all respects to his friend had ridden through Harston

in the late afternoon, with a little valise on his saddle. At Trump-
ington he heard of him again, and at Grantchester he met a man
who had seen the same traveller ride slowly through in the fog.
The traveller must have been confused by the mist, for he had
hallooed, and asked if he was near to Cambridge. And he could
hear no more of him after that.

The next day the matter went from bad to worse; the express
from Hitchin brought clear news of Mr. Peach, who had lain the
night there and ridden away in the morning. Then Mr. Leadbetter
went to the constable of the town and told his story; and he was
told that a horse without a rider, with broken knees, and much
disordered, had been found in Silver Street the night of Mr. Peach's
arrival. Mr. Leadbetter saw the horse and the saddle, which was
one made at Trowbridge, near Steeple Ashton; so he had no doubt
that it was Mr. Peach's horse; but Mr. Peach himself had wholly
disappeared; and though they searched the roads all about, they
could find no sign of him.

The same day he went in his distress to Mr. Burton, and told
him all the story. Mr. Burton had a shocked and pinched look, and
seemed averse to hearing and talking alike. Mr. Leadbetter himself felt very ill and weary, and he thought at first that perhaps
Mr. Burton was sorry that he had spoken ill of a man who, it
seemed, must have met with some evil fate.

But suddenly a very horrible thought came into Mr. Leadbetter's mind, so horrible that for a minute or two he could not
speak. He seemed to see, as in a vision, a weary man on a horse,
riding past a College gate, and that the man was struck by a thought
and had alighted and gone in, and up a stair, and rapped at a door;
and then words had been spoken and anger had blazed up, and
then he saw two men struggling together; and then his dream came
over him; he knew only too well whose figure he had seen in the
turret chamber.

He sate lost in his thoughts, and looking up saw that Mr. Burton was very pale and looking at him in a singular way.

Hardly knowing what he did, Mr. Leadbetter said in a low voice,
"Mr. Burton, may I look into your little turret now?"

Mr. Burton seemed to him to frown and wink, and then to gather himself together; then Mr. Burton said in a loud uneasy voice, "My turret, sir?" adding, "Oh, look at it by all means. Why not, sir, why not? I must own it seems to me strange."

Mr. Leadbetter rose and went across the room, and, opening the door, saw that the books had been shifted, and that the cupboard had been washed and scrubbed.

"What have you been doing here?" said Mr. Leadbetter in a faltering tone.

"What have I been doing?" said Mr. Burton, in a harsh and gusty voice. "This is strange behaviour, sir! I was ashamed of the disorder, and have had it cleaned, sir. Cleaned out and washed! Is that not permitted?"

Mr. Leadbetter stood in silence and surveyed him. His tired brain could not bring the ends of the puzzle together, but he was certain now that something very dreadful had occurred. He sate down faintly in a chair, and he said, "Oh, dear sir, I have had dreams, terrible dreams, in which the turret played a sad part. . . . Oh, dear sir, let me hear all; I shall not shrink from anything you may have to tell me . . . if passion overcame you . . . we are poor worms, but we may find grace and forgiveness for all."

He looked furtively at Mr. Burton, who sate white and open-mouthed, and seeming ready to burst out into a rage; but he controlled himself and said, "Mr. Leadbetter, you are speaking very strangely and wildly, and I do not understand you. You are disordered, dear sir, with trouble and anxiety, and you are not well. Let me give you a glass of wine, and let me entreat you to return home and rest. This unhappy man. . . ." Mr. Burton fell into silence, and then said, "Let me walk home with you, dear sir—you will permit that? And when you have rested, we will talk more of the matter."

"Nay, nay," said Mr. Leadbetter, "I am well enough; it is you that are sick; let me have but a word, dear sir—a word of contrition; there is instant access to the Throne of Grace!"

"You distress me inexpressibly," said Mr. Burton, "but I would not revive the matter now; be content, sir; go home and take some rest; you are not fit to talk now; indeed, I will soon tell you all that is in my mind."

Mr. Leadbetter looked at him for a moment; and then refusing the wine which Mr. Burton pressed on him, and declining all assistance, went home in great heaviness and dismay.

The loss of Mr. Peach began to be noised abroad in Cambridge and was much talked of in all places of resort. There was an old and much dilapidated inn called the Anwyl Inn, from the name of an ancient extinct family. It stood in Chesterton Lane, opposite St Giles' Church, in front of a close named the Green Peele, at the corner of the Magdalene Pondyard, now the Fellows' Garden. It was a high, lean, sinister building, with a gable, where hung a battered sign. Its yard-gates opened to the west of the inn, and the yard ran far back among the houses. The landlord of the inn was a big, sly-looking man, very civil in his manner, and lengthy in discourse, much blown upon in repute; he was the friend of all the poachers and hucksters that lived about the Castle Hill, and was supposed to do a nefarious trade. But it was he who had found the riderless horse in Silver Street, and night after night there was a concourse to hear him tell the tale. "Ay, it was a misty night and shivering cold," he was saying one evening to a ring of topers in the tap-room, "you may wager your money on that, and none to take it up! Cold it was, cold in the bones: I was standing at the yard-door there and I heard a horse go jiggety-jig down N'thampton Street! There's something wrong there, said I, the man's drunk or stupid, to ride breakneck like that in a fog, that's what I said, not aloud but in my mind. So I went off after the horse, and couldn't come by him in the fog; but I'm a pretty fair goer, I am, if I mean to go; and then I catch a sight of him under the trees, and I see it was a horse and no rider; and I say to myself, there's something cruel wrong here; there's been a slip; and so on I go till I come up with the horse in Silver Street, and find him all bloodied and sweating. Well, I coaxed him, and got up to him, and took him round to the watch-house; and next day I come up before the Mayor, and tell him the tale straight, just as I am telling it to you: and the Worshipful say to me, 'You're a man, Cates, as is a good man and

no mistake; you have ears and eyes of the best, and you are a merciful man too, Cates, a good merciful man and no mistake; and it
would be better for the town if there were more such, and no mistake.' That's what the Worshipful said, and the others said the
same."

There was a murmur of applause, and then a voice said, "No,
there's no mistake about that, Mr. Cates, and so say all; and what
might your opinion be, Mr. Cates, about the gentleman as was
riding, or as ought to have been a-riding that bare horse?"

"There," said Cates, looking round, "so might you ask me and
so I might say, he might have fallen off, or I might say again, he
might not have fallen off; or he might have had a knock that was
meant for him, or he might have had a knock as wasn't meant for
him, and so we get no nearer."

"That's a true word!" said the others, "no nearer, that's it; no
nearer to what we might know, or again, to what we might not
know. A knock meant for him, that might be, for there are those
we know, as might be more careful, or then again, they might not!"

"That's it, Sir," said Mr. Cates, "you're a man of sense, like the
Worshipful. 'You are a good man, by God,' he says to me, 'and no
mistake,' and I says nothing to the Worshipful; for it's best to be
silent if you are rightly praised, and know it's right; 'it would be
better for the town if there were more of your sort, Cates,' says he;
and I say nothing, gentlemen, but I ask, 'did I find the horse or
not? Did I fear that something wasn't right, or did I not?' That's
what I ask, gentlemen. It was a cold night, that was, shivering-
cold in the bones . . ."; and the story began again.

A week later—there was still no news of Mr. Peach—Mr. Leadbetter was about again. He was still in a very heavy frame of mind.
He had written a letter to Mr. Burton, and had received no answer. There weighed on him the dread of some shocking discovery; and though he had no evidence in his mind, the dream was for
ever with him, and gave him no peace. If he sate at his accounts, or
with a book before him, the thought of the bare turret and the struggling figure painted itself horribly on the air. The light at the top,
what was that? and what was that which fell so heavily from above?

He could not tell; but only thought with horror of the newly scrubbed boards, and the ladder, and the anguish written visibly on Mr. Burton's face. He had indeed enquired once at St John's, but Mr. Burton had gone into the country and had left no address; and this added to his suspicions.

He was obliged, in the course of the week, to go and see about some repairs in an old house in Magdalene Street. It was a rickety old tenement which ran some way back; Mr. Leadbetter went out into the back-yard to look at the hinder part of the house. To the east towered up the gaunt and sinister roof of the Anwyl Inn, with the elms behind.

As he stood there an odour, horrible, choking, insupportable, assailed his nostrils. "What is this detestable smell?" he said to the tenant, Mr. Halliday, who was with him. "There's something very nasty here, that should be cleaned away!" "I don't rightly know, sir," said the tenant. "It comes from Mr. Cates's yard—I have spoken to him about it, and he was angry with me; he said it was some hides a-drying in his yard, and it would be all right in a day or two. But there's something going on there I don't like, Sir, for there was a man out working there all the night, working quietly with a spade; and I heard the noise of something that kept falling and falling."

"Well, I must speak to Cates about it," said Mr. Leadbetter. "He must not be allowed to poison all his neighbours. I never smelt anything so horrible: the College must see to this."

"I shall be much obliged to the College, Sir," said the tenant. "Mr. Cates isn't an easy man to deal with."

Mr. Leadbetter went round to see Cates. He found him standing in the yard of the inn, looking down to the west; he had a curiously preoccupied air, and gave a strange start when Mr. Leadbetter spoke to him, immediately assuming a very civil demeanour and touching his hat.

"Mr. Cates," said Mr. Leadbetter, "I have come to speak to you about a most horrible smell in the yard. The College cannot allow a nuisance to continue. Mr. Halliday tells me you have some hides drying. They must be removed at once, if you please."

As he said this he walked down the yard, with the inn-keeper following him. "They are in this shed," said Cates obsequiously, "and they shall be took away at once, I promise you, Sir—I didn't think they would be so strong—I did not indeed! The College won't be hard on a poor man who finds trade bad, and has to do many a bit of a thing for a living; it is a little tanning, Sir, that I have been a-trying."

Mr. Leadbetter looked around him with a dissatisfied air. The scent hung heavily in the closed-in yard. "What have you been doing here, Mr. Cates?" he said presently, "it looks as if you had been building!" He pointed with his cane to a heap of what looked like dried mortar, and a spade beside it.

"It's a bit of lime, Sir," said Cates in a very uneasy way, "it's for the hides, to bring the hair off—that's what it is, Sir."

"Why, the smells seem to come from the well!" said Mr. Leadbetter, pointing to the orifice of a brick well, with a roller above, for drawing water.

Mr. Cates looked at him very strangely, and wiped his brow with his hand. "It does seem to have poisoned the water," he said, "but I'll put an end to it all in a day or two, if the College'll give me time: it's a mistake, Sir, and I'll own it. I thought I could do a bit of tanning on the quiet, Sir—and that's my mistake, and I'm sorry for it."

"Well," said Mr. Leadbetter, "the thing must be put straight at once—I will pay you a visit to-morrow, and see if all is right. If not, I shall have the whole place cleaned out myself; the College will not have a public nuisance. We must be just and fair, Mr. Cates, and merciful too, even in the matter of smells, if we hope to obtain mercy."

"Yes, Sir," said Mr. Cates, "just so! To obtain mercy!"

And Mr. Cates took off his hat and held it in both his hands, as if mercy might somehow fall into it, like rain from Heaven.

"It shall be all right to-morrow, Sir—I promise you," said Cates very humbly.

As they walked back together through the yard, the inn-keeper seeming to breathe more freely, Mr. Leadbetter said, "You are not looking well, Mr. Cates—this horrible stench is bad for you; you must be sensible. By the way, it was you, I think, who found poor Mr. Peach's horse astray?"

"Yes, Sir," said Cates, "I followed 'im all down the road in the fog; but about what you were saying, I'm not well. It's the time of the year; and tanning 'ides, that's an un'ealthy trade; and it was the chill I took that night in the fog."

At this moment a young woman came out of the house, with an old coat, which she shook out as if to air it, and threw it down upon a bench in the yard. Mr. Leadbetter's eye fell upon it, and he drew in his breath sharply, as if he were about to say something; it was an old-fashioned riding-coat with long skirts, blue-green with use and weather. But he said nothing, and turned sharply away with a nod to the inn-keeper.

Mr. Cates took off his hat, and waited until Mr. Leadbetter was out in the street. Then he caught up the coat, and with an oath to the girl who stood in the doorway, he went into the house with the coat. Then he went into an outhouse and got a wheelbarrow, and with a sigh, as though he were feeling ill, he wheeled it off into the street. Half-an-hour later he returned, with the wheelbarrow full of lime; and then he went back to the taproom, drew a jug of beer, sate down very wearily by the fireside as if he were faint, and drank the beer off, presently dozing away in his chair.

Mr. Leadbetter, looking very thin and pale, went back towards the College, then hesitated, and finally limped away into the town.

That night when the moon was down, about three of the morning, all lights having long since been put out in the street, a little group of men, walking quietly, gathered in the darkness of the wall of St Giles' churchyard. Two of them carried a heavy looking bundle slung to a pole which they bore on their shoulders; they arrived, not all together, but singly, all saving these two, until eight men were assembled in the shadow of the wall. They hardly spoke at all, or only in whispers. At a quarter past three, two men, one of them walking lame, in low-crowned hats and cloaks, came gently along from the direction of Magdalene. As they came, they stopped and spoke to two other men, who stood one on each side of a little entry that led out into Magdalene Street from among the houses, called Copped Passage. When they arrived opposite the Anwyl, where the others were gathered, they spoke quietly with the men that were there met; and then, as the half-hour struck on St Mary's clock, the two men who had arrived last, with two others, crossed the road and knocked loudly at the Anwyl door.

After a short pause they knocked again, and presently a window in the gable was thrust up, and a head was put forth, while a female voice asked shrilly what they wanted. "Come down, madam, and open at once without question," said a clear and decisive voice. "In the King's name!"

The window was put down, a light was kindled, and presently the door was opened by a young woman much dishevelled, reported to be Mrs. Cates. After a short parley with the men, she was pinioned, and made no protest. The door of the yard was then opened, and the other men were admitted. On hearing the sounds, a man who had been working quietly out in the yard by the light of a lantern, put his lantern out, and went quickly and silently up a little ladder that leaned against the wall. The men all then came into the yard, and waited in silence, the young woman standing beside them.

Presently footsteps were heard in the street, and the two men that had been waiting by Copped Passage came up; between them walked Mr. Cates, now also pinioned, bare-headed, and evidently in an extremity of fear, from the husky way in which he spoke, often moistening his lips.

When they were all assembled, some orders were given. The lame gentleman, who it was now observed was Mr. Leadbetter, with the young woman and two of the other men, moved into the house. Mr. Cates had tried to slink up to his wife, but was prevented, and a meaning look passed between them. The others went down the yard towards the well. Lanterns were then lighted, and it was seen that there was a heap of white dust, or lime, close to the well, with a spade stuck in it; and the rim of the well was dusted with the same. The packages were undone, and were seen to consist of long poles, like punt-poles, to the ends of which were attached hooks of

iron. The stench from the well was horribly perceptible, and the
other gentleman in the cloak, who was now seen to be the Mayor, a
leading burgess of the town, held his handkerchief to his face, as
did some of the others. Two of the men then went to the well, and
plunging down their hooks, began to prod about with them, and
when they encountered anything to draw up. But whatever it was
that they hooked, again and again it escaped them, and plunged
back into the waters of the well. At last, however, something was
firmly hooked, and was hauled up to the well's mouth, the odour
being now nearly intolerable. The men drew round, and the Mayor
coming near looked a moment at the thing that was drawn up,
which seemed like a ragged and oozy heap of something, much
sprinkled with white, of the bigness of a man. The Mayor turned
away, very pale and troubled, spat several times upon the ground,
and presently drew out a pipe and tobacco, at which he puffed very
fiercely, some others doing the same. The Thing was then laid in a
sheet of canvas which had been spread on the ground, and was
securely tied up. One of the men then went away, and returned in
a few minutes with a hand-cart, on which the Thing was set, while
water dripped and dribbled from the canvas.

Presently they were softly called from the house; the Mayor
went in, and in the tap-room, which was dimly lighted, was a
strange scene. Mr. Cates sate on a chair as pale as death, his eyes
seeming to start from his head, and every now and then he coughed
an ugly cough. On the table were spread a little valise and some
articles of clothing. The young woman stood by, her hands clasped
together in a despairing manner.

The Mayor then drew out a paper and read out a couple of warrants; then he said that he must ask some questions, and he stated
that one Thomas Peach having disappeared, in or near Cambridge,
ten days before, and a horse having been found which was now
known to belong to the same, much enquiry had been made; and
he went on to say that Mr. Leadbetter, the Bursar of Magdalene
College, having seen a riding-coat which he recognised as belonging to Mr. Peach, in the yard of the Anwyl Inn, warrants of search
had been issued.

Mr. Leadbetter then said that having searched the house by the Mayor's authority he had found a valise and wearing apparel belonging also to Mr. Peach, laid away in a cupboard.

The Mayor then said further that a body believed to be that of Mr. Peach had been drawn from a well in the yard; and that Mr. Cates, the landlord of the inn, had been working at the edge of the well, and had made his escape by the entry known as Copped Passage, there to be caught by two posted constables. He therefore committed the bodies of the two prisoners, John Cates and his wife, to the Town Gaol, to take their trial. But that if they chose to say anything, they might do so, if they could give any lawful explanation of what had been found; but he cautioned them that anything they said would be brought up at the trial.

There was a silence, and then Mr. Cates, making a strong effort, and speaking low and huskily, said, "It's bad, Worship, it looks bad, and no mistake, but it ain't as bad as it looks, before God. The gentleman, Mr. Peach as may be, came to my yard with his horse on a foggy evening ten days ago. He said he was going to Magdalene College, and asked me to put up the horse. We went into the yard together, and the horse trod on a bit of a board, which brought down a pile of planks that leaned up against the wall; and he was startled like, and let out with his heels, and struck Mr. Peach on the head and breast, and he fell down where he stood, and the horse ran out of the yard. There was no one about, and I took the gentleman to the house and laid him on a bed, and then I started off to catch the horse, and caught him down by Silver Street; and then I come back, and the gentleman lay never so still, a-bleeding from his head, and I took the clothes off him, and there was a hole in his head under the ear, where the hoof 'ad tore him, and another great wound in his chest; and I saw he was dead and gone. Then I was cleaned mazed out of my senses. I knew that the house had a bad name, through no fault of mine, and p'raps I had a bad name too, all through my misfortune of being poor and that, Worship. And then I thinks I'd better hide him away and say nothing. I don't say I oughter done it, but I was that worried I couldn't think, and then

I put him in the well, and put the things away, and then in the morning I see I done wrong, and dursn't speak of it for fear they should ask me why I put him down the well. That's all the truth, before God, Worship, and I ain't done no wrong, so to speak, in a way." The wretched voice choked and was silent, but it was evident that the words made an impression—the story at least hung together.

But an unforeseen interruption occurred. Mr. Leadbetter, as pale as death, came forward, and, with hand outstretched, said, "Cates, you lie—you have told half the truth, which is the worse of lies. Mr. Mayor, this man is lying."

"Gently, gently, Mr. Leadbetter," said the Mayor. Mr. Cates has told his story clearly. You must have some evidence, you know!"

"Why," said Mr. Leadbetter, "my poor friend was not dead. He was thrown down the well, and he struggled for his life: he called on the name of God, and he twice cried for help in God's name. And this man threw something down upon him and stunned him, so that he went beneath the water and was choked. And if you ask me how I know it, I saw it with my eyes and heard it with my ears"; and then he added, with a solemn and uplifted air, "in the spirit!"

No one spoke. There was a silence, and then there was a sound as of something breaking. The landlord collapsed together, and fell out of his chair, striking the ground with a heavy thud, and lay there. His wife screamed out, "Yes, John, confess . . . you told me all that, you know, when you came back to bed."

A year later Mr. Leadbetter and Mr. Burton were seated one on each side of a comfortable fire in a little study of the parsonage in Steeple Ashton. Mr. Leadbetter's health had given way after the strange events above recorded, and he had felt obliged to leave Cambridge, so he had taken the living of Steeple Ashton, and Mr. Burton was paying him a visit.

"Yes," said Mr. Leadbetter, "this was poor Peach's room, and most of the furniture is his. Who would have thought that I should so soon be at home here and he gone from us. The ways of God are indeed unsearchable."

Mr. Burton pulled rather a wry face and said, "after all it was a College living!" Mr. Leadbetter smiled and shook his head.

Presently Mr. Leadbetter said, "I have not liked, dear Sir, to speak much of the sad events of last year; they are better forgotten. But I should like to ask you two questions."

"By all means," said Mr. Burton.

"This, then, is my first question," said Mr. Leadbetter. "What made you act so strangely to me when I came to your rooms to question you—the day when you had the cupboard cleaned out?"

"That is easily answered," said Mr. Burton. "In the first place, I was not well myself. I had been much shocked that I had spoken so angrily about poor Peach—though indeed he did me a great wrong—and had refused all reconciliation; and then, if I may speak bluntly, your own manner, dear Sir, was so strange, that I feared for your mind—I thought you had lost your senses!"

Mr. Leadbetter smiled. "Very natural!" he said: and then resuming: "Now the second question," he said, "is addressed to myself as much as to you. I have often questioned with myself why it was that in my dream I mistook the well that I saw for your turret. It was marvellously like the turret, and it set me on a wrong scent from the first. Was it a mere chance that I had seen your turret first that very day, or was it the work of the Devil, that I might be thus confused and helpless, or was it the Providence of God, for some end that I cannot discern, that I might see how easily I could fall into vile suspicions of a good man?"

Mr. Burton shook his head. "Who can tell?" he said. "For myself I do not much believe in chance, nor indeed very much in the Devil either!"

"Tut, tut," said Mr. Leadbetter. "We have warrant of Scripture for him, to say nothing of our own corrupt hearts."

Presently he resumed again. "Now I ask myself too, how it was that he was enabled to send a message to me at the last—for that it was a message, I doubt not. I could not help him; it but enabled me to avenge him—and I like that least of the whole affair!"

Mr. Burton still said nothing, and Mr. Leadbetter continued, "I have indeed wondered whether his fate was so evil after all; he was suddenly summoned, it is true, and he was thrust roughly into a painful and grievous death; but his passage was swift, and perhaps we think too much of our poor bodies. It may be that it is better thus swiftly to enter into life eternal, naked and wounded, and swimming in a foul well, than to fade out of life, fretful and peevish and dismayed, with physic by the bed and the blankets tucked beneath the chin?" and Mr. Leadbetter smiled to himself, and stirred the fire on the hearth.

Quia Nominor

Mr. John Byron, who held a John Smith Fellowship at Magdalene until his death in 1788 at the age of sixty-three, seems to have been a man of noted inefficiency. He had gone to the Bar as a young man, where it was certain he had obtained a single brief, given him apparently by the kindness of the College, in an action against a tenant for cutting and selling timber privately. This much, I say, was certain, for Mr. Byron mentioned it very frequently in his talk; but it was held to be no less certain that he had never obtained another brief, for he would assuredly have made mention of it. He subsisted miserably enough in London on his Fellowship, which was poorly endowed; and he then returned to Cambridge, where he was not much welcome. However, the College made him a lecturer, and here he failed again grievously, being quite unable to command the attention, or even assure the silence, of his class. After which experiment, when he was not again appointed, he lived in his rooms the greater part of the year. But, strange to say, this proved incompetence in all practical affairs was accompanied by a most inordinate vanity.

Mr. Byron was vain of his name, of his appearance, which was meagre and slovenly, of his experience, which was small, and most of all of his conversation, which reached a degree of tediousness impossible to describe. He was both voluble and embarrassed in discourse, fond of telling a few very dreary anecdotes, so that his company was much dreaded by all merry men. He was something of a free-thinker, and spoke very scornfully of the intelligence of

351

others; and he was, moreover, a greedy man, eating profusely and
in a very slatternly manner, his waistcoat being generally garnished
with the drippings of gravy and ale; so that, indeed, he was no orna-
ment to the table. But being a man of no natural affection, he cared
very little how distasteful he was to his fellows, and lived a sloth-
ful life, walking much about the town in the mornings, and staring
at all whom he met; while in the evenings he sat alone in his rooms
and was very peevish; and so the years moved on, with but little
change.

Mr. Byron sate one day in Hall next a visitor, a courteous and
ingenious philosopher, learned in all sorts of curious knowledge;
when Mr. Byron, as was his wont, spoke of his excellent handling
of the case against the tenant of the College, and went on to talk
very lengthily of the ancient family to which he belonged and all
the glories of his name; he said to the visitor that no one had ever
been able to tell the origin of the name, at which the philosopher
laughed and said that it was plain enough. It was a Scandinavian
name, he said, of common use in Norway, where it was called Björn,
and had the signification of a Bear. The family, he said bore a bear's
head as a crest; at which Mr. Byron said that his own arms were
three bendlets enhanced gules, and that he had a mermaid proper
for his crest. To this the visitor courteously said that Mr. Byron
must then be akin to the Lord of that name, to which Mr. Byron
said that he took little interest in such vanities, but that he believed that the Lord Byron was an offshoot of an inferior branch of
his family. The visitor went on to talk of the strange way in which
certain animals and fowls were attached to certain clans and families, and spoke of some curious customs that seemed formerly to
have existed in Northern tribes, by which it was forbidden to any
tribesman to slay the animal which was the sign of the tribe, "and
I daresay, Mr. Byron," he said, "that some of your ancestors had
trouble enough with bears which they met in hunting and were not
permitted to slay."

"Very like, very like, sir," said Mr. Byron, who was displeased
that the talk should pass out of his hands; and Mr. Byron went on
to tell stories of his family and of their greatness, and especially of

his great-uncle, who in Mr. Byron's description of him became a very notable man, though he had been, in fact, but a tallow-chandler in Ipswich; but this made no appearance in Mr. Byron's talk. The company would have wished to hear more of the philosopher's conversation, but Mr. Byron allowed him no second chance, and talked very wearifully all the afternoon.

A day or two after, Mr. Byron was walking about the town in the morning, and, as was his wont, staring at all those he met, when he saw a little ring of people in the corner of the market-place. He hurried thither to see what the affair was, and, pushing into the gathering, he saw that a circle had been formed round two men, of foreign appearance, who led with them a great brown bear. The bear wore a little coat on his shaggy shoulders, and a cocked-hat on his head, and shouldered a pole, which he held in his long claws. He seemed to be very friendly and obedient to the men, and, at a word of command, danced a little in the ring, lifting up and setting down his flat feet very clumsily. His little eyes and his red tongue, which lolled out of his mouth across his white teeth, seemed very curious to Mr. Byron, and he pressed further into the ring till he was on the inside. The bear came round still dancing, but when he got close to Mr. Byron, so close that Mr. Byron could perceive his strong and acrid odour, he came to a stop, regarded Mr. Byron very curiously, and dropping his pole, came towards him in a decided way, as if recognising an old acquaintance. Mr. Byron was taken with a sudden terror, and cried out faintly. One of the men called the bear off, who picked up the pole humbly enough and continued his dance. But Mr. Byron conceived a great disgust of the whole matter, and slipped out of the throng, feeling sick and shaky and entirely unmanned. He had a sense that he had been in some danger, he knew not what, and that the bear would have hugged him in his arms, if the men had not interfered. He could not get the business out of his head, and for some days after that he was ill at ease, sleeping brokenly, and often dreaming of the little sullen eyes of the bear and the red tongue which lolled out of his mouth. He gave up his usual walk in the town and strolled instead in the College garden.

It was a week later that in some dumb hour of the night, Mr.
Byron woke suddenly up in his bed and wished for day. His rooms
were on the ground floor, on the South side of the Court, near the
Porter's Lodge. He woke with a sense of great discomfort, feeling
as though something had leaned over him and touched his arm; he
had felt, he thought, a hot and fetid breath on his face; and what
added much to his alarm was that he could discern the heavy scent
of a bear, just as he had smelt the one in the market-place. He
dared not move at first, but presently he took courage, made a light
and looked fearfully round. All was as it should have been; he got
up at last with the taper in his hand, and went out into his ugly
and comfortless sitting-room, and even so far as his outer door,
which was securely closed. He felt clearer now, and opened a little
cupboard, where he kept some brandy; he took a dram, and was
soon very valiant again. The clock presently struck three, with a
very solitary sound; Mr. Byron betook himself to his bed again,
but he could not sleep, and he was glad when the light began to
filter in among his curtains, and the sparrows fell to twittering in
the ivy.

Soon after this the vacation came on; the scholars all departed,
and most of the Fellows travelled away. Mr. Byron was left alone
in the College, except for the Dean, an old somnolent man, who
had no use for talk; and very dull were the dinners for the two. But
Mr. Byron could not hold his peace, and bit by bit told the old Dean
the story of his meeting with the bear, and his fancy of the night.
The old man heard him very inattentively, and said that such fancies were uncomfortable things, and that Mr. Byron had better go
off for a visit, and shake all such thoughts out of his head. "It's an
ill thing," said the Dean, in his slow and husky voice, "when a man
gets to brood upon bears, and such outlandish cattle. It's a disorder of the mind, Mr. Byron; there is an old story of a family, the
name of which I cannot call to mind, the head of which is visited
on occasions by the sight of a great white bird, poising in his chamber—and it means no good. I would not have any Fellow of this
College to tamper with the thought of birds of the air or beasts of
the wood visiting them in their chambers at dead of night. That's

an ill thing, Mr. Byron, and it's a boding thing. A man should read
the Scriptures at such times, and pray a little; for both of which
exercises I fear you have but little stomach."

Mr. Byron said that he thought that strong ale and brandy were
a more manful cure, but the Dean shook his head and would say
no more on that head, or indeed upon any other head at all.

Mr. Byron was now left quite alone in the College, for the Dean
departed soon, and Mr. Byron was in great dudgeon. He parted
with his appetite, and could only palter with toast and tea, which
he laced with brandy. He gave up going into Hall, and sate much
in his rooms, beating a tattoo with his fingers on the table. It was
then that he took to writing a good deal in a little notebook, from
which the event that followed is closely taken. It appears from this
book that he was not at peace with himself, and that he had a sore
heart about his wasted and selfish life; he made some entries, too,
about the strange doom which befalls certain families; and he wrote
down, too, some silly tales of his boyhood and youth, which had
no beginning or end, as thus: "When I was in the garden, I remember that Marjorie came to me, and showed me some pears which
Mrs. Vickers had given her, and offered me to share them; but I
said no, and that I would play her for them at a game we much
used, called Pattle-pottle; then I cheated her, and won all the pears,
and ate them all and laughed at her, so that she did not contain
her tears. I wish I had not cheated Marjorie. She died April 8, 1748,
of a quinsy, but that was long after. I did not like her husband well;
he spoke injuriously to me" . . . So the notes rambled on, without
any order. Then comes the following entry, written in a very wild
hand, the lines sloping every way: "The worst thing I ever saw in
my life, but I am constrained to set it down, for fear of I know not
what. May God spare me and have mercy on me, and forgive my
disbelief. It was thus: I woke very unquiet, I suppose about three
in the morning (this was Wednesday, I think—I am not sure of this
or of anything), and getting up I heard something go softly to and
fro in my outer chamber; something brushed by the door, and it
was thrice pushed and rattled, but it held. Then I heard something
sniff and blow under the bottom of the door, and the smell, I

cannot write of that, for it sickens me. . . Oh dear, how I am undone— Oh dear! Then I heard it pad about again; and again it
sniffed and blew beneath the door. All this time I stood amazed
and dared not even move, so that I grew stiff and cold. Then the
day came in very slowly, and silence fell; and at last I took courage,
and opened the door. The room was grey and dim, but— Oh dear!
how can I write it— God be merciful; for the bear sate as I feared,
all hunched up opposite the door, and looked at me out of its little
eyes, and I saw its teeth and the redness of its tongue. It was there
at last— Oh dear, what can I do? I shut to the door and I fainted
after that, and crept to my bed; but now I cannot put the smell
away from my nostrils: was ever man in such a horror— Oh dear!"

This passage is followed by some unintelligible scrawls, which
appear to be fragments of Psalm *xcv.*, "Whoso dwelleth," etc., very
imperfectly remembered.

There is but one more entry, two days later. "I have seen nothing further, and the horror is a little abated; but I cannot get the
stench of the beast out of my rooms; my clothes seem infected with
it, and it hangs about my food. I have sat indoors too much of late.
I must go abroad more, and walk more; this and a regular course
of life and diet, with prayer, may help me. I dare not go to any
physician, and if I went to a clergyman, I know not where I should
make a beginning. I cannot rid myself of a burden of thought, and
some disaster is awaiting me, I cannot conjecture what. It is too
late, I fear, to live differently. Now if it had been twenty years ago!
The curse of my house is fallen upon me, through my own great
fault. If I had but one friend in the world, I could go forward in
hope. If little Marjorie had lived, she would understand."

The end came very swiftly; but the only record I can find of the
event is a brief obituary notice of Mr. Byron, which appears in the
Gentleman's Magazine of July 20, 1788, about a week later. It was
as follows:

"On the 18th of July, at the Fish and Duck Inn, Cottenham, died
Mr. John Byron, Fellow of Magdalene College, Cambridge, a face-
tious and well-respected man. His death was occasioned by a singular accident. The deceased gentleman, who was in excellent

health, was accustomed to take long walks in the neighbourhood
of Cambridge, where he resided. On the morning of July 18, two
Norweyan sailors, known as Swain and Burn, were showing a
trained bear in the street at Cottenham, when Mr. Byron turned
suddenly out of a side street. The bear, for some cause not explained, broke loose, and made as if it would embrace Mr. Byron,
who stood by as if irresolute. He turned to run, with the bear close
upon him, but collapsed to the ground, and the bear took hold of
him. He was at once extricated, but he seemed to be in a fit, occasioned by terror, from which he did not rally, and died the same
afternoon. At an enquiry which was held, Swain, the bear-guard,
gave the bear a good character, and said that it could be trusted
safely with the smallest child. He said, indeed, that the behaviour
of the animal seemed to shew that he recognised in Mr. Byron an
old friend, and wished to testify affection rather than any enmity.
It had been intended that the bear should be destroyed, but the
man Swain pleaded very earnestly for it, as an old favourite and as
his means of livelihood; and as the doctor said that Mr. Byron had
received no hurt from the bear, Mr. Cutlack, the magistrate, decided in Swain's favour, and let the Norweyans go. Mr. Byron will
be buried in St Peter's Churchyard at Cambridge, and is sincerely
regretted by all who knew him."

The Stone Coffin

The year was 1754, the month October. The Chapel at Magdalene had been undergoing renovation all the summer, at the hands of the ingenious Mr. Collins, of Clare Hall—indeed, since the beginning of the Easter Term the College services had been held in St Giles' Church adjacent.

Mr. Dobree the Bursar, a big bluff man, was pacing in the Court in the autumn sunshine. Some workmen were carrying planks and poles out of the doorway of the Chapel staircase. The Bursar's companion, a little meagre figure in rusty black, peering about him through big horn spectacles, was Mr. Janeway, the President of the College. Presently they went in at the Chapel door, and stood regarding the building. "Dear now!" said Mr. Janeway, staring about him, "I hardly see where I am! A great change, no doubt! But it is a chaste design!"

It certainly was a change! but out of a Gothic building with an open roof, much as we see it now, the ingenious Mr. Collins had made a place more like, one would have said, the dining-room of a Roman consul than a Christian church. The roof was cut off by a flat plaster ceiling, heavily ornamented. A classical arch spanned the sanctuary, and the East window was obliterated by a columned piece of statuary. The floor was elegantly paved with black and white marble.

Mr. Dobree looked complacently about him. "It is not such a change to my eyes," he said, "Because I have watched the work from the beginning. It seems to me a very respectable place!"

"And pray what does the Master think of it all?" said Mr. Janeway.

"That I cannot tell," said Mr. Dobree rather curtly. "Has he seen the progress of the work?" said Mr. Janeway.

"The Master," said Mr. Dobree, "has been, to my knowledge, twice in the chapel since the work began. He ran in once without his wig, in a greasy cassock, and spoke rudely to the workmen about the noise they made—as if such work could be done in silence! He was disturbed at his accounts, he said. Once again he met Mr. Collins in the chapel, when the carved piece over the table was up. He said to Mr. Collins that he was given to understand that the figures were those of saints and angels, but that they appeared to him to be something much more indelicate. Then he laughed, and said he supposed it was the effect of the plaster work, at which Mr. Collins was greatly mortified. But so long as he can find fault and has nothing to pay, the College may go hang for him. He has gotten a Prebend of Durham, they say, by interest, this last week, and that is all he cares for."

"Tut, tut" said Mr. Janeway soothingly.

"Now," said Mr. Dobree, striding up the chapel. "Come hither with me, and I will relate to you a curiosity. About six weeks ago the workmen were laying the floor, and one came to me and said they had found somewhat. It was hereabouts, by this step." He stamped on the pavement, and then continued, "When I came in, they had uncovered and broken in pieces the lid of a stone coffin just here, and I bade them take the bits out. I tell you it was a strange sight underneath! There lay a man, his head in a niche made for it in the stone, robed from head to foot in an embroidered robe, of the colour of a butterfly—one of the orange-brown ones that you may see sitting on summer flowers—with figures and patterns inwrought. The flesh was all perished, and the skull, with its dark eye-holes, stared very dismally out, with something like hair atop of it. I doubt he had lain there since monkish days, and it displeased me very much. I stooped down and picked at the robe, and it all came away in my hands, falling to dust, leaving but a few coloured threads. The bones had mouldered too, all but the thigh-bones, and they were brittle. 'Come,' said I, 'the less we look on this the better!' So I took a besom in my hand and swept the whole carcase, bones and dust and robe and all, to one end of the coffin; and it made but a little heap there. I prodded the skull out of its niche, and that all came to dust too. But while I brushed, I heard a tinkling, and I picked out of the mess a little cup and platter of some metal, very dark, and a big ring with a blue stone—all very Popish and disgraceful to my eyes. I have them in my chamber, and I shall send them to Mr. Gray, at Pembroke Hall, who cares about such oddities. Then I had the coffin broken up, and carried to the stonemasons' yard, and dropt all the dust into the hole thus made, saw that they put soil on the place and battered it well down. A good riddance, I think!"

"Dear now!" said Mr. Janeway, musing. "That is a strange story—a very strange story! But, Mr. Dobree, if you will pardon me, I do not like your action very well. It seems to me that the man, whoever he was, was piously bestowed here, and had a right to his rest—so it appears to me, but I speak under correction!"

"Pish!" said Mr. Dobree. "Here's a pother about a parcel of old Popish bones! I am one who hold by the glorious Reformation, and I would cleanse the temple of all such recusants, if I had my choice. Why, the thought of that ugly figure, under my feet, would have made me very squeamish at my prayers. I wonder at you, Mr. Janeway, indeed I do!"

"Well, well," said Mr. Janeway, "There are many opinions; but I cannot like the business. May be he was a holy man, even if he died in sad error. I doubt if he could have known better."

"A sincere study of the Word would have shown him his abomi-nations," said Mr. Dobree. "I am a Protestant, born and bred, and I have no patience with old mummeries."

Mr. Janeway sighed and said no more, and presently they went away.

It might have been a week later that Mr. Dobree awoke sud-denly at night in his room, which was in the right-hand corner of the first Court, as you come in by the gate, on the ground floor. He awoke half in terror and half in anger, troubled by a dream, and thought that he heard someone moving very softly about his room; which was lighted only by a little high window in a deep recess that looked out towards the river, on to what was then a little street or lane of houses, running parallel to the College. The window was bare of any curtain, and Mr. Dobree thought that he saw a very faint figure cross the glimmering panes, it being bright moonlight without.

Mr. Dobree was as bold as a lion. He sate up in bed and shouted out in his great voice, EH, WHAT? HOLLA-HO! WHO IS THAT? EH, WHAT DID YOU SAY? WHAT DO YOU THERE, SIRRAH?

His voice reverberated in the little bare room, and died away, leaving a shocking silence. Nothing moved or spoke. He felt for his tinder-box and made a light, and then jumping out of bed, in nightcap and nightgown, looked about everywhere, first in his bed-room, then through his two keeping-rooms, and even in his cup-boards, but he saw no sign of anything living. After some time he went back to bed, but not to sleep. He was angry with himself for being afraid, and half suspected a trick; but his door was firmly latched, and no one seemed to have come in that way, while the windows into the court were safely shuttered.

In the morning, after a draught of small beer, which he used for his breakfast, and when he had made his toilet, he felt better; but for all that he wished for company, and made his way to Mr. Janeway's rooms in the second Court as soon as might be. He found Mr. Janeway reading in a book, with coffee beside him, and sitting down he told him his adventure rather shamefacedly. Mr. Janeway nodded his head and said very little, save this, that he too, when his stomach was at all disordered, suffered from disturbing dreams. "A little sick fancy, no doubt!" he added comfortably.

"It may be!" said Mr. Dobree moodily; "But I think there was someone with me in the room. Yet what sticks even more in my mind was a dream I had dreamed, which I cannot fully recall."

"What was it like?" said Mr. Janeway.

"What was it?" said Mr. Dobree; "That I cannot quite tell—but it was an ill dream. I was in a dull place, methought between buildings. They were buildings, I believe; and a dark sort of thing poked its head out in front of me in an ugly way. It seems to me now that it had on a parti-coloured robe, of black or white, or both—like a gown, and like a surplice. There was something drawn over the head of it; and the face was very white; now, as I think of it, I believe it had no eyes; it said something to me, which still sounds in my ears like Latin, in a very low voice; and it seemed to be angry—Yes, Sir, it was angry, was that person!"

"Dear now!" said Mr. Janeway, looking over his glasses at Mr. Dobree, "That's a bad story and a confused story! Is it your way to dream like that, Mr. Dobree? It seems to me a dark affair."

"Why, Sir!" said Mr. Dobree with a sudden anger, "It appears to me that you are but very poor company this morning! I come to my old friend to be made cheer with, and you can only shake your head and look dismal. This is not friendly, Sir! You are not speaking your mind!"

"Nay, Sir," said Mr. Janeway, "Be not so peevish! There is something that presses upon my spirits, since you spoke your dream, and I am grown very heavy. You must think no more of it, Sir. It was but a touch of vapours, such as comes to us lonely men, as we get older and more solitary."

Mr. Dobree got up, shaking his head and looking very sullen, and marched off without a word. He went about his business as usual, but found himself day by day in a disordered mood. He ate little and spoke not at all, though he had been ever ready with his tongue. He slept brokenly; and presently as he sate alone in his room, he began to hear whispers in his ear, or he would think that he was called; and his brother Fellows began to be concerned about him, wondering why he peered so often into the corners of the room, and why he wheeled round so sharply in the street to look behind him as he walked alone.

It was a very wet and dull afternoon at the end of November, and Mr. Dobree had sate all day indoors. Just about dusk he remembered that he had a word to say to the stonemason who worked for the College, about some tiling on the roof. He went out of his rooms and found the whole place very still, with a light rain falling. He walked out of the gate, and turned to the left at once, down the lane that ran close by the College, the stonemason's yard being at the end of it, by the water's edge.

When he got there he found the mason with a lantern in his hand looking about among some piled-up stones in the yard. Mr. Dobree went to speak to him, and broke off in the middle. He felt very much displeased to see what was evidently the head-piece of the old stone coffin lying on the ground. "How comes that there?" he said with a sudden sharpness. "Why, Sir," said the mason "You ordered me to take it and break it all up, and it has lain there ever since." "What is that which lies inside it?" said Mr. Dobree in a loud voice. The mason turned his lantern on the piece. It was roughly worked, the strokes of the chisel being visible where the head had lain, and it was pierced with a hole, the use of which Mr. Dobree did not like to guess. "There is nothing here!" said the mason. "No," said Mr. Dobree, "There is not—I see plainly now. I was dazzled—It was but the shadow. Yet I certainly thought . . ." He broke off, turned on his heel and went away, the business being still unsettled. The mason stood, lantern in hand, watching him as he marched out of the yard. Then he shook his head, and went into the house.

A moment later Mr. Dobree was hurrying up the lane. It was very dark, and the rain kept all men at home. On his right, the wall of the College towered up in the misty air, and he could see a few lighted windows, very high above. The houses on his left seemed all dark and comfortless. He went on until he was close outside his own rooms, which lay next the street.

Suddenly out of the window of his own bedroom, just above him, not a yard away, there came with a silent haste the head and shoulders of a man, wrapped up, it seemed to Mr. Dobree, in a parti-coloured robe, black and white, with a hood over the face, but the face itself was visible, a dead yellow-white, like baked clay, with holes for eyes. There came a faint, thin voice upon the air, and words that sounded in Mr. Dobree's agonised ears like *"Quare inquietasti me ut suscitarer?"* But Mr. Dobree heard no more. He fell all his length in the wet road, and presently turned over on his back, where they afterwards found him, still looking upwards.

The Hole in the Wall

"What is the matter with you, Melon?"

"What do you mean by 'the matter' with me?"

"Well, you are quite different—snappish—jumpy—you may call it what you like!"

"I suppose a man may be a bit below the mark without having it called attention to?"

The first speaker sate silent for a time, and looked at his companion, who fidgeted under the scrutiny.

They were two undergraduates, sitting in a big comfortable room on the first floor of the front court of the college. The questioner, Jim Redford by name, whose room it was, was a tall, thin good-humoured looking man, with a face at once indolent and intelligent. He looked as if he took life easily, and found it interesting. The second man, Harry Bradley, was a short, sturdy, shaggy-haired man, commonly called Melon, from a supposed resemblance to the rugged plumpness of that fruit. They were in their second year at Magdalene, and were close companions and friends.

It may be added for the sake of clearness that the college at that date, the early sixties, was by no means full. On the particular staircase, which contained six sets of rooms, both the ground-floor sets were tenanted, but only one of the first-floor sets, Jim Redford being the occupier of them. Higher up, only one of the two attic sets was in use, Harry Bradley being the occupant; his rooms were over the empty set, while the attics over Redford's room were vacant.

It was the afternoon of a sunny day in May; the two had been having tea together; Redford's room was comfortably and handsomely furnished, and gave evidence of considerable wealth.

They sate thus in silence for a time, and then Bradley said:

"Yes, you are right, Jim! It's no use snapping and growling as I am doing—I'm not well, and it's difficult to explain—but I'll tell you about it. I *should* like to tell you, though it won't be of much use, and yet I ought to have spoken before."

Jim sate up in his chair and looked at Harry, who showed signs of considerable agitation. "All right, old man," he said, "out with it—take your time."

Presently Harry said, "You remember that day about a month or five weeks ago—it was Wednesday, the 21st of April, as a matter of fact—when I had that nasty tumble on the stairs here? I slipped on the narrow step at the corner near the top, and came down, giving my head a bump. Well, it was that which began it, I believe; I have never been right since, and it was the next day that . . ." he broke off and looked rather gloomily at Jim, "that the dreams began. That's the mischief!" he went on. "I can't sleep properly. I don't know half the time if I am asleep or awake, and the dreams, or whatever they are, come and go."

Jim bent forward and said, "Yes, it's the devil if you can't sleep; but tell me what the dreams are!"

"That's just the difficulty!" said Harry. "They are like nothing else I ever had—they are so confused and indistinct, but the same thing is always happening; it will all sound so idiotic, but I'll try. Let me have a moment to think."

He thought with knitted brows for a moment. Then he said, "I begin always by thinking about a little place, or village, near my home—it is called Kirkby—I always seem to think of that first, but I don't know why; it has no connection with what happens. Then suddenly in the middle of it, I become aware that someone is drawing near. I don't know who or what it is, but he—or it—comes upstairs, I think, very cautiously, as if it was all dark, feeling his way; he is afraid of something, afraid of being seen, and he is carrying something. I don't know what he carries—it is all so mixed. There

is something red about it, with a pattern; then there is something
to do with Virgil. I can't describe it. Something printed or written.
Perhaps it is a book, but it isn't quite like a book. It's heavier, but
I can't make out what it is, because the person who carries it does
not want me to know. I don't think he likes to think of it himself."
He stopped and shook his head. Presently he went on. "Then suddenly he is quite near me; and he pushes something away with his
foot and he puts his hand down to the floor. I don't know what he
does. I can't see him, I can only hear him. It takes a long time.
Then there comes a noise, a curious noise, loud but muffled, not
very near—a thud, and something clicks; and then an awful fear
comes over me. That's the worst part of the whole thing. A *horrible* fear. I don't know what about; and then I know that the man
has crept away.

"I wake sometimes then, all in a sweat, in a perfect agony; but
it's no use; I can't do anything; or stop what is going on, and after
a bit he is back again. I never can make out what happens. I see
curious things; a stick or rod—it is a yellow colour, rather bright,
but spotted, and there is something white twisted round it, and
there is a thing like a hook, two hooks, the sort of hooks they hang
meat on in a larder, and there comes a curious scratching sound,
very soft; but it all seems of no use, and then I hear sighs; whatever it is that is done, it's of no use—and then I am afraid again,
but afraid in a different way, and sometimes I see men sitting in a
lighted room round a table, talking rather seriously; that does not
always come,—and then the whole thing begins again; the man
creeping near, the sound which frightens me, and then there's the
soft scratching."

"What an *extraordinary* dream!" said Jim, leaning forwards
with a curious look on his face. "Is that all—does nothing more
happen?"

"No," said Harry, "nothing more happens, that's the worst of
it. It sounds perfectly idiotic, and *is* idiotic; but it simply drives
me mad; night after night it goes on, and I can't help thinking . . ."
he broke off with a gesture of misery.

"Thinking what?" said Jim.

THE HOLE IN THE WALL

"Why, is that how people do go out of their minds?" said Harry, "for ever thinking of something they can't stop or forget, and thinking it over and over again—that knock on the head I mean—did that set up something wrong? You see, I feel I'm in a bad way, and can't get out of it. What *can* you advise me to do? Oh, I'm so *wretched*!" He broke off suddenly.

"I suppose you won't see a doctor?" said Jim.

"What's the use?" said Harry. "There's nothing wrong with me in other ways; and I can't tell him all this nonsense."

"Do you ever feel it by day?" said Jim.

"Not much," said Harry. "I don't like being alone in my rooms—you have noticed that I'm always dropping in here. I feel in my rooms that there's something bad about, but I don't feel as if it meant any particular harm to me; it is more as if I had just got in the way of something that was going on."

"You won't get leave to go home for a bit?" said Jim. "I think that would help."

"I can't," said Harry. "I have nowhere to go to; my people are away, and my exams are coming on. I must just stick it out."

Jim pondered for a bit. Then he said, "How would it be if you could change your rooms? I think that it is possible to get a place on one's nerves. Why not get leave to change into the empty attics? You can easily make an excuse to Cooper. He won't care; they are the same rent, and rather better rooms. Then you would be over my head, and if you thumped on the floor, I could come up, and have a talk. I *really* believe that might be of some use."

Harry looked a little relieved, but presently shook his head. "I would be glad to get out of the rooms at any price," he said, "but it would cost something, and I haven't a halfpenny to spare!"

"It wouldn't cost anything," said Jim. "You haven't got much to move, and you could do most of the moving yourself. The empty rooms don't want doing up. We could just get a man in for an hour or two to help, but you could settle in all right in an afternoon. I'd come and help."

"I really believe it *would* be a good plan," said Harry. "I don't want to move off the staircase. I'd like to be near you. What could I say to Cooper?"

"Just say you would like the other rooms better," said Jim. "He's a good-natured old boy, he wouldn't mind. He would only say, 'Certainly, Mr. —, by all means; the other room's a bit more cheerful, hey?'" He imitated the genial accents of the worthy tutor, and Harry smiled. "I'll do it to-morrow," he said; "I'll get leave to-night—it's a good idea of yours!"

"And I'll come up to-night and sleep on your sofa," said Jim. "It will rather amuse me. Then you can sing out if you are inclined."

"What do you think about it all?" said Harry.

"I think it's all natural enough," said Jim. "I expect that little knock you had started it, and now you have got into a habit of remembering certain things which have got all mixed up together, and which you probably happened to see without particularly noticing—it seems a regular mess of absurdities. You are all right, old man! You look better already!"

Jim did as he suggested; he took possession of the sofa in Harry's room, and slept well. Once he awoke, hearing Harry cry out, and lighting a candle went into the bedroom. Harry was lying on his back, his hands twisted into the counterpane, breathing heavily, much flushed. Jim did not like the look of him; and he suddenly had a sense that there *was* something very uncanny about—was there someone standing behind him? He turned hurriedly, but there was nothing visible but the bare white attic, with a row of pegs, and clothes hanging on them. He was rather afraid of waking up Harry suddenly, but he stood by him, put his hand on his shoulder, and called him softly by his name. Harry woke with a start, and sate up, in an obvious agony of fear. "Good God!" he said, "get away—get away, I say—let me alone . . ." . . . he recognised Jim suddenly, and sank back with a look of relief. "Oh, it's you!" he said. "Well, I've had a damnable time; it has all been going on as usual, over and over again." "Never mind, old man!" said Jim. "Now just lie down and go to sleep. I'll bring a chair in here, and you won't mind if I have a pipe?" He dragged a chair in, sate down, wrapped a rug round him and smoked. Harry slept again, tossing about at times, and once or twice crying out. Jim did not wake him again; and at last the daylight came softly in,

and the birds began to twitter in the ivy; and then Harry sank into
a quiet sleep. Presently Jim went softly out, and down to his own
rooms, where he went to bed; but he did not sleep; he lay open-
eyed, wondering and pondering. He did not like the look of things
at all.

The next morning Harry declared that he had had an *awful*
night, worse than ever; but he had got leave to move his rooms;
and that afternoon the two men, with a carpenter to help them,
got the furniture across, nailed up pictures, hung curtains. The old
bedmaker entirely approved. "I always thought, sir," she said, "that
there was something nasty-like, in a manner of speaking, about
the other room. And I have wondered why you didn't change, sir;
but it was not in my duty to say so. And I have been thinking, too,
sir, that you was not, as one may say, quite yourself."

Harry was much delighted with the change, and declared that
he felt quite different already; Jim told him to be sure and knock
on the floor if he felt disturbed; but no knock came, and Harry,
marching into breakfast, announced that he had had an excellent
night. "Just a touch of the old thing," he said, "but no more. The
person was about, you know. Yes, he was creeping about a bit—but
he didn't bother *me*."

In the course of the morning, Jim, who was a decided young
man, went off and told the whole story to a doctor in the town whom
he knew, a kind-hearted old fellow, who heard him attentively. "You
did quite right, Mr. Redford," said the Doctor, when he had heard
all. "Most sensible! I wouldn't press your friend to come and see
me, till you have seen how the change works. I think you are right—
there has been a little mischief resulting from the blow. He ought
probably to have rested, and he ought to rest; but he is evidently
not much amiss, and I daresay it would worry him less to go in for
his examination. In a state like that he had better have something
ordinary to think about, if the work doesn't bother him; get him to
take exercise regularly and not overdo it; and come and tell me
again how he is getting on. I expect it will be all right now."

From that moment all went well. Harry ceased to be troubled
by dreams, his spirits came back to him; it was Jim's turn to be

preoccupied. He wrote down all he could remember of the dream—
he had a taste for the investigation of problems, and he now in-
dulged it to the full. He discovered a lot of old Boat records and
account books in the Library, and he studied them with infinite
care. He got the bedmaker to let him have the keys of the two vacant sets, and he made a careful examination of Harry's former
bedroom; while he did so, one fine morning, he was conscious of
very great uneasiness and considerable qualms, so that once or
twice he thought he must desist. What he found he kept to himself.

Another day he sent for a carpenter, and made a similar investigation of the rooms opposite his own. The side of the room further from the door, and thus immediately underneath the wall
which separated the attics above, was panelled. He got the carpenter to take down and remove with very great care the panelling
which was in the corner of the room near the window, and thus
more or less under the corner in which the bed in the attic above
stood. A dusty wall was revealed, with immense festoons of cob-
webs, among which he made a very careful search, removing them
with the utmost care.

At last the examination was complete. He arranged with the
bedmaker that the room should be kept carefully locked, and that
evening he made a number of notes on some sheets of paper. When
he had finished, he read it all over very carefully, and looked round
with an air of satisfaction.

The same day Harry finished his examination. The two spent
the evening together. Harry was in high spirits at the recovery of
his health, and rather rallied Jim on his thoughtfulness. "You would
think I had shifted it all on to you!" he said. Jim smiled and said
nothing at the time. But the following morning, when Harry pro-
posed that they should go out together, Jim said to him, "Now, are
you perfectly sure you are all right, Melon?"

"Yes, indeed," said Harry; "what on earth is the matter?"

"Well, sit down there," said Jim, "and let me tell you a story,
which I think will interest you." He spread his notes before him.
"Do you mind if I ask you some questions about your dreams?"

"Not a bit," said Harry, "it would rather amuse me—by Jove, though, they were bad at the time!"

"There's only one thing I don't understand," said Jim. "You said that your dreams always began with your thinking about a village, near your home. Kirkby, you said it was. I can't get that in."

"Yes," said Harry, "Kirkby Basset—Kirkby for short!"

"Kirkby *what*?" said Jim sharply.

"Kirkby Basset!" said Harry. "There's a Kirkby Lestrange some miles away, but we always spoke of Kirkby Basset as Kirkby."

"Well, upon my word!" said Jim, striking his hand on the table, "but this simply tops everything. That was the very thing I wanted!

"Now, look here! You must attend to this. In the year 1826 there was a man here called Basset—he was an extravagant man, I have reason to believe, and he got into difficulties. He wanted money. The Boat subscriptions were kept in a cash-box, which stood on the secretary's table. One day it was missing. There's an entry about the theft of the money in the Boating-book, and it was thought to have been bagged by an errand-boy.

"Basset kept in these rooms of mine. The attics were both empty. Well, it was Basset who took the cash-box. No, don't interrupt me now! He kept it in his room for a day or two, but when it all came out about the theft of the box, he got frightened. He wrapped it up in a bit of paper—I don't quite know why, but we shall see—he had a reason; and he wrapped it all up in an old handkerchief, a red bandana handkerchief with an odd pattern on it, which he took, I believe, from another man's rooms. Then he got the key of the empty attic—your rooms—then one night, very late, he crept upstairs, and he went into your bedroom, and he got a bit of the wainscot off, and he pushed the cash-box into the wall; but he hadn't examined the place. There was a hole through the wall there, which communicated with the sitting-room; and the flooring comes to an end, so that anything pushed in there falls down behind the panelling of the sitting-room beneath. And when he pushed it in, it fell down, and made an awful clatter down below.

"He was in a horrible fright, thinking it would wake up the man who kept there; but I suppose it didn't wake him.

"Then he was in a dreadful state. I don't *quite* know why. I am not sure whether he had taken the money out or not. I rather think not. He did nothing more that night, but went back to bed.

"In the morning, he felt he *must* get the box up again: and I suppose he had been planning how to do it. He stole a meat-hook, which he tied on to an old curtain-rod, and then he pushed it down into the hole, and tried fishing for the box; he felt it, I believe, but he couldn't hook it up; and then he let go of the rod by accident, and it slipped down out of his reach, and then he gave it all up as a bad job, pushed the wainscot back, and made it as firm as he could. And then I don't know what happened."

Jim stopped for a moment, and Harry sate staring at him. "I see," he said, "I more or less see, it fits in some of the things, but it's only a bit of clever guessing, it seems to me. Have you any proof of all this, or is it just a detective sort of affair?"

"Come and see," said Jim, getting up. Harry followed him; Jim went out on to the landing, and opened the door of the rooms opposite. He looked at Harry, "You are quite sure you won't mind?" he said. "It will be rather a surprise to you."

"Mind?" said Harry, "No, we'll see this out!"

Jim opened the door of the room opposite, and they went in together; then Jim carefully closed the door. They stood together in a big room, bare of all furniture. The wall opposite them was panelled, and a piece of the panelling had been removed. Jim pointed at an object which lay on the floor close to the wall. Harry went over to it. It was a small bundle, tied up in an old red wrapper, covered with dust. Against the wall, partly concealed by the panelling which was still standing, stood a thin metal rod, with traces of brass veneer upon it; at the end of the rod which touched the ground was a big double meat hook, tied to the rod with a piece of what had once been white window-cord.

"There it all is!" said Jim. "I haven't touched them. Now we will examine them."

He took the bundle and laid it on the window-seat. It was fastened up with a rough knot, which Jim undid. He laid the corners on the window-seat, and there appeared an object tied up in what had once been white paper with a piece of red tape. He undid the red tape. A bit of manuscript appeared, and an old japanned cash-box. "Wait a minute," said Jim. "Just look at these." The MS., on examination, appeared to be a piece of Latin hexameters, in the Virgilian style. There was a name at the top, "Sedley." "Yes, that was one of the names in the club," said Jim. "Stop—look at the handkerchief."

He turned it over, and a name was visible, written in a space, "H.P. Sedley."

"There!" said Jim. "That's the last clue, or nearly the last! He tied it up, you see, in Sedley's paper, and in Sedley's handkerchief. He meant the suspicion, if there was any suspicion, to fall on him!"

Then Jim took up the cash-box. It was heavy, and he shook it in the air, so that money clinked within. "Yes," he said, "he left the money in it, sure enough—let us get back and examine this!"

He put the paper and the handkerchief carefully together; both were frail, stained and tattered. He looked at Harry, who stood seemingly bewildered.

"Good Heavens!" said Harry, "it all comes back to me bit by bit—it's all here! It was *that* he was feeling for in the wall—*that* was what he was after!"

They went back to Jim's room, who after a minute's fumbling with the rusty cash-box, prized it open and tumbled the contents out on the table—several gold coins, guineas and sovereigns, some tarnished silver, and a few coppers.

"Count it all!" said Jim; and they slowly counted the contents. It came to a sum of £32 4s 8d. Jim looked on his table, found an old account-book, and showed Harry the same amount totalled up on one of the pages. Underneath was a blurred note. "This sum in the club cash-box was abstracted from J. Faning's rooms on May 10, 1826. A fresh levy of subscriptions was made. The thief remains undiscovered."

The two looked at each other in silence. Then Harry said, "This man Basset, what became of him?" Jim searched among the papers, and held out a slip of print before his eyes. It was an obituary notice, of some two years before, of the death of Mr. Henry Basset, of

Friars' Norton Hall in the County of Hunts., who, the paper said, had been educated at Magdalene College, Cambridge, and had taken his degree in the year 1826. The notice went on to speak of him as an active magistrate, and a man of many charities.

A few days later, the two were sitting together; there had been a long silence, when Harry suddenly said, "I'm hanged if I can make anything of this business, Jim! I don't like it, it's very uncanny; but I don't really see that it can be coincidence or imagination. I should like to think it could."

"Yes," said Jim, "it would be convenient, no doubt! But it's rather a grim affair, you know! I would like to think of the old man as better occupied, and more piously engaged over there. It rather knocks one's idea of Heaven on the head; because he seems to have ended by being a good old man, and yet forced to come back here, and go fretting about over this old prank of his; and what good could he do either, tell me that? It isn't a case of restitution, because all the people whose money he took are gone long ago. No-one is being wronged in consequence. It's just a windfall for the club, and, by the way, I propose to pay it in quietly, through the Bursar. It's no use talking about all this; we should only be thought to be mad."

"Well then, what *do* you think?" said Harry.

"If you ask me," said Jim, "it looks to me as if dying didn't make very much difference to us! I expect that the old man had worried and fretted all his life long about the cash-box: he didn't like to own up, but I expect he went through the performance simply millions of times, thinking what a fool he had been; and now it is such a habit with him, that he comes back here and worries us to death. I tell you, I was frightened about *you*; but it was as you said: it wasn't you he was after. You merely got in the way."

"But he died some time ago," said Harry, "and why did I suddenly become aware of it?"

"Oh, that was the knock you got," said Jim. "I have no doubt of it. A thing like that shakes one up; it's like starting a leak in the mind, and the water rushes in. You simply became aware of something that had been going on for a long time. And I'm thankful—

yes, I'm devoutly thankful that something worse didn't happen! But for all that I don't believe that the old man meant any harm— he wasn't thinking about you."

There was a pause, and then Harry said, "It makes me rather uncomfortable to think of all sorts of things like that going on, shadows running all kinds of errands, going in and out. Do you really think we are in the middle of all that, Jim?"

Jim looked at him very seriously. "Yes," he said, "I think that is so. I believe we are right in the middle of some very queer things indeed, and I believe it's lucky for us that we so rarely knock up against them!"

The Hare

Dick Bramwell had just arrived at Magdalene as a freshman, and had been directed by the porter to his rooms in Staircase G, on the right side of the front court. He had not been able to take any steps about furnishing, as he had only been offered a set in College by wire a day or two before, the tenant of which had unexpectedly decided not to return to Cambridge. It was a ground-floor set, not far from the street, with one high window looking toward the river, and one on the court. Without pictures, without any furniture but a dull-looking table and three hideous chairs, a damaged sofa, a faded and stained carpet and some sunburnt curtains, the room looked entirely slovenly and woe-begone. It smelt nasty and smoky too, and there was something, Dick thought, unfriendly and even sinister about it. He did not like it at all, and even wished he had stuck to his lodgings.

As he stood surveying the room with a growing disgust, a loud and voluble voice behind him said, "Yes, you may well be surprised, sir—Mr. Bramwell, I believe—which I can see without asking that you're not pleased, and it didn't ought to look so." Dick turned round, and saw a large, cheerful elderly lady with a bonnet, standing before him with a broom in her hand. "Mrs. Humphrey, sir, your bedmaker," she said with a pleasant smile, and continued with great gusto, "Yes, it's a pore room to look at now, and well it may be called so; but it ain't a bad room to live in, as it's been in my work for thirty years, and gentlemen get to like the set, as it's always cheerful from the look-out, and never neither too hot nor too cold. You'll like it well enough, sir, with a few pictures and that, and some pleasant company."

Mrs. Humphrey, called Mother Hump from time immemorial, bustled about the room, showing off its conveniences. Dick felt an immediate liking for the pleasant old dame, with her loud inconsequent, rambling talk. A curious recess met his eye in the corner of the room. It looked like a small fireplace, except that it had been bricked up and painted, and it had a trace of Tudor carving in the stone spandrels, which gave it the appearance of being the top of a door, if it only had not been but a couple of feet above the floor of the room. It was a curious object, and Dick whose observation was of the keenest, halted before it. "What on earth is that for?" he said. "Oh, sir, it ain't of no concern that," said Mrs. Humphrey, "it was a door, may be, for the old monks as they say lived here once, in their Cathedral or what not—but it's been a Christian room for many years now, thank God!" Mrs. Humphrey was evidently a sound Protestant. "What were the monks doing here?" Dick said. "Well may you ask, sir," said Mrs. Humphrey, "and it seems to me a pity they were ever allowed in the College— but here they were, Mr. Simpson tell me—he's the Bursar, sir, a nice gentleman—conjuring and thieving and that, and worshipping heathen images between whiles, I make no doubt!" Mrs. Humphrey's views of history seemed likely to be interesting, Dick thought, but before he could enquire further, Mrs. Humphrey was showing him a convenient cupboard, which she assured him was free from mice "which is ever a plague in College rooms, sir, do what you will. Now there's Mrs. Bradley, sir, she's bedmaker on staircase Q, and she's a one to talk wild, if ever; she tell me only yesterday that her mice had a wonderful taste for malted liquor, and I only laugh and tell her that my mice had but a taste for groceries, and for all that a mouse might by nature desire. But malted liquor!" And Mrs. Humphrey laughed a hollow laugh of derision. "I thought in my mind, though I kep' it back, that it'd be a mouse in Christian petticoats that went after malted liquor—though to be sure it ain't 'ardly delicate for me to relude before a young gentleman to an article of female wear!"

Dick burst into a loud laugh, and Mrs. Humphrey smiled approvingly. She liked to have her sallies enjoyed. "That's right, sir," she said. "Now you and me'll get to work on these rooms, and we'll soon have you as neat as a ninepin!"

Dick Bramwell knew two or three men in the College, but they were not back yet—he had come up a day or two early to get straight. He unpacked, he went to report himself to the Tutor, he dined in Hall with half-a-dozen silent and desperately polite freshmen; and he spent the evening rather ruefully in his bare room, writing a letter or two and reading a book. But somehow he did not like the room. What was it? He could not tell. It was sombre and grim. He heard vehicles go past in the street, and the room shook with the passage of waggons; people clattered through the court, and he heard odd scraps of talk. But he found his eyes persistently dwelling on the little recess with its carved corners, much obliterated with old coats of paint. It seemed as if something must be inside it, bricked up, immured, forgotten, but not wholly forgetful. It looked rather a wicked little door, he thought. He would cover it all up somehow, put a table in front of it. And as he sate reading, looking about, wondering what it was all going to be like, the little recess seemed to watch him too with a secret air of disapproval.

Dick soon settled down at Magdalene, and the sense of loneliness and strangeness wore away very quickly. He found that the freshmen were not either so silent or so polite as he had fancied. His friends of the second and third years were glad to see him, and he was soon very much at home. He was a simple-minded and cheerful young man, with no fancies or prejudices, and prepared to take people as they came; he was neither embarrassed nor superior, but fell into line at once. He had made a very different place out of his rooms, with pictures, arm-chairs, books and ornaments, and people took to dropping in a good deal, for Dick was never inconveniently busy. But he could not quite get over his dislike of the room, though he found that he became entirely oblivious of the noise of the street. The little doorway continued to be unpleasant to him. There was not room to put a table in front of it, so he

nailed a curtain over it; but he found that he had a curious dislike
to sitting with his back to it, a sense as if someone or something
might look out of it, even lean over him. It was all right when other
people were there; but if he had been sitting with his back to the
recess all the evening, when he was left alone, he always took a
chair opposite it. He thought at one time of having it opened, but
it was evidently carefully built up, and it seemed likely to be a
troublesome job to hack the brickwork away. Neither, he found,
did he quite like to speak about it.

One evening he had been sitting and talking with half-a-dozen
friends. They melted away, and he was left alone. He was sitting
smoking and reading in a low chair opposite the recess; it was a
chilly evening and the fire was a little low. He got up to poke it,
and put a bit of coal on. He laid his pipe down on the chimney-
piece, when out of the corner of his eye he suddenly saw something run out of the recess and across the room. It was a very curious object, so far as he could make it out—but the light was dim,
and it was gone before he could fix it. It looked about the size of a
hare, and it seemed to him to have long ears; it did not run on all-
fours, but on its hind-legs, with its fore-paws stretched out in front
of it. It flitted quickly across the room and vanished in the shade.
To say that he was surprised would be a very mild expression to
represent his feelings. He was startled, horrified, almost sickened.
The creature had the look of escaping from captivity. He stood staring after it for a moment, and then he had a wild impulse to rush
out and find someone; but he did not know what he could say to
explain himself. Then he pulled himself together, and decided that
it must be a cat, which had got in from the garden. He took the
poker in his hand and made a thorough examination of the room.
He thrust the poker under the sofa, he turned up the table-cloth,
he beat the room out, but there was no trace of any living thing—
and then he saw that the window on the garden was closed. He did
the same with his bedroom, but in a few minutes it was clear to
him that there was nothing there. At last he decided that he must
have been mistaken, and went to bed. But he could not sleep; he
read, he tossed about, and he could not bring himself to extinguish

the light, while all the time he kept his glance apprehensively fixed on the door into his sitting-room. But sleep intervened; and he woke at last with a start, to find his candle burnt out, and to hear the welcome sound of Mrs. Humphrey clattering the fire-irons. With the morning light his confidence returned to him, and he called himself a silly ass with deep conviction.

However, when Mrs. Humphrey came to take away the breakfast things, he felt an irresistible impulse to speak to her. "Mrs. Humphrey," he said standing before the fire, "I want to ask you a question. Don't think it ridiculous, but I want to know . . ."

"Ah," interrupted Mrs. Humphrey, "I know what you are going to say, sir, without talking. I saw in a minute when I come in that something had happened. . . . I said, 'Mr. Bramwell ain't had a good night, and he's hurt in his mind'; I said so, sure enough."

Dick smiled uneasily, "Well, then, if you know about it, Mrs. Humphrey," he said, "I needn't tell you—but *you* shall tell *me* what you think."

"I suppose then, sir," said Mrs. Humphrey, "that you seen what they call the Hare—well, and what if you have, sir? It don't do no harm, that little thing, sir. I see it myself half-a-dozen times, and some of my gentlemen have seen it too—but it ain't a thing to talk about, if I may be bold to advise. I tell the Bursar about it once, sir, and he said it was stupid nonsense, and so I hold my tongue and mind my business. But it's there, sure enough! And it's my rule, sir, not to talk about things what I don't understand, because if you do, why other folks get jerking up their arm and talking about the whiskey bottle and that. But there ain't a soberer woman than myself in the place, sir, and yet I see the Hare plain enough. Now, Mr. Makins, that's my last gentleman but one, he see the Hare, and he never touched no form of strong drink. But it never done no harm, sir, that I heard of. It just do skip out, once in a while."

"But what it is?" said Dick.

"Well, in my mind, sir," said Mrs. Humphrey, "it's some conjuring of the old monks, drat 'em! They never should have been let into the College, I say—there was the mistake!"

"But I don't like it," said Dick.

"Well, it did give me a start, sir," said Mrs. Humphrey. "But I look at it like this. Let it 'ave its run, pore thing, if it 'as a mind to. It won't do right-thinking people any 'arm. Why, I take no more notice of it than if it were poultry."

"Well, I don't know," said Dick. "It makes me feel rather queer. I think I shall tell the Tutor about it."

"You take my advice, sir," said Mrs. Humphrey, "and say nothing about it—it makes people think you are queer in your head, if you say you seen a Hare in your room at midnight, with the door sported. They don't come about College rooms much, don't Hares! Mark my words, sir, it ain't going to do you no harm; what'll do you harm is if you get brooding about it and talking of it. There are many queer things about, and this is one of them. The less said the better, says I!"

"You're quite right, Mrs. Humphrey," said Dick. "I won't say anything about it. And now that I know that you have seen it and other people have seen it, I don't care a rap."

"It's numbers as does it!" said Mrs. Humphrey. "But if we let the pore thing alone, it'll let us alone. It's prying into things as does the 'arm."

The matter of the Hare slowly faded from Dick's mind as the weeks went on, and the more he thought about it all, the wiser it seemed to hold his tongue. Also the fact that there were others who had seen the little apparition gave him much comfort, especially when one of these was the robust and cheerful Mother Hump. It would have depressed him to think that he was exceptional in the matter, and exposed to psychical experience. Dick took a very straightforward and concrete view of life, and had no curiosity whatever about the Borderland. Moreover, the oppressive atmosphere of the room seemed to have been cleared away by the vision.

However, some four weeks later, the sense of tension began again quite suddenly, and in a new form. He could hardly have put the feeling into words, but it was as though someone, he could not tell where or how, was waiting for an opportunity to communicate with him. He saw and heard nothing; but when he was alone, there was a sense of some entreaty in the air. This did not exactly frighten him, but rather aroused a feeling of adventurous expectation. There was no hint of ill-will about it, but more as if someone or something was attempting to familiarise him with its presence. It hardly interrupted him in his work; and if he could have made a comparison, it was almost as though there were a friendly dog in the room, not intrusive, but hoping to be summoned for a walk.

One day this was very strong indeed; so strong that, as he sate in his room alone and late at night, he raised his head quickly once or twice as if some acquaintance had drawn near. When he went to bed it was stronger than ever; and though he did not put his feelings into words, he went to sleep with a half-formed invitation in his mind—as though he had said "Well, tell me if you can, and whatever you can?" It was like a little surrender of his will to an insistent influence which he had learned not to mistrust. At some dumb hour, late in the night, he awoke with a start, with the impression of a very vivid dream upon him.

He had seen a large room, sparely furnished, with a heavy roof of wooden beams and white-washed walls. There were seats along the walls, and dark figures seated; but this was all a very faintly perceived background. His attention had been riveted on a particular group. An old man, in a loose dark robe, clean-shaven and ascetic-looking, with an air of some nobleness, but as if deeply perplexed and anxious, sate at a table, leaning back in a chair, with his hands clasping the arms of it; on each side of him sate two others similarly attired; and he knew from their shaven scalps that they were monks. Immediately opposite the three, on the other side of the table, stood a figure which absorbed the interest and compassion of Dick. He was a young man, hardly more than a boy, with beautiful features, but indicating by the open lips, the dark shadows under the eyes, the pallor of the whole face, that he was labouring under a sensation of deep anxiety and terror. But what most surprised and struck Dick was that he held clasped in his arm a hare, evidently very tame. Its fore-paws were resting on the boy's arm, its ears were pricked up, and it was regarding the old man in the centre with wide-open hazel eyes. Presently the old man began to speak in a low, severe and yet regretful tone. What he said was

hardly intelligible to Dick, but it appeared to be the announcement
of some decision. When it was finished, the boy said some hurried
sentences, which seemed to be an explanation and a plea of some
kind. But presently the old man shook his head, and looked first to
one and then to the other of the men who sate beside him. One of
them frowned and shook his head, and the other laid his hand on a
paper which lay on the table, and said a few words.

Then two of the dark figures in the background came forward
and stood beside the table; and presently, at a sign given, they came
close to the boy, who bowed low to the three seated figures, and
was then led away, his guides bowing similarly. They left the room;
when the old man, who had given the decision, rose up, and made
a sign; and the whole assembly fell on their knees. Some sentences
were said and responses made; but they all remained kneeling in
silence, till at last the two guides came back, but without the boy,
made a short statement, and then the whole assembly silently dispersed.

Dick had a sense that something very solemn and dreadful had
happened. The emotion of the whole company was evidently pro-
found, as of men who, in spite of natural compassion, had felt
obliged to carry out some stern decree; indeed, Dick had no doubt
that the death of the boy was involved, rather than any lesser punishment.

He woke with a sense of deep depression and anxiety, and at
the same time became aware that his presence was needed in the
next room. He lit a candle, and holding it high over his head hurried into the room, which stood quiet, just as he had left it. He
fixed his eyes upon the little recess, and as he did so, in a moment,
the figure of the hare appeared. But instead of moving across the
floor, it stopped, sate down just by the recess, and Dick became
aware that its yellow eyes were turned upon him. Then for the
briefest instant a cloudy figure appeared standing by it. There was
no question of recognition; indeed, he never saw the figure clearly
enough for that; but he had no sort of doubt in his mind that it was
the boy of his dream. The figure outlined itself very faintly on the
air like a reflection in a dim glass; he saw a hand outstretched, a

youthful hand, pointing to the recess; and then followed the strangest sound he had ever heard, thin and faint and infinitely remote—
no word audible, just a cry of poignant entreaty, and then both the
figures faded slowly from his view.

To his amazement Dick found himself hardly terrified; he had
one moment of intolerable awe, as though his body rebelled against
being confronted with a presence so incorporeal; but there followed
a sense of entire reassurance, and a clear knowledge as to what
was demanded of him. He made his way back to bed; while so strong
and secure was his belief that the purpose of the secret visitant
had been made clear, that soon after he got into bed he fell asleep
quietly, and slept undisturbed until the morning.

The next morning Dick went to work with a will. He went round
to the shop of the decorator who had done up his rooms for him,
and he arranged for a bricklayer to be sent into College that very
afternoon, saying that he wanted to have an alteration made. When
the man arrived, Dick sported the outer door and instructed him
to pierce the wall of the recess. It proved to have been filled with
brick-work and plastered over, and he noticed that a curious device, like a five-pointed star, had been scratched deep on the plaster. Some boards of the floor had to be taken up, as the recess went
down beneath the flooring. This was soon done and the bricks were
disengaged. A dark little passage appeared, leading into the wall,
with a close and musty smell. Dick then sent the man away for a
quarter of an hour, flashed a ray of light from his reading-lamp
into the recess, procured a broom and a shovel, and cleared out
the contents of the passage. It was mostly dust of a fine white kind.
But among the dust he could discern some bones, both entire and
in fragments, and also some teeth. He put the whole mass into a
box, and then when the man returned, the wall was built up again
and plastered over, and the curtain replaced. Dick heard several
people come to his door and go away; but the whole was finished
by Hall-time, and he went into Hall with an extraordinary sense of
relief. He spent the evening in a friend's rooms, but late at night,
when he returned to his own room, he filled up the spaces of the
box, above the dust and bones, with straw and paper, fastened it

all securely and went to bed, where he spent the first entirely tranquil night that he had for some time enjoyed.

A few days later the term came to an end, and Dick went home, taking the box with him. The Vicar of the country parish where Dick lived was an old friend of his family, John Marsh by name, and Dick had known him ever since he was a boy. The Vicar was a considerable antiquarian, and he was further a very kindly and sensible man. Dick went to see him, and told him that he had found in his rooms at Magdalene some things which he did not understand, and asked if he might show them to him. The Vicar wanted to know some particulars, but Dick said that he would like him to look at the things first. He carried the box with him, and presently the whole contents were turned out on some newspapers on the Vicar's huge oak table, which was cleared for the purpose. The Vicar began poking and prodding among the dust. "H'm," he said, "bones—yes human bones! teeth, I see—yes, teeth of a young man or woman, age about twenty or a little less. Hullo, what is this? H'm, teeth of some small rodent, a rabbit, I think. No, too big for that! A hare, I expect. Ah, a horn button, a bit of cord, some fragments of frieze or serge. What on earth is this?" He drew from the fragments a rough metal crucifix. "Very interesting that!" he said. "Early fifteenth century, I should say—beads!—yes, probably attached to the crucifix—well, that seems to be all!" He turned and looked at Dick through his spectacles. "A queer find!" he said. "I should say it was some *monk*, to judge from what remains—a young monk. But I'm blessed if I know how the hare comes in. He can't have swallowed it whole, hey? In that case, probably the cause of death! You know we ought to have a coroner's inquest over all this!"

Dick thereupon told him the whole story from first to last. The Vicar heard him with amazement. He asked a few questions, and then he said, "Now does anyone know about this?" "Not a soul," said Dick. "Very well," said the Vicar, "that was very sensible of you! I'll think it all over; and look here; I'll just get the sexton to dig a hole in the churchyard, and I'll put the bones and dust away—perhaps say a few prayers when no one is looking. If the young fellow has had Christian burial already it won't matter—but I very much doubt it!" Presently the Vicar said, "What about the crucifix, by the way, and the cord and button?" "Oh, you keep them," said Dick. The Vicar beamed with delight, the instinct of the collector rising to the surface. "Are you sure, my dear boy, that you wouldn't prefer to keep them?" "Not I," said Dick with a shudder. "Well, that's very kind," said the Vicar. "I'll think it all over—very interesting problem! But mind, Dick"—he held up a warning finger, "No more dreams and visions!"

Dick heard no more about it, except that the Vicar one day after Church walked with him round the Churchyard, and pointed to a little heap of earth in a quiet corner, by a yew-tree. "There he lies," he said, "all that is mortal of him! Poor fellow! Well, it's over and done with now!" But a few days after Dick got back to Magdalene, the Vicar wrote to him as follows:

> Standish Vicarage
> Jan. 20, 18—
>
> Dear Dick,
> I have ferreted it all out, and it is pretty bad, I think. Just read the enclosed, which I have translated from the Croyland Register, some fragments of which are preserved. It's disgraceful Latin, and you wouldn't be able to construe it. It's only a fragment, and it belongs to the middle of the 15th century or thereabouts:
> "... great and heavy trouble among the novices, Brother Paul, much beloved, and of whom much was hoped, being grievously drawn away by Satan into magical practices and devices hated of God. The Lord Abbot himself went thither to examine and enquire into the matter. Testimony there was little, but many heinous things were alleged; and this was at least certain, that an evil spirit resorted to him in the shape of a hare, that was seen to have a devilish craft and wit surpassing the wit of hares, which are silly creatures, it is well-known. Being much exhorted to

make confession, he was dumb and stubborn, and when holy relics were applied to him, he was much oppressed and astonished, and the hare itself spake in a human voice, and said, 'I am Sycorax the accursed.' And when all this had been done and observed evidently, the Lord Abbot condemned him for his soul's health to be immured alive, as the law is, for the practice of magical arts; which was done presently, with great fear and trembling, and to the glory of Mother Church. And the Lord Abbot made charge that no one to whom the place of his death was known should reveal it under pain of excommunication. So that it is said of him, as it was said of the Prophet Moses, that no man knoweth of his sepulcher . . ."

That is the whole passage, and I leave it to you to draw your conclusions; it gives me a turn to think of it—but we have done the best we can.

Believe me, dear Dick, your affectionate old friend.

John Marsh

Dick sate musing over the letter when a voice broke in upon his reverie. "Excuse me, sir," said Mrs. Humphrey, "but I seen what you 'ad a-done to the wall there. I know I ought to tell the Bursar, but I shall hold my tongue, you may be sure; and the air does seem a bit fresher after all; and I seem to know in myself that the pore creature won't be seen no more. Let it rest, I say! If ever there was a Hare that 'ad a secret on its little mind, it was that! And I make so bold as to thank you, sir, for having done what was right and proper; and for having given them old monks a set-back, in a manner of speaking." And Mrs. Humphrey gave a short laugh of satisfaction, and went her way.

Coachwhip Publications

CoachwhipBooks.com

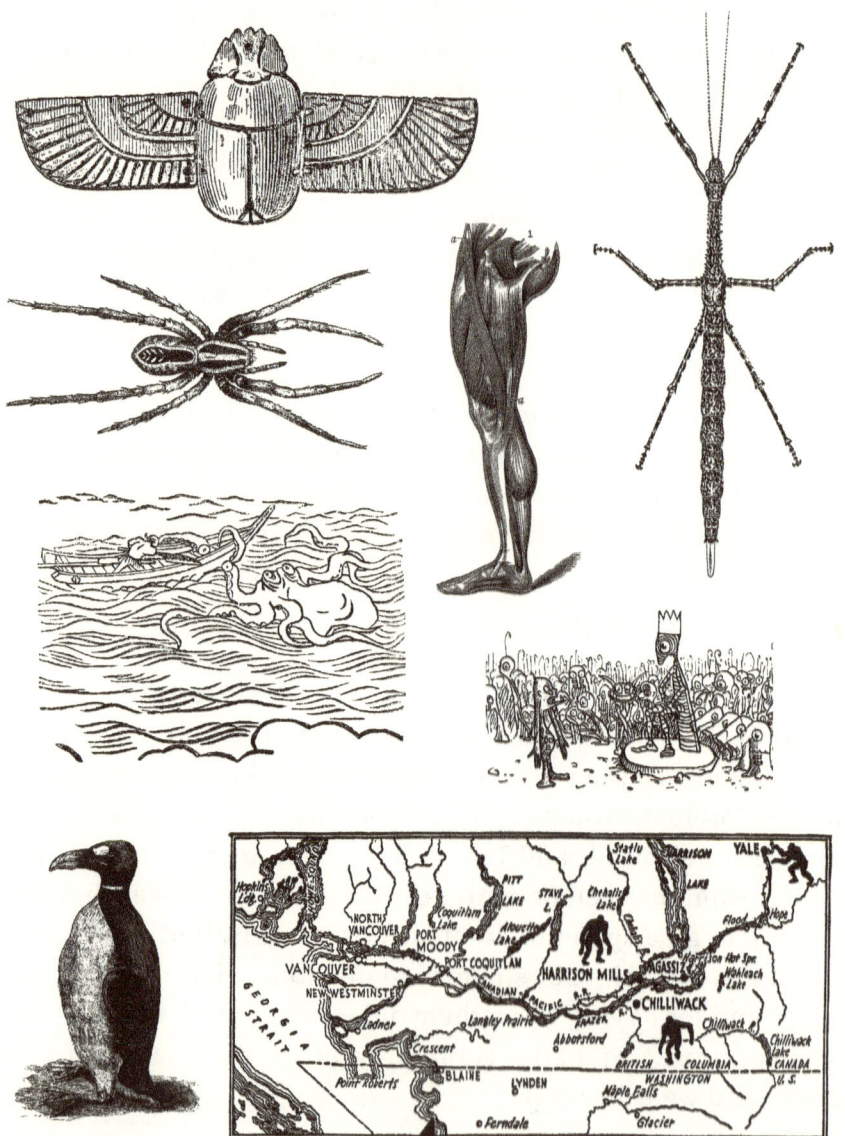

Coachwhip Publications

Also Available

The Supernatural Stories of
Monsignor Robert H. Benson
ISBN 1-61646-004-0

Dark Canon
ISBN 1-61646-020-2